****

Full-Sailed Surrender

****

Kathleen L. Gregory

For my late husband Dan.
Our love will transcend time and space.

Acknowledgements

I would like to thank my sister, Maureen, and my heart-sister, Susie. They graciously suffered through reading my initial raw draft of this story, chapter by chapter. It was their constant encouragement and undying enthusiasm that compelled me to finish this book.

I would also like to acknowledge my editor, Jo Kiester. She helped me to find my writing "voice", patiently guiding me through my long forgotten English skills, forcing me to elaborate, and to dig deeper to express my thoughts. She was not only an editor; she was a teacher and an artist. I thank her for her expertise, and for her painting (which became the cover of this book.)

Finally, I thank you, the readers who have taken a chance on a story from an unknown author. Please enjoy the book and feel free to contact me at facebook.com@kathleengregory with any thoughts or questions.

Kathleen L Gregory

Prologue

S everal school-aged children stepped off the yellow bus onto the clean, white sidewalk set in the breezy sunshine of their peaceful neighborhood. They immediately ran down the elegant, tree-lined street all that is, except for seven-year-old Vanessa, who stood hesitantly, anxiously looking down the road in the opposite direction for her mother. Vanessa's mother always waited for her bus to arrive, but today she wasn't there. As the bus pulled away, Vanessa began tentatively walking towards her home, cautiously passing by the three spectacularly larger homes situated on the same side of the street as her own. Abruptly, a strong gust of wind blew against the back of Vanessa's legs, giving her the uneasy sensation of her feather-light body lifting up towards the sky. Frightened by the strong wind, she ran the remainder of the distance, around the towering green hedge and onto the lush lawn blanketing her front yard. Her frantic pace slowed at the comforting sight of her beloved tire-swing dangling from the massive oak tree, feeling soothed by its steadfast presence. Smiling, she remembered fondly the day her father had carefully tugged and tested to find the sturdiest branch, before he'd hung the swing, just for her.

Discovering her long-absent father's car parked at the end of the driveway, she giggled, happily. Skipping toward her home, she slipped silently through the side door and into the laundry room, wanting to surprise her dad. Her backpack flung carelessly to the floor, she turned eagerly to enter the kitchen, but paused, hearing her mother's angry voice drifting through the closed door.

"I can't believe you'd just show up like this! After not so much as a word for the past six months, you walk in, *demanding* that I give you a divorce," her mother screamed.

"I thought it would be easier this way. Didn't my lawyer send you the papers?" Her father's voice sounded sad to Vanessa. She'd missed her father desperately, but not their fighting. Removing her hand from the doorknob, she leaned her back against the wall and slid despondently down to the floor. Hugging her knees close to her chest, she dropped her forehead wearily to rest on top. The bitterness in her parent's raised voices caused tears of hopeless heartache to spill down her flushed face.

"Why are you here now? What's the big rush?" her mother demanded.

"I'm getting married." Her father's barely whispered words were almost inaudible, and at first Vanessa thought she'd overheard him wrong. The kitchen chair scraped the floor and she pictured her mother lowering herself into it.

"I don't want to hurt you—I just stopped by to get the rest of my things. I *need* you to sign these papers." Her father's voice varied from faint to loud, as he paced back and forth across the tiled kitchen floor.

"Who is she?" her mother demanded. "Don't tell me, it must be Christine, your trusty little assistant." Vanessa cringed at the vicious sarcasm that laced her mother's voice.

"It's not what you think," he said, defensively. "I'd originally planned to come home. But when Christine unexpectedly lost her lease—I let her stay with me—and everything just happened. At first it seemed practical, we worked together all the time," he sighed. "And, I finally got that promotion I've been working so hard for."

"I always thought you were smarter than that," her mother exhaled with a defeated sigh.

"I'm sorry. I never intended to tell you about her. Now will you *please* sign these damn papers?" her father's voice rose, pleading insistently.

"Why the pressure? Tell me the truth or I'll contact a lawyer. I probably should anyway. I haven't worked since before Vanessa was born—how am I going to take care of her alone?" she sobbed.

"I promise, I'll keep supporting you for the next year while you decide what to do. But you might as well know, Christine is pregnant, and she's insisting that we get married immediately."

"You poor foolish man. Here, give me those, I'll sign your damn papers." Neither spoke for several moments. "What about *our* daughter?" her mother asked softly. "The one you haven't seen or spoken to in six months? She'll be home soon, what will you tell *her*?"

Vanessa leaned closer to the door, straining to hear his response. Her father didn't answer right away, and when he did, his voice sounded strained and distant. "I'll always take care of her...and I'll always love her, but I don't think I can see her today. I think it would be best if *you* told her." Vanessa heard the rustling of papers. "I'd better leave now, before she gets home. Tell her—I love her."

"You're a reckless coward. You know the day will come when you'll regret this," her mother called after him.

Her father never answered. Vanessa heard the front door slam and the roar of his car engine. He disappeared, leaving her disheartened mother sobbing alone in the recently deserted kitchen. Vanessa roughly dashed the tears from her face, pushed herself into a standing position and reached for the doorknob, silently entering the kitchen. Her mother sat at the table as she'd imagined, her head resting on her arms, her shoulders shaking, sobbing with uncontrollable despair. Feeling Vanessa's small, warm hand touching her shoulder in comfort, she lifted her head, realizing that her innocent child had overheard their spiteful conversation. The dried tears on Vanessa's face, and the spark of fury in her eyes worried her and she opened her arms, pulling Vanessa's small form onto her lap.

"I hate him!" Vanessa said, heatedly. Her mother gently pressed Vanessa's head against her chest and began stroking her long, smooth, auburn hair, in an attempt to soothe her only child.

"He's stupid! And I hate him!" Vanessa repeated, insistently. Her mother wanted to defend her husband, but the words caught in her throat, so she silently cuddled and comforted her innocent child instead.

Vanessa pulled out of her mother's embrace. A look of wild-eyed determination crossed her innocent face. "Don't worry Mommy, I'll always love you!" Her mother responded with a ghost of a smile.

Outside, the bitter winds wailed, while inside a grieving Vanessa and her mother huddled together, sharing their abandonment and harsh disappointments. An occasional blast of wind rattled the windows, but no amount of blustery clatter could disturb the heartbroken mother and daughter, holding each other close, within the desolate walls of their recently shattered home.

* * * * *

Chapter 1
Vanessa and Haley

*C*ountless years later, the warm, wild Santa Ana winds swept off the desert with a devastating force, whistling uncontrollably through the congested streets and neighborhoods of Los Angeles. Known by old-timers as *Devil Winds*, these destructively vicious winds cause power outages and downed trees. The disturbingly warm, crackling ionic atmosphere that routinely accompanies these electrifying winds significantly affects the moods of everyone within its path, notorious for whipping both wildfires and residents into frenzied states. Law enforcement and emergency rooms across the region report an increased number of violent suicides and homicides during these blustery periods. When the Santa Ana winds begin to blow, locals know to lock their doors and stay alert. Today was just such a day, with both electric, wild wind, and violence palpable in the air. Anything could happen!

Haley

Haley swiped impatiently at her uneven bangs, irritated by the long, tangled strand of pale-walnut colored hair hanging limply in front her face. Frantically, her heart pounded out of control as she urgently stuffed what little she owned haphazardly into an old grocery bag. Then suddenly she froze, like a deer caught in the glare of a car's headlights, as she listened to the ominous sound of squeaking floorboards accompanied by heavy footsteps clomping outside her door. Her heartbeat and breath temporarily suspended within her chest, while hysterical panic and fear bubbled in her throat. Quickly recovering, she scurried frantically across the room to the old, stained, torn up mattress on the floor. Hastily, she tossed the bag of clothes into the closet in a desperate attempt to hide all evidence of her intended escape, and dove for the grungy mattress on the floor. Positioned on her side, facing toward the wall away from the door, she struggled hopelessly to calm her pounding heart and quiet the sound of her gasping breath echoing throughout the cramped apartment.

Jimmy burst through the door with such force, the hollow door bounced back off the wall. Even though the apartment was filled with putrid odors of old food, and the filthy, rotting carpet, Haley could smell the unmistakable stench of stale booze from across the room. Unable to control her fright, her muscles responded, instantly contracting, rigid and tense with dread. She cowered, preparing for his approach, her breaths mere gasps and her heart palpitating furiously in her throat. Haley silently willed her body to remain statue-still as she trembled helplessly in terrified anticipation.

Jimmy reached down and plucked her off the mattress with one massive hand, lifting Haley's tiny frame high into the air until he held her suspended, feet dangling, so near to his reddened face that she was overcome by his foul breath. She'd never seen such fury and contempt in his eyes before. With his full weight, Jimmy slammed Haley up against the wall, viciously tightening his punishing grip on her throat.

"Damn it bitch, are you going to cooperate, or am I going to have to beat the ever-loving shit out of you?" he yelled, his beady, bloodshot eyes narrowed with rage.

Haley shivered, a final thought passing through her hazy, fear-soaked mind. 'Why didn't I run when I had a chance? Now I'll never get away...' The vision of Jimmy's incensed face blurred and her body wilted. The room gradually faded away into darkness. Motionless and desolate, Haley mercifully slipped away into a temporarily safe state of oblivion.

Fiercely, the Santa Ana winds howled and raged outside the dilapidated building, as they whipped angrily through the shabby neighborhood near downtown LA. The fourth floor, condemned studio apartment offered shelter, but little more, as the constant wild winds screeched relentlessly through the filthy, cracked windows.

Jimmy callously dropped Haley's limp body onto the grimy mattress. Unconcerned, he turned away, in search of another beer. There was no one but the inebriated Jimmy who knew of Haley's grim predicament, or that she currently lay helplessly sprawled in a vulnerable, lifeless, unconscious heap on the floor.

Vanessa

Meanwhile, life was a different story thirty miles away from the dregs of downtown LA, where the same Santa Ana winds whirled unheeded through the prosperous canyon community of Bitton. This upscale, privileged community situated off the freeway, safely tucked away from curious eyes, was well known for its luxuriously secluded homes.

As Haley lay helpless on her dingy floor, a persistent ear-piercing alarm clock sounded inside one of these perfectly manicured homes. Unable to stand the irritating noise, Vanessa reached over and blindly swatted at the annoying clock. Her fluffy calico cat leaped gracefully off the bed and onto the floor. Callie had slept peacefully all night curled up in the crook of Vanessa's bent legs. Pausing briefly for effect, the irritated feline swished her fluffy tail and shot a vexed look over her shoulder, haughtily displaying her indignation.

Rolling onto her back, Vanessa threw an arm over her eyes and groaned. *How can it be five am already?* After tossing and turning all night, she'd somehow managed to escape into a restless sleep sometime during the wee hours of the night. Try as she may to avoid her dreaded fate, Vanessa knew the nightmare that had interrupted her sleep was about to come true, next week she'd turn the unimaginable fifty-five years old! Senior citizenship here I come. The very thought made her cringe.

Life had sped by far too fast. In truth, Vanessa had not become the woman she thought she'd be today. Years had blown by, and all she had to show for herself were empty dreams and broken promises. No husband, no children of her own; her current life was not at all the one she'd dreamed of as a small child. A great, big, happy family was what she'd visualized! But, instead of the perfect family, the closest she'd come to having children in her life had been the acquisition of her young team of executives and a demanding career that had monopolized her entire world. Sighing, she realized she no longer felt the same level of pleasure, or satisfaction, from her high-powered position, as she once had. Instead lately, she found her professional role emotionally draining, and a constant reminder of her advancing age and limitations. Callie interrupted Vanessa's woolgathering, meowing plaintively from the doorway; at least she wasn't completely alone. She lifted her arm to peek at the only other living soul who shared her home, her very own, very demanding cat.

For years Vanessa had lived comfortably in her home, safely settled within the suburbs of Bitton. The three-bedroom ranch-style home was the perfect size for just her and Callie, sitting snuggly away from the road on the back end of a large one-acre lot. When she'd first begun house hunting, Vanessa had been attracted to its privacy, with a large wooded lot situated directly behind the house and an abundance of leafy, sheltering maple and pine trees dotting the yard. The securely fenced-in backyard pool had added to its overall appeal.

3

Higher in the hills above Vanessa's home were the mansions of several movie stars. These multimillion-dollar homes belonged to the rich and famous, and were kept extremely private down long tree-lined driveways and surveyed by closed-circuit cameras. The homes, unseen from the road, remained protected by high wrought iron fences and locked behind electric gates. Vanessa never saw any of the residents of these homes. Bitton was a community that valued privacy.

As a newlywed, Vanessa had purchased this very safe, private house, attracted by its size and location. She enjoyed the relaxing short mile walk, along tree-lined streets into the town of Bitton, whenever she found the time. After her brief marriage fell apart, she struggled with her options, but ultimately decided to remain in the home she'd single-handedly selected and grown so attached to. It was a difficult decision for her at the time. Painful memories of when she'd lived in her house as husband and wife still haunted Vanessa, even though they'd lived together for less than a year, a lifetime ago.

The annoying alarm clock sounded again. Frustrated, Vanessa forcefully tossed off her covers. It was now five fifteen. A fanatically punctual person, she detested wasted time. Even the idea of sitting idly in the LA traffic gridlock drove her crazy, so she'd arranged for a chauffeured car service to convey her to and from work years ago. Her driver, Tom, was scheduled to pull into her rock-lined circular driveway in less than an hour to collect her. Vanessa knew she had no time to waste hanging around in bed.

Reluctantly, she climbed out of her comfy, warm bed and sleep-staggered down the hallway into her kitchen for the fortifying, automatically dripped cup of coffee that awaited her. She poured a quick splash of cream into her coffee, and poured a generous amount into Callie's dish. Still out of sorts, Callie rubbed insistently against Vanessa's legs to complain. Picking up her grumpy cat, Vanessa affectionately stroked her in an attempt to gently soothe her only companion.

"Hey Callie, we girls need to stick together." Callie squirmed insistently out of her arms and leapt to the floor. She walked arrogantly over to her dish of cream while her fluffy tail waved her supreme displeasure like a flag. Vanessa smiled warmly at the lovable cat's flagrant display of her unfailing, independent spirit.

Absently pushing the strands of her messy, shoulder-length, auburn hair out of her face, with her coffee and a Power Bar in hand, Vanessa dashed back down the long hallway to her bedroom. Sighing bleakly, she gazed pensively into the bathroom mirror at her mop-head and droopy-eyed reflection. 'Time to put on my war paint,' she said to herself halfheartedly as she began tackling her tangled hair vigorously with a comb.

Half an hour later, impeccably dressed in her usual business attire (a white blouse, straight navy-blue skirt, and matching jacket) Vanessa scooped up her briefcase off the chair, clamping today's mail and newspaper firmly under her arm. She took one final look around her house, armed her alarm for the day, and locked the door behind her as she stepped outside. Turning from the secured door she smiled at Tom, who stood with his arms folded, nonchalantly leaning against the long black car as he waited patiently for her appearance.

"Good morning, Tom," Vanessa called. Although Tom had been her driver for the past ten years, they still maintained a formal greeting each morning, which suited Vanessa just fine.

"Good morning, Ms. Golden," Tom smiled, pushing off from the car.

After Vanessa had settled herself comfortably in the back seat, Tom slowly pulled out of her driveway, keeping his eyes squarely focused on the road ahead as he drove. He knew from experience that Vanessa preferred silence during her forty-minute commute to work.

Picking up her mail, Vanessa began absently sorting through the various magazines and letters. The first piece of mail she opened looked interesting, until she realized it was an offer for a senior citizens discount card, and she threw it down on the seat in disgust. This must have been mailed to her by mistake! She huffed indignantly. *No one could possibly consider me a senior citizen.* After all, her closet was filled with the same size six, exceptionally pricey dress suits that she had worn for the past twenty years. *Okay,* she thought, *maybe my ankles do swell a little by the end of the day. And, I admit I can't run as far or as fast as I used to, but I'm still in excellent shape. I look younger than most forty-year old women!*

Sighing in mild despair, Vanessa stared bleakly out of the window, silently agonizing over the significance of her upcoming birthday. Meanwhile, Tom quietly weaved his way through the horrific, downtown LA traffic snarl, unaware of Vanessa's gloomy mood.

The car slowed, pulling up to the curb in front of the *Gemma* building. Vanessa stopped her brooding and returned to reality. Gathering up her belongings, she thanked Tom for a pleasant ride and stood for a moment, shielding her eyes against the morning glare with her hand, gazing up at the impressively shiny building. Rising eight stories from the pavement, *Gemma* was a massive white stone and tinted glass building in the heart of LA's coveted prime commercial business district. The imposing structure contained the staff of the most influential magazine designed for the corporate woman, repeatedly recognized internationally as the most popular magazine dedicated to fashion and savvy advice for businesswomen.

Deliberately placing her three-inch stilettos on the sidewalk, Vanessa straightened her jacket, squared her shoulders, and marched confidently up the front steps with an air of dignified determination. She pushed through the heavy glass doors, entering the immense, white-tiled lobby, and waved informally to the security guard as she passed by. Stepping briskly into the elevator, she pushed the button for the top floor. Silently she took three deep, fortifying breaths as it rose, mentally preparing for her first meeting of the day.

As the head of the magazine's advertisement department Vanessa was scheduled to meet with her young, six-member executive team in twenty minutes. Her editor, Max, had uncharacteristically requested to join today's meeting. She cocked her head to the side, puzzled why he would take time out of his busy schedule to attend a routine weekly run-down of the current advertising accounts. Vanessa had known Max for years, both having had a long history with *Gemma* magazine. Max's father actually owned *Gemma* magazine, and after he'd confirmed Max was satisfactorily married and settled down, he had bestowed the position of editor-in-chief upon his only son. Max, who was just a couple years older than Vanessa, had been the one to hire her; first as his intern, later as a junior advertising executive, and finally promoting her to the head of *Gemma's* prestigious advertising department nearly twenty-eight years ago. Making them both the youngest senior executives at that time. He had once confided to her how impressed he'd been by her intelligence, and how he'd admired her creative initiative and fiery drive.

Reflecting back on her rapid promotion to head of advertising, she remembered her predecessor and mentor, Gloria. At Gloria's retirement party, she had taken Vanessa aside, confiding to her how she'd regretted that she'd never found time for a life outside of the magazine. Gloria, younger than she was today, had warned Vanessa not to make the same mistake. It had taken Vanessa a lot of years, but unfortunately, she now understood what her predecessor had meant.

Although Vanessa struggled with the daily stressors of her position, she hid it well. Quickly composing herself, she shrugged off her curiosity concerning Max's behavior and stepped smartly out of the elevator, immediately running into one of her team members in the hall.

"Good morning, Ms. Golden," Jack greeted her. *Always such a polite gentleman*, Vanessa thought, as Jack reached over to open the etched glass door of their office suite for her.

"Good morning, Jack." She returned his smile warmly as she walked past him. Jack, currently the most senior member of her small team, was tall and thin, and always wore a slight smile, as though he knew a secret that no one else knew. Jack was her rock. Vanessa could always count on his professional abilities as well as his well-timed finesse with clients.

Approximately two years ago, most of Vanessa's team had either moved out of state, changed roles within the company, or left for other opportunities. Training the new team presented a constantly exhausting challenge for Vanessa. Jack had been her first replacement, and a valued member of her team for nearly three years now, while the remainder of her team had only come onboard during the past two years, with Vanessa's newest and youngest team member, Maureen, joining them only four months ago. Two years out of college, Maureen had some previous experience as a freelance advertiser. She seemed smart and grateful for the opportunity to join the team. Vanessa enjoyed working with both Maureen and Jack.

Passing the spotlessly glassed-in offices of her junior executives, Vanessa didn't stop to chat, but continued past her executive assistant's desk to enter her own spacious office. Vanessa set her briefcase on her desk and wandered over to her window, pausing briefly to admire the magnificent view of the city below, just as she did every morning. Her towering view of the surrounding tall, shiny, dark-tinted, glass buildings made her feel invincible.

Her assistant, Marie, magically appeared in front of her desk with a fresh steaming cup of coffee and began a brief review of Vanessa's schedule. Collecting the six account files off of her desk, Vanessa nodded her approval, checked her watch, and picked up her coffee. Completely at ease and in charge of her world, she strolled down the familiar hallway to meet with her team.

The designers of the conference room had placed a large, dominating circular table in the center of the room. They claimed it promoted team cooperation. Her junior executives were already seated around the table, notes and files before them, all except for Mindy, who had not yet arrived. Vanessa nodded to each of them as she seated herself facing the door, leaving an empty seat to her right.

"Good morning, everyone. We've got a lot to accomplish, so let's get to work." Vanessa belatedly realized she'd made this statement in a firmer voice than she'd intended. Noticing the concerned looks around the table, she modified her tone in an attempt to lighten the mood, and indicated the empty seat next to her. "I'm sure you will all remember that Mr. Edwards will be joining our meeting shortly. In the meantime, I'd like a brief run-down of each of your accounts," she instructed professionally.

The door slammed loudly as Mindy rushed into the room. Throwing her account folder carelessly onto the table, she immediately interrupted Vanessa, babbling enthusiastically, "I'm so excited Max is coming today. I have so many ideas I want to run by him," she said, primly seating herself directly across the table from Vanessa, an obvious position of conflict.

The rest of the team busily looked down at their files, each of them pretending to be fascinated by their notes.

Mindy, was a young, perky, willowy blonde, who had joined Vanessa's team less than a year ago, at Max's insistence. Vanessa had strongly objected at the time and had openly expressed her concern that Mindy was the wrong fit for her team. But unfortunately, Mindy had been Max's intern the year before, and he was determined to find a place for her within *Gemma*.

A recent graduate with an MBA in marketing, Mindy had graduated at the top of her class. Aggressive and argumentative, Mindy frequently undermined Vanessa's advertising strategies, claiming Vanessa's research was obsolete and outdated. Overly eager to shine and take credit, Mindy had managed to make more than one enemy at *Gemma*. Vanessa found her to be a constant irritant, and an annoying distraction to the success of her team.

Without acknowledging Mindy's comment, Vanessa shifted her eyes and attention toward Matt, who sat quietly to her left. She located his file from within the stack and addressed him. "Matt, how is the Washburn account coming?" She tapped her pencil, impatient for his response, and anxious to complete the run-down before Max's arrival.

Matt, usually a self-confident young man, became unnerved by his boss's sudden attention, especially after he'd witnessed Vanessa's obvious annoyance with Mindy. He began nervously shuffling through his notes. "Well... I met with their advertising director. We're definitely in the running for a series of full-page ads," he stammered, and looked up without finding his notes.

"Sounds great Matt, we'll talk more about it later in the meeting," Vanessa encouraged, and switched her attention to Odessa, who sat next to Matt. "Odessa, what's happening with the Cover-All lipstick advertising contract?" Vanessa raised an eyebrow expectantly. She considered Odessa's professional experience and expertise an exceptional addition to her team.

Odessa responded with a quick smile. While maintaining direct eye contact with Vanessa, she spoke decisively with self-assured confidence. "The contracts will be signed as soon as their legal department approves them."

"Excellent." Vanessa nodded appreciatively in Odessa's direction. Then turned to face Alexis Chavez. Alexis was the quiet, observant member of the team. Pleasant to work with, she seemed to like everyone, even Mindy. "Okay, Alexis. What can you tell us about your progress with the bilingual advertising campaign?" Vanessa inquired.

Alexis replied without hesitation. "I've completed ten rough drafts to share at our meeting today."

"Thanks, that's great. I'm sure Max will be very pleased!" Vanessa made a note in her file, extremely satisfied by her progress. Vanessa knew she could count on Odessa and Alexis to impress Max. Although, she was still at a loss to understand why he'd decided to join today's meeting.

Next, Jack gave a quick update on his long-term account. He'd recently succeeded in persuading his client to purchase more advertising space in *Gemma*. Maureen, on the other hand, was having some trouble with her account. Primarily due to a complete restructuring of the firm, which is always a difficult process, her client was reluctant to make a commitment to continue advertising in *Gemma*. Vanessa made herself a note. She'd need to provide additional support and mentoring for Maureen. She refused to allow even one account to slip away.

Just as she was turning to address Mindy, Max arrived. An impressive, immaculately dressed, graying gentleman, who immediately commanded the attention of everyone present, Max oozed charisma and charm. Towering at an impressive six foot three, he had a sturdy frame, and a quick, captivating smile. Surveying the nervous faces around the table, his gaze landed on Mindy, sending her a noticeable wink and nod along with an approving smile.

"Welcome, Max. I was just about to ask Mindy to update us on her account. She's been working closely with the Blissful Hair Care advertising department," Vanessa informed him formally.

Max settled himself comfortably into the seat next to Vanessa. His gaze rested fondly on Mindy and he immediately gave her his undivided attention. Mindy returned his smile, basking in the light of Max's scrutiny.

"Well, I've met with Stephen Wright, the head of their advertising department," Mindy began.

"Mindy, you mean Mike O'Hare." Vanessa frowned, correcting Mindy's mistake. "Stephen is one of his *junior* executives," she stated confidently.

"No, I mean Stephen," Mindy chimed; her voice syrupy sweet, implying she knew something that Vanessa was unaware of. She coyly tilted her head to one side as she continued. "I believe Mr. O'Hare retired last week...anyway, Stephen is now head of the advertising department. I've had several meetings with him already this week." Mindy flipped a strand of her long blonde hair over her shoulder, punctuating her confidence.

Vanessa, embarrassed at being corrected by Mindy in front of Max and her team, sat in stunned silence, absorbing the unexpected news of Mike's retirement. She'd always enjoyed a close working relationship with Mike. Hadn't she attended his fiftieth birthday party just last month? Temporarily rendered speechless by Mindy's disturbing news, she concentrated on the file.

"That's great Mindy, please continue and tell us the results," Max encouraged, as he shot Vanessa a quick stern glance to squelch her display of irritation with Mindy.

"Stephen and I work very well together," Mindy continued in a childlike voice. Vanessa shook her head slightly in disgust, and felt like rolling her eyes, but surprisingly Max failed to notice Mindy's phony baby talk. "You know, we both graduated from UCLA, so we speak the same language," she boasted. "We're in complete agreement. Past approaches to advertising do not speak to today's consumers. His company is about to launch a brand-new product line, and they want our assurance that we'll be forward-thinking in our approach. Stephen pitched a wonderful campaign all about modernization. That's the reason *he* was selected for the promotion!" Mindy stopped her enthusiastic monolog long enough to catch a breath and send a beaming smile in Max's direction.

Max returned her smile. His voice carried a warm, appreciative tenor as he praised her. "It seems to me that you were in the right place at the right time. Great job!" His stunning white smile shone directly on Mindy.

Vanessa, appalled by the praise Max lavished on Mindy, could feel her blood pressure start to rise. Her face flushed and her head felt like it was about to explode. Leave it to Mindy to single-handedly find a way to make a fool out of her. Vanessa's reaction, which typically would have been a biting response to Mindy's nasty little insinuations, was thwarted by Max's preferential treatment toward his ex-intern. Instead, she glanced discreetly over at Max. She speculated for the first time whether his paternalistic smile and unusual attentiveness toward Mindy, might actually represent something other than simple approval.

Mindy continued to monopolize the meeting as she discussed the particulars of her account with Max. He leaned closer and seemed to listen intently to every detail, captivated by her elaborate assessments. Once she'd finished, Max responded affectionately. "We really value this account. If you run into any roadblocks..." he frowned pointedly at Vanessa, "Establishing or promoting it, please feel free to let me know. I'll happily run interference for you."

The unveiled look of contempt in Vanessa's eyes toward Mindy had not been lost on Max, and he sent her a brief, stern look. The warning tone of his remark along with his look, made the hairs on the back of Vanessa's neck stand on end. She was shocked into submission by his uncharacteristic, blatantly public admonishment.

Although Vanessa managed to conduct the remainder of the meeting with adequate decorum, it passed in a blur, and her heart wasn't in it. Max seemed genuinely interested in the qualifications of each member of her staff, making several comments of appreciation. He frequently deferred to Mindy's suggestions, as the team reviewed their accounts, adding only minor recommendations himself. Vanessa jotted down notes, but sat quietly and scarcely listened. Max's sudden interest in her team seemed out of character. She struggled to shake the sudden sense that Mindy and Max had been colluding with one another, while deliberately keeping her out of the loop. Vanessa felt as if she'd lost control of her own meeting, and sensed that something was definitely amiss.

Vanessa concluded the meeting with her usual efficiency, and Max stood up to leave. His gaze shifted back toward Mindy. "Keep me posted on your progress," he instructed as if she now reported directly to him.

"Yes sir," she responded, smiling smugly as she gathered her files.

Max returned his gaze to Vanessa and asked, or rather commanded in a very serious tone, "Walk me back to my office Vanessa, I've something I need to discuss with you."

Vanessa picked up her own files off the table and informed her team she would be available after lunch to meet with them individually. She paused, awkwardly aware of the questioning, confused looks from a few of her team members. Each quietly picked up his or her notes, all except for Mindy, who remained seated and smiled nauseatingly as she began to hum softly. Smiling confidently, Vanessa nodded in response to her team's curious looks, and followed Max obediently out of the room.

Once they were out in the hallway, walking swiftly toward Max's elegant office, he nonchalantly asked her, "Have you been feeling all right these days?"

Leery of this unexpected line of questioning, Vanessa noted the mild look of concern in his eyes. "I'm fine, is there some reason you're asking?" She eyed him suspiciously.

Max looked straight ahead as he casually added, "I don't know, you've just looked a little tired recently. I hope you won't hesitate to let me know if you're having any difficulties with your health."

"I can assure you Max, I've never felt better," Vanessa stated with more confidence than she felt at the moment.

"Well..." Max began as they entered his immense office, measuring twice the size of hers, with a sweeping panoramic view. He continued reluctantly, seating himself and leaning back in his high-backed leather chair, attempting to get to the point. "Last Friday, I was given a stern talking-to by HR. Apparently you've only used about ten days of vacation time since you became head of our advertising department." He rested his arms casually on the armrests and raised his eyebrow in dismay.

Thrown off balance and a little confused, Vanessa frowned, "Is that a problem?"

"According to HR..." he slowly elaborated. "You've managed to accumulate almost a full year of vacation time."

"Again, is that a problem?" Vanessa struggled to understand the issue as she sat down warily across from him. She was caught off guard and a little worried by the subject he seemed to be cautiously dancing around.

"I'm sorry, Vanessa." Max attempted to sound official, but sympathetic. "But I was forced to appease the HR manager. I'm afraid you'll be required to take a two-week vacation. Beginning on Monday. Believe me, I had to do some fast negotiations in order to meet our HR requirements." He held his breath as he watched her expression.

"I—I can't possibly leave on Monday!" she faltered. "My team...my accounts...require *my* personal attention, and how can I possibly make any reasonable vacation plans in less than a week?" She had never expected this horrific news. "Max..." she reasoned. "Couldn't I just work from home for two weeks, in order to use up my vacation time?"

"Sorry." Max shook his head. "I already tried that, and HR scolded me for being an ogre. I hate to tell you, but this is only the beginning." He paused, searching her eyes to judge the effect of his previous directive. "You'll be required to take two weeks off every month until your vacation bank is reduced to four weeks." Vanessa blinked and her mouth fell open.

He rushed on to the next topic. "That's the main reason why I wanted to get up to speed with your team today. I'll be troubleshooting your team in your absence. Also, I want Mindy to act as the team leader. She's smart and she can help the others. I'll be working very closely with her, so I can stay informed of any pressing issues as they arise." He held his breath and hoped she wouldn't fight his promotion of Mindy, well aware of her contempt for the girl.

Vanessa felt the blood drain out of her face. For years, she and Max had enjoyed a close, collaborative working relationship. They'd never crossed the lines of professionalism, but she'd always considered him to be a good friend. "Are you unhappy with my performance?" she asked hesitantly, fearful he could see the apprehension on her face. Squelching her feelings of vulnerability, she forced herself to maintain direct eye contact with him, as she gauged his response.

"Heavens no!" Max returned her gaze and offered her an affectionate smile. "You know how I feel about you; you're invaluable to me. I'm as upset as you are by this dictate from HR, but my hands are tied." He shifted uncomfortably in his chair, abruptly averting his eyes from her, and examined the calendar on his desk. "Now, I've set aside Friday morning to meet with you and Mindy. I'll need you to wrap everything up for me in a nice, tidy bundle. I want to make sure we're both fluent on all of the current and prospective accounts. Thank you so much for your understanding in this situation." Max rushed through his speech before she had time to think or respond. Awkwardly, he concluded their painful discussion, and Vanessa sighed, feeling resigned.

"Very well," she said, quietly.

She knew Mindy was the real reason she was suddenly being sent on 'vacation.' Standing on shaky legs, she attempted to muster her tattered pride, and straightened her suit jacket. Turning away, she had reached the door, her hand resting on the knob, when she heard Max call to her softly.

"Vanessa?" He spoke hesitantly from his seat, safely protected behind his massive teakwood desk.

Hearing his change of tone, she turned uncertainly from the door to face him, hoping he wouldn't notice the tears glistening in her eyes.

"Yes Max?" she inquired softly.

"I hope you can look at this opportunity as an unexpected gift." His voice softened, tempered by more than thirty years of friendship and respect.

Feeling the sting of his sympathy, Vanessa couldn't respond to him. Instead, she simply turned and closed the door quietly behind her, striding quickly toward the safety of her own office, desperately struggling to preserve her rapidly fading dignity.

Once cocooned within her office, with her door tightly closed, she swiveled her chair to face the window. Looking out at the familiar landscape, she no longer felt a sense of empowerment. Her eyes blurred, watering with anger and frustration. Isolated in her once cherished space, she allowed her lower lip to quiver, and previously restrained tears spilled down her flaming cheeks. Triggered by bitter feelings of rejection and despair, her tears smarted with the unexpected awareness of her boss's betrayal, and the uncertainty of her once secure future.

Chapter 2
Office Politics and Survival

*H*aley awakened reluctantly from her deep stupor. The sun was shining high in the sky when she finally became fully aware of her immediate surroundings, and discovered Jimmy asleep on the dirty mattress beside her. He faced away from her with his arm resting protectively across her waist. Briefly, she remembered how she used to feel about Jimmy, back when they'd first met. He'd seemed like such a sweet, funny man, immediately capturing her naïve heart and imagination. A smooth-talking, easy-going guy, Jimmy had had a charm all his own. Much older than she, he'd become the heartthrob of her limited world, easily convincing an innocent fifteen-year-old girl to run away with him. Oh, he'd painted such a beautiful picture of a life filled with incredible, romantic, carefree adventures. Haley had been enchanted, blindly trusting her future to him.

Looking back now, Haley realized if there hadn't been friction with her parents, Jimmy could never have seduced her into leaving the security of her family and home. Her parents, both good-hearted, devoted people, dearly loved each other and all of their children. But work had become their priority, which had left Haley to look after her little brother and four younger sisters. Bitterly resentful of the way her parents had simply expected her to take over parenting responsibilities and duties, Haley found Jimmy's fanciful promises of freedom irresistible. Nothing had sounded better to her than speeding out of her small Ohio town on the back of his motorcycle.

But, by the time they'd arrived completely broke in Los Angeles, Jimmy had changed. He'd become a contemptible, desperate man. At first, he tried to work sporadically, but eventually his uncontrollable drinking consumed him, and he didn't work at all.

Haley had also tried to work, but she quickly discovered her opportunities were limited. As a runaway, and a minor, she lacked proper identification. Her inability to obtain a job, along with Jimmy's incessant drinking, had further complicated their ability to survive.

One night Jimmy had decided, in his desperate attempt to support his drinking, that he would allow some of his so-called friends to enjoy 'alone time' with Haley. Instantly pleased by the easy money, it hadn't been long before he'd allow just anyone to enjoy her company.

Haley shuddered, thinking about the constant humiliation, shame, and physical abuse she'd suffered. She'd begged Jimmy endlessly to stop, and *frequently ran away. But, having nowhere else to go, she'd always returned to this same old, dingy room with him. Ultimately, Haley's childish fantasies of Jimmy had disappeared. Looking over at him now, Haley felt nothing, and his mere touch disgusted her. Gingerly, she removed his possessive arm from her waist without waking him.*

Haley had managed to free herself from Jimmy, but she remained perfectly still beside him, afraid to move or risk waking him. I've suffered enough abuse from him, she thought angrily, feeling nothing but hate and contempt. But where can I go? Deep in her heart she knew she could never return home, so her options were limited. No matter how much she ached to return to the safety of her own home and family, she knew they would never understand or forgive the repulsive choices she'd made to survive with Jimmy.

Jimmy, always looking for easy money, had cooked up a brand new get-rich scheme, and yesterday he'd casually informed Haley of her role in his witless plan. Horrified by his reckless behavior, she wanted nothing to do with it, or him. This was the absolute last straw! But Haley knew if she continued to refuse to cooperate, she'd be subjected to his cruel, punishing wrath until she agreed. She quivered, remembering how close he'd come to killing her last night. In order appease him, and avoid more of his tortuous beatings, she would need to play along. Only then could she remain strong enough to escape him, once and for all.

Jimmy stirred, his movement interrupting her troubled thoughts.

He leaned up on one arm, closely studying her face, noticing that her eyes were wide open. He suddenly reached over and pulled her roughly against him. "What the hell's going on in your damn head now, girl?" he growled.

"Nothing!" Haley cried, shrieking in pain as he twisted her arm roughly behind her back. She would have to leave him soon, or die trying!

Vanessa knew she must look a mess after her tearful outburst. Being a senior executive of *Gemma* magazine meant she had a private bathroom attached to her office. She inspected herself closely in the mirror to check the damage; her dull eyes and dramatically swollen face shocked her. Her eyes looked like tiny, red slits inserted in her puffy face. *Darn*, she thought. Her composure had slipped. She detested losing her self-control! To remedy her humiliating situation, she splashed cold water on her face, which temporarily helped her eyes to focus. Valiantly, she struggled to hold back more tears of self-pity, as she carefully reapplied her makeup. Her futile efforts were interrupted by a knock at the door. Vanessa called to her assistant, Marie, to enter.

"I just wanted to remind you, Maureen's appointment is in fifteen minutes. Also, Mindy arrived right after your team meeting requesting an urgent appointment with you at four o'clock. Should I confirm her appointment?" Marie, who had never seen Vanessa so distraught before, hesitated, "Or... should I reschedule?" she asked thoughtfully.

Vanessa shuddered involuntarily. Even the thought of being in the same room with Mindy today made her skin crawl.

"Please reschedule Mindy for tomorrow at ten am. I've decided to leave early today. Call my driver and have him pick me up at three thirty." Vanessa remained focused on her reflection in the mirror as she spoke.

Knowing her usually resilient boss had been crying, Marie had deliberately waited until she saw her get out of her chair, before disturbing her. What on earth could possibly have happened to upset Vanessa to the point of tears?

"Can I get you anything else?" Marie asked kindly.

"I don't think so, thanks." Vanessa's voice sounded meek even to her own ears. She drew in a fortifying breath, exhaling it slowly as she'd been taught, and struggled to reclaim her usual inner strength. "Wait Marie, can you find me the contact number for that travel agent I like to use for my business trips?" Vanessa began formulating a shrewd plan. She was determined to save her position at *Gemma,* if she could.

Vanessa managed to repair most of the ravages of her crying jag in time for her meeting with Maureen. Maureen walked in and instantly became the complete focus of her attention. Enjoying the challenge, she quickly developed several clever tactics to keep her account from slipping away from the magazine. Building a business strategy kept Vanessa's mind occupied. Maureen listened attentively and hung on her every word, absorbing Vanessa's mentoring like a thirsty sponge. Respectful and quiet, Maureen sat in rapt attention as she busily typed reams of notes. Although she frequently looked directly at Vanessa, nothing in her demeanor indicated she was aware of her boss's recent anguish. Her confidence bolstered, she gradually felt her customary sense of control reemerge. After they'd agreed upon a plan of action, Vanessa concluded her meeting with Maureen.

Vanessa leaned over to press the intercom. "Marie, can you find me copies of the last six issues of *Gemma*?"

What an odd request, Marie thought. But she trusted Vanessa knew what she wanted. "Your car will be here in thirty minutes. I'll have those issues to you before you leave. Would you mind if I also leave for the day?"

"Of course not, but come see me once you find the copies of *Gemma*. There's something I'd like to discuss with you before I go." Vanessa's voice had the strength and steely determination Marie had grown accustomed to.

Marie had been Vanessa's assistant for over twenty years, and she was her secret weapon. Vanessa depended on her, trusting her implicitly. During her untimely absence, she knew Marie would be willing to gather pertinent information and report back to her. After all, it was the executive assistants at *Gemma* who knew firsthand what happened behind closed doors.

Meanwhile, Vanessa decided it was time to change her image. She'd prepare herself physically and emotionally to seek other employment opportunities if it became necessary. The first thing on her agenda was to actually read *Gemma* magazine. What better way to improve her image than to absorb the styles and strategies from the most popular magazine designed for today's successful businesswomen? Vanessa felt confident that Mindy would make such a mess of things in her absence that Max would beg her to return. But she'd formulate a contingency plan, just in case.

Marie arrived with the requested magazines and found Vanessa lost in deep thought. "You wanted to talk to me?"

"Oh, thank you. I wanted to let you know that beginning on Monday I will be taking an HR mandated vacation for two weeks out of every month." Vanessa wrestled with her feelings of injustice.

"For how many months?" Marie stood frowning across the desk. Her mouth fell open and her eyes widened.

"I'm not sure." Vanessa tried to sound nonchalant, struggling to keep her tone optimistic. "But, for at least a year."

Marie sat down hard in the chair facing Vanessa. Appalled, she asked, "Can you tell me why?" She feared Vanessa might be deathly ill.

"I wish I knew," Vanessa sighed. "Max claims HR insists that I use a portion of my vacation days each month until my vacation bank is reduced to four weeks," she smiled weakly.

"Do you think that's true?" Marie had never heard of such a thing and squinted skeptically.

Vanessa shrugged, attempting not to react emotionally to Marie's incredulous response. "That's what I've been told."

Vanessa had a pretty good idea what had actually happened. The whole thing was just a ruse to get her out of the office. She believed it was Max's way of giving Mindy an opportunity to audition for her position.

"I'm going to need your help while I'm gone," Vanessa rushed on.

"You know I will do anything you ask." Marie had no idea what she could do to help her, and searched her eyes for clues.

"Can you be my eyes and ears while I'm out of the office?" Vanessa gave her a conspiratorial smile.

"Of course." Marie knew there must be more.

"Will you call me if anything happens that I should know about?"

"Yep, as often as you like."

"You should know Max is promoting Mindy." Vanessa tried to sound casual as she added, "She'll be working in my office and reporting directly to him during my absences."

Marie nodded slowly; now she understood the situation. She had already heard an earful about Mindy from Max's assistant, Jane. "Oh *really*? Now I get it," she nodded with a smirk.

"Come on, what do you know?" Vanessa coaxed, leaning forward in anticipation.

"Well, I heard... that while Mindy was Max's intern, they frequently went out to dinner together."

"I know, he was mentoring her," Vanessa shrugged unimpressed, settling back into her chair with a sigh of disappointment. Marie leaned forward, lowering her voice dramatically.

"According to Max's assistant, it often turned into more than just dinner."

"Do you think?" Vanessa's eyebrows rose, genuinely surprised.

"Jane says Max's wife is divorcing him." Marie seemed eager to share more office gossip. "She's citing Max's relationship with Mindy as her primary reason."

"As in the present tense?" Vanessa assumed this was old information. "I can't believe he would leave his wife for Mindy." Vanessa wrinkled her nose as if she smelled something foul.

"That's the story." Marie sat back in her chair with a nod of conviction.

Vanessa rested her forehead in her hands for a minute, and then she looked up resolutely. "It will take more than office gossip to get rid of Mindy. I need proof! I need evidence that Mindy is totally in over her head. That she's destroying my accounts while I'm away. Can you help me?" she implored.

Marie nodded in affirmation. In her opinion, Vanessa had been the heart and soul of *Gemma* for years. She'd supported her through her glory years and her disasters. She refused to sit back now and watch Vanessa be ousted by a twit like Mindy.

"You can count on it. I know the board will never tolerate Mindy stepping in for you. I've known Mattie Howe since grade school. You know, as in our chairman of the board's sister? A few choice words in her ear, when you're ready, will reach the board in no time at all. I'm certain they care a lot more about the profits of this magazine than they do about a mercenary like Mindy!"

Once Vanessa had filled Marie in on the details of her predicament, she felt completely supported. Marie had never liked Mindy anyway. Mindy had repeatedly treated her with disrespect; talking to her in a singsong, condescending voice, as if she were some kind of moron. Marie might be a quiet, middle-aged woman who generally maintained a low profile, but she knew more about how *Gemma* ran than most executives. Unlike Mindy, Vanessa was tough, brilliant, and considerate. She'd always treated her with the utmost respect. Marie would do anything within her power to make sure a greedy usurper like Mindy didn't run Vanessa out of *Gemma*!

Comforted by Marie's encouragement, Vanessa gathered her belongings to leave. She left by the back elevator to avoid any unwanted contact with Max or Mindy. Walking out of her beloved *Gemma* building, she glanced back at her office window sparkling in the bright afternoon sunshine. Before stepping into her awaiting car, she defiantly lifted her chin, determined to save her job at all costs.

At Vanessa's request, Tom stopped by the store on the way home. She craved some comfort food, which included a rare indulgence of Jamoca Almond Fudge ice cream. Tonight, she planned to open a bottle of wine, eat the whole pint of ice cream, and contemplate the next step for her future. Then, she would give some serious consideration to her ideal vacation spot. Preferably someplace that would leave her well tanned, rested, and youthful-appearing.

After two glasses of wine, Vanessa picked up her copies of *Gemma* and selected one to skim. It only took a few moments for her to realize how completely outdated her professional look had become within the corporate world. Mentally reinventing her image would add a touch of needed strength to her waning self-confidence.

Vanessa texted her travel agent to request that some specific vacation brochures be sent to her office first thing in the morning. She knew she could count on Marie to find her a good personal shopper, and maybe even contact a couple of headhunters on her behalf. She planned to investigate a few business opportunities, just in case. It felt good to make definitive, positive decisions.

Vanessa downed the rest of the bottle of wine, and staggered wearily down the hall to bed. What a remarkable day, she reflected with an ironic chuckle. She marveled at how just one day had completely changed her predictable, serene life. *Tomorrow*, she groaned inwardly, *I'll be forced to endure an extremely humiliating and painful day. Beginning with Mindy's ten am appointment.* How she dreaded that meeting! But she'd always been a survivor, and she would simply suffer through Mindy's simpering and gloating, and then move on.

Vanessa's alarm sounded with its usual irritating ring the following morning. She rolled over and groaned. *Is it only Tuesday?* Today she would need to be alert and, on her toes, especially while dealing with Mindy. Afterwards, she'd spend the remainder of the week preparing for her Friday sign-off meeting with both Max and Mindy.

Vanessa's head pounded and her stomach felt twisted in knots. For a brief second, she considered calling in sick. Instead, she headed to the medicine cabinet for a couple of aspirin. *Calling in sick was for weak cowards*, she told herself. A vacation was beginning to sound better and better.

When Vanessa walked into her office, she found Marie typing at her desk. Her assistant usually arrived early to look over Vanessa's schedule and complete any last-minute tasks from the previous day. She followed Vanessa into her office and seated herself, her memo pad poised and ready for action.

"Have you heard through the grapevine of any executive positions that may be opening up soon?" Vanessa asked, abruptly.

"Actually... I have heard of a couple recently." Marie said her eyebrows rising in surprise, caught off guard by Vanessa's directness. "Do you want me to find out more about them?" she asked hesitantly

"That would be great, but be discreet," Vanessa hedged. "Also, I think I'll need the names of a couple of excellent headhunters. Any suggestions?"

"I'll check with my husband." Marie paused and responded thoughtfully, "You know he works in HR over at Myer and Myer?"

"That's right, he does." Vanessa had indeed known this before she'd asked. "Thank you, he would be an excellent resource."

"I don't suppose you would consider taking me with you?" Marie quaked at the idea of working for Mindy permanently.

Vanessa walked around her desk and sat on the edge facing her. "I would love to. *If* I decide to leave, I'll see if I can negotiate a package deal."

"Is this it, Vanessa?" Marie frowned. "Are you set on leaving *Gemma?*"

"No, I'm just looking at all my options." Vanessa moved back behind her desk. "I'll keep fighting Max's little head in the hope that his big head will kick back into gear."

"And if it doesn't?" Amused by her frank tone, Marie couldn't help but chuckle.

"Like I said." Vanessa sat, leaning back into her leather chair and answered calmly. "I'm just considering all my options. Now on a lighter note, I need you to make some appointments for me."

"Shoot." Marie lifted her pad and pen.

Vanessa enlisted Marie's assistance in scheduling a complete makeover, including an update on her wardrobe with a personal shopper. She specifically wanted *age-appropriate* versions of those found in *Gemma* magazine.

Marie smiled at the newly energized Vanessa.

"Oh, and I'm expecting some vacation brochures. Any questions or clarifications?"

"No, I think I have it all." Marie closed her pad.

Vanessa made one more impulsive request. "One more thing...would you please interrupt me every couple of minutes during my meeting with Mindy?" Vanessa gave her a sly smile causing Marie to laugh out loud.

"Gladly." She stood to leave as Vanessa added casually, "Also, make us a reservation for lunch today, somewhere nice."

22

Marie furrowed her brow in confusion. Vanessa always ate alone at her desk, unless she had a business lunch.

"You and I?" she clarified.

"Yes." Vanessa shrugged, sending Marie an appreciative smile and a nod. "I think we both deserve a nice long lunch today. Make it for noon. If Mindy's still in my office at eleven thirty, interrupt and inform me it's time to leave for my next appointment," she directed.

"All right Boss, whatever you say," Marie smiled to herself. This was turning out to be a very interesting day.

After Marie left her office, Vanessa's bravado disappeared. She suddenly realized there was literally no one else to commiserate with, other than Marie. Her career had become her entire life. She had no immediate family except her mother, who currently lived in France with her new boyfriend. Her mother no longer traveled, and rarely talked on the phone anymore. Her father, who had not been a part of her life since she was a small child, had died several years ago. She had no siblings or cousins, and her closest friends from college had busy families and demanding careers of their own.

Vanessa swiveled in her chair to gaze pensively out of her window. Outside of work, she rarely went anywhere or spoke to anyone, except her cat. Suddenly she felt very desolate, lonely, and overwhelmed by a soul-drenching sensation of regret. Time was not her friend, and now there was no going back. Hindsight couldn't undo the choices of her past, or change her present. She literally had no one!

Vanessa shook her head to clear the cobwebs of her past regrets. Forcing herself to stand, she moved into the bathroom to check her appearance. As she surveyed her image in the mirror, she gave herself a pep talk. "You still have a lot of life left. It's time you went on a fabulous vacation and found some sort of soul mate! Or at least someone you can count on in times like this. Being alone sucks!" She nodded at her reflection with finality and determination. Returning to her desk, Vanessa called her first client to share the news of her unexpected vacation schedule.

Mindy arrived at her office ten minutes late, an obvious power move that Vanessa easily recognized. Mindy overheard Vanessa on the phone and Marie silently motioned her to the chair across from her desk to wait. Mindy belligerently glared at her, and Marie had the fleeting thought she might stick her tongue out at her like a spoiled child. Instead, Mindy settled herself with exaggerated dignity into the offered chair.

When Vanessa thought enough time had passed to make her point, she pressed the intercom button. "Please send Mindy in," she requested formally.

"You may go in now," Marie smiled, speaking in a forced, overly pleasant voice.

Mindy smiled back at her like a Cheshire cat. *The first thing I'll do when I take over*, Mindy thought silently, *is to demand that this smug woman is fired*.

Making direct eye contact with Mindy as she entered her office, Vanessa ceremoniously indicated the chair across the desk from her. Once she was seated, Mindy's eyes slowly wandered around the room, examining it closely, as if she were an interior decorator.

Vanessa noticed Mindy eyeing her view, and interrupted her daydreaming. "You wanted to see me?" she asked politely.

Mindy's affect instantly changed. She became almost giddy with excitement, as if she were a small child who'd just discovered ice cream. "I was so excited when Max told me I would be filling in for you while you're away on vacation. I could hardly wait to meet with you. I want you to tell me everything I need to know in your absence." She spoke rapidly with breathless anticipation.

"I see. But you asked for this meeting right after our meeting yesterday." Only minutes *before* Vanessa had found out herself!

"I know, Max let it slip out last weekend, and I just couldn't wait." Mindy's eyes were bright, sparkling with excited anticipation

Vanessa's phone rang and she picked up the receiver. It was her co-conspirator, Marie.

"Here's your first interruption."

Vanessa hid a smile and responded in a businesslike tone. "Very well, I will call him back right now. Excuse me Mindy, I need to reassure one of my clients that I'll still be available to him for the remainder of the week."

Vanessa called Marie back and spent the next ten minutes reassuring her fake client. She informed him she would be returning in two short weeks, and promised there'd be no interruption in servicing his account during her absence. She went on to assure him that the editor would personally be available if there were any issues during her absence. Talking casually, she acted as if they were old friends, frequently smiling and joking, which was easy since it was actually Marie. Mindy listened absently as she wandered around Vanessa's office, busily redecorating it in her mind.

Vanessa wrapped up her conversation. She frowned, irritated by the way Mindy gazed dreamily out her window at the city below, seemingly lost in a world of her own making. "Sorry for the interruption, I've spent the entire morning reassuring my clients that my brief absences will not affect their accounts. Where were we?" she asked, directing Mindy back to her seat.

"These are different accounts than the ones we discuss every week." Mindy frowned with a slight hint of confusion.

"The accounts I give to the junior executives are the ones this company can afford to lose. I personally handle all of the major accounts. You know, the ones that keep *Gemma* in business." Vanessa said calmly.

"How many accounts are you referring to?"

Vanessa's phone rang again. "Put her through, Marie." *Sorry,* Vanessa mouthed to Mindy's anxious, perplexed face.

Mindy literally squirmed in her chair as Vanessa reassured another 'concerned client.'

The constant interruptions continued for over an hour. Vanessa never directly answered any of Mindy's questions. Instead, she watched Mindy's gloating turn into real anxiety. Mindy's casual wanderings during the multiple phone calls began to slowly transform into agitated pacing.

At eleven thirty, Marie informed Vanessa it was time to leave for her next meeting.

"I'm so sorry, but I'm on a tight schedule this week. I'm trying to get everything done before my vacation. I hope you understand." Vanessa attempted to sound sympathetic.

Mindy stood and wrung her hands. "When can we meet again?" she asked, her voice high-pitched with stress.

Vanessa shook her head, "I'm sorry, you can check with Marie, but I'm booked solid this week. We'll just have to wait until Friday, at our scheduled meeting with Max."

"Are you sure you can't find some time for me before then?" Mindy pleaded.

Vanessa almost felt sorry for the girl. Almost! "I am sorry, but Max wants everything in a tidy package by Friday. There's still a lot of work for me to do before I leave. Don't worry, I'll review all of the accounts with you and Max at our meeting. Trust me, you'll have a clear picture of your responsibilities after that."

Mindy stood there with her mouth gaping. Consumed with apprehension, she suddenly wished Vanessa would stay. She turned slowly toward the door, clearly perturbed and deep in thought. Once she stepped outside, she stomped away rapidly in frustration, so preoccupied with her own agitation, she didn't even acknowledge Marie's smile.

Vanessa and Marie laughed all through lunch at the multiple moods Mindy had displayed during her meeting.

"I can't believe how angry Mindy looked when she left your office," Marie chuckled.

Vanessa felt a twinge of guilt for the unsuspecting girl, until she remembered she was the one responsible for her current circumstances. "You saw how giddy and excited she was when she first walked in," she said, defending her behavior as she sipped her water casually.

"You're an evil genius!" Marie saw a side of Vanessa she never knew existed before; it was impressive. They toasted with their water glasses.

"You know..." Marie confided cautiously. "When I first began working for you, I thought you were the strongest, toughest, smartest executive at *Gemma*. But...for the last few years I've often worried that *Gemma* might be the only family you have. Will you be all right, I mean if you choose to leave?" she asked.

"To tell the truth..." Vanessa put down her glass and stared deeply into the remaining contents as she answered solemnly. "I really don't know."

Vanessa spent the remainder of her day contacting her *real* clients, informing them of the changes in her upcoming schedule. She gleefully gave them Max's private phone numbers. Most of her clients were concerned, knowing what a workaholic she was, which left them puzzled and confused regarding her sudden extensive vacation schedule. Those clients with whom she had the closest relationships inquired about her health, and discreetly, about her job satisfaction.

Riding home that evening, she thought back on her day. She'd managed to temporarily unnerve Mindy, her clients had stepped up to support her in ways she'd never expected, and Marie had once again proven to be her strongest ally at *Gemma*. All in all, today was a big improvement over yesterday, turning out much better than she'd expected. The satisfaction she felt with her small victory faded however, as a disturbing thought invaded her mind. *Do I really want to put up a fight for my position? Is it worth the trouble?* She gazed uneasily out the car window and sighed as she pondered this monumentally unsettling question.

Chapter 3
Soggy Hand-off

*F*riday morning, Haley barely noticed the faint pink rays of sunshine peeking out over the mountaintops, as she reluctantly returned to her filthy, dilapidated apartment. Every step up the stairs caused her agony. Blood slowly oozed from inside her swollen, split, lower lip, leaving an unpleasantly salty taste in her mouth. Unusually cruel during their 'appointment' last night, Scott had appeared stoned beyond reason, and he'd seemed to get more pleasure out of pounding on her, than screwing her. Haley paused in mid-step, cautiously struggling to catch her breath. With each gasp, she winced. Broken ribs again, she thought. Scott's brutality had left her feeling battered from head to toe.

In the past, Jimmy had always insisted that Haley perform her services within the confines of their own apartment. Sadistic-natured, he enjoyed watching her humiliation, and the close proximity guaranteed his immediate payment. Last night, however, he'd seemed eager for her to be elsewhere. He'd forcefully informed her that she'd be spending the night at Scott's, expecting a fight from Haley. But last night was different for her as well, and she had left without argument.

The last time Haley went to Scott's apartment with Jimmy, she'd discovered an interesting little item. While looking for something besides booze to drink, she'd accidently found Scott's secret stash of money and drugs. He kept a surprisingly large roll of bills, stuffed carelessly inside an old coffee can. Desperate to get far away from Jimmy, Haley had made up a risky plan.

Scott, exhausted after nearly an hour of vigorously torturing Haley, had passed out cold. She'd waited for her opportunity before silently tiptoeing into the kitchen. Noiselessly, she removed the money from the can, without stopping to count her loot. Instead, she rapidly replaced the inside bills with wadded paper, leaving an outside bill secured with a rubber band, and left his drugs untouched. Slipping quietly out of the apartment while Scott still slept, she escaped frantically down the dark, windy streets. It was the first time she had ever resorted to theft. Running faster, her adrenaline pumping, she silently prayed he wouldn't check his stash until after she was long gone; escaping from violent men like him, and this dreadful city.

Haley groaned, taking her final step up onto the landing outside her dingy apartment, to return grudgingly to Jimmy. Even though it was barely dawn, loud music and boisterous talking could be heard filtering out into the hallway from beyond the closed door. Wary of what she might find, she *cracked the door open, seeing both Jimmy and his friend Marvin busily creating something in the kitchen, while rowdy country music blasted from a laptop. She frowned in confusion; neither of them knew how to cook. Not that there was ever any actual food in the apartment. She watched their exaggerated, animated movements around the kitchen as they giggled and yelled at each other over the noise, periodically stopping to huddle over the laptop resting on the counter. Softly closing the door behind her, she moved cautiously toward them. Her nose wrinkled in confusion as she was assailed by the pungent odor of sulfur filling the room, which caused her tentative footsteps to halt apprehensively.*

Jimmy heard her approach and whipped around to face her. His eyes danced wildly and he grinned from ear to ear. "Hey, Haley. Guess what we're making? Dynamite for tomorrow! Marv's an absolute genius. Right Marv?" He slapped Marvin on the back to show his appreciation. Jimmy turned away and returned to mix ingredients with Marvin, ignoring Haley or her abused condition. Their laughter and senselessly joking troubled her. Jimmy's red eyes, jubilant behavior, and the fresh pile of empty beer bottles on the floor made her suspicious that they might be drunk, high, or possibly both.

Feeling a disturbing ache of fear deep within her chest, Haley gasped in pain. A cold sense of alarm swept through her, and she began slowly backing away from the crazy-eyed men in the kitchen. Terrified, she frantically searched for the farthest point away from them. Across the main room was a tiny bathroom, where she fled, ignored and unobserved. Tears of fear and helpless frustration began to fall as she closed the door, and pushed her hand firmly against it in despair. Petrified, she was unsure of how to protect herself, until she vaguely remembered her tornado training, and climbed gingerly into the discolored, filthy tub to sleep. Oh please, she prayed, just let me survive through one more day.

Vanessa arrived at *Gemma* earlier than usual. She'd remained sheltered in her office all week while she updated her client files. She squirmed a little, remembering the information she'd deliberately omitted from her account reports, including an assortment of simple little tidbits and personal data, she'd spent years collecting. Deception was not really her style, but in this case, it seemed a necessary part of her corporate survival.

Mindy had tried multiple times to meet with Vanessa, but Marie had skillfully run interference for her all week. Max, on the other hand, didn't seem interested in meeting with her at all. He'd avoided contact with her, and had even cancelled their routinely scheduled meetings. Now that the time had come, she felt confident and completely prepared to hand off her accounts.

Vanessa leaned forward to buzz Marie, "Can you bring in some tea and muffins? And please come in and join me." She counted on a few moments of peace to fortify her emotionally and keep her mentally agile.

As soon as they were both seated, she began. "First of all, I wanted to thank you for keeping Mindy at bay this week."

"That was my pleasure," Marie smiled, relaxing into her chair and leisurely sipping her tea.

"Also, I wanted to apologize in advance for leaving you here to deal with her while I'm away." Vanessa set her teacup down and looked sympathetically at her.

"That's not your fault," Marie shrugged. "Please don't apologize, I'll be fine."

"It is my fault," Vanessa sighed, shaking her head in disgust. "I should have gone with my gut. I should have refused to let Mindy join our team in the first place."

"As I recall, Max didn't really give you a choice," Marie reasoned.

"I know," Vanessa said, shaking her head regretfully. "But I should have convinced him to send her to another department within *Gemma*."

"Jane did mention that Max had briefly considered making Mindy his editorial assistant." Marie set her teacup down on the desk and added, "That was before his wife got wind of their relationship."

"I guess we're paying for their lack of discretion," Vanessa smiled wanly. "The only person who seems to be getting everything she dreamed of is Mindy." She leaned back in her chair in defeat.

"Not yet," Marie said encouragingly, leaning toward Vanessa. "Think about it this way. What if Max is using your position to appease Mindy, and perhaps avoid a sexual harassment suit."

"So? What are you thinking?" Vanessa prodded.

"If Max gives Mindy what she thinks she wants, and it's too hard for her, she could bail out of your position, without any consequences for him."

"Okay... What if she moves into my office and discovers she loves it?" Vanessa sighed, gazing longingly around her office, unconvinced by Marie's hypothesis.

"Jane thinks Mindy will cave the minute she has to juggle more than one account," she continued. "Max's wife, Kitty, and Jane are close. She believes Max wants to go home, but he can't, not until he deals with Mindy."

"So...?" Vanessa urged, still not quite sure what she was getting at.

"So, you and I may not be the only ones who want to see Mindy fail and leave *Gemma* magazine permanently." She smiled, reaching for her teacup.

"That would be very nice, if it were the truth." Vanessa reluctantly acknowledged Marie's inference and noticed the time. "Wish me luck," her voice strained and falsely cheery. Gulping the rest of her tea she stood up to gather her bulky files.

"Vanessa, you don't need luck." Marie stood to clear the dishes. "Remember who you are!" She raised her fist once in the air to demonstrate her support.

"You're right Marie, thank you." Nodding once with more bravado than she felt, Vanessa deliberately straightened her spine before resolutely marching out the door to her fate.

Walking briskly, Vanessa ignored the plush, carpeted hallway and the constant activity within the offices she passed, but her previously confident steps began to falter slightly as she approached Max's office. She scolded herself mentally for her cowardly hesitation, and stood tall before she entered his office with renewed strength.

Max and Mindy sat side by side, deeply engrossed in conversation, their eyes focused on Mindy's laptop screen. Vanessa groaned inwardly at the sight of the two of them intimately cuddled up together. *Such a cozy team*, she thought sarcastically. The only empty chair in the room was directly across from them. She moved toward it, discreetly clearing her throat.

Max looked up, surprised by her presence, "Please, have a seat Vanessa." He motioned to the chair as his eyes met hers. He continued without breaking eye contact with her. "Mindy, let's look at this again later. Right now, I'm anxious to review the accounts with Vanessa," he added in his businesslike tone.

Max rolled his chair away from Mindy and positioned himself directly across the desk from Vanessa. This placed him in a neutral position, equidistant from both women. "I hope you can get us up to speed on all your accounts today." He looked at Vanessa expectantly. "We need to be able to maintain them during your absences—uh—vacations."

Vanessa smiled inwardly at his slip of the tongue. She knew the information she was about to share with them could be easily accessed on the company server. She visualized her briefcase currently located in her office, containing her *confidential* files, including all of the background checks and personal client information she'd gathered over the years. She had generated detailed reports following each formal office encounter, friendly luncheon, and even a few intimate dinners, attaining invaluable client material through years and years of careful observation. Vanessa *knew* her clients.

She'd maintained her poker face, but noted Max's curious stare, and quickly sent him a reassuring smile as she answered. "Of course, Max, it's all right here," she said, and calmly placed twenty-six account file folders on his desk.

"Alright then, let's dive in." He rubbed his hands together in nervous anticipation. "I want you to review each account with us, one by one. Spare no details." Max reached for the first file. "Wow Vanessa, how many accounts are we talking about? This is impressive!"

"Well, there are the six accounts that the junior executives are managing. We've already reviewed those," she reminded him and smiled proudly.

"And the rest here?" Max inquired, raising a questioning eyebrow.

"Those are twenty accounts that I maintain myself." Vanessa flipped through the folders, moving a few of the files to the top of the stack. "These folders represent the accounts that keep this magazine afloat," she said, indicating the top folders.

Mindy let out a soft groan. Max, who was engrossed in the files, appeared not to notice. But Vanessa did, and couldn't resist flashing her a sweet smile.

"Okay, let's start with our money makers," he directed.

"Let's," Vanessa responded, knowing she'd captured his complete attention. "You'll notice a dollar amount on the corner of each folder."

"I do, what's that?" He glanced at the top file.

"That's how much money each client represents to *Gemma* in revenue," Vanessa instructed.

"But this one says one million?" Max exclaimed. Vanessa responded with a proud smile and nodded.

"Wow, there are five more folders like this one. Each one is worth over a million dollars?" Max shuffled through the folders. He knew she had a strong clientele, and he knew the bottom line, but he had never bothered with any of the specifics. The files signified considerably more work than he'd anticipated.

"I had no idea," Mindy whispered. Vanessa noticed the color draining from her face and believed she might actually faint.

Vanessa looked expectantly at Max. *Maybe his big head is kicking back in,* she thought. His furtive glance at Mindy, and his exasperated exhalation said it all. Frowning deeply, Max pushed his intercom. "Jane, cancel my appointments for the rest of the day, and order us some lunch."

"Should I also notify Vanessa's assistant to cancel her appointments as well?" Sitting at her desk, Jane smiled. She could tell by his gruff tone that Max had gotten himself into a well-deserved pickle.

"Yes!" Max barked his impatient response. "And I need you to come in to take some notes for me. Now!"

Throughout the morning, Vanessa pored over every detail of each individual account. Max listened thoughtfully and asked insightful questions, while Mindy sat noticeably mute, focusing on her laptop and making an occasional notation. By the time the caterer arrived with their lunches, they'd only reviewed a few of the top accounts. Jane and Vanessa stood simultaneously to ask Max to excuse them for lunch.

"Won't you join me for lunch?" he asked Vanessa, annoyed by the interruption to his workflow. "Remember, we still have a lot of accounts to review."

"I'll be back as soon as I can," she said calmly, noting his obvious irritation.

Once both Jane and Vanessa had left the room, Max turned to Mindy, his voice low and serious. "Do you think you can handle all this?" He spread the stack of files with his hand.

Mindy stunned by his lack of confidence, sat up visibly straighter as she answered with exaggerated bluster. "I have an MBA in marketing. I know all of the latest statistics and strategies. As long as I have your support, Max, I'm sure I can handle anything Vanessa can," she spat out in contempt.

Max sat back to study her for a moment. "All right Mindy, we'll see how well you handle Vanessa's first two weeks of vacation," he said, skeptically. He was seriously regretting many of his recent decisions. "I want you to promise me, that you'll involve me early on if you run into even a minor difficulty. I don't want you to come to me after you've lost one of Vanessa's accounts!" he demanded.

"Fine, Max," Mindy pouted. "I promise. I cannot believe that you don't have more faith in me." She flipped her long, blonde hair over her shoulder, offended. "After all, Max, I was *your* intern for over a year!" With that, she stood up, and escaped childishly into Max's private bathroom, shutting the door firmly behind her.

Max sighed in frustration. Alone in his office, he gazed down at his favorite lunch, resting untouched on the desk before him. "What have I done?" he muttered remorsefully to himself.

Back in her office, Vanessa was greeted by a cardboard box resting on the corner of her desk, overstuffed with all of her personal items. She wandered aimlessly around her desk. The room appeared as bare and sterile as the first day she moved in. This had been her home for many years, she thought. The room hadn't changed at all, but she had. Somehow, she'd lost her sense of pride regarding her precious position at *Gemma*. She felt betrayed!

Marie peeked in from the doorway. "How's it going?" she asked cautiously.

Vanessa looked up, her forehead creased, her face showing the intense strain of the morning. "I can't begin to tell you how painful this day is for me," she answered softly.

"Try to hang in there," Marie frowned, concerned by Vanessa's somber tone. "I just talked to Jane. She says you're really doing a number on Max and Mindy," she encouraged. "Apparently, Max looks like he wants to kill someone. Be careful Vanessa, or he might just cancel your vacation," she warned.

"You know, it would break my heart if those two destroyed everything I spent years building," she sighed, smiling weakly. "I'm beginning to run out of stamina. I think I'll try to skim through the remaining accounts." But she knew in her heart that she'd complete her report like the professional she was. "I guess I'd better get back before Max has a fit," Vanessa teased, although her smile didn't reach her eyes.

"Try to have some fun tormenting Mindy," Marie suggested, attempting to lighten her mood. "And don't worry, Max will eventually come to his senses."

As Vanessa reluctantly pushed through her glass doors to return to Max's office, piercing fire alarms shrieked in the hallway. Overhead sprinklers spewed a steady stream of cold, murky water, instantly soaking her to the skin. She rounded the corner to see Max, Mindy, and Jane dashing into the stairwell, and she quickly followed.

Once inside the stairway, which was mercifully dry, Max shook off the excess water from his suit and attempted to pull himself together. "We've managed to save your files. Jane dumped them inside the wastebasket and wrapped them in the plastic liner."

Vanessa looked over to the now very wet Jane. "That was fast thinking."

"This fire situation is a mess," Max continued, sounding discouraged. "It could take hours before they clear the building. I don't know when we'll be able to resume our meeting." He shook his head in disparaging frustration.

Jane suggested they continue the meeting at the Drake Hotel. She knew Max had moved there after his recent separation from Kitty. Max nodded approvingly, readily agreeing to her plan.

They descended the stairs, with Max in the lead, closely followed by Mindy. Shortly his breathing became loud and labored, and he was far too breathless to converse comfortably. Vanessa and Jane hung back a little to chat quietly about the fire alarm and sprinkler deployment.

Jane's cell phone rang several times. After a brief conversation, she called down the stairs, "Max?"

He stopped on the landing and gulped air as he looked up at her.

"We're all set with a conference room at the Drake. A car is waiting for us down the street by the coffee shop."

After catching a few breaths, he nodded up at her. Meanwhile Mindy continued down the steps in front of him. She didn't stop or look back.

An hour later, seated around a luxurious conference table at the Drake Hotel, Vanessa attempted to resume her review of the accounts with Max and Mindy, but Max's cell phone constantly interrupted her presentation. Even Max's elderly father had called to get filled in on the fire.

"Jane..." Max finally barked at her in frustration. "Find someone to screen these damn calls! I don't want to be disturbed unless it's urgent!"

"What about Vanessa's assistant, Marie?" Jane suggested. "Fine, contact her now, and here, take my phone." He nearly threw it at her.

His phone began ringing in her hand as Jane walked out of the room to call Marie. Once Jane had located Marie in the mob outside the Gemma building, Marie made the quick trip to the hotel, and was situated in an office down the hall. Relieved, Jane then returned to the meeting in progress.

Relaxing back in his chair, without the irritation of his phone constantly ringing, Max was finally able to concentrate on Vanessa's accounts. He preferred to simply listen, and relied on Jane's notes for the details.

Mindy sat quietly throughout the entire meeting, and had even stopped making notations. After several hours of collaborating with Vanessa, Max turned to Mindy, before rapping up the meeting. "Do you have any last minute questions for Vanessa?" he prompted. "After all, I'm counting on you to run point on this." He smiled at her in an attempt to display a confidence that he didn't currently feel.

Mindy looked up briefly and merely shook her head. "No, I got it," she said, insolently.

Vanessa stood up and gave Max a quick nod and a wistful smile. "I guess I'm off for my vacation. I'll see you in two weeks."

"You will be available by cell phone, won't you Vanessa?" Max beseeched.

Vanessa, disappointed in Max and the whole situation, made a snap decision. "I'm sorry Max, after our discussion earlier this week, I arranged for a trip that is well out of cell phone reach. Should I change my travel plans?" she baited him, wondering how he would respond.

Max turned his head and ran his hand through his damp hair in frustration as he glanced over at Mindy. Vanessa knew he only displayed this particular mannerism when under extreme stress. But he turned back toward her and forced a weak, uncertain smile. "Of course not, after all, it's only two weeks, what could possibly happen?" He sent Mindy a tentative glance. "Please, enjoy your well-deserved vacation." Max's nonchalant response failed to match his concerned expression. He shifted his attention to a very pale Mindy, as he reached down to help her out of her chair, and requested firmly, "Come with me please. I think we need to talk in private."

Mindy stood without responding. She sullenly accompanied her boss out the door and they disappeared down the hall. Marie caught sight of Max and Mindy from the office. She observed them as they silently entered the elevator that led to the upstairs suites.

"I take it the meeting's over?" Marie asked, walking into the conference room to join Vanessa and Jane.

"Yes, it is, and that had to have been the strangest meeting I've ever attended." Vanessa shook her head in bewilderment.

"You can say that again!" Jane exclaimed as she gathered the files along with her notes. "What's up with little Miss know-it-all? I've never seen her so quiet. She didn't make one single valuable contribution all day."

"I know what you mean," Vanessa had to agree. "Oh well, that's Max's problem now."

Suddenly, Vanessa felt reluctant to go home, craving a little female companionship. "Ladies," she asked, "may I buy you both dinner? The bar looks like it might have just what we need after a long day like today. After all, I'm on vacation!" She laughed as Marie handed her purse and briefcase over the conference table.

The three women sat down at a table in the cozy, dimly lit lounge, close to the bar. Guitar music floated softly to a handful of people scattered around the room. Exhausted by their long week, they ordered drinks to celebrate their endurance and Vanessa's vacation. Their conversation slowly turned to speculation over the day's unusual events at *Gemma*. Each one had arrived at a tentative theory regarding the cause of the mysterious fire alarm and sprinkler deployment.

Max's cell phone rang loudly in Marie's pocket, and she jumped at the unexpected sound. "This is Maximilion Edward's cell phone," Marie answered formally. "No...this is Marie, one of his executive assistants," she said, attempting to sound official. "Thank you." Marie's eyebrows rose as she listened. "I'll be sure to give him the message." She set the phone down on the table and backed away like it might bite her.

Vanessa and Jane leaned toward her and looked at her intently. "Well?" they asked in unison.

"That was Max's wife." Marie shrugged. "And I'm too much of a lady to repeat what she just said." She pushed the phone toward Jane. "Here, you take this!"

Vanessa and Jane exchanged looks, but silently agreed they could guess what Max's wife had to say.

"Okay, then tell us about the other calls you fielded regarding the fire," Vanessa prodded.

"It seems..." Marie leaned in, eager to share. "They found no indications of *any* fire at *Gemma*!"

Vanessa and Jane's mouths flew open.

"What do you mean no fire?" Jane asked.

"What caused the sprinklers to activate?" Vanessa indicated her soaked jacket.

"The fire investigators found a smoke bomb on the fourth floor." Marie leaned farther across the table and lowered her voice conspiratorially. "They believe the sprinklers were activated remotely from somewhere in the basement."

"Who would do such a thing?" Vanessa choked on her daiquiri. "And why?"

"They don't know yet," Marie shrugged. "They think it may be some kind of corporate espionage. Someone may have been after computer information or *Gemma's* private files. They haven't uncovered any clues yet."

Marie glanced up from her drink just in time to catch a glimpse of Mindy darting out of the elevator. Running heedlessly through the crowded lobby, she bumped into several people without stopping, slowing, or even attempting to apologize.

"Looks like their private meeting is over," Marie observed sarcastically, motioning toward Mindy with her head. "Mindy looks like the devil is chasing after her."

Jane looked over the rim of her margarita in time to see Mindy knock over a suitcase in her haste. "There was something really strange and spooky about that girl today," she said, slowly watching as Mindy disappeared from view.

The three women nodded in silent agreement and continued to thoughtfully sip their drinks. Each had witnessed Mindy's dramatic personality swings over the past week, leaving them all to wonder; *exactly which personality represented the real Mindy?*

Chapter 4
Winds of Change

*H*aley kept her eyes closed, but the sound of cascading water drew her hazy attention. The splashing reminded her of a familiar, crystal clear waterfall, tumbling down a steep mountain slope, over mammoth boulders, and into a pristine, clear, blue lake nearly sixty feet below. It was her family's favorite destination, a place where they had enjoyed several steep hikes up a rocky trail, bordered by blankets of tiny wild lavender flowers, to a secluded picnic area next to Lost Lake. The tantalizing aroma of her mom's fried chicken and potato salad made her mouth water. She could almost hear her little brother and sisters laughing and playing nearby in the lake. Blissfully she listened, lost within her memories, deeply appreciating the serenity of the setting. She floated euphorically, only semi-awake in her peaceful state, until an electric, searing sensation of pain shot up her spine, rapidly returning her to the harshness of her reality.

Haley peeked through one eye, but instead of the beautiful waterfall she had just imagined, she saw Marvin peeing into the toilet only inches from her head. He stood with his eyes closed and didn't seem to notice her uncomfortably curled up in the tub. He finished, farted, and left, not bothering to flush or wash his hands. Carelessly, he'd left the door ajar, and she struggled to see through the portal into the room beyond, now shrouded in partial darkness.

Haley winced in pain as she tried to shift positions, wondering, how long have I been in here? It felt as if she'd slept off and on for hours. The tub she'd piled with filthy, stained towels and clothes for cushioning this morning had proven to be monstrously uncomfortable.

Her arms failed her as she pushed futilely against sides of the tub to stand upright. Finally, in frustration, she crawled over the edge, and landed awkwardly onto the hard, urine-stained floor. Burning shards of pain shot through her body. She leaned lightly against the edge of the tub for support, struggling to catch her breath. The agony brought unwanted tears to her eyes, but she fought through them, finally hoisting herself upright, and forcing herself to stand erect.

Looking into the darkened room beyond, Haley could scarcely distinguish the outlines of Jimmy and Marvin, now asleep on opposite ends of the mattress. She found their arrhythmic snorting and snoring oddly reassuring. Closing the door noiselessly, she put the toilet lid down and sat gingerly on the toilet seat. Stealing some private time, she began to think *through her escape plan. First, she'd need to see how much money she had. She pulled the wad of bills out of her back pocket and began counting. She'd only counted about half of the stack, more than six hundred dollars, when the door crashed open.*

Jimmy towered over her, his mouth gaping in astonishment. "Where the hell did you get that?"

Haley cringed. She felt her heart sink into the pit of her stomach. Holding her breath, she waited for him to strike her, like the rattlesnake he was. Speechless with terror, instead of responding, all she could muster was a slight shrug of her shoulders.

"Dammit Haley! You stole that from Scott, didn't you?" His booming voice shook the tiny room, rattling the fractured mirror over the sink. Haley ducked and covered one ear, while her other hand desperately clutched her newfound wealth.

Tears streamed uncontrollably down her face, blurring her vision. Without looking directly up at him, she watched helplessly as his big mitts ripped the money from her hand. All of Haley's hopes for a getaway tomorrow were crushed! Now, she prayed Jimmy would finish the job and kill her. At least then she'd be free from him, and her dismal, wretched life would be over at last.

Instead, Jimmy left her sitting in misery. He flipped the lights on in the other room and kicked at Marvin's legs. "Hey, get up. It's after eight at night!"

Marvin pulled the tattered blanket over his face, grumbled inarticulately, and refused to open his eyes.

Jimmy danced around the room ecstatically, waving the bills in his hands like a fan. "Look, my bitch got us some cash. Now we can rent a car for tomorrow, so we don't have to worry about getting traced or nothing."

Marvin's snoring had resumed beneath the blanket. Jimmy paced the room, until he became infuriated and lifted the edge of the mattress, rolling Marvin onto the hardwood floor. "Dammit, get up Marv! We have things to do!"

Vanessa's chauffeured car pulled into her rock-lined driveway much later than usual that night. All the way home she'd pondered over the mystifying day she'd just experienced. Her routine meeting to temporarily hand over her clients had dissolved into some kind of bizarre, three-ring circus. Was someone actually working to sabotage *Gemma?* She couldn't imagine that *Gemma* had any unique business plans worth stealing. And what about Mindy? Not one word of her usually confident chatter today. Instead, she'd seemed uncharacteristically meek, skillfully avoiding any direct eye contact throughout the meeting. Why had she exited the hotel in such a frantic state? What was she hiding? Was she somehow involved in today's office commotion? *Crucial pieces of this puzzle are definitely missing*, Vanessa mused, shaking her head in bewilderment.

Vanessa's high-heeled shoes crunched on dry leaves, recently blown up against her front door. Tripping through her doorway, she was greeted by her surly cat. She reached down and cuddled Callie, making a silent resolution. What happened this week has happened! There was no point in wasting any more of her time or energy thinking about *Gemma*. No need for her to worry about *Gemma* at all. Marie would keep her updated on any office drama that might evolve. Instead, it was time for her to focus on her own plans! The next two glorious weeks would be about nothing but her.

She lifted her cat in front of her face and exclaimed, "I'm on vacation, Callie, beginning right now!"

A bit tipsy from dinner with the girls, she swerved a little on her way into the kitchen. Her message machine on the counter blinked ominously. Unable to contain her curiosity, she pushed the play button. The pleading voice, easily identified as that of an extremely inebriated Max, filled her empty kitchen. "Vanessa, can you ever forgive me? I'm such a foolish old man. Please? Please..." The dial tone droned briefly, then the line went dead. Vanessa stared at the machine momentarily, as if the cold, black box could interpret the meaning of his cryptic message. Aggravated by Max's drunken plea, she switched off the recorder, and impulsively turned off her cell phone as well. "Max can just deal with everything himself until I'm officially back!" she declared with finality.

Walking to the sink, she filled a glass with water and popped a couple of aspirin into her mouth. After feeding her cat, she leaned against the counter and toasted the preoccupied Callie ceremoniously with her raised glass. "Here's to us, my friend!"

She traversed the rotating hallway, periodically swaying out of control against one wall or the other. Once she'd reached the safety of her room, she peeled off her previously soaked suit, regarding the ruined clothes with regret. Into a dry cleaner bag, they went, without expectations.

The hot shower felt heavenly. Every muscle in Vanessa's body relaxed under the steaming, soaking water stream. The past week had tied her body into tight knots. Now, she felt the alcohol and the soothing warm water release her tensions, along with her uncertainties regarding her future at *Gemma*. Closing her eyes, she allowed her fuzzy mind to wander, envisioning a new Vanessa with an inspiring hairstyle and a captivating wardrobe. *My transformation will astonish the modern world of fashion—and Max,* she predicted smugly.

Vanessa examined her face in the mirror, lathering on the anti-wrinkle cream from the previously unopened jar that she'd bought years ago, in honor of her new resolutions. She lifted the nightshirt over her head and let it fall. It stuck to her freshly washed body, causing her to giggle at the absurdity of the fabric that clung to her, like old, wrinkled skin.

Once in bed she stared blankly up at the ceiling. Wide-awake, the room began to spin around her bed. Throwing off her covers, she opted for popcorn and the ten o'clock newscast, instead of struggling to sleep. Slipping on her robe, she staggered only slightly on her way back to her kitchen, with Callie trailing close behind.

Vanessa settled herself on the cozy living room couch in front of the TV set. With a bowl of popcorn resting on her lap, she pulled a fuzzy, soft blanket over her legs. Callie jumped up to cuddle beside her as she flipped on her usual, nightly news program.

Her favorite reporter announced the first big story of the day. *"Breaking news, there was a mysterious fire at the Gemma building today. Although they found smoke, no evidence of a fire was uncovered by the fire marshal. Water damage to the building was quite extensive and estimated repairs will run into the millions. Authorities are currently suspecting foul play. Local police were unwilling to share any theories regarding the cause of the damage at this time, but simply state that they're in the middle of an ongoing investigation. Stayed tuned for Marty, with the local high surf advisories, and the latest news on the Santa Ana winds. He'll let you know how they may both affect your weekend plans."*

"That's enough of that," she said, thoroughly disappointed by the lack of new information regarding the incident at *Gemma*. She clicked off her seldom-used TV in disgust.

Eyeing her briefcase next to the door, Vanessa thought, *Just a quick look at some of the travel brochures might clear my mind and help me sleep.* She located the brochures she wanted, buried beneath her client files, and fanned them in her hands. Glancing briefly at the file resting on top, she noted it was Mindy's account. *Something seems peculiar with her account,* she thought. *And, Stephen, of all people, had replaced Mike!*

Vanessa had never liked or trusted Stephen. He was rude, and he'd frequently hang around to eavesdrop on their business and personal conversations. Stephen had seemed particularly creepy at their last meeting, constantly interrupting Mike with irrelevant, irritating questions, and dominating their conversation. It was after that meeting that Vanessa had chosen Mindy to take over the account. At the time, she'd had no idea that there was any connection between Stephen and Mindy. She shook her head at the irony. *Apparently, now I'm in the same position that Mike had found himself. Perhaps ladder-climbing was a popular class offered in their college.*

Vanessa carried her popcorn bowl and water glass into the kitchen, with the packet of travel brochures securely tucked under her arm. She tipped the remaining popcorn into the garbage and placed the bowl inside the dishwasher. Fresh water in her glass, she returned to her bedroom with Callie, who immediately curled up comfortably against her, purring contentedly as Vanessa absently stroked her back.

Spreading the brochures out in front of her on the bed, Vanessa quickly scanned them and began to sort them by locale. She plucked out six of them to read more thoroughly, stuffing the remaining brochures back into the packet, which she tossed to the floor next to her bed. With the wire-rimmed reading glasses from the nightstand placed on her face, she settled back in bed with only the soft glow from the bedside lamp illuminating the room, and began to read through the details of her potential vacation destinations.

Vanessa was attracted to the cruises, but quickly eliminated the ones leaving from LA. Being stuck onboard a ship with one of her clients was definitely out! That narrowed her selection down to the Caribbean cruises leaving from the Florida ports. *A five-day cruise would be best*, she thought. *That will give me plenty of time to prepare myself, with ample travel-time.* She loved to scuba dive and thought maybe she'd try parasailing, so she found a cruise featuring the type of activities she found appealing. She set the one she liked on her bedside table. *Choice made, tomorrow I'll book my trip!*

Vanessa was about to turn off her bedside lamp, when a loud noise filled the room, sounding as if the roof might have caved in. The lights flickered, and then she was immersed in pitch darkness. She had to know what had happened. Leaping out of her bed, she blindly groped inside her nightstand for a flashlight, and located her robe.

Moving cautiously toward the kitchen, after Vanessa felt adequately reassured that her roof was intact, she discovered nothing disturbed within the house, even when she slowly focused the flashlight around the front yard. Everything seemed normal. However, when her flashlight skimmed over the backyard, she found all of her patio furniture overturned, and dried maple leaves scattered and formed into asymmetrical piles. She shone her light farther out into the yard, until it landed on her favorite maple tree, which had been viciously uprooted by the wind and tossed, upended, into the pool. Lowering her flashlight, the devastating, senseless destruction overcame her.

Shocked by the mess, she continued to stare and watched the tree tossing and twisting in the wind, mesmerized by the way the moonlight shimmered on the tree's exposed roots. The gnarled, dirt-clad roots appeared to stretch up into the sky, like a drowning victim reaching up from the water, pleading to be pulled to safety. She felt a chill travel up her spine and turned away from the ghostly sight. *Damn that crazy wind!* She shivered, feeling strangely isolated and alone.

With a sudden sense of urgency, Vanessa headed toward the garage. Her security system was hard-wired, but she remembered that the back-up battery check had been neglected for quite some time. Now, as she stood unnerved in front of the panel, she could tell the security system was indeed dead.

Callie had reluctantly followed Vanessa through the dark house. She reached down and picked her up for solace. "I guess I won't be swimming laps in the pool tomorrow morning," she chuckled, nervously.

Still unsettled and unable to sleep, Vanessa began to create a mental list of all of the calls she'd need to make in the morning. First off, she'd call the power company, but more importantly, she'd call her gardeners. She wanted everything back to normal as soon as possible. And, even though it broke her heart, her maple tree would require removal, before her pool could be thoroughly cleaned. Anything out of place in her personal space drove her nuts.

"Looks like I'll hit the jogging trail tomorrow instead," Vanessa said, optimistically pushing a damp strand of hair out of her face.

Hating the feeling of vulnerability, she rummaged around in the kitchen junk drawer for her portable alarms. Methodically, she moved around her house with a flashlight, setting the alarms on every door and window, testing the locks as she went. Even after securing the house, Vanessa still couldn't seem to shake the uneasiness she felt. She picked up her cell phone from the kitchen counter before returning to her room. Living all alone, she used her cell phone as her security blanket at night.

Returning to her room, before she plugged in her phone next to her bed hoping for the power to return sometime during the night, an earlier text message from Marie caught her eye. It read, "On my way home I saw Mindy. She was with some guy on the sidewalk by Sacs having a very heated argument. She seemed angry, and I watched her punch him on the shoulder. Couldn't hear anything, except I think she called him an idiot. I'm sending you a picture of the guy. Talk to you soon."

Vanessa shook her head; she didn't really care about Mindy's private life. But she began to wonder if what Marie had witnessed was somehow related to the odd phone message she'd received earlier from her boss. Intrigued, she pulled up the photo Marie had sent. Mindy faced away from the camera, looking towards an angry-looking, red-faced Stephen. *Huh*, she thought, *looks like those two are working on more than just the Blissful Hair account!* She'd see what else Marie knew in the morning.

Stretching her arms over her head, she felt ancient and exhausted. Yawning involuntarily, she saw by the illuminated time on her phone, that it was now well after midnight. Outside she could still hear the wild, deafening winds storming around her home. Shivering, she pulled her covers around her tightly and snuggled in close with Callie. "It's going to be a long night, girl."

The next morning, Vanessa woke feeling sluggish, stiff, and achy all over. The sunshine streamed through her window, and she watched tiny swirling dust particles dance in a ray of light. The house was absolutely still. The winds had ceased, but her bedside alarm clock was still dead. *Looks like there's no power,* she thought. Lifting her cell phone, she noticed that it was after nine am. She hadn't slept this late in years! Callie stirred, standing beside her, the cat stretched her back into a rainbow shaped curve, causing her long, feathery fur to stand on end. She jumped nimbly to the floor and looked expectantly up at Vanessa, which made her smile. "All right, all right, I'll get your breakfast."

Callie disappeared down the hallway while Vanessa pulled back her covers and climbed out of bed. Cell phone in hand, she slowly followed her cat. She had lots of calls to make today. But, coffee first!

Once Callie was fed and Vanessa had endured a cold glass of coffee latte, she nibbled on a Power Bar as she began to make her calls. First, she dialed the gardener. She explained the condition of her yard to Juan, who readily agreed to take care of it that afternoon. He'd been her gardener for years, and she was pleased by his prompt response.

The next call was to the power company; reaching a recorded message, she hung up feeling mildly annoyed. She tried her club, thinking maybe they had power, but the message simply said the line was temporarily out of service. Great, that meant no hot shower, and no swim this morning. She finished her Power Bar and returned to her room to throw on her running clothes. The jogging trail around the reservoir would have to do, that is if it wasn't too littered with fallen branches. She needed to burn off some of the nervous energy coursing uncontrollably through her tense body.

Vanessa felt unusually trapped this morning. An inexplicable, compelling urge to escape her temporarily damaged home, engulfed her. The house was still and eerily quiet. Gone were the fierce winds from last night. Today, her wind-tousled yard would be completely restored. Soon her usual, calm, orderly life would return to normal. But that didn't console her. Vanessa felt consumed by her restlessness and overwhelmed, urgently needing to flee from her weather-beaten home.

Chapter 5
Unexpected Guests

*H*aley sat solemnly in the back seat of the rental car, while Jimmy pulled slowly into the alley beside the First National Bank of Bitton. It was ten thirty in the morning, and although the power had been off when they left their apartment, several lights now shone inside the businesses of downtown Bitton. The small town seemed quiet and deserted. Timing was everything.

Marvin, who sat next to Jimmy in the front seat, had a friend who worked at the armored car company. She had selected this particular bank based on the armored car routes, schedules, and the bank's low security measures. They had everything they needed to successfully pull off the job.

Earlier, despite Haley's protests, Jimmy had dumped green dye into her freshly chopped off hair and spiked it straight up, punk style. He'd added fake tattoos on her arms, and had forced her to wear an obscenely low-cut top and skimpy shorts.

Angry and terrified, Haley was positive she was about to be killed or sent to prison. *At least if I go to prison*, she thought, *Jimmy won't be able to control or hurt me anymore.* Trembling uncontrollably, even though it was eighty degrees outside, her hands felt icy cold and she rubbed them together nervously.

Marvin and Jimmy grabbed the dynamite vests from the back seat beside her. Jimmy narrowed his cruel eyes and sent her a lethal look as he reached for his vest, threatening, "If you ruin this for me, I'll make you wish you were never born! Got it?" The look, and the low fierce voice Jimmy used, sent waves of fear through her. Haley nodded, afraid to utter a word.

"We need you to keep that guard looking toward the street, and away from the door. Can you handle that?" Jimmy asked, his challenging voice making it clear there'd be painful consequences if she dared to disobey him.

Terrified, she nodded silently again, her eyes widening as big as saucers.

"Haley?" he threatened, his dark eyebrows drawing menacingly together. Obviously, he'd expected a more definite answer from her.

"Yes, I got it," she said, forcing her bravado, even though her voice quivered uncontrollably. He knew he'd intimidated her, and feeling his brutal power over her, he sent her a cruel smile of sadistic satisfaction.

Haley kept her head down, suppressing her nauseated reaction to his smug performance. She'd already decided that the minute Jimmy and Marvin turned their backs on her she'd run. She might not get away, but it *was worth the risk.*

Jimmy and Marvin buckled their dynamite vests, slipping thin jackets over the top, while they waited in the car. She thought it humorous how they'd made paper signs, full of misspelled words, with instructions for the tellers. Marvin assumed they'd be safer wearing masks and not speaking, thereby making themselves unidentifiable. Now, as they tried on their masks for the first time, they nervously hammed it up with each other.

Content with their clever get-ups, Jimmy turned back to Haley. "Okay, get going. You know what to do. You'd better not screw this up, or you'll damn well regret it!" he warned, seeming even more intimidating as he growled at her through his gorilla mask.

Terrified and nervous, Haley had no idea how to divert the guard's attention. "He looks pretty old. How... will I distract him?" she stammered.

Jimmy scoffed. He reached back and whacked her on the side of her head to make his point. "He might be old, but he's not dead," he leered obnoxiously, removing his mask as he spoke. "Just talk to him, Haley. You'll think of something. We'll watch you from the corner until we're sure he's not looking, then we'll slip in."

She reluctantly placed her hand on the inside handle, waiting for Jimmy to unlock the door. Getting out, she stood on the sidewalk and pulled futilely at the hem of the shorts that had ridden up indecently between her thighs. Hesitantly, she looked down at her red stiletto heels and racked her brain for a way to distract the unsuspecting guard. Her hideously bruised and battered legs, compliments of Scott and her many other 'appointments,' helped her to settle on a plausible solution.

Haley walked around the corner and cautiously entered the bank through two sets of glass doors. A kindly, grandfatherly-looking security guard sat quietly on a high chair reading the local paper, just to the right of the doors. She walked up behind him and deliberately stood between him and the plate glass window looking outside. Speaking in a soft voice, she forced him to turn and lean closer to her in order to hear.

"Sir, can you please tell me if there's a women's shelter close by?" Haley asked politely, her appropriately timid voice laced with apprehension. She could see by the sympathetic way he regarded her that her ruse had worked.

The security guard considered Haley's condition, seeing a troubled young girl. Despite the heavy makeup and obscene outfit she wore, he could see she was just a child. 'My granddaughters are older than her!' he thought, and was thoroughly convinced by the abundance of bruises on her body, that someone had been repeatedly brutalizing her. His protective, fatherly side kicked into gear.

"I'm sorry, I don't know of one here in Bitton," he said, sympathetically. This was his retirement job, and he loved it. His neighbors all banked here, and he enjoyed chatting with them. Nothing out of the ordinary ever happened in Bitton, and he'd never required any of the local community services.

Haley shifted a little to one side. The security guard leaned toward her, facing away from the interior of the bank and the entrance.

"Honey, can you tell me what's going on?" he asked. Haley was convinced she'd captured his complete attention. The security guard appeared genuinely worried about her, unaware that he'd turned his back to the door, and was now oblivious to any activity occurring within the bank. He spoke to her with such kindness that Haley began to cry. No one had been kind to her in such a long time.

Marvin watched from outside as Haley manipulated the guard. "Look Jimmy, now's our chance. Haley's doing great."

"I told you my bitch could do it," Jimmy said, sneering possessively. They took their masks out of their pockets and pulled them in place as they rounded the corner, just before they quietly entered the bank. Fortunately, the lobby was completely empty except for Haley and the guard.

Haley, peering anxiously over the guard's shoulder, watched with trepidation as Marvin and Jimmy approached the teller's window and began silently flashing their instruction cards at the terrified tellers. She had to leave right now! Haley's heart began pounding in her ears as she backed away from the sympathetic security guard.

"I'm sorry I bothered you," she said, apologetically.

Scooting past the confused guard, she ran headlong through the first door. Having reached the second door, she pushed frantically against it with her back, and found herself unexpectedly facing the anxious guard who had followed her and was closing in behind her. Then suddenly, without warning, an unexpected explosion blew her forcefully through the partially opened glass door.

Haley flew out into the street, landing hard in the bed of a pickup truck. Stunned for several minutes, she eventually pushed herself up enough to peer over the side of the truck bed. The bank was dark inside, streams of acrid black smoke billowing out of the windows and doors. A small crowd of local shop owners began to form in the street outside the bank, but no one seemed to notice her. Instead, the crowd's focus remained on the black smoke inside building.

Haley found strength she didn't know she possessed; she pushed herself upright, jumped out of the truck, and ran down the deserted alleyway. She sped away from the crime scene without daring to look back, fear and adrenaline pumping steadily through her body. Time became meaningless, but eventually she noticed that the nameless city streets had become wider and lined with fancy houses, many of them surrounded by immense, lush, manicured lawns.

Hearing police sirens in the distance, Haley quickly ducked out of sight inside a huge, rectangular shaped, leafy green hedge. Struggling to catch her breath, she felt temporarily protected by the enormous bush, and oddly safe for perhaps the first time in years. Thoroughly exhausted and terrified, she lay down in the dirt, resting her head on her folded arms; she allowed her tears to fall. Glass fragments covered her entire body and fresh blood oozed from her head, arms and legs, all of which she paid little attention. 'Great! Now what,' she thought, despondently. 'No plan and no money!' The reality of her precarious situation slowly dawned on Haley. 'At least I don't have to worry about what Jimmy will do to me.' Desperately alone, Haley curled up on the ground in the middle of the sheltering hedge, where she whimpered and cried, until she exhausted her supply of hopeless tears.

Vanessa's cell phone rang just as she was about to leave the house. She rapidly postponed her plans for a run in order to take the call. It was Marie, wanting to know if she'd received her text the night before.

"You know, that was Stephen from Mindy's account, in that picture you sent me." Vanessa attempted to make the connection for Marie.

"I had no idea, who knew?" Marie responded. "By the way, talk about odd behavior, a few minutes after we drove past them, Max called Jane. Apparently, he was very drunk, rambling on and on about how he'd hurt everyone he cared about." She took a deep breath, lowered her voice and continued confidentially. "He let it slip out, that Mindy really let him have it once they were alone. Apparently, she *demanded* that he help her with your accounts, so he was calling Jane to ask her to find time in his schedule." She paused before she added. "He was also muttering some nonsense about his father making plans to replace him at *Gemma*." She paused, waiting anxiously for Vanessa's response.

Vanessa shook her head in disbelief. "Max left me a very strange message on my machine last night, too. He seemed to be apologizing for something." She wondered what had happened between Max and Mindy. She'd known Max for years and she'd never seen him drunk before.

"You might want to screen your calls, or your vacation could come to a screeching halt," Marie warned.

As soon as Vanessa hung up, she checked the time on her phone. It was already eleven thirty and the lights had come back on while she was on the phone with Marie. Giving up on her run, the kitchen phone began ringing while she was busily taking down her portable alarms and resetting her clocks. It was Juan, asking if he could come a little earlier. She readily agreed, eager to have everything back to normal.

After she put away the alarms, she walked past the front door on her way to her bedroom to change out of her jogging clothes, and Vanessa heard a faint, barely audible knocking sound coming from the door. *Now what!* She thought. Hardly opening her front door, a strange young girl literally fell through it, and sprawled gracelessly onto the tile floor of her entryway. Speechless with shock, she watched as the unusual-looking girl collapsed at her feet.

At first Vanessa thought she might be dead. Her clothes were covered in glass shards and her body dripped with blood. She noticed the young girl sported short, completely lime-green hair, except for a bloody streak over her left ear. She bent down to inspect the questionable black soot and ash that clung to the girl's clothes. Her breathing seemed shallow, scarcely there. Vanessa stared, fascinated by the girl's unusual appearance. Heavy black, gothic-looking makeup and dirt had smeared down her tear-streaked face, and her skimpy, worn-out clothes clung to her frail-looking body. The colorful tattoos on her arms caught Vanessa's eye, and she wondered if they were somehow gang-related. In her left hand, the girl clung to a single high-heeled red shoe, as if it held some unknown significance. Vanessa, concerned for the girl's welfare, immediately reached for her cell phone to dial 911.

The girl roused enough to flutter her eyes open. "Please don't call anyone. Just help me... Please?" The unfortunate girl sounded desperate.

Vanessa clicked off her phone. *I guess I could wait,* she thought, *at least until I clean her up a little.* She decided to see how extensive the girl's injuries actually were, before calling for help. Vanessa walked to the front window and scanned the street outside. *There's no sign of a vehicle, so she must have walked here,* she thought. Also, she quickly noticed that no one seemed to be following her. Turning back, the girl's bare feet seemed unusually dirty, as if she'd walked quite a distance. How she had arrived here in her current condition was a complete mystery.

Vanessa knew her reluctance to finish her 911 phone call defied her initial instincts. Now, standing there indecisively, she recognized exactly why she'd hesitated to notify the authorities. There had been a time in her own life when she too had sustained horrendous injuries, and she'd also refused to seek out any medical or police assistance, fearing that their interference would result in unsolicited, and possibly lethal consequences.

The girl slipped in and out of awareness, and was either unable or unwilling to talk. Vanessa had difficulty obtaining any clues from her regarding her current condition. Being small in stature and able to walk with minimal assistance, Vanessa guided her into the guest bathroom, where she kept a first-aid kit in the linen closet.

Vanessa helped her step into the bathtub to prevent blood from dripping onto her bathroom rugs. Carefully she supported the girl, who seemed barely able to stand on her own, while she removed her tight clothing. Vanessa turned on the shower and rinsed away the glass and blood with the hand-held showerhead. She watched in fascination as not only the green hair-dye washed out, revealing light brown hair, but her black makeup and tattoos went down the drain as well. Once washed, she appeared quite young, maybe only sixteen. Incredibly, the young girl beneath her entirely fabricated exterior had the face of an innocent angel.

While inspecting her for injuries, Vanessa noticed that not only was she thin and appeared malnourished, but her body also displayed multiple bruises and scars; all in varying stages of healing. The way she flinched when she dried her with a towel made Vanessa think she might also have one or two broken ribs. She was furious! She shook her head in utter disbelief. *How could anyone treat this child so callously?* She didn't ask outright who had hurt her, but cautiously bandaged her wounds and applied adhesive closures to her open cuts. Finding nothing she considered to be serious injuries, she attempted to gently prod the girl for information.

"Can you tell me your name?" Vanessa asked, taking care to keep her tone low, as if she were addressing a skittish colt.

The girl answered softly, without returning Vanessa's inquisitive gaze. "Haley," she whispered.

Encouraged by her response, she pushed on. "How old are you, Haley?"

"I'll be eighteen next month." Again her response was whispery, and her stare remained fixed on the floor.

Vanessa thought about the cuts and glass shards. "Were you in a car accident?" she asked.

Haley didn't answer. She quietly shook her head no.

"Are you hiding from someone?" Vanessa asked, concerned about her reluctance to elaborate on how she arrived at her home injured and bleeding. Haley began to cry silently, her shoulders shaking almost imperceptibly.

"It's okay, we can talk more later," Vanessa said calmly, not wanting to upset her further.

Gingerly drying Haley, she wrapped her tiny, battered frame gently in one of the big, fluffy, white robes she kept on hand for guests. Her tiny figure was dwarfed by the robe, and lost within its generous folds. Vanessa walked the girl carefully into the guest bedroom, one arm wrapped around her waist for support, while the other held up the hem of the robe. After Haley had nestled into the soft, queen-sized bed, Vanessa left her briefly, reappearing with a glass of juice and a couple of aspirin. She turned off the lights and drew the blinds.

"You're safe here," Vanessa reassured. "Try to get some rest. We can talk more later, when you're feeling better." Haley's face relaxed into a serene expression. She didn't verbally respond, but she silently thought, *I don't care what happens next, just being wrapped in clean white linens, in a real bed, feels like heaven!* Closing her eyes, she felt temporarily secure, and drifted peacefully off to sleep.

Vanessa returned to her guest bathroom to assess the damage. Every surface of the room had been spattered with blood and covered with tiny shards of glass. She hated disarray in her personal space even more than outside. Without hesitation she gathered assorted cleaning supplies. She tossed Haley's bloody clothes, the used first-aid supplies, bloody towels, and bathroom rugs into a large plastic leaf bag. Washing down the bathroom thoroughly with bleach, she replaced the missing towels and rugs with a backup set she kept in the linen closet. Meticulously, she scoured the rest of the house for traces of dirt or blood. When she'd finished, she placed the full garbage bag into the laundry room to deal with later.

Vanessa had finally changed her clothes, when she heard the gardeners in the backyard. Convinced everything inside of her house had been restored to its normal appearance, she went outside to greet Juan.

Juan, with his two brothers, had arrived in a large, red pick-up truck. Vanessa greeted them on her patio, grateful that Juan's brothers had righted her patio furniture straightaway. She looked around her yard and gave Juan specific instructions regarding the tree removal and cleanup. Juan had been her dependable gardener for years, and he routinely followed her instructions faithfully. She sighed, and thought, *Thank goodness the yard will be normal again soon.*

Satisfied, Vanessa headed back into the house to check on Haley. She peered through the cracked open door. Hearing her soft snoring convinced her that Haley was asleep, and she returned to the kitchen. She considered what she should do about Haley's unfortunate situation.

Callie joined her, grumpily reminding her of the protein bar hours earlier, and she decided to make them both a light lunch. She searched through the meager supplies of her refrigerator for food to serve her guest later. *Looks like I'll need to do some shopping*, she thought. Fixing herself a salad, she fed the cat and sat down alone at her kitchen table to quietly reflect. Haley's body had shown definite signs of repeated abuse; she cringed inwardly at the thought of what the girl had suffered. After all, Vanessa knew the signs of abuse from an exceedingly personal perspective.

Finishing her lunch, Vanessa stood and walked to the sink to rinse her dish. Seeing Haley's bruises and scars had brought back her own suppressed memories of Mark, the man she'd married right out of college. After having dated him for several years during college, she thought she knew all about Mark. But she'd been painfully disappointed.

Vanessa returned to the table, thoughtfully sipping her iced tea, as she reluctantly recalled her disastrous marriage to Mark. The year before they'd graduated, Mark had received the devastating news that his mother had suffered a crippling stroke, and she'd been moved into a long-term care facility. Following graduation, Mark had been offered a two-year assignment as an engineer in the Middle East, in exchange for student loan forgiveness. Mark wanted to go, but was anxious about leaving his mother behind. Impulsively, he asked Vanessa to marry him. They'd been a couple for years, and she'd believed they were in love. Taking his circumstances into consideration, she readily agreed.

Rubbing her throbbing temples, she recalled how recklessly she'd made the worst decision of her life. They'd both been so confident, believing they'd created a perfect life-plan. She would focus on her career and watch over his mother, while he completed his two-year commitment in the Middle East. They would begin their lives together professionally established, and debt-free. Hastily, they were married two days later in the college campus chapel. They'd agreed to keep it a simple ceremony, with only their closest friends in attendance.

Everything had progressed on schedule. Vanessa had quickly moved up the ranks in *Gemma* and had bought them the perfect home. After two years in the Middle East, Mark returned home as planned. Vanessa had arranged for an extended vacation, to stay home with him as they adjusted. At first, married life seemed like the honeymoon they'd never had, full of laughter, sex, and lazy mornings spent together in bed.

Vanessa shuddered involuntarily, recalling how rapidly her idealistic life had become a total nightmare. It began the first day she'd returned to work; back to her new, extremely demanding position. Once he was left on his own, Mark's behavior promptly changed. Looking back now, it seemed unbelievable that she'd managed to survive his constant verbal abuse, jealous paranoid accusations, fierce mood swings, and drunken beatings. Humiliated by his violence toward her, she'd gone to great lengths to assure that no one ever knew of the berating and savagery inflicted on her at home. Convinced that he would some how miraculously change back into the man she'd married, and assuming her marriage was her own personal failure, she'd found clever ways to treat and hide all of his brutal, physical attacks.

Vanessa realized she had her fists clenched, and forced her damp hands to open and relax flat on the table. She knew from experience how fearful Haley would be to confide in her. She understood all too well how shame and self-degradation had prevented her, as it did most abused women from speaking out against their abusers. But she was sure, if she could somehow gain Haley's trust, she could rescue her.

The roar of a chainsaw in the backyard broke into Vanessa's thoughts, shifting her attention, and stirring her to action. She went outside to check on Juan's progress. He stood on the patio proudly watching his brothers repairing her yard.

"How's it going, Juan?" she asked casually. Vanessa could see multiple bags of debris already stacked in the back of his truck.

"We should be done in about an hour."

Vanessa surveyed her yard, delighted by their rapid progress. She watched the three brothers work, noticing how different they each looked. His older, taller brother was much darker, and sported a distinctively bushy mustache. He seemed a bit introverted, focusing intently on chopping her treasured maple tree into pieces. In contrast to his serious older brother, his younger brother appeared shorter, rounder, and clean-shaven. His cheery smile filled his ample face, as he merrily whistled and scooped up the leaves from her pool.

"Everything looks great. How much do I owe you?" she asked, admiring her rapidly improving yard.

Juan shrugged. "For you, two hundred and fifty dollars?" he suggested. Vanessa considered that more than fair.

"That's fine, can you put it on my bill?" she asked, smiling sweetly at him.

"Sure, no problem." He returned her smile; he'd do anything for her. Vanessa was one of his favorite customers. She reached out and formally shook his hand to seal their deal.

"I really appreciate your coming today."

"I got lots of calls after the storm, but I take care of my regular customers first." Tall, dark and muscular, he removed his wide-brimmed hat, bowing to her in exaggerated flourish.

"Thank you, Juan." Vanessa smiled, amused by his showmanship.

Things were quickly returning to normal in her yard, so Vanessa wandered back inside to sit at the kitchen table and start a shopping list. She was concerned by Haley's malnourished appearance, and hoped she would eventually wake up famished.

Callie jumped into Vanessa's lap, demanding her immediate attention. Distractedly, she scratched her cat lightly behind her ears. "Well Callie, this vacation has started off considerably different than I'd planned." Her cat purred in contented response. Cuddling with her cat helped Vanessa to dispel some of the lingering disquiet she felt after reliving her bitter past with her ex-husband, Mark.

Vanessa took a deep breath. Gradually she relaxed and returned to the task of creating her shopping list. She had just jotted down protein bars on her list, when her concentration was rudely interrupted again. Startled by the unexpected chiming of the front doorbell, Callie abruptly jumped off her lap. Vanessa slowly stood, feeling mildly confused and irritated. She typically had very few visitors. Frowning, she turned to glance toward the front door. *Who could that be now?*

Chapter 6
Opening Old Wounds

Vanessa, feeling more than a little curious, moved swiftly to her front door. She fumbled momentarily with the lock in her haste. Callie, who'd followed her to the door, now stood guard between her legs as she swung it open. However, at the sight of the large German shepherd, sitting harmlessly on the stoop, the cat reacted with a loud hiss and sprinted down the hallway. Despite her cat's lack of hospitality, the dog sat politely. The docile dog remained unperturbed, resting at the end of a long loose leash, at the feet of a tall man turned slightly away from Vanessa. The strange man stood there, quietly gazing across her yard.

Appearing roughly six foot two, with well-groomed salt-and-pepper hair, the stranger slowly turned to face her, casually removing his dark sunglasses. Towering over her, his clear, crystal blue eyes instantly drew Vanessa's rapt attention. His eyes weren't an icy blue color, but instead they appeared to be warm, reassuring, almost comforting. Vanessa couldn't be sure, but something about his eyes seemed vaguely familiar to her. Speechlessly, she stared up at his chiseled, ruggedly handsome, well-tanned face. The hair near his temples, along with his neatly groomed mustache, had turned entirely white, and she presumed he was several years older than her. Dressed informally, his opened tan sports coat clearly displayed an intimidating badge and a holstered gun, both firmly attached to his belt. He stood still, intently watching her reaction.

"Good morning, I'm Detective Andrew Kelly. I'd like to ask you a few questions, Mrs....?"

Andrew had recognized Vanessa immediately. And, he'd instantly noted the wary, vulnerable look in her eyes, before she quickly shielded them from him. She's tough, he thought as the corners of his mouth lifted slightly, but she wants everyone to think that drama has no effect on her. *Incredible, but even after all these years, she still looks the same*, he thought. *Beautiful!*

It had been nearly thirty years since he'd last interviewed her, and she'd had that same exposed look on her face then. Her despondent, ethereal eyes had haunted him for years. He would never forget this brave, remarkable woman, whom he'd quickly grown to respect. She was unlike any other woman he'd met before, or since.

Vanessa was surprised by the way his deep, baritone voice resonated deep within her, making her immediately feel safe. It was as if she'd known him her whole life. She didn't realize it, but she had physically taken a small step toward him, as if he had some unseen magnetic pull on her.

"It's Ms., but please call me Vanessa. What can I do for you, Detective?" she answered formally, covering her discomfort.

Andrew smiled broadly. *Still the little toughie*, he thought, relaxing his shoulder nonchalantly against the doorjamb. "Were you aware that there was an attempted robbery at the Bitton Bank this morning?"

"No, I had no idea! I've been dealing with the fallout from last night's windstorm. My power was out all morning. Was anyone hurt?" Her expression made it clear that she was genuinely shocked and maybe slightly alarmed by this unexpected information.

Dropping her guard ever so slightly, it was just enough for Andrew to see the distress clearly reflecting in her eyes. *Bitton's a small town*, he reminded himself. It was likely that she personally knew everyone who'd worked at the local bank.

"The two would-be bank robbers..." He straightened up, attempting to relay the information to her in a gentle, considerate tone. "Blew themselves up with some kind of homemade bomb. Unfortunately..." he paused, waiting for the news to sink in before he told her more. "They also blew up two of the tellers and critically injured the guard. It's touch and go for him, I'm afraid."

Vanessa paled visibly at the unexpected news. She banked there routinely. "Was it Jeanie or Helen?" she asked, her voice hushed and fearful.

Damn, he wished he hadn't been the one to tell her. He looked down at his notepad, where both of the names she'd asked him about were listed as deceased. "I'm sorry Vanessa, I can't release their names until their families have been notified."

"I'll assume they were." She bristled a little when he hesitated. "I know for a fact that John was the guard on duty. Will he make it?" she asked, pain etched on her face.

Andrew shuffled his feet and returned his gaze to his notepad. Why did he have to be the one to cause her suffering? He hated this! "Sorry, all I know is that he's still unconscious, and listed in critical condition." Although Andrew actually knew, but couldn't say, the man in question was scarcely clinging to life.

Watching as her eyes began to well up with tears, he swallowed hard. From his previous personal experience with Vanessa, he knew how tenderhearted she could be, even though she would never admit to it.

"Detective..." Vanessa began, struggling to regain her tightly held control.

He wanted her to say his name.

"Andrew, please." His voice was as soft as a caress.

"Alright, Andrew, what brings you to my door?" Vanessa got back down to business and the reason for his untimely visit, regaining her composure and once again shielding all expression from her eyes.

Andrew reached into his pocket and pulled out a sketch. It depicted a young girl, with spiky, lime-green hair, heavy dark makeup, and arms covered with tattoos. Vanessa forced herself to swallow down her gasp of surprise.

"We've...been tracking her since the attempted robbery." He looked down to include his dog. "That's why we're here. Have you seen this girl?" he asked, holding up the sketch.

Vanessa kept her face expressionless as she pretended to examine the sketch closely. The picture was obviously Haley, although the girl asleep in her guestroom looked nothing like that now. She'd only just met Haley, but she would protect the poor, battered child at any cost. Wrestling temporarily with her civic duty, she discovered that the welfare of the young girl she'd just met was her main concern.

Andrew relaxed against the doorjamb again. He studied Vanessa's reaction, fascinated by the multiple emotions that flickered in her eyes, as she worked through what to say next.

"Why are you looking for this girl?" she shrugged, trying to keep her voice neutral, acting as if the girl was of no concern to her.

"At this point, she's simply a person of interest in this case," he said, casually watching Vanessa's face for clues.

"You mean *she* helped rob the bank?" She raised her eyebrows in disbelief, stunned by the mere suggestion that Haley could be involved in a bank heist.

"We don't know yet. Witnesses saw her flee the scene shortly after the explosion." Hoping to prevent any unnecessary alarm, Andrew kept his tone neutral while maintaining his relaxed stance, leaning against the doorframe.

"Well, I haven't seen *this* girl," she said, handing the picture back to him. Vanessa had quickly decided to give Haley the benefit of the doubt. She would wait until she could discuss the situation with her in private, before she'd decide if and when she would speak with the authorities.

"Are you absolutely sure?" He frowned slightly and pulled a plastic bag out of his pocket. "How about this shoe? Have you seen anything like this? Perhaps abandoned in your yard?"

The bag contained a red high-heeled shoe. Vanessa recognized it immediately, but she was sticking to her story. "No, I'm sorry. You could check with the gardeners. Maybe they've seen your unusual Cinderella, or her shoe," she lied poorly. She refused to look closely at the shoe; instead she worked hard at keeping a straight face.

Andrew rubbed the back of his neck in frustration. He knew she wasn't telling him the truth, although he wasn't sure why. Chewing on the earpiece of his sunglasses, he pondered the right approach to take with her.

"Since Shep led me here, would you mind if we quickly searched your house?" He looked her squarely in the eyes as he asked, silently challenging her to refuse his request.

Panicked and defensive, she used her haughty, authoritative voice. "I'm sorry Andrew, that is out of the question."

"Why?" He kept a straight face, but secretly found her vehement response amusing.

"My cat's already in a snit about your dog," she continued lamely. "Besides, I have a guest who is still asleep. We didn't get much sleep last night." She attempted to infer that she'd had a wild night with a male guest to throw him off the scent.

"It will only take a minute," he coaxed, sending her a reassuring smile. He was sure now that the girl was here, and that Vanessa was fully aware of her actions. He admired her protective streak, but he had a job to do. He used an easygoing but firm approach. "You do know...I can get a search warrant in a matter of hours."

"If you feel you must," she said dismissively, although she began chewing on her bottom lip.

Maybe he could reason with her. After all, she must negotiate all sorts of deals in her fancy, big-time job. "Do you understand what obstruction of justice is?" he asked officially, pulling away from the doorframe. He straightened to his full height, resting his hand casually on his gun.

"You said she was just a person of interest. Do you have a warrant for her arrest?" Vanessa was not about to let this charming man bully her.

"I don't need one." He decided to call her bluff. "You can't interfere with an ongoing investigation," he said, maintaining his aggressive stance, but using a kinder tone.

She stepped closer to him, closing the door behind her. Glancing down at his passive dog, she noticed with alarm the tiny shards of glass, along with a few blood drops evident on her doormat and she hastily covered them with her foot, desperately hoping he hadn't already noticed them. Frantic to buy Haley some time to explain herself, Vanessa's soft, brown eyes pleaded with him, and she flashed him a tentative smile. "Would you consider coming back at, let's say, four o'clock? By then my guest should be awake, and I can make arrangements for my cat while you conduct your search."

She'd moved closer, and now stood so near to him that Andrew could smell her tantalizing, floral fragrance. All he wanted to do was kiss away her torment. He took a deep breath. He had to get hold of himself! What was wrong with him? This was one of his last assignments before he retired. He hadn't so much as looked at another woman since he'd lost Grace, but suddenly he was eager to find a way to console Vanessa.

"You do realize that's not how investigations work?" he said, speaking rationally.

She looked at him directly. "Yes," she whispered anxiously.

He exhaled loudly; he couldn't help himself. "Do you promise to cooperate completely when I return?" Leaning forward, he searched deep within her eyes for the truth.

The sincere, candid look he gave her made her heart beat loudly in her ears and her knees tried to buckle. Breathlessly, she answered, "Absolutely!"

Their eyes locked in challenge, and his tone became deadly serious. "You're asking me to break with procedure. Can I trust you?" He asked, though he knew the answer even before he'd asked the question.

"Yes," she whispered. Her low, husky voice sent Andrew's dormant hormones into overdrive.

He tried unsuccessfully to pull his gaze away from her inviting mouth, and finally had to force himself to take a step back. He draped his coat over his gun and badge, looked down to button it, and dropped his authoritative posture. His gaze shifted down to his dog, and he cleared his dry throat. In an official-sounding tone, he commented, "Apparently, there was no one at home today. I will return to complete my investigation—at four pm." His voice cracked a little when his eyes returned to hers and she sent him an endearing smile of relief.

"Thank you, Andrew," she whispered; stepping back inside the house, she quietly closed the door behind her.

Once safely inside the house, Vanessa leaned her back against the closed door. She felt adrenaline rushing through every part of her body.

Sighing to herself, she thought, *this has got to be the most eventful week of my life! First the turmoil at Gemma, the crazy windstorm last night, then the battered child asleep in my guest room, and now an encounter with law enforcement. Extraordinary,* she marveled. Not to mention, Andrew, whose unexpected masculinity had sent sensual shivers all the way to her feminine core, unlike any other man had before. She closed her eyes, attempting to calm her ragged breathing, compelling her clenched fists to relax open. She had just begun to calm herself when her eyes popped open wide. *Oh no, I'd better get busy before he comes back!*

Quickly Vanessa replaced the front door mat, and had just tossed the old one into the garbage bag in the laundry room, when Juan's knock at the back door startled her. In all the excitement, she'd completely forgotten about Juan and his brothers in the backyard.

"We're finished, Ms. Golden. Is there anything else you would like us to do?" he asked, removing his work gloves.

Vanessa walked outside with Juan. Order had been restored to her yard, and her beloved maple tree had vanished. Her eyes moistened as she remembered how she'd planted it as a sapling, faithfully tending it for years until it grew into a spectacularly colorful shade tree. Now the spot where it had once flourished was barren. Juan noticed the forlorn look in her damp eyes as her gaze lingered across the yard where the tree had once stood tall.

"Would you like me to plant another tree, just like the one you lost to the wind?" he asked.

Vanessa couldn't bring herself to explain the significance of what that particular maple tree had meant to her. "That would be wonderful," she said, absently.

"Is that garbage in your laundry room?" he inquired. "We'll be going to the dump to take the tree and leaves. We could take it if you want?" he offered as he walked back inside to pick up the bag.

Vanessa thought for a minute. What else could she do? Juan had no idea what was in the bag. There'd be no legal implications or entanglements for him. "That would be great. Did a detective talk to you earlier?" She kept her voice neutral, attempting to sound unconcerned.

"Yes, he asked about someone he was looking for. I told him we hadn't seen her." He paused for a moment. "I sent him to talk to you. I hope that was okay?" he asked, hesitantly.

"Yes, of course. Here, let me tip you," she smiled, reaching into her purse to hand him a hundred dollar bill.

"Please, Ms. Golden, no need," Juan objected and tried to wave away the tip.

"I insist. Thank you for doing such a wonderful job, and thanks again for coming so promptly." She assertively pressed the bill into his hand.

Accepting the tip, Juan waved goodbye. "No problem, señora. Adios." He tucked the bill away and hoisted up the garbage bag, effortlessly tossing it into the truck with the other bags. His brothers were waiting in the truck as Juan turned to wave before he stepped up into the cab.

"Bye Juan, see you next week." Vanessa felt only a slight twinge of guilt as she watched him drive away with what she thought might possibly be incriminating evidence.

Haley had roused from her slumber long enough to overhear Vanessa's conversation with Andrew earlier. But she had fallen back to sleep by the time Vanessa returned to check on her. Lulled by the comfy bed, she slept deeper than she had in years.

Vanessa searched until she'd located some of her clothes tucked in back of her closet that were too tight on her. They included a pair of running pants and a long sleeved T-shirt she thought might fit Haley. Her thought was to try to cover Haley's wounds completely. She picked up her flip-flops and decided they would do. Carrying them into the guest room, she woke Haley. Sitting up abruptly in bed, Haley searched the room, feeling momentarily disoriented. Once she remembered where she was, she relaxed back against the fluffy pillows.

"I brought you some clothes, please get dressed. I need you to come into the kitchen to talk," Vanessa instructed softly. "And I'll fix you something to eat. Do you think you can manage to get dressed by yourself?"

Haley nodded yes and Vanessa closed the door on her way out to allow her privacy. Gaining Haley's trust was going to be a challenge. But it was imperative that she clearly understood Haley's involvement with the robbery prior to Detective Andrew's return.

A short time later, Vanessa heard the toilet flush, and Haley appeared in the kitchen doorway. The clothes were a little loose on her, but normal looking. Her skin seemed pale, and her attitude hesitant and somber.

"Please, have a seat," Vanessa said, gently ushering her into the kitchen.

She indicated her small wooden kitchen table with four chairs. Haley sat down silently, unsure of what was expected. Vanessa served her a peanut butter and jelly sandwich resting neatly on a Wedgewood china plate, along with a glass of milk. But although Haley eagerly ate, she remained quiet.

"Thank you," she said, so softly that Vanessa barely heard her.

Vanessa decided to let her eat in peace before she tried to talk to her. She sipped her iced tea while covertly observing Haley. How this normal looking, sweet girl with impeccable manners, could be the same scruffy, punk-rocker who'd arrived on her doorstep earlier today, seemed unimaginable. Vanessa studied her attractive, light chestnut brown hair. It had been chopped into varying lengths, as if she'd cut it herself. It wouldn't be too hard to even out, she thought. Thankfully, her clothes effectively hid most of her present and past injuries. *Maybe Andrew will think that Haley was another girl, not the punk-rock teen he was searching for.*

After finishing her sandwich, Haley sat sipping her milk, anxiously waiting for Vanessa's inevitable questioning. She'd overheard Vanessa's conversation with the detective and was grateful for the temporary reprieve this kind woman had negotiated. It made her feel safe and protected, even if it would only be short-lived. She believed Vanessa deserved some sort of an explanation, but she had no idea what to tell her, or where to begin. At least now the ringing in her ears had stopped, making a normal conversation possible.

Vanessa cleared her plate and put it in the dishwasher. She sat down across from Haley and began to explain. "There was a detective here earlier. I got him to agree to wait until four o'clock, but he'll be back." Seeing the fearful expression on the girl's face, she continued gently. "He just wants to ask you a few questions about what happened at the bank this morning."

Haley began to cry quietly. She didn't want Vanessa to know what a horrible person she was. She'd made far too many unforgivable mistakes in her life. She hung her head, feeling foolish and humiliated by her weaknesses.

"I'm so sorry. I wouldn't pressure you if he weren't coming back soon." Vanessa put her hand over Haley's. It broke her heart to see her cry. "I know how hard things have been for you. I can only imagine how you must feel. I've been there myself."

Haley raised her head and cocked it to the side questioningly. She could see the sincerity and telltale traces of pain evident on Vanessa's face.

Convinced that the best way to gain Haley's trust was to share her own sordid past, Vanessa confessed. "I was married once," she said, unsure exactly what to tell her, since she'd never told her story to anyone before. "My husband was once a wonderful man. But his employment in the Middle East separated us for the first two years of our marriage, and when he returned to me, he'd become a vicious, drunken monster. Eventually, he was diagnosed with post-traumatic stress disorder, or PTSD."

She paused to gather her courage. The next portion of her story was painful and extremely private. "I didn't care if he was sick. I just didn't want to be his punching bag. I begged him to get help! Sometimes, after he beat me, he'd apologize the next day, promising he would stop. He'd make an appointment with a therapist, but then he'd get angry again, and refuse to go. Afterward, if I even mentioned that he needed help, he'd hurt me even worse than he had before."

She looked directly at Haley. "I felt so ashamed!" she exclaimed. "Here I was, a successful businesswoman. People respected me, looked to me for leadership, and I couldn't even manage my own marriage. I worked hard to conceal my pain. I wore long sleeves, and discovered that tan tights helped cover the bruises on my legs. No one had the slightest idea what was happening to me." Tears fell, as she spoke of that nightmarish time in her life.

Haley didn't say a word; she silently watched her with muted, empathetic eyes as Vanessa ripped open her old wounds, and allowed her past to pour out of her tormented heart.

"That's why I have all those first-aid supplies," Vanessa explained. "I wanted to protect him. I never went to a hospital. I surfed the Internet instead, gathering information to help me to doctor myself. Once, I even set my own broken arm," she said, boasting her skill ruefully. After keeping her painful past secret for so many years, Vanessa hesitated before saying more. But she knew if she wanted to reach Haley, she'd have to confess everything. Vanessa took a deep breath and went on. "His abuse continued on and off for eight months. That's when I became pregnant." She looked down at her hands, gathering her strength.

"I chose my child over my husband!" Her voice grew strong with anger and her hands shook with rage. "I refused to place my unborn child in danger. I decided to contact a lawyer. He advised me to file a restraining order. I filed one immediately and initiated divorce proceedings against him." She gazed up at the ceiling and her lower lip quivered with anguish. "But I was too late." She bitterly shook her head in disgust as she relived his crazy allegations. "I arrived home that night to find him pacing furiously and guzzling beer after beer. He accused me of cheating on him, and twisted my wrist so forcefully he broke my arm, once again. Angry and out of control, he beat me without mercy, knocking me to the ground. While I lay there dazed, he kicked me repeatedly in my stomach." She shuddered at the memory of her terror; of the dreadful night she'd scarcely survived. Her eyes glazed over, tears of recrimination flowed freely down her cheeks.

"I made it as far as the bathroom, where I locked the door," she whispered, recalling the nightmare. "He pounded on the door—tried to break in—but I called 911. I was bleeding heavily—terrified I'd pass out. This time I wanted him arrested! I only hoped they'd reach me in time to save my baby." Sobbing at the memory of that disastrous night long ago, she clutched her stomach, instinctively rocking in her chair. Talking about and reliving her traumatic terror left her dazed and temporarily oblivious to Haley's presence.

Haley tentatively reached over to touch Vanessa's arm in support, feeling intrusive, powerless to comfort her.

Vanessa's voice took on an eerie tone as she continued, "He shattered the bathroom door just as the paramedics arrived. They rescued me, whisking me off to the hospital, but it was too late. I lost my baby, and when they couldn't stop my bleeding, and they had to remove my uterus too! I lost everything!" Vanessa suddenly became still and trancelike, while her detached, scalding tears of regret bathed her flushed face.

Haley impulsively threw her arms around Vanessa and began sobbing. Vanessa's arms slowly responded, gently holding her, returning gradually to the present moment in time. They silently embraced each other, two kindred, victimized spirits, with abused and tattered hearts. Vanessa had never trusted anyone enough to share her suffering, or the painful events of that day. Talking about it now made it feel as if it had just happened yesterday.

Time passed in tiny increments. Haley reluctantly pulled away from Vanessa to ask timidly, "What ever happened to your husband?"

Standing, Vanessa walked to the sink to grab a paper towel. Wetting it, she began dabbing deliberately at her tear-drenched face, attempting to regain some smidgen of control over her emotions. She remained at the sink, but turned back toward Haley to finish her story between shuddering gasps. "They arrested him. He had no idea about the baby, and when I testified about it in court, he cried and begged for my forgiveness. But I had none to give, for either one of us." She sniffled, preparing to share the worse part. "Our baby was dead! And my *husband*...got off with only a one-year sentence with counseling. I divorced him while he was still in jail," she said, coldly.

Vanessa's eyes narrowed, her fury palpable. "The day he got out, he came to see me. He begged me to forgive him and take him back," she spat out with disgust. "But I couldn't even look at him. I simply closed the door in his face. We've never spoken since. Our friends tell me that he moved to Denver, remarried, and now has four kids," she hiccupped.

Haley's mouth flew open, horrified by the injustice. "I'm so sorry."

Facing away from Haley, Vanessa struggled to regain her composure. Pouring a soothing glass of water, she fought to stem her uncontrollable tears. Finally, she squelched her painful memories back down and returned to sit at the table with Haley. Focusing her thoughts on Haley, she wondered if her open display of emotions had created a safe enough place for Haley to share her own agonizing story.

"I'm sorry for dumping my disturbing past onto you. I didn't mean to tell you quite so much," she apologized. "I just wanted to let you know that I truly understand how it feels...when someone you love abuses you."

Haley nodded.

"Do you think you can tell me your story now?" Vanessa asked.

"Yes, I guess so."

The meekness of Haley's voice, along with her stunned look of shock made Vanessa doubt she could talk openly just yet. She sensed they both needed a break from the morbid spell she'd just cast. "Before you begin, do you like Jamoca Almond Fudge ice cream?"

Caught off guard, Haley answered bashfully. "I think it used to be one of my favorites. I can't remember the last time I had ice cream." Her answer had a wistful undertone.

"I think we're going to get along just fine!" Vanessa smiled.

The two of them sat, each with a pint of ice cream, in companionable, thoughtful silence. The sweet creamy coffee and chocolate flavors of the decadent delight temporarily soothed the distaste from their previous conversation. Indulging in the frozen treat together helped create an emotionally safe space in time, allowing Haley's nervousness to subside a little, giving her a welcomed distraction, before she attempted to articulate her own painful story. Haley's troubled past was an unknown mystery, one that Vanessa could only imagine and one she was anxious

Full-Sailed Surrender

to understand.

Chapter 7
Haley's Story

Vanessa watched Haley scrape the ice cream off the side of the carton with her spoon, close her eyes, and relish the last bite. They'd been sitting together in silence as they devoured their comforting, sweet treat. Now, it was time for Haley to open her heart, and divulge her own harrowing story to Vanessa.

Haley thought she was ready, but the words caught in the back of her throat. She averted her eyes, gazed at her fingers, and realized she had no idea how, or where to begin. "I'm sorry ma'am, I'm still feeling a little embarrassed about telling you everything—I'm not exactly sure where I should start," she faltered timidly.

Vanessa detested being called ma'am. It made her wince, like fingernails scraping across a chalkboard. She already felt old enough, particularly this week. Obviously, Haley had been raised with manners, which included respect for her elders. Sensing her reluctance to unburden her soul in her presence, Vanessa realized she'd need to create a more casual, relaxed atmosphere. She felt confident that once Haley began telling her story, she wouldn't be able to stop.

First, she had to address this "ma'am" business. "Haley, please call me Vanessa." She cringed inwardly at the thought of hearing *ma'am* from her lips again.

Haley blushed, surprised by Vanessa's adamant request. "I'll try." Her pursed lips relaxed and the corners of her mouth lifted slightly at the idea. Vanessa smiled back, but Haley's obvious discomfort remained, so she attempted to steer the conversation to a neutral topic.

"How would you feel about telling me something about your family? For example, where you were born?" she asked.

"I guess that would be all right," Haley shrugged.

"Then, as you get to the hard stuff..." hearing her reluctant shyness, Vanessa tactfully suggested, "What if I trimmed your hair while you talk? Would that be all right with you?"

"Yeah. I always liked it when my mom used to cut my hair. I think that would be nice." Haley sent her a bashful, relieved smile. The idea of Vanessa having a task, and not watching her every expression as she spoke, appealed to her.

We're making progress, Vanessa thought. "So, tell me about your parents?"

"They live in Ohio." Haley began without hesitation, having no problem talking about her past life with her family. Her voice became stronger and slightly animated. "My parents were high school sweethearts. They went to junior college together, but they both dropped out after their first year to get married. I guess I was born about six months later," she said, shrugging with a charming crooked smile across her face.

"Then what?" So far Vanessa had found nothing uncommon about Haley's story.

Haley swallowed. Her mouth suddenly felt parched as she struggled to continue. "At first—my dad worked at the post office while Mom stayed home with me. I remember when I was really little, she'd take me to the park, and I'd play on the playground. I was happy then," she sighed sadly, remembering her early childhood.

Vanessa smiled, nostalgically remembering a piece of her own early childhood fondly. "I'm an only child," she shared. "My parents spent hours with me. That is, until they divorced," she said resentfully. "Were you an only child too?" she asked.

"Far from it." Haley laughed at the absurdity. "My brother was born when I was four, then I got a new sister about every two years. I am the oldest of six kids." Her voice had turned bitter and resentful, as if her siblings had deliberately intruded on her happy childhood.

"Wow, I can't even imagine what that must be like. I've always wished I had lots of brothers and sisters," Vanessa said, impressed by Haley's sizable family.

"My parents both worked six days a week, all day long. Guess who gave up her entire life to take care of all of *their* kids?" she asked sarcastically, rolling her eyes. Her statement oozed with anger, and Vanessa could hear her deep-seated resentment.

"I can't imagine what that must have been like either." Wanting Haley to continue confiding in her, Vanessa kept her tone neutral, without judgment.

Frowning, Haley began recalling what she saw as a gross injustice. "My parents woke up every day at five am. Dad drove our only car to the post office, while Mom had to catch two busses to get to her job at the dry cleaners. They'd return home late, eat, and go to bed," she said, regretfully. "Every morning I got everyone out of bed, fed the kids, and sent them all off to school. Then I'd pick everyone up on my way home from school, make dinner, help them with their homework, bathe them, wash the dishes and the laundry, until finally, I'd put everyone to bed," she said, reciting her schedule with disgust. She went on to plead her case. "The only time I spent time with my parents was on Sundays. That was the day we all went to church. On Sundays, mom would make a big afternoon meal, and it was the only day we all ate together. For one day a week, we were all one big, happy family." She might be resentful of her old life, but at least she wasn't ashamed of it.

"Did you think your parents loved each other?" Vanessa asked, cautiously, wishing that her own parents had been able stay as committed and in love.

"Yes." She teared up, obviously missing them.

Sensing Haley needed a break, Vanessa stood up and excused herself, giving Haley a moment alone to reign in her feelings. Going into her bathroom, she retrieved a pair of scissors, a curling iron, and a new, unwrapped comb. When she returned to Haley, she found her pensively contemplating her hands.

Time to liven up the mood, Vanessa thought. "Okay then, why don't I trim your hair now? Did you cut it yourself?" she asked, lifting a strand of Haley's uneven hair, trying to decide how short to cut it.

"No, my boyfriend cut it with his pocket knife. I used to have really long hair, all the way to the middle of my back," she said, indicating a spot above her waistline.

Vanessa bristled. Haley had confirmed what she'd already suspected. She knew exactly who'd been brutalizing this poor child, but she struggled to keep her voice light and nonjudgmental as she gently ran the comb through her ragtag hair. "Please continue with your story," she encouraged. "How did you end up in Los Angeles?"

Haley exhaled, loving the feel of Vanessa's gentle touch, as she stood behind her, smoothly running a comb through her hair. It made her feel braver than she'd felt in a long time. "The Sunday before I left home, my parents sat us all down and told us they had some exciting news. I thought of all kinds of wonderful things. I thought maybe we were going on vacation or something. But when my mother smiled and said, 'We're having another baby,' I was furious!" Haley's body tensed as she relived her outrage.

"I take it that wasn't good news for you?"

"I had just gotten my youngest sister out of diapers!"

"So...what did you do?"

Haley felt the same overwhelming anger she'd felt on that day, and her voice sounded exasperated. "I told my parents they were crazy! I said they couldn't even take care of the kids they already had! Then I took off," she said, swiveling her head to look back at Vanessa, attempting to gage her immediate reaction.

"You left home that day?" Vanessa asked, confused that Haley would leave home over having one more sibling.

Haley sighed, and her shoulders visibly slumped. She continued in a quiet, somber voice, "No, I left a couple of days later. My parents had tried to talk to me, but I'd already met Jimmy, before their 'big news.' Jimmy was older than me, and he rode a motorcycle!" She blushed and hung her head, realizing how foolish she sounded. "I really believed he loved me," she whispered quietly. Then she lifted her eyes, pleading in a stronger voice, "He promised he'd take me far away from my ungrateful family. He said he had big plans for us. That we'd have nothing but fun and excitement every day for the rest of our lives!" She lowered her head, whispering again, "He said he'd take really good care of me." She choked back a sob as she finished her last statement, her gaze self-consciously returning to her hands on her lap.

"Did he take care of you?" Vanessa asked softly, her scissors still.

"No!" Haley wept.

Setting down the comb and scissors, Vanessa retrieved a box of tissues, and handed them to Haley.

After Haley had wiped away her tears and caught her breath, she bravely resumed. "Jimmy and I rode out of town on a Wednesday, when the kids were all in school, while Mom and Dad were at work. I left town on the back of Jimmy's motorcycle. I knew my parents would be called when I didn't pick up the kids after school. I was fifteen, completely clueless as to what that would mean to them," she said remorsefully. "The next day I knew I'd made a big mistake. I tried to call home from a truck stop, but I got scared, and hung up as soon as I heard my mom's voice. I knew she'd stayed home from work that day and I was afraid she was mad at me." Guilt and pain resonated unmistakably in her voice.

"Please continue," Vanessa gently prodded. "When did you arrive in Los Angeles?"

"We just rode for days, sleeping at truck stops in a sleeping bag under the stars. It took four days to get to LA. We got there early in the morning and pulled into some deserted looking, sleazy bar. Before he went inside, Jimmy told me he'd run out of money. He made me sit by myself in the parking lot for hours, watching over his dumb bike, starving," she recalled bitterly. "When he finally came out, he'd met up with some loser, who took us to an old, condemned apartment building. He said the owner of the building only rented under the table, mostly to illegals and drug addicts. It was the most disgusting place I'd ever seen! The walls were crumbling and there were lots of creepy people hanging around. But Jimmy said we had to stay there." Haley's voice trembled as she spoke.

Vanessa heard her disappointment and disillusionment. "Did you consider going home?" she asked gently, continuing to style Haley's hair.

"Yes, but my parents are very religious people. By the time I knew I wanted to go home, I couldn't. I'd let them down in so many ways. Plus, Jimmy did things to me that I couldn't undo. I can never face them again! Ever!" she exclaimed vehemently.

"Exactly what kinds of things did Jimmy do to you?" Vanessa asked, attempting to hide her mounting anger.

"Well..." Haley began shamefully, "The second night after we left home, he drove his bike out into the middle of an orchard to spend the night. He hit me a bunch of times, and tried to rape me. I screamed and screamed, but no one could hear me. I was so scared of him; he just kept hitting me, ripping at my clothes and acting mean, until I finally gave up. I stopped fighting him off, and just lay there. I let him do what ever he wanted," Haley whimpered, tormented by the memory of her violently lost virginity.

Vanessa felt her face flush, and her blood boiled in fury. Thank goodness that slimy man was dead, or she'd have to kill him herself. "Did you try going to the police?" she asked sympathetically.

Haley shook her head no. "The first time it happened, I told Jimmy I was going to the police. He said go ahead; they'd just send me back home. He knew I could never face my parents again," she sobbed.

"How long did you live with him?" she asked, concealing her revulsion.

"We've lived in that disgusting apartment together for two and a half years," she said, sighing as she thought back over the nightmarish life she'd shared with him. "After we got settled, I tried to leave him lots of times, but he always found me, and then he'd beat me. I didn't have any money, so I never got very far. The last time I ran away from him, he said he'd kill me, and that no one would even notice." She shuddered as she remembered how cruel he had been to her that night.

Charming, Vanessa thought. "How did you two survive? Did he have a job?" she attempted to sound casual as she used the curling iron on Haley's cropped hair.

"Jimmy worked sometimes," she continued slowly, "And I tried to work, but it was hard. No one would hire me because I had no ID, and no skills," she explained. "Some of the illegals in the building paid me to watch their kids while they worked, but it was never very much. Sometimes, they'd give me food instead," she said, gratefully.

Haley's voice became so soft, Vanessa could barely make out what she was saying as she continued. "But one night, when Jimmy was drinking, he'd decided to let one of his friends have some fun raping me. I fought him at first, but he was strong, and very drunk. He just kept beating on me until I passed out. I woke up the next morning with all my clothes ripped off. They were shredded all over the floor." She grew silent, reliving the horrendous mistreatment she'd endured.

Vanessa, sensing Haley's need for another break, dropped her hands to her sides while she waited patiently in silence for her to complete her story.

Haley's voice sounded flat and strained when she resumed. "Jimmy's friends always seemed to have money. So he decided that charging them for sex with me was a good way for *him* to make money. He kept me inside that horrid apartment all the time, insisting that I wear only lacey underwear. Whenever his friends showed any interest, he'd tell them, 'pay me and you can have her.' Soon all his friends knew they could have me anytime they wanted, as long as they had the cash." She wondered what Vanessa must think of her. Remaining perfectly still, she felt Vanessa gently fluffing the curls in her short hair.

Haley wanted Vanessa to know that she hadn't gone along with Jimmy's moneymaking scheme, and pleaded, "I begged Jimmy to stop, but he just laughed at me. Finally, he went off and left me on my own. One of the moms I used to babysit for brought me some clothes. She insisted I go to a free clinic, where I got shots and birth control. They took good care of me there, but I had to sneak out the back door. I overheard them calling the police." She spoke rapidly as she tried to make light of one of the worst days of her life. She didn't need or want Vanessa's pity.

Concentrating on Haley's hair, Vanessa was too shocked to react. She thought of all kinds of sympathetic responses, but controlled her impulse to comfort Haley. She wanted her to finish her story first.

After a moment or two, when Vanessa had failed to comment, Haley continued, "I tried to run away the day I left the clinic, but I didn't get very far. Jimmy found me and he was really angry. I could barely walk when he'd finished with me, and he insisted I lay around completely naked for a week, even after I pleaded for his forgiveness. Finally, I promised him I wouldn't try to leave him again until after my eighteenth birthday," she whispered. "Once he began to trust me again, he eventually gave me back a few of my clothes. He even seemed a little nicer. Everything was fine for a while, as long as I did what he told me." She'd never revealed her appalling life to anyone before. Now that she had, she was too ashamed to look at Vanessa. She couldn't stand to see her disgusted reaction.

Jimmy's cruelty infuriated Vanessa. Haley had made a big mistake when she'd left home, but no one deserved to be treated like that. Standing behind her, she rested her hands gently on Haley's shoulders for a minute before she spoke. "I'm so sorry you found yourself in such a horrible situation," she said, sympathetically. Vanessa paused, then changed the subject. "Your hair is trimmed and curled. I think it looks great. Hold on while I get you a mirror."

"Thank you," Haley whispered. She began weeping silently in response to Vanessa's kind words, as shame overwhelmed her. Sitting motionlessly, her blurred eyes fixated on her twisting hands in her lap.

Vanessa handed her the mirror. Haley glanced at the first real hairstyle she'd had in a long time and then she set the mirror faced down on the table. Vanessa seated herself across from her and waited, hoping that she would be strong enough to continue their conversation.

"Can you tell me about the bank?" Vanessa asked, changing the subject away from Jimmy's exploitation.

Haley's face relaxed and she dashed away her tears. She was glad to focus on the bank robbery, instead of her shameful sex life.

"Jimmy and his friend, Marvin, decided to rob the bank using bombs they made in the kitchen," she rolled her eyes at their foolishness. "My job was to distract the security guard." She leaned toward Vanessa to stress her dilemma. "I didn't want to, but Jimmy said he'd kill me if I didn't do exactly what he said," she clarified defensively. "My plan was to run away while Jimmy was distracted with the bank tellers. I thought they wouldn't bother to look for me, since they'd be too busy hiding out from the police themselves," she said, logically.

Guilt washed over Haley's face as she recalled what Andrew had said about the guard. "Is that nice old man going to live? I was running out the door when he followed me. I hope he's going to live," she pleaded. "I should never have been there. I shouldn't have helped those two freaks. I'm so sorry." Her eyes glistened with tears of remorse. Then she whispered, "Will I go to jail?"

Vanessa reached for her hand. Compassion filled her heart for this poor girl, who'd obviously been living in hell for years. Justice would not be served if she went to jail. "We'll see what the detective says, but I think you have a good case for a complete acquittal," she said confidently, reaching over to fuss with one of her stray curls. She'd tried desperately to cover the cut over Haley's ear with curls, believing that if she covered the cut, maybe Andrew wouldn't notice.

"Do I have to tell the detective everything?" she moaned. "I don't want him to think I'm a slut." Haley's eyes were wide with shame and fear.

"If you'd like…" Vanessa offered, "I'll explain the first part of your story regarding your relationship with Jimmy. But after that, we'll have to wait to see what else he wants to ask you." Vanessa gave her a reassuring smile and squeezed her hand gently.

"Please don't tell him I'm a runaway," she said, fearfully. "I don't want him to call my parents."

Vanessa believed it was well past the time for Haley to contact her parents. She imagined they must be out of their minds with worry. As she was still a minor, she assumed Andrew would have a legal obligation to contact them, despite Haley's objections. Vanessa would let Andrew handle it. "I won't say anything about your parents, if that's what you really want," she smiled, reassuringly.

Haley exhaled the breath she'd been holding, mildly relieved. "Thank you." Appearing pale and exhausted, she asked nervously, "Do you think it would it be okay if I lay down until he comes? I'm still feeling a little dizzy," she said weakly. Vanessa wasn't sure if she was simply tired, worried, or actually injured more than she'd initially thought. She surreptitiously checked for any signs that might indicate Haley needed further medical attention, while she pretended to survey her new hairstyle. "Of course you can, but I'm worried about you. Should we go to the emergency room?" she asked, casually.

"No!" Haley said vehemently, then softened her tone as she rationalized, "I'm just a little tired. I haven't slept for a very long time. This is the first time I've felt protected enough to sleep soundly." She stood behind her chair, clearly holding onto the back for support.

Vanessa wasn't entirely convinced. "All right, if you're absolutely sure?"

"I'm fine, really I am." Haley relaxed. Vanessa clearly wasn't going to drag her to the hospital against her will.

"Go ahead and lie down. I'll come get you when he arrives," Vanessa said, although unconvinced by her protests.

Haley started to walk down the hall, then turned around and called shyly over her shoulder, "Vanessa?"

Busily cleaning up after the hair cutting, Vanessa answered without looking up. "Yes?" she said, automatically.

"I can't thank you enough for everything you've done for me. I had forgotten how nice normal could be."

Vanessa raised her head. The look in Haley's eyes broke her heart, but she managed to smile back. "You're welcome, hon. Go get a little rest, it's three thirty now, and he'll be here shortly." She spoke quickly, covering the sudden flood of tender emotions she felt for the young girl.

Haley walked slowly down the hall. Every muscle in her body ached, leaving her completely drained. She closed the bedroom door softly, kicked off her flip-flops and snuggled back under the wonderfully soft, clean comforter. The faces of her parents, brother and sisters floated before her. Suddenly homesick, a sob of guilt caught in her throat, before she plunged back into an exhausted slumber.

Vanessa swept the clippings off the floor and tidied her kitchen. She turned on the coffee maker as she anxiously prepared for Andrew's arrival. Inspired, she pulled out the frozen cookie dough she kept in her freezer for unexpected guests, and turned on the oven. Thinking of Haley, she placed a full cookie sheet in to bake.

A plate of warm chocolate chip cookies might sweeten him up, she thought. And, possibly keep him from hauling both her and Haley off to jail. Feeling enormously protective of Haley, Vanessa went over and over in her mind the best method of handling Andrew's questions.

Both the oven buzzer and the doorbell ran simultaneously. She pulled out the cookie sheet and turned off the oven. After a hurried check of her appearance in the hallway mirror, she gulped a quick breath, and slowly opened the front door.

This time Andrew stood alone on her doorstep. He'd changed his clothes and presently wore a light blue cotton dress shirt with the top button left open, and the sleeves rolled up to his elbows. Vanessa thought he looked very handsome, if overheated. She looked past him to his car parked under a shady tree in her driveway. It was a shiny, black, station wagon, bearing an official emblem with the words Canine Unit on the side panel. Slowly, he removed his sunglasses, and his eyes captured hers hypnotically before he spoke. The look he gave her was like a possessive, tender caress, and his voice, heartfelt and intimate.

"Vanessa?"

What was wrong with her? She had a crazy impulse to wrap her arms around him. Again, she felt an unnatural desire to seek comfort and support from this complete stranger. He stood in her doorway, silently observing her; while she continued to stare back, utterly transfixed by his probing, blue eyes.

Andrew hesitated, thrown off balance by her lack of a verbal response. Puzzled by the dazed look in her eyes, he repeated his cautious endeavor to elicit a coherent response from her. "Remember, you promised your complete cooperation if I returned?" He raised a questioning eyebrow.

Vanessa quickly pulled herself together. "Of course, Andrew, please come in," she stammered.

Andrew looked back at his car to explain; "I decided that maybe Shep should stay in the car with the windows open, for now." His voice softened fondly as he referred to his dog.

"Thanks, Callie will appreciate it." Vanessa felt the unexpected blush rapidly warming her cheeks.

"Vanessa?" Andrew inquired, his voice vibrating in a seductively low tone.

"Um?" She stared at him, still a bit dazed.

"May I come in now?" he smiled, amused by her blush and lack of response.

Vanessa suddenly realized she'd been standing in the middle of the doorway. "Oh, of course..." Her blush deepened as she stepped to one side and motioned him in. "Please, come in, Andrew."

Chapter 8
A Warmhearted Touch

*T*he minute Andrew walked through the door of Vanessa's cozy kitchen, the tantalizing aroma of fresh coffee and chocolate chip cookies overwhelmed his senses. "Umm, something smells delicious." He inhaled, his pleasant smile lighting up his face.

Hiding her own smug smile of satisfaction, Vanessa ushered him to the table and graciously offered him a cup of coffee. Parched from the sweltering heat, he settled for a cold glass of iced tea instead.

His eyes danced with delight when she placed a plate of freshly baked cookies in front of him. Breathless with anticipation, she watched him close his eyes as he savored his first bite. When he opened his eyes, he caught her anxiously studying him. The broad smile that filled his face was contagious, and they broke out in spontaneous laughter.

"I can't remember the last time I had one of these." He indicated the warm cookie in his hand.

Vanessa, pleased by his spontaneous praise, sat down next to him and waited patiently for him to begin his investigation.

"Where's your guest?" He licked the chocolate from the corner of his mouth below his mustache, casually remarking, "I thought she'd be up by now." He glanced down the hall toward the bedrooms.

"I don't recall telling you my guest was a female." Baiting him coyly, Vanessa stalled in an effort to allow Haley more time to rest.

"You didn't actually, I just assumed." He checked for chocolate smears on his face and casually wiped his fingers on a napkin. *I see*, thought Andrew, *we're going to play a little cat and mouse now. Okay, I'll play*.

"Well, you're correct, my guest is in fact a young girl. She was awake earlier, but she's resting now. We had our own, very intense conversation just a short time ago." She relayed this information to him with a tone of formality.

"I see…" Andrew pulled out a notepad. "You wore out my witness." He reached in his pocket for his pen. "In that case, I'll ask you some questions instead. What is your guest's full name?" Pen on paper, he awaited her response.

"Her name is Haley," she said, primly.

Andrew sensed Vanessa was trying to deliberately drag out his investigation by answering vaguely. He endeavored to be patient.

"Haley what?" he prodded.

"I'm sorry..." Her wrinkled brow indicating to him that she was genuinely perplexed. "I don't think she ever told me her last name."

"Fine, I'll ask her later." He moved on. "How old is Haley?" He began to tap his pen on the notepad in frustration.

"She told me she was turning eighteen next month," she said, truthfully, watching him jot down another notation without comment.

"Do you know her current address?" he asked, without looking up from his pad.

She realized belatedly she hadn't actually gotten any useful information from Haley. Vanessa's queries had fixated specifically on the girl's traumatic experiences instead.

"No, I'm sorry. I know that she's been living in a condemned apartment, somewhere in LA." She shuddered, remembering Haley's description.

"I see. And where are her parents?" He focused on his notepad trying to hide his irritation.

Knowing her parents were a touchy subject, Vanessa paused. She struggled to respect Haley's privacy without aggravating the detective further. "I don't know exactly. She mentioned something about Ohio. I wish I knew more, but she was hesitant to talk about her parents." She gazed at the table as she apologized.

"Runaway," he said, matter-of-factly, as he made a notation.

"That would be my guess." She nibbled on her lower lip.

"But you're not saying exactly." He laid his pad on the table. This was a waste of time, he thought.

"So far you've been a wealth of information," he said, mildly sarcastically. "How is it that this girl is here today, at *your* house? Did you know her prior to this morning?"

"No." She cautiously avoided his penetrating stare.

"But you plan to do anything and everything to protect her, is that right?"

"Yes!" She looked defiantly into Andrew's blue eyes. "I'm afraid you're right." Her assertive tone taunted him, with just the right touch of rebellion, and no sign of remorse.

He saw how she planned to impede his investigation, and elected to approach another sensitive subject instead.

His voice suddenly changed, turning soft and mellow, while he returned her intense, challenging gaze. He'd been studying the flashes in her eyes, reflecting her many emotions, while they conversed. His previous experiences with criminals had convinced him that a person's eyes never lie, even when their mouths did. Vanessa's expressive eyes certainly confirmed his belief.

She squirmed a little under his unnerving gaze. She felt a sudden shift in his questioning from interrogation to personal curiosity, which made her feel even more uncomfortable.

"Vanessa?" He said her name like a whispered caress, laced with familiarity.

"Yes, Andrew?"

"Do you remember me?" His eyes searched hers for any sign of recognition.

"No..." She crinkled her forehead, struggling to place him. "But there is definitely something about your eyes that makes me think that I might. Do I know you from somewhere?"

He paused to grapple with his conscience. He didn't want to callously remind her of what was probably the most painful day of her life. The tone of his voice dropped to an intimate whisper. "I took your statement in the hospital almost thirty years ago."

Recognition jolted through her body. She whispered sadly, "I remember now. I met you when I first came out of surgery."

"Yes." His voice became low, as he compassionately watched her wrestle with her painful memories. Her face became devoid of all expression. But Andrew wasn't deceived. He'd immediately sensed her anguish, and thought she might flee the kitchen. Instead, she quickly shielded her expressive eyes from him. When their eyes met again, he could see her composure had returned.

"Actually..." she said, "I'd just finished telling Haley all about that day. I thought she was the first person—that I'd ever shared my entire story with." She looked back at him, murmuring, "I'd completely forgotten—I 'd told you as well."

Andrew smiled slightly, but remained perfectly still as he watched her work through her emotional past.

"I remember..." She flashed him a shy, appreciative smile, recalling their interactions of that day, years ago. "How gentle and kind you were when you questioned me. You seemed unusually upset by my surgery." Her own devastation was understandable, but she'd been puzzled at the time by his furious reaction and his unexpected anger toward her husband. It left her with a lasting impression of him.

"I was. My wife had been going through horrendous fertility treatments, and I'm afraid I empathized with your case more than I should have. Your unnecessary loss—felt so personal. Your senseless tragedy infuriated me. I've never forgotten you, or the look of suffering reflected in your eyes." This he confessed for the first time. Such a remarkable woman, Andrew thought. Even on the most tragic day of her life, she'd noticed and remembered how he had reacted. He suddenly realized that he'd unexpectedly shared more of his private thoughts than he'd meant to, and didn't elaborate.

"Forgive me for asking..." her voice trailed off and her eyes watered a little as she reluctantly voiced her own sensitive question. "But did you and your wife ever have a baby?" She instantly knew she'd overstepped. The torment that filled his eyes was answer enough.

"No." He cleared his throat, preparing for what he was about to share with her. "After two years of infertility testing and treatments, instead of having a baby, my wife was diagnosed with ovarian cancer." Simply voicing this painful, harsh reality, dragged him back into the darkness, one he'd only recently escaped.

Vanessa could hear his suppressed bitterness, and wished she hadn't asked. She'd opened a festering wound for him, unnecessarily.

"I'm so sorry," she whispered sincerely. Without thinking, she began to reach across the table to touch his hand with hers, but she stopped short of physically touching him. Instead, she allowed her fingers to rest on the table, so close to his, that she could feel his warmth. Disillusioned and disappointed, they'd both desperately yearned for a family that never materialized.

He sat silently brooding as he gazed deeply into his glass of iced tea, wishing it were a beer in some darkened bar instead. His hands wrapped tightly around the glass, attempting to draw support from the amber liquid within. Lost, and re-experiencing his own tormented past, he seemed completely unaware of Vanessa's attempt to comfort him, but remained consumed by the endless shattering of his heart.

"Once she was diagnosed..." His voice sounded eerie and far away as he began to speak again. "All thoughts of having a child were irrelevant. I knew I was losing my wife. She lived longer than expected, but she suffered horribly," he recalled without emotion. He lifted his glass to sip his tea, suddenly remembering that he wasn't alone, and became uncomfortable. "How about you? Did you ever remarry and adopt?"

"No, I married my job instead." The complete irony of her current situation made her statement sound flat and pathetic, even to her own ears.

He watched her guarded response closely. Glancing down at the table, he was surprised to find her hand resting so close to his. He released his hand from the cool glass and placed it on the table, positioning it so that the tips of their fingers barely touched. He absently studied the points where their fingers intersected, then a strange feeling of warm energy traveled through his fingertips and up his arm. Incredibly, he felt tranquility radiating deep within his entire body.

Both of them remained completely still, absorbed in quiet contemplation, the raw memories of their past slowly fading. He moved his hand closer, gradually entwining his fingers with hers, and looked up into her eyes. A look of complete wonder appeared on her face as she stared, wide-eyed, into his eyes. The warm sensation was simultaneously calming and faintly electrifying.

Overwhelmed by the tingling sensation pulsating through her body, she remained frozen in time, completely spellbound. When the warm vibrations settled into her feminine zones, she reluctantly removed her hand, folding them self-consciously into her lap. She felt her face burn with a betraying blush and she kept her dilated eyes hidden from his penetrating gaze.

Andrew felt cold and desolate after she removed her hand from his. He straightened in his chair as he struggled to compose himself. Clearing his throat, he continued to speak to her tenderly.

"I didn't want to hurt you with the past." He leaned forward to apologize, wishing she'd look at him. "I just wanted you to know how much I admire your courage. I understand the reason that you feel so protective about this young girl that you've only just met."

"I sensed that I knew you the first time I looked into your eyes." She felt the flush recede from her face and was able to look up to face him again. "Thank you for reminding me. As for Haley, when you meet her, you'll see she's innocent. She may have made a few bad choices in her life, but she's already paid dearly for them." She wanted to touch him, but instead she implored him to understand with her expressive eyes.

"I'll trust your instincts, but would you care to enlighten me about a few of these bad choices she's made?" Andrew asked, back to the business at hand. He turned the page on his notepad.

Somehow, they'd transitioned back to a professional-sounding conversation. Vanessa missed the intimacy that they'd momentarily shared, but it was imperative for Andrew to understand Haley, before he actually met her.

"First of all, she made the mistake of hooking up with a loser." She emphasized *loser*, attempting to explain Haley's situation. "Not only did he rape her repeatedly, but he has kept her a virtual captive for the last couple of years, pimping the poor girl out to support himself and his sickening lifestyle." She spat out her words with contempt.

"Poor kid." He shook his head sadly. "I don't suppose this *loser* has a name?" He cocked his head to one side and examined her closely, to determine if she knew the answer.

"She called him Jimmy. Sorry, I don't know his last name either," she smiled weakly.

"Okay, then..." He knew it was time to ask some of the tough questions. "Can you tell me if she was at the bank this morning during the robbery?"

"She was, but only because Jimmy threatened to kill her." Adamantly, she defended her guest in the other room. "Andrew?" She panicked, realizing she may have just incriminated Haley. "I'm not sure how much she, or I, should say about the bank without a lawyer present." Terrified, she worried she may have already said too much. She couldn't be responsible for sending Haley to jail!

He leaned back in his chair and chewed on his pen as he considered her dilemma for a minute. He had a law degree, and knew she was correct in her assumption. "I see your point. Does she know the identities of both of the bank robbers?" he asked, switching his focus to his defense lawyer mode.

"Yes." Her questioning eyes carefully searched his.

"Will she continue to stay here with you?" He returned her direct gaze, no longer taking notes.

"For as long as she wants." She leaned closer; her glistening eyes and her assertive tone indicating she was following his train of thought closely.

He pondered for another minute or two. The DA happened to be a good friend of his and he believed they could agree on a good solution to Haley's problem.

"All right..." He leaned back toward Vanessa. "I'd like to meet briefly with Haley today." He looked for her approval. "I'll hold off on the details of the robbery. Instead, I'll approach the DA first. I think he'd be willing to grant her full immunity, in exchange for the names and her testimony against the other two suspects." He grinned at Vanessa, certain she'd agree with his clever plan.

Relief spread over her like warm sunshine. He had to be the most decent man she'd ever met. "Thank you," she exhaled in relief. "Would you like to meet with Haley now?" She hesitantly stood up.

"Yes, if you think she's ready and can handle a quick interview."

"I'll go check on her." Her facial features relaxed. She had almost exited the kitchen, when she stopped and turned back toward him. "Thank you, for understanding." She beamed him an appreciative smile.

Vanessa had the unbelievable power to melt him where he sat. The mere idea that he might upset or disappoint her in any way was unthinkable. Questioning Haley could place him in emotionally hazardous territory.

When Vanessa returned, Andrew was shocked by the appearance of the petite, pale, childlike girl, who accompanied her. She looked like any other shy child pulled out of class and sent to the principal's office. Gone were the green hair spikes, dark make-up, and tattoos of the girl in the photo. He found it hard to believe this child was almost eighteen, let alone turning tricks and robbing banks.

Haley saw the disbelief in his eyes when he stood to greet her. Mustering her courage, she looked him straight in the eyes, sent him a shy smile, and reached out to shake his hand. "Hello sir, my name is Haley." Her voice was faint and her hand trembled slightly, but she bravely maintained eye contact.

He found himself immediately charmed by her and felt secretly relieved. No jury on earth would convict this child for even so much as a parking ticket, let alone a bank robbery.

"Hello Haley, please call me Andrew. I am a detective with the Bitton Police Department." He formally introduced himself to her. "Would you be willing to sit down and maybe answer a few questions for me?" He helped her into a chair. "Please remember; anything you say to me can be held against you later."

Sitting between them, Vanessa kept her eyes constantly fixed on Haley. He noted her wary look and the tautness of her body.

"I'll try." Haley's weak response concerned him.

Observing Haley fidgeting nervously with her hands, he sat back to carefully formulate the best line for his inquiry.

"Haley, because you do not have a lawyer present..." his tone still official. "I won't ask you anything that might incriminate you. This is just a preliminary investigation. All I need from you right now is information regarding your identity. Can you please tell me your whole name and date of birth?" Picking up his pad, he prepared to write.

She paused, gazing down at her hands, fearful that he'd contact her parents. "If I tell you the truth, will you promise not to call my parents?" Her pleading voice and her frightened expression quickly derailed his determination. He'd been in tough, touchy spots like this before, and he chastised himself. *I must be getting soft in my old age.*

"When I run your information through the data banks, it will automatically alert any authorities on the lookout for you," he informed her truthfully. "The only thing I can offer you is to delay running it, at least until after you've secured an immunity deal with the DA. Will you please give me your information?" Her eyes had grown wide with fear after he'd stressed that he was obligated to obey the law.

"I appreciate your offer. I realize you're only doing your job," she said, a single tear rolling unheeded down her face. "My name is Haley Martin. My birthday is July 19th, so I'll be eighteen soon." Although her answer was brief, it was polite.

He jotted down the information. "Can you tell me when you last saw your parents?"

She considered refusing, but instead she responded hesitantly. "About three years ago."

"And where was that?" he asked.

"In Ohio." She hoped to delay the notification of her parents by answering vaguely.

He decided it was best not to push for an address. He would get it later. He studied her for a moment; a piece of clear tape above her right ear drew his attention. He wondered what other injuries were hidden under her loose clothing.

"May I take a picture of you for my files?" His kind tone reassured Haley, but her eyes darted anxiously toward Vanessa.

Vanessa nodded back and tried to reassure her. "I'm sure it's standard procedure."

"Okay, I guess so," she reluctantly agreed, but instantly began fidgeting with her hands again.

He caught Vanessa's eye. She could tell he was miffed about something. "Would you please escort me to the car to get my camera?" He sounded unusually terse, speaking through his now gritted teeth.

"I'll be right back." She reached over to pat Haley's hand.

Following close behind him, she wondered what it was that he needed to talk to her about in private. He turned to her as soon as they were out of earshot. She nearly ran into him when he stopped short in front of her, immediately noticing the unexpected sparks of anger in his eyes.

"What's the matter?"

"Have you taken that child to a doctor?" His concern for Haley made his tone sound accusatory.

Immediately ashamed and feeling defensive, Vanessa responded, "I wanted to, but she refused to go!" Her excuse sounded lame even to her own ears.

"Look, I saw the cut over her ear, it's very likely she's suffering from a concussion!" He continued relentlessly with his assault, maligning her ability to care for Haley.

"All right, Detective." She didn't appreciate his insinuation that she'd somehow been negligent. "What do you suggest we do?" His high-handed attitude annoyed her.

"How about this?" He calmed as he tried to think rationally. He rubbed the back of his neck, thinking aloud. "What if I ask her a couple more questions, then tell her that legally I'll need her to get medically checked out?"

When they returned with camera in hand, they found Haley staring off into space, twisting her hands in her lap, her mounting level of anxiety clearly visible. After snapping a few photos, Andrew picked up a small recorder, and clicked it on. "Just a few more questions." He feared she would reject the idea of going to the hospital and softened his tone, sounding friendly. "I need to record this for the DA."

Vanessa stood behind Haley with her hands on her shoulders for support. Haley nodded, quietly facing him with her wide, innocent eyes.

"Were you in the Bitton bank this morning?" he asked.

Haley didn't flinch, since she'd previously decided to answer all of his questions truthfully. "Yes."

Andrew continued officially, "Do you have any information regarding the attempted robbery of the bank this morning?"

"Yes."

"Do you know the identities of the two bank robbers?"

"Yes."

"Will you give us that information in exchange for immunity from prosecution?" He looked at Haley directly.

When she paused, Vanessa tried to explain. "He means that if you tell them what they want to know, you won't be charged with anything."

He noticed how calm and effectively Vanessa explained the situation and he rapidly confirmed her statement. "Vanessa is absolutely correct. Will you agree?"

"Yes, I will." Haley nodded in relief.

He switched off the recorder and watched as the young girl visibly sagged back into her chair. But, her momentarily relieved expression unexpectedly became a worried frown. "Andrew?"

"Yes?" He raised an eyebrow, surprised that she'd used his name.

"Can you tell me how the security guard is?" The wringing of her hands in her lap began again.

"I'm happy to report that although he's in serious condition, he's currently stable." He felt the sincerity of her concern, and wanted to reassure her. "He's expected to be up for questioning sometime tomorrow."

"Do you think I might be able to visit him?" She gazed at him with childlike expectation after making her simple request.

He was in the process of picking up the recorder and camera, but the hopeful tone of her voice made him stop. "Probably not tomorrow, and maybe not for a few days." She nodded and nervously glanced back at her hands. The remorse she felt was apparent.

"Haley, look at me. Did you have anything at all to do with the bomb that exploded?" he asked.

She shook her head no.

"Then his condition is not your fault," he reasoned firmly. "Speaking of injuries, what about yours?" He began to scan her from head to toe with his eyes.

"I'm fine!" Haley ducked her head dramatically.

"It's very important." He walked calmly over to her and squatted down in front of her. "I need to get official medical verification of your injuries from a qualified doctor for our records." He spoke softly, but authoritatively, as if he were quoting the law.

Haley looked pleadingly toward Vanessa.

"I was able to patch you up, but I can't tell if you have anything seriously wrong. I promise I'll stay with you the whole time." Vanessa used her most persuasive sweet-talk voice.

"I won't go if my parents have to be called." Haley knew about the hospital requirement for parental consent, from the time her sister broke her arm.

"That means you'll go to the hospital, if I can arrange for you to be seen without notifying them?" he negotiated. *Aha, she's about to agree*, he thought triumphantly.

"I suppose..." Haley said, hesitantly. "But I have no way of paying."

"How about if I get the DA to pay for it? As a part of the deal for your testimony." He had already decided that if the DA refused, he'd cover the bill himself.

"Okay," Haley pouted, and reluctantly agreed.

"One more thing. Would you be willing to give the doctor permission to discuss your injuries with Vanessa and me?" He included Vanessa, knowing she would appreciate the gesture.

Haley hadn't trusted anyone in years. Today, she'd trusted Vanessa with her past, and now she found herself trusting Andrew with her future.

"Okay," Haley nodded cautiously. She only hoped that she wasn't about to make another big, life-altering mistake.

Chapter 9
Life Hurts

*T*he Bitton Memorial Hospital was on the edge of town, two blocks south of the Bitton Bank. The hospital was an incredibly landscaped, modern facility, operating with substantial financial support from local philanthropic residents. Andrew walked in like he owned the place, and was greeted like one of the family. Addressing the admissions clerk, he introduced Haley as his witness, who was currently in his protective custody. The young clerk listened with intense curiosity as he explained that she'd been a victim of the early bank bombing, and now required medical clearance from the emergency room doctor. No one challenged his authority, and Haley was swiftly escorted to an exam room with Vanessa trailing close behind.

Vanessa felt self-conscious under the staff's scrutiny, wondering if the hospital personnel assumed that she was Haley's mother, even though Andrew had answered all of their questions regarding Haley's identity from his notepad. He watched them go down the hall and disappear into an empty exam room. Leaning against the counter, Andrew lingered at the familiar nurse's station, joking comfortably with the staff.

After Haley had endured a multitude of lab tests, x-rays, and an ultrasound, the doctor asked to speak privately with Vanessa and Andrew in his office. His findings shocked and saddened them. Haley had suffered multiple untreated fractures. The x-rays also showed several newer fractures, and a break just above her right ankle that required immediate treatment. He voiced concerns about several past and recent rib fractures. The scan of her head revealed several previous skull fractures, and she currently suffered from a mild concussion. Her right eardrum had ruptured during the blast, and the laceration over her ear needed suturing. He also noted that Haley's spleen had developed a slow leak, and he was concerned about possible blood loss. The good news was that Haley was not pregnant. But the doctor had discovered evidence of multiple rape events, and probable STD's. He concluded that she'd been a long-term victim of severe physical and sexual abuse. His recommendations included admission to the hospital overnight for close observation, and consultations with both the general and orthopedic surgeons.

After he finished his report, the doctor threw the chart down on his desk in fury. "Damn it!" he said, glaring at Andrew. "Tell me you locked up the son-of-a–bitch who did this to her?"

Andrew nodded. "We did one better doctor, he's dead."

"That's a relief," the doctor muttered without remorse. He bent down and retrieved Haley's chart before he reached out to shake Andrew's hand, and calmly returned to the ER. *Maybe there was some justice in this world after all*, he thought.

Vanessa and Andrew remained alone in the tiny office, sharing their shock and disbelief. Suddenly, she collapsed, shaking and sobbing uncontrollably. Andrew didn't hesitate, and pulled her close while she cried. He realized her highly emotional state represented more than just Haley's unspeakable injuries. Everything about Haley's circumstances had struck a very deep, personal chord with her own violent past. Embracing her now, he felt helpless in the presence of her intense grief and pain. *If I had a magic wand, he thought, I would end all the suffering in the world.* But he didn't, so he stood powerlessly, gently rubbing Vanessa's back.

Never had Vanessa allowed herself to release her private emotions in public. But hearing the graphic details of Haley's unbearable suffering had been more than she could stomach. Haley's despair had become strangely entangled around her own repressed agony. No matter what happened in the future, Vanessa knew she'd always feel a protective bond with the frail young girl.

Gradually, Vanessa became aware of Andrew's strong, comforting arms around her, and the wet spot on the front of his shirt. He'd been there for her once before, years ago, when she'd believed her tragic life had ended. Now here he stood again, holding her close, supporting her through another horrifically brutal episode of her life. Vanessa sniffled a few times as she gently extricated herself from his warm embrace. Looking up into his beautiful, kind blue eyes, his look of utter helplessness and genuine concern, touched her troubled heart.

"I'm sorry," she said, lowering her eyes in embarrassment. "The doctor's report was even worse than I'd expected."

Andrew tenderly brushed the hair away from her face, resting his hands lightly on the sides of her face, waiting patiently for her to lift her head enough for their eyes to meet.

"You never need to apologize to me," he whispered softly, his tender touch matching his affectionate tone. "You've been through more than your share of heartbreak. I know how much Haley's situation hits close to home for you." He dropped his hands to her shoulders and gave her a gentle squeeze of encouragement.

"Thank you, for your kindness and understanding." Vanessa's sad gaze met his. "You've been wonderful." Her attention shifted to the middle button on his shirt. "I think I'll go make myself presentable. I'm sure Haley's frightened by everything that's happening. She'll need me to be strong." She tucked away her raw emotions, switching back to her usual, rational mindset.

She's back to being a little toughie again, Andrew thought. Her resilience never ceased to astonish him. "Do you think you'll be okay here for a while? I want to touch base with the DA"

"I'll be fine. It's Haley I'm worried about." She stepped back, chastising herself for her humiliating display of weakness.

"Of course you will," he said. "I'll be back in about an hour. I'll come find you both when I return." Charmed by her false bravado, he impulsively bent over to give her a quick kiss on the cheek, before turning to leave.

"Andrew?" she called after him.

"Yes, Vanessa?" He swung back toward her.

"I can't thank you enough for being here with me today. And for everything you're doing to help Haley." Even though his quick kiss had stunned her, she tried to sound composed. "It's incredibly kind, and very much appreciated." She searched his face, not wanting him to leave her just yet.

"You're welcome. I think it's about time someone looked out for Haley, don't you agree?"

Vanessa nodded as another humiliating tear spilled out of the corner of her eye. Andrew felt his heart stop. He slowly returned to stand in front of her, reaching down, he tenderly wiped the solitary tear away, before he bent down again to kiss the haunting torment from her eyes. This time his kiss landed full on her mouth. His kiss was gentle and brief and when he lifted his head, he immediately noticed that the torment in her eyes had turned into a look of shocked surprise. He sent her a pleased, slightly crooked smile, and turned toward the door to leave.

Watching him walk away, Vanessa reached up to touch her tingling lips with her fingertips. Andrew's kiss felt incredibly caring, and yet it seemed casual, like it was something that happened every day. Spellbound, she stared at the closed door he'd just passed through, instantly missing him. Slowly she shook her head in astonishment, and then she suddenly recalled Haley, being poked and prodded down the hall, urgently needing her support.

Standing in front of a mirror in the nearest ladies' room, she endeavored to restore her normal appearance. She thought it was important for her to emerge calm and composed, for Haley's sake. But she couldn't get Andrew, or his surprisingly endearing kiss out of her muddled mind.

When Vanessa returned to the examination room, she found Haley reclining on the exam table, quietly enduring stitches. She immediately went to her side to hold her hand as if she were a small child. Pale as the paper white sheets she lay on, Haley remained stoically still as the doctor sutured the cut above her ear. Vanessa squeezed her hand in silent support. "How are you holding up?" she asked cautiously.

The drape covered most of Haley's head and she faced away. "I'm fine." Her full concentration was on remaining perfectly still for the doctor.

"It looks like you'll be spending the night here in the hospital." Vanessa struggled to make the news sound cheery.

"I guess so." Haley's muffled voice sounded sullen.

"I'll stay with you for as long as I can." She squeezed Haley's hand gently.

"Thank you. Thanks for caring, and for being my friend."

"You know you've got me, and Andrew too. He left for a little while to talk to his friend about your deal, but he'll be back soon." Somehow, she thought chatting would ease the intensity of Haley's apprehension.

"You've both been incredible. I mean it." Haley's voice sounded slightly stronger. The doctor looked over at Vanessa, his concern for Haley etched in a wary expression across his weathered face.

"We both plan to stick around. We'll make sure you're as good as new." Vanessa felt a weak squeeze from Haley's hand.

"Thank you."

"Well, that's it for me." The doctor finished and turned to explain, "An orderly will come in a little while to take you to your room." He set his tray aside, smiling affectionately at Haley, turning to address Vanessa. "You're welcome to stay with her for as long as you like."

"Thank you, Doctor." She didn't want to be kicked out as soon as visiting hours were over.

"Yes, thank you for everything, Doctor," Haley added, sitting up straighter to face him.

"You're very welcome, young lady. You're an excellent patient, but I hope this will be your last time here in the emergency room." He sent

Haley a warm, paternal smile. *Such a pleasant young girl*, he thought. *Her abused condition is unforgivable!* He patted her leg as he turned to leave.

"How are you feeling? Any pain?" Vanessa asked anxiously, pulling up a chair beside her while they waited.

"No, I'm fine," Haley smiled, though she remained deathly pale.

"If it's alright with you, I'll stay with you until you fall asleep," she said, convinced Haley was simply putting on a brave face for her sake. "But I do think that at some point, I should go home to take care of my cat."

"I'm sorry, I'm being selfish, please don't feel you have to stay with me. I know how to take care of myself." Haley didn't want to become a burden.

"I know, but hospitals can be a little scary. I'm happy to stay as long as you need me." It broke her heart to see Haley trying to act courageous. She suspected she'd never been in a hospital before.

"I really appreciate that you're here, but please leave whenever you want. I'll be fine." Her hands continually opened and clenched in her lap, that along with her quivering lip gave her true misgivings away.

"I'd really like to stay. I promise, I'll leave when I need to. Okay?" Vanessa reached over to fuss with the dampened curl over her right ear.

"Okay." Haley giggled nervously, feeling relieved.

Conversation ceased when an orderly arrived with a wheelchair. A police officer followed them inconspicuously through the hospital to Haley's room on the second floor, and then settled into a chair right outside her door.

Once they were alone, Haley quietly whispered to Vanessa, "Am I under arrest?"

"No, I think Andrew must have arranged for police protection," she assured her confidently.

"Why? Jimmy's dead."

Vanessa thought for a minute. She was right. Her abuser had died in the bank explosion. "I don't know exactly why, but I'm sure he must have his reasons. He said he'd return in a while. We'll ask him then." She frowned, glancing toward the door. "Hopefully he'll return with good news from the DA, which reminds me, I need to call my attorney first thing Monday morning." Reaching inside her purse, she pulled out a pen and paper.

"No thank you, you've already done too much for me. I can just use the free guy."

"Don't worry about it." She jotted down her reminder note. "I know it will be hard, but please don't answer any questions regarding the bank robbery until we talk to my attorney. We need the deal in writing and approved by her first. All right?"

"Right," she conceded gloomily.

A nurse walked in with a tray filled with tubes and a bag of fluid. "Hi Haley, is that the name you'd like to be called while you're here?"

"Yes, please." Haley liked the friendly woman right away.

"My name is Mary. I need to start an IV, so we can give you some fluids and medications. Are you ready?" the nurse asked cheerfully.

"I guess." Haley frowned surveying the suspicious looking supplies.

"Have you ever had one before?" Mary asked

"No, I've never been in the hospital before."

Vanessa hated needles of any kind, but knew Haley needed her support, so she attempted to focus on her instead of the suspiciously painful looking objects. "Here, why don't you hold my other hand? Tell me about your favorite pet?" she suggested.

"Thanks." Haley suddenly ached for her mom. "I was about four when my Dad gave me a dog named Roger. He was a tiny, cute, black and white puppy, and he peed on everything." Haley seemed lost in the memory of her dog. She didn't even notice that the IV needle had been inserted.

"What else do you remember?" Vanessa enjoyed hearing about Haley's happier memories.

"I remember, after we got Roger, my mom told me I would also be getting a new little brother or sister." Haley frowned. "She made it seem like it would be so much fun." Her voice was peppered with disappointment.

"What did you think about that?" she asked cautiously.

"I thought I was getting one the same age that I was. I thought we could play together." Haley's response carried the disillusionment of a small child.

"That's it, I'm finished for now." Mary began picking up. "I hope that wasn't too bad for you, Haley?"

"I didn't even feel it." She looked at the fluid running into her arm with surprise.

"Great. Your nurse, Dee, will be in to see you in a few moments. Can I get you anything?" Mary asked cheerfully.

Haley automatically shook her head no, so Vanessa remarked, "She hasn't had dinner yet."

"No problem, I'll make sure she gets a menu." With that settled, she left the room.

"Are you all right?" Vanessa thought Haley still looked pale. She needed sleep and nourishment.

"I'm fine. You haven't had dinner either," Haley pointed out.

"I know, I thought I might grab a bite after Andrew gets back."

"Vanessa?" Haley, as a matter of survival, had become unusually perceptive for her age, learning the hard way how to discern people's feelings.

"Yes?" She had no idea what Haley was about to ask.

"I really like Andrew, don't you?"

"Yes, I suppose." Haley noticed her flush as she fumbled around, checking for the TV remote. "Would you like to watch some TV?" Vanessa quickly changed the subject.

"I think you two are really great together." Actually, Haley believed Andrew was perfect for Vanessa, whom she envisioned as a lonely cat lady.

"Honestly! I just met the man today." She couldn't believe how audacious Haley was. Her unanticipated, harmless suggestion caused Vanessa's cheeks to burn. After all, she was just beginning to sort out her puzzling feelings for Andrew.

"I'm just *saying*." Haley flashed her a knowing smile.

"What would you like to watch?" Vanessa asked, determined to put an end to the uncomfortable subject.

Haley knew better than to push. She'd wait; maybe later Vanessa would share her feelings, once she recognized them for what they were.

"Whatever you want."

They both sat quietly in comfortable silence, but neither one paid attention to the TV program flickering across the room. Preoccupied and lost within their own conflicting thoughts, they stared at the screen, until a new nurse arrived at Haley's bedside. She addressed Haley as Andrew slipped into the room close behind her.

"My name is Dee, and I'll be your nurse tonight," she introduced herself. "Here's your menu, please let me know what you'd like to eat," she instructed, handing her a slip of paper. "May I listen to your heart and lungs?" Haley nodded yes, and with the stethoscope in her ears, she continued, "I'll need to ask you a bunch of personal questions. Would you prefer privacy?" She motioned with her head toward where Andrew and Vanessa now stood beside each other.

Haley looked over at them. They had already begun to whisper in quiet code to one another. Wanting to give them a little push in the right direction, she asked, "Vanessa? Would you mind if you and Andrew went to eat while she's here?"

"Of course. I'll be back in about a half an hour." Feeling flustered, she walked over to Haley's bed to give her a quick hug for support. Then she addressed Dee, "Do you think you'll be finished by then?"

Dee lifted the stethoscope out of her ears to respond. "That should be about right."

"You have a very nice mom," Dee said, after they'd left the room.

Haley just smiled in response. She decided her relationship with Vanessa was far too complicated to explain. And the fact was, she *did* have a very nice mom, back home in Ohio.

As soon as Andrew and Vanessa were out of Haley's earshot they began to talk openly. Andrew explained that he'd met with his friend, the DA, at the dog park. They'd informally discussed Haley's case. After hearing all about Haley's involvement in the attempted bank robbery, including the circumstances that led to her being in the hospital, the DA readily agreed to grant her full immunity from prosecution. He had three young daughters of his own, and found Andrew's description of what Haley had been through for the past few years unimaginable. He agreed to draft the paperwork first thing Monday morning, and interview Haley as soon as she was deemed medically stable. In the meantime, he wanted her to remain in protective custody. She was the now key prosecuting witness for his case.

Vanessa relaxed, feeling relieved by the deal, until Andrew dropped the next little bombshell. "The DA gave me no option. Haley's information was placed into the police computer immediately after I met with him today. I was also forced to notify the FBI of her status as a runaway."

"You did what you had to." Her calm demeanor surprised him. "Frankly, I'm glad you did. She needs her parents. From what she's told me about them, I think she may be pleasantly surprised by their reaction to finding her." Going against Haley's expressed wishes made her feel disloyal, but it was for the best.

"I'm glad you agree. I was really nervous about telling you." Andrew flashed her an apologetic smile. He'd expected recriminations from her.

They split up after they entered the cafeteria, each heading for different food choices. Once they settled into a quiet booth together, Andrew continued their conversation. "Are you staying the night with Haley?"

Vanessa realized she was starving, so she quickly swallowed her forkful of salad before she answered. "Just 'till she falls asleep. I need to get home to feed the cat."

"I'll come back to make sure you get home safely."

"I'm sure I'll be fine," Vanessa objected, used to managing on her own. She waited for his predictable, male reaction.

"Please don't take what I'm about to say the wrong way." He knew she'd reject his offer, but he planned on insisting. "I think I should spend the night on your couch tonight, to make sure you're safe."

"Oh, really?" Vanessa couldn't believe he'd be so bold, or assume she'd be so naïve.

"Listen, it's not like that." He paused, sipping his coffee. "Haley will have protection here...and I just think you might need some protection as well." He leaned back away form her. "I'm simply having one of my gut feelings. I really believe there's still a threat out there." When she didn't respond, he offered half-heartedly, "I'll stay in the car with Shep if you'd prefer?"

"Don't be silly," she laughed. "We're both adults. I have a spare bedroom, if you really think it's necessary for you to stay. I'll just need to change the sheets as soon as we get home."

"No need." He shook his head to refuse. "I'll sleep on top of the covers with the door open. I'm a very light sleeper. Tell me you have some sort of home alarm system."

"I do, but only if the power's on." Vanessa thought about the trouble she'd had with her system during the recent windstorm.

"Okay, that'll work for tonight." He finished his hamburger, wiping the secret sauce off the corner of his mouth. "I think we have a plan." He quickly drained his coffee cup and stood. "I have some phone calls and paperwork to attend to at the office. Here's my cell number. Just call me later when you're ready to go home," he said, handing her his card.

Leaving Vanessa at the elevator, he walked directly to his office, three blocks away. The comforting low tones of the bullfrogs and crickets' songs filled the peaceful quiet of the pleasantly warm evening air, giving him a much-needed chance to clear his head. But his mind wandered back to Vanessa. *What is it about Vanessa that made my protective*

Kathleen L. Gregory

instincts run wild? Why do I always want to reach out to touch her, to hold her, and comfort her? He'd never felt as powerful of an attraction to anyone before. The random questions in his mind remained unanswered. A totally unsolved mystery, as he shook his head in bewilderment and ran up the steps into the station.

His office seemed unusually dark and deserted when he arrived. But a handwritten message had been left for him, resting carelessly on top of the scattered papers cluttering his desk. The note simply read that he'd missed an urgent phone call regarding Haley. He quickly scanned to bottom of the slip of paper, noting the return name and number.

The urgent call was from Haley's parents!

Chapter 10
Identity Quandary

*T*he sun shone brightly as a tall man with clean-cut, short black hair, and a dark five o'clock shadow stepped out of the twin-engine plane. He'd been traveling all night. The glare of the sunlight, as he emerged from the plane, temporally blinded him. Thankfully, he'd bought a pair of sunglasses at his last stop, which he instantly lowered over his beady, blood-shot eyes. His new suit, wrinkled beyond recognition, was clearly unsuitably warm for the sweltering climate. Laughing carelessly, he hoisted the two large satchels, now both currently locked and chained to his wrists, as he gingerly stepped down the stairs. All he needed now was a beer, a soft place to land, and at least ten hours of undisturbed sleep.

Shackled to his only luggage, he walked directly through the tiny airport to an awaiting cab parked at the curb.

"You speak English?" he demanded suspiciously, addressing the driver leaning against the cab to smoke.

"Si, Señor." The cabbie smiled broadly in response.

Satisfied by his answer, the man climbed into the back seat of the cab, tightly clutching his two treasured satchels, as the driver ground his cigarette into the curb and jumped in.

Andrew woke to the tantalizing aroma of freshly brewed coffee. He'd slept all night in his clothes on top of Vanessa's feathery guest bed. Quickly changing into the clean shirt he routinely kept at the office for emergencies. He smiled, relieved that the night had been quiet and surprisingly uneventful. He'd slept deeper than he'd expected, undoubtedly exhausted by the whirlwind of events of the previous day, but he felt surprisingly refreshed this morning. Regretting that he'd slept much later than planned, he hastily freshened up. Andrew was still shaking the remaining sleepy cobwebs from his mind, when the enticing aroma of freshly brewed coffee drew him down the hallway, directly into Vanessa's cozy kitchen.

Vanessa, having already showered and dressed hours ago, sat at the table deep in thought, leisurely sipping her coffee. Andrew's sleeping in the room next to hers had resulted in some disturbing dreams during the night. Flashes of fondling, kissing, and erotic caresses floated through her mind. Struggling to understand her disturbing dreams, she made a futile attempt to erase the sensual images from her waking thoughts.

Andrew noticed the confused look on Vanessa's face as he entered the room, just before she hastily set her coffee cup aside to greet him. Watching her expression closely, he sat down and rested his hands casually on the table, surprised by how natural he felt invading Vanessa's intimate space.

"Good morning sleepy-head. I thought you said you're a light sleeper?" she teased, as she graciously poured him a cup of coffee. "All I can say is, thank goodness Shep was on duty last night." She frowned, her gaze directed toward the front door. "Do you think he was all right sleeping on the front porch?"

"Sorry, I guess yesterday took its toll on me. Shep's fine," he assured. "You're up early?" The steaming cup of coffee she placed into his hands smelled heavenly. "Ah, thank you." He closed his eyes in pleasure as he took his first sip of the morning.

"I've been sitting here worrying for a while now." She shifted in her chair. "I feel guilty for leaving Haley alone last night. Do you think I should have stayed?"

"No, you'll be a lot more supportive after having had some sleep," he said, confidently. "Speaking of Haley…" He scooted his chair closer to her. "I have something else I need to tell you." He broached the subject uncertainly. "I would have discussed this with you last night, but we were tired and I didn't want to upset you." He paused, momentarily distracted, his train of thought temporarily derailed by the fragrant bouquet of the fresh, clean, lavender soap she'd showered with this morning.

"What is it?" she asked, anxious for him to finish his statement.

He closed his eyes briefly, dragging himself back to the delicate situation at hand. "When I returned to my office last night, I had a message from Haley's parents."

"So soon?" she asked.

He nodded before proceeding with caution, unsure of her feelings on the subject. "I called them back, and it turns out that the local detective on Haley's case is also the father of one of her classmates. He'd set his home computer to alert him as soon as any leads came in about her location. When I posted her information yesterday, he called her parents right away, and gave them my contact information."

"I assumed it would take a lot longer for them to find out she was here." Her shoulders drooped and the knuckles of her fingers, gripping her coffee cup, turned white.

He reached over, lightly brushing the side of her cheek with his knuckles. When she flinched and backed away from him, he accepted her rejection, respectfully dropping his hand back onto the table. His mere touch caused the vivid, sexual images Vanessa had struggled to suppress, to reappear. She blushed uncontrollably.

"They've been looking for her for years," he whispered, misreading Vanessa's embarrassing reflections. "They've never given up hope of finding her, and they're both ecstatic to discover that she's alive." Their overjoyed voices on the phone echoed in his mind.

Andrew watched as Vanessa sat quietly, deliberately avoiding his questioning gaze. He knew she wasn't ready to turn Haley over to them yet. Unaware of the discomfort his touch had aroused in her, he worked on persuading her to understand, to share in his satisfaction of reuniting Haley with her parents.

"I warned them about Haley's condition, including a few of the unsavory experiences she's suffered. I also informed them of what she may still be facing regarding the bank robbery," he said quietly. Pausing, he searched her face sympathetically. "They didn't care about any of it. They immediately booked a flight last night. I expect they'll be arriving in town later this afternoon."

"I'm glad for Haley. I really am, and I hope she'll be able to reconnect with her family," she said, struggling to place her focus back on Haley, instead of her erotic dreams from the previous night.

"Would you like me to explain everything to Haley? I can tell her that her parents will be arriving later today, unless you'd prefer to..." He gave her a face that reminded her of a puppy dog begging.

"You want me to tell her?" she asked with disbelief. "Oh no..." She said vehemently, shaking her head. "Wow, I never took you for a coward." She'd successfully squelched her lingering dreams and socked him on the shoulder playfully.

"Okay, I'll tell her." He held his hands up in surrender, relieved by her good nature. "I just have some errands to run first."

"I know... you're hoping I won't be able to keep it a secret." Tilting her head to the side, she eyed him suspiciously. "You think I'll spill everything to her, so that you won't have to, don't you?"

"Honestly, the thought never entered my mind," he said, as he air-crossed his heart, a spark of mischief in his baby blues.

"Yeah, right!"

The hospital room where Haley slept felt safe and peaceful, until early in the morning a nurse abruptly bustled into Haley's room, the unexpected noise rudely awakening her. The nurse made no effort to be quiet, but cranked open the blinds, letting the brilliant sunlight burst into the room.

"Wake up sleepy-head, its time for me to check you out. How did you sleep?" the nurse asked in a falsely cheerful voice.

"Okay, I guess." Haley squinted as the bright light poured in through her window, shining painfully into her heavy-lidded eyes. She'd never been much of a morning person.

"My name is Patti," she said, as she simultaneously read and pointed to her nametag.

Haley noticed how this nurse looked different than the others. She had long red fingernails, high heels, dangling earrings, dark red hair, eye makeup with bright red lipstick, and the dark blue scrubs she wore seemed too tight on her. She didn't look anything like the nurses she'd seen last night.

"I'm your nurse. Can you tell me how you're feeling?" she asked briskly.

Haley didn't feel much like talking. Hoping the gaudy nurse would leave sooner, if she didn't encourage her by chatting.

"My head hurts a little, but I'm fine."

The nurse attempted to check her pulse while she continued chatting. "By the way, I'm John's niece, you know, the security guard from the bank?"

"How is he?" She sat up. The subject immediately captivated Haley's interest.

"Oh, he's tough, I know he'll be fine," she said carelessly, aggressively fluffing her pillow. "I understand you were with the men in the bank yesterday, the ones who almost killed him," she accused mildly.

"Sort of." Shamefaced, Haley avoided her probing gaze.

"Would you know if there was anyone else involved in the robbery?" The nurse, Patti, narrowed her eyes. "Like say, someone who helped them plan it?"

"Jimmy never told me any plans. He just told me what I had to do, or he said he'd kill me." She tried earnestly to explain her circumstances to the pushy nurse.

"Oh, you poor dear," she responded, patting her roughly on the top of her head. "You're sure he never said any other names?"

"No! It was just Jimmy and Marvin, they're the only ones I know." She ducked, trying to move away from Patti's hammering head pats.

"Well, I am relieved to hear that," she said, and seemed oddly pleased. "I was afraid, when I saw the guard outside your door—maybe there was someone else out there. Someone who planned the robbery? I just couldn't stand it if my Uncle was in any danger." She dramatically placed her hand over her heart.

"There's no one else I'm telling you, only those two, and they're both *dead*!" she whispered. Patti stopped patting her head abruptly and began backing toward the door.

"Thanks for telling me kid." She stood by the door hesitantly. "Um, someone will be in shortly to check your temperature and stuff. I'll see you later. Bye-bye." She exited Haley's room so quickly, she didn't even get a chance to say thank you.

Haley shrugged off the intrusion, closed her eyes, faced away from the bright window, and snuggled back into her comfy bed, quickly falling back to sleep.

She walked out of Haley's room, and avoiding any eye contact she passed the unobservant guard, currently preoccupied with his sports page. Her heels click-clacked down the hall as she rapidly entered the nurse's changing room. She placed the badge back in the unlocked locker and stripped off the hideous, borrowed scrubs. Once she'd changed back into her own flamboyant garb, she touched up her vibrant red lipstick using the locker mirror. Keeping her head down, she proceeded to the nearest exit, taking care to avoid the overhead cameras. Purposefully, she'd parked about a half a mile away, where she would cleverly elude any parking garage cameras or attendants.

Once she safely reached her car, she exhaled a sigh of relief. Thank goodness Marvin had never said her name around that idiot girl. Now that both Jimmy and Marvin were dead, it was as if the whole thing had never happened. She was totally in the clear.

Shortly after her unusual nurse's hasty exit from her room, another nurse arrived at Haley's bedside, waking her gently with an efficiently quiet calmness. Haley immediately trusted her, preferring her soft, respectful tone, to the brashness of the other nurse.

"Good morning Haley, my name is Jean. I'll be your nurse today."

"What happened to Patti?" Haley asked.

"Patti?" Jean frowned and didn't seem to understand.

"Yes, she was here just a few minutes ago. She said *she* was my nurse."

Jean began to shine a penlight carefully into her eyes; concerned that Haley's confusion may be a worsening sign of her head injury. "Can you please follow my finger with your eyes?" she instructed. Haley quietly complied. "Do you know what day it is?" Jean asked.

"Sunday the 15th," she answered patiently.

"Do you know the year?"

Answering all of her questions correctly, Haley finally attempted to reason with Jean. "Look, I'm not mixed up. There *was* a nurse in here just a few minutes ago. She said her name was Patti, and her nametag said Patti C. You must know her, she said she's the bank security guard's niece."

"I'm sorry, Haley. The only Patti C. who works here left for vacation three days ago. She's in Hawaii."

"Then who was that nurse?"

"Excuse me, Haley, for just one minute, I'll try to find out which nurse came in here." Her voice remained steady, but her haste gave her concern away.

Jean stepped out of her room, but Haley could still hear her talking insistently to the guard. Next, she heard a code something-or-other paged overhead, and then she heard a lot of whispering in the hallway outside her door.

The guard stepped authoritatively into her room. "I'm sorry, Miss. I need to ask you to describe the woman who was in your room."

After Haley gave him a complete description, he stepped back out into the hallway to talk on his radio. He returned immediately to stand quietly, just inside her door. "I apologize Miss, but I need to stay in here with you until Detective Kelly arrives."

"Can you tell me what this is all about? Who was that woman?" she asked.

"We don't know yet, Miss." The officer kept a straight face as he answered her in his calmest, most professional tone of voice. "The detective will be here shortly to give you more information."

Haley hadn't felt threatened by the woman, but she belatedly realized she'd ignored Vanessa's instructions not to speak to anyone. Instead she'd openly answered all her questions in a foolish attempt to comfort the woman, believing she was John's niece. Haley wondered if maybe she had been a reporter of some kind.

"Officer, please have a seat and get comfortable," she offered, pointing to the chair in the corner of her room.

The guard stared at Haley, appearing far from comfortable. He looked troubled as he maintained his post by the door. She felt bad for him.

"Don't worry, Andrew won't bite your head off. Have a seat," she enticed.

The officer sat down reluctantly. And they waited.

Andrew's radio interrupted his intimate breakfast with Vanessa.

"Change of plans, grab your stuff, we have to go now. Someone got into Haley's room this morning posing as a nurse," he said cryptically, gulping the rest of his coffee.

"Was she hurt?" Vanessa asked, standing immediately.

"No. She just now mentioned the incident to her actual nurse. They're searching the hospital as we speak."

He noticed Vanessa bite her lower lip with concern as she obediently followed him out the door.

"She's fine," he said, soothingly. "The guard's in the room with her now. We'll get more information as soon as we get there. Ride with me, it'll be faster. Let's go!"

Shep jumped into his cage and Andrew appeared at the passenger door to help Vanessa in.

At first, she felt strange and conspicuous riding in a police car. Then seconds later she felt exhilarated; the thrilling speed of his car, with its lights flashing and sirens blaring, made her hold on tight, feeling her heart pounding with the sudden adrenaline rush! Andrew had been right, he pulled into the emergency room parking lot in less than ten minutes.

Kate hid her face when she saw the canine car speeding past her. After it disappeared around the corner, she inconspicuously pulled out into the quiet street. She knew she could return to Los Angeles unnoticed. It didn't matter if anyone saw her now. She planned to disappear, permanently.

While Andrew stopped to talk to a group of police officers standing outside the emergency room, Vanessa rushed to Haley's side. "Are you all right?" she asked fearfully.

"I'm fine, I slept really good, until that strange woman came into my

107

room this morning."

"Did she do anything to hurt you, or upset you?" She shot a chastising look toward the officer sitting in the corner. Haley sat comfortably in bed, her hands relaxed in her lap, which reassured Vanessa even more than her words had.

Vanessa heard the door open behind her. She felt Andrew standing close behind her, his presence oddly comforting. She held her breath, waiting for Haley to answer her question.

"No, nothing like that," she shrugged. "She said she was the bank security guard's niece. I'm sorry, she asked me a lot of questions about the robbery. I answered them without thinking. Do you think she was a reporter or something?"

Before Vanessa could answer, Andrew placed his hand on the small of her back as he calmly stepped forward, signaling that he would take over the questioning. "You might be right, what did she look like?" He pulled out his pad to make notes as he looked expectantly toward Haley. He continued to ask Haley questions until he was satisfied that he had all the details surrounding the encounter. "Is that everything you remember? Can you think of anything else?" he asked, before he wrapped up his questioning.

There was something in the back of her mind that she couldn't quite recall. Haley gazed upward as she concentrated on the question he'd just asked. "I'm sorry, I know there's something else, but my mind won't work," she said, apologetically.

He closed his notepad and consoled her. "That's perfectly understandable. You've had a concussion along with a very busy morning. Try not to think about it any more, but let me know if anything pops back into your mind."

"Thanks for understanding," Haley said, and she leaned back into her bed, relieved that the questioning had concluded.

He motioned to the guard, who followed him reluctantly out into the hallway. She heard Andrew's firm, controlled, angry voice as he questioned the guard. Then Andrew went to the lobby to coordinate the search of the hospital and grounds.

Haley's breakfast arrived and she chatted calmly while she ate. Noting her healthy appetite, Vanessa decided she'd suffered no ill effects from the strange, early-morning encounter.

Vanessa knew she should inform Haley of her parent's impending arrival, but instead she attempted to distract her, and began making a list of all the things she might need during her hospital stay. When a nurse came in to help Haley get up to shower, she gently hugged her, and trusting Andrew to protect Haley, she disappeared to go shopping.

Later, Vanessa returned to the hospital, spotting Andrew across the busy lobby. The increased security included wanding for weapons, and presenting official identification. Andrew clearly was taking no chances of another event. His face lit up when he noticed Vanessa approach.

"Where have you been, beautiful?" he asked, curiously.

"Just a little shopping." She raised her arms, holding multiple bags.

"That's nice," he chuckled.

"You know, I've been thinking. Let's not tell Haley about her parents right now. Let's wait until we're sure they're on the way to the hospital," she said, wanting to avoid a scene that might upset Haley.

"Does that mean you've decided to be the one to tell her?" he asked.

"Yes, I'll tell her." Vanessa rolled her eyes at him and sighed. "I just want to wait. I don't want her to be anxious all day in anticipation, or be disappointed if they're unexpectedly delayed."

"You're such a tender-hearted woman. It's one of many things I love about you." He sent her an appreciative smile, stepping closer.

He rested his hands gently on her waist as he leaned down to give her a quick, tender kiss, right in the middle of the hospital lobby. She closed her eyes, feeling the deliciously warm sensation travel all the way to her toes. Opening her eyes, the intensity reflected in his crystal, blue eyes mesmerized her. His kiss released some of the hollow, dead feelings that had occupied her heart for so many years. This incredible man appeared to be slowly bringing her back to life. Since they stood in the middle of the bustling lobby, he gradually stepped back, reluctantly breaking their intimate contact.

"Here, give me some of those bags to carry," he instructed, reaching for the bags. "I'll see you to Haley's room. Maybe she's remembered that detail that eluded her this morning." He tried to sound casual, but the slight rasp in his voice gave his true emotions away.

Entering the elevator, she hid her smile after hearing his telltale emotional response. It was nice to know he'd been just as affected by their kiss as she had.

When they entered Haley's room, she sent them a curious glance, causing Vanessa to blush. Her hair freshly washed, she rested with her leg back up on pillows, balancing an ice pack on her shin.

"I remembered what bugged me about that woman this morning," Haley exclaimed exuberantly, her eyes sparkling with excitement.

"All right, shoot." Andrew set down the bags and pulled out his notepad.

"I remembered that Marvin once said that he got the bank information from his friend at the armored car service. Does that help?" she asked hopefully.

"Marvin? He was one of the bank robbers?" Andrew clarified. Jimmy had been the only name he'd heard her mention so far.

Haley nodded.

"Thanks, Haley." He gave her a thumbs-up sign, jotted down the name, and tucked away his pad. "I think this is the first good lead we've had on this case so far. I'll check it out." He nodded to Haley and sent Vanessa a smoldering look, melting her fragile composure.

"I'll see you for lunch," he said, tugging gently on a strand of Vanessa's hair before he walked out the door.

"It looks like you have a hot lunch date," Haley said, grinning.

Vanessa and Haley simultaneously broke into laughter, helping them spontaneously release some of the nervous energy triggered by the morning's unexpected events.

When their laughter subsided, Vanessa felt a thickness in the back of her throat. *Exactly when would be the best time to inform Haley they'd betrayed her confidence*, she secretly wondered. Not only had they contacted her parents behind her back, the family she'd been emphatically avoiding, would be appearing, face-to-face with her, at any moment.

Chapter 11
New Beginnings

*T*he tall man in the hopelessly wrinkled suit stepped into the cab. Leaning forward, he asked the "English speaking" cab driver to take him to a comfortable downtown hotel.

After a minute or two, he casually began to pump the driver for information regarding someone who could forge identification papers. It took multiple attempts to get his inquiry through to the cab driver, since he actually spoke very little English, regarding what it was he looking for. Specifically, he wanted a forged ID that would allow him to stay in this country indefinitely.

The cab driver smiled, nodding his comprehension. "Si, Señor, my cousin makes the most excellent papers."

The man became impatient. "How much?"

Shaking his head, the cabbie frowned and replied, "Very expensive señor, five thousand American dollars."

"Fine! When?"

The cabbie grinned. "I'll meet you in the lobby of your hotel tonight at nine, okay señor?"

"Fine," he answered dismissively, settling back in his seat.

The cabbie dropped him off in front of a modest-looking hotel. He got out with his satchels and tipped the driver fifty American dollars, assuring his return later tonight. He watched the cab pull out of sight, before he walked confidently through the empty lobby, continuing unnoticed out the back door. Walking the short, three-block distance up the street, he checked into a very elegant, high-priced hotel. The luxurious hotel he had chosen catered to many wealthy Americans, and they'd advertised wall safes large enough to accommodate his two cumbersome satchels. The questioning glances from the bellhops made him stop briefly in the well-stocked gift shop for suitable clothing before taking the opulent elevator up to his room.

His room had ornate touches of gold everywhere; it was far more luxurious and impressive than any place he'd slept before. He ordered and consumed an inordinate amount of food and beer from room service. Satiated and spent, he planned to sleep until it was time to meet the cabbie in the lobby of the other hotel. Tomorrow he would open a bank account with his fresh ID and begin his new life.

He'd unlocked his satchels from his wrists and locked them inside the safe. Pleased with himself for his resourcefulness, he placed the do not disturb sign outside his door. Wake-up call arranged for eight thirty pm, he burrowed deep inside the king-sized bed, safely tucked in. He smugly lapsed into a deep, exhausted stupor.

Haley and Vanessa visited comfortably, while Andrew remained preoccupied investigating the incident in Haley's room. After Haley's lunch, an orderly arrived with a wheelchair to transport her to ultrasound. *Another bothersome test to check my insides*, she thought.

Andrew had yet to return, so Vanessa made her way to the cafeteria alone. She wondered if he'd managed to track down the mysterious woman, and dreaded that the time had come for her to tell Haley about her parents. She had almost finished eating her solitary lunch when Andrew joined her.

"Sorry, I got delayed." Andrew shot her a sheepish smile.

"That's alright. Haley went to ultrasound, so I came downstairs. What did you find out?"

"Well..." He pushed his food around his plate. "As you know, the only picture we had of the woman in Haley's room shows her general appearance, but not her face. I took it to the armored car company, the one that the Bitton Bank uses, and they recognized her immediately. Her name is Kate Sweeney."

"That's great! Did you talk to her?" she asked, appreciating his excellent detective skills.

He shook his head slowly and swallowed a large bite of his sandwich before he spoke. "She quit her job last week. However, we discovered that her position gave her access to all the information any would-be robber could possibly want."

"Now what?" Vanessa slumped back against her seat, her momentary excitement deflated.

"We have an all-points bulletin out for her. You might even see her company picture on the news tonight." They ate for a while in silence.

"Do you think she'll come back?" Vanessa asked, playing absently with the silver bracelet on her wrist. Her level of concern impressed him. *It's too bad*, he thought, *she would have been a great mom.*

"No, in fact, if she hadn't gone to Haley's room in the first place, we'd never have known she existed."

Vanessa wondered if Haley would be safe, which reminded her of Haley's parents' impending arrival. "Have you heard from Haley's parents today?"

"Yeah," he answered offhandedly between bites. "I meant to tell you. They took the red-eye, and their plane landed about an hour ago. They plan to check in to their hotel first. They should be here pretty soon now. Have you told Haley yet?" He raised his eyebrows hopefully.

"No, I thought there'd be more time," she said, looking at her hands on the table. She felt guilty for postponing her talk with Haley.

Knowing how hard this was going to be for Vanessa, he reached over to place his hand over hers. "Would you like me to come up? I'll tell her myself. After all, I'm the heavy here, not you."

"Thank you." She let out a sigh of relief. "I just don't know how to tell her. I'm afraid she's going to feel terribly betrayed."

"She's a smart girl. I think she'll understand once I explain everything to her. She'll see that I had no choice. Also, while I'm there, I wanted to update her on today's findings. I want her to relax and feel reassured regarding the intruder in her room this morning."

He finished his lunch and looked directly at Vanessa for strength. *Together*, he thought, *we present an indomitable force*. Helping her out of her seat, they went upstairs to deliver the upsetting news to Haley.

Walking into her room, fully prepared for conflict, they discovered an empty, freshly made bed. Andrew sat down on the bed to wait, while Vanessa paced the room.

"Try to relax." Her pacing made him nervous.

"I just don't know how Haley will react to the news." She imagined the worst-case scenario. "Plus, her parents are about to arrive here any minute!" She wrung her hands together as she continued to pace, eventually coming to rest in front of the window.

Andrew joined her and they stood together gazing out at the calm, slow-moving white clouds for comfort. He placed his hands on her shoulders as he gently turned her around to face him. Tucking a stray strand of hair behind her ear, he spoke gently. "What are your plans for the rest of this week? Are you working?" he asked. His tone of voice insinuating that he had more interest than simply idle curiosity about her plans.

Flashes of last night's dreams invaded her brain. His intimate gesture made her pulse race. Suddenly feeling breathless by his close proximity, she whispered, "Actually, I'm on vacation for the next two weeks."

His hands slowly ran down her upper arms to her elbows. "Oh really?" He moved a little closer as he asked softly, "I don't suppose you'd like to spend some time with me? I mean away from hospital rooms?" His inquiry definitely sounded intimate and suggestive.

Oh my, Vanessa thought, *he's flirting with me*. She decided to flirt back. Casually she placed her hands flat on his chest, secretly gratified by the soft gasp of his response. "What exactly did you have in mind, Detective?" she teased.

Vanessa watched him bend down to kiss her, pausing just before their lips touched, when the sound of Haley's wheelchair interrupted their intimate moment. The smoldering heat between them rapidly cooled, and they swiftly broke apart from each other.

"I see you two are getting to know each other." Haley watched their guilty reaction and flashed them a knowing smile.

Andrew placed his fist over his mouth and cleared his throat. Vanessa could feel her warm blush rising. It seemed silly to be embarrassed! Maybe it was simply the circumstances that made it seem so inappropriate.

With the orderly's assistance, Haley settled into bed. Her nurse bustled into the room, fluffing pillows and making sure Haley was comfortably settled before she gave her a paper cup full of pills.

"How did the test turn out?" Vanessa asked, attempting to lightened the mood.

Haley waited until the nurse left. "Well, the technician wasn't supposed to tell me anything, but he explained that all of the squiggles on the screen meant my bleeding has stopped. So, that's good news, right?" she asked, pleased with her cunning discovery. "Oh, but I'm supposed to act surprised when the doctor tells me." She sent them a conspiratorial wink.

They all laughed. Haley seemed to be in great spirits. Now it was time to give her the facts. Andrew pulled up a chair close to her, while Vanessa slowly wandered back to look out the window at the fluffy clouds. She couldn't bear to watch the look of betrayal when it crossed Haley's face.

"I have a few things to talk to you about," Andrew began.

"Wow, sounds serious." His demeanor troubled her.

"You were right." He decided to update her on the mysterious woman first. "We found out that the woman in your room this morning was from the armored car company. That was a great lead!" he smiled, praising her shrewdness.

"Did you get her?" she asked, gleefully.

"No, but have you ever heard the name Kate, or Katherine Sweeney?" He watched for any sign of recognition.

"No, is that her name? You can find her, can't you?"

"Unfortunately, she quit her job last Friday and no one, except you, has seen her since. We're still looking though," he said, looking down briefly, searching for the right words to tell Haley about her parents.

"What else do you need to tell me?" Haley's eyes narrowed, questioning him suspiciously when he made eye contact with her.

"Remember—when we discussed the process of putting your information into the computer system?" he asked, using his professional tone.

"Yes?" She didn't like where this was going.

"The DA insisted that I enter your information yesterday. He said he couldn't make a deal until I did."

"When are they coming?" Haley's shoulders slumped, and she looked down pensively at her hands.

"They're here—they're in town." He reached for her hands resting in her lap, as he continued in a gentle tone, "They'll be arriving shortly."

Haley's eyes flashed to Vanessa, who stood by the window, quietly watching her reaction from across the room. There was no sign of betrayal in her eyes. Instead, Vanessa saw raw pain.

Haley didn't speak, but silent tears of remorse filled her eyes. Vanessa went to the opposite side of the bed and scooped her up into her arms.

"I'm sorry I didn't tell you sooner. Andrew says they love you very much, and they've been suffering horribly ever since you left home," she cooed, holding her empathetically and hoping she'd be forgiven.

"I understand," she said. Her expression turned stoic, but Vanessa felt her trembling.

Andrew handed Haley a box of tissues. She pulled away, blew her nose, and bravely dried her tears.

"That's right," he confirmed. "I talked with them on the phone last night. I told them everything, and they don't care one bit. They're completely overjoyed to find you alive." Culpability for contacting them behind her back made him want to make everything nonthreatening for her.

"You really told them everything?" She stared up at him with watery eyes. She didn't want to face her parents, but she was grateful that at least he'd given them some inkling of the disreputable life she'd been living.

"They don't blame you. They don't care about anything that's happened," he affirmed. "They love you."

"Thank you," Haley said. She sent him a weak smile and reached out to touch his hand. She knew it wasn't his fault. But still, she dreaded facing her parents sooner than she'd anticipated. She knew she would have to explain why she left them, and how she'd manage to survive these past few years.

The three of them had just finished quietly discussing her parents' expected arrival, when the sound of boisterous talking, and laughter outside Haley's room abruptly assailed their ears and ended further conversation.

Haley dabbed at her wet eyes and began laughing. "That would be my family!" she said, apologetically.

Andrew stepped out into the hall to instruct the guard to admit her enormous family. Haley's mother threw her arms around him the minute he introduced himself. Five lively children of varying ages gathered around Haley's parents. Her father, carrying a shy toddler, shook his hand vigorously.

"We can't thank you enough, son, for finding our daughter. You're a godsend," he exclaimed, beaming at Andrew.

Completely overwhelmed by the large, demonstrative family smothering him with gratitude, Andrew simply nodded and smiled. He immediately understood why Haley seemed like such a delightful young lady.

"Vanessa actually found her." He attempted to deflect their gratitude. "She's been here supporting Haley the entire time, in fact she's with her now," he said, attempting to usher them into Haley's room.

Haley's mother hadn't let go of his arm, but took a step back and pulled him aside. "Does Haley know we're coming?" she asked, anxiously.

Andrew smiled at her apprehension and simply nodded in response.

Her father choked up as he asked, "Can we see her?"

"Of course, go on in. I'll answer any questions you have later. Here's my card, please call me anytime." He handed him the card and held Haley's door wide open, and her anxious family excitedly rushed past him.

"We can't thank you enough, Detective," her father repeated. Then he followed his family in to reunite with his eldest daughter.

Vanessa, completely overwhelmed by the exuberant family that surrounded Haley's bed, retreated back to her spot near the window to quietly observe the noisy reunion.

Haley's mother gathered her missing child in her arms, crying over and over, "My sweet baby, I've missed you so much."

Her father set the toddler on the floor and knelt down beside his daughter, wrapping his arms tightly around the two of them.

Haley's younger sisters tried to corral the toddler, while her sullen teenage brother leaned against the wall. Although he tried to stand apart, Vanessa could see by his moist eyes that he'd been just as emotionally affected. He watched intently while his parents greeted his long-lost older sister.

Feeling intrusive, Vanessa watched the large, loving family welcome Haley back into their fold. She quietly slipped out the door, where she literally stumbled into Andrew's waiting arms.

He felt her tremble as he held her in his comforting embrace. Eventually Andrew became aware of the guard and hospital staff eyeing them. He tentatively set her away from him and tipped her chin up until their eyes met. "Would you like to go somewhere alone? With me?" he asked, softly.

"Yes," she whispered, instantly relieved.

He took her by the hand and led her to the elevator. Once they were settled in his car, he steered towards his home. "We're going to my place."

"Sounds good to me," she smiled, relaxing back in her seat and closing her eyes. Intense emotions, awakened by the sight of Haley's large family reunion, seeped out of her. She understood why Haley might have felt compelled to escape the overwhelming chaos.

The scenery sped by in a blur, until the car slowed and Andrew pulled into the driveway of an impressive two-story house on the beach. Helping her out of the car, he politely escorted her inside.

Upon entering his home, Vanessa immediately noticed a photograph on the entryway table, resting in solitude. She felt compelled to pick it up and inspect it closer. A solitary woman sat on the ground in the middle of a field of morning glories, her pink floral dress mushrooming out over her legs. She looked directly at the camera with a serene smile on her face, and although she appeared frail, her classic beauty was undeniable.

"That's my wife," Andrew said quietly, as he gently took the picture from her and set it back in its place. Without further comment, he escorted her into his living room.

117

Entering the massive room, the floor to ceiling picture window astonished her, captivating her complete attention with the stunning ocean view. "Wow, detectives make a lot more than I thought."

Enchanted by the impressive backdrop, she visually explored the room, noticing the wide variety of fascinating ocean landscapes covering the walls. The room, impeccably decorated in neutral earth tones, felt incredibly elegant, yet surprisingly inviting and comfortable.

"Your wife had excellent taste."

Andrew followed her questioning gaze. "I bought this place after her death," he stated simply, and she studied the room with fresh eyes. The lack of personal photos or memorabilia made her feel sad.

"I'll explain everything to you later." He caught the glimmer of unease in her eyes and easily read her thoughts. "For now, I'll just tell you that a well paid decorator and my housekeeper can take all the credit for the design of this place."

Shep loped into the room wagging his tail; he'd brought him home for a nap earlier in the day. An attractive young woman carrying a dog leash followed Shep into the room. She was elegant, very tall and lanky, sporting a perfect tan and a stylishly short, blond haircut.

"Oh, hi Andrew, I didn't expect to see you today. Shep just finished his walk." Shep ran over to Andrew's side, wagging his tail enthusiastically to greet him.

"Thanks, Shelby, this is Vanessa. Vanessa, this is Shelby, my dog walker." He smiled fondly up at Shelby as he squatted to scratch Shep behind his ears. Shelby acknowledged Vanessa briefly with a nod, explaining to Andrew that she was running late to meet some friends, and left.

Once they were alone again, Andrew turned toward Vanessa with a look in his eyes that said he meant business. He approached her cautiously, leisurely wrapping his arms around her waist, before he pulled her close against his body, bestowing a deep, passionate kiss on her inviting lips.

Caught off guard, Vanessa's arms dangled loosely at her sides at first, but then, swept up in his passionate kiss, she threw her arms around his neck, responding with reckless abandon to his unexpected advances. *His mustache tickles my nose*, she thought briefly. Lost and fully adrift with forgotten sensations stimulated by his long, intimate kiss, she became extremely aware of the subtle, unanticipated sensual heat pulsating between them. But before she could explore the curious sensation further, Andrew broke off their passionate kiss, far too soon for Vanessa's muddled mind.

The dazed, thoroughly kissed look on her face bewitched him. Taking her hand, he murmured softly, "Come with me. I have something I want to show you."

"I'll just bet you do," she laughed.

Her sarcastic wit made him smile. She'd proven to him once again what a truly remarkable woman she was, in any circumstance. He couldn't remember the last time he felt so relaxed, so happy. He led her outside through the sliding glass door to the elegant pool area overlooking the expansive beach below.

Vanessa gasped at the unbelievable view. "Oh Andrew! The beach—the ocean, its all so incredible! You live here?"

"Yep, when I'm not chasing after criminals."

She bent down to scoop up a handful of the lukewarm pool water. Then, walking to the edge of the patio, she inhaled the fresh sea air, feeling the breeze gently blowing her hair away from her face; she stood spellbound, gazing out over the magnificent ocean horizon.

Andrew walked up behind her and she leaned back into his eager embrace. Affectionately, he kissed the top of her head, and they stood together for a moment in total harmony.

"Come along," Andrew coaxed. She turned to face him, her eyes sparkling with childish enchantment. He couldn't resist her charm, and gave her another quick kiss. He laughed with delight, excitedly stepping out of their embrace, before taking her hand, and guiding her swiftly to the steps leading to the beach below.

"Here, sit down on the step and take off your shoes," he instructed. "We'll grab them when we return."

Vanessa gleefully kicked off her shoes and began to pick her way through broken seashells and scattered driftwood to the smooth, sandy water's edge. Standing in awe, she gazed out over the rolling, azure-blue ocean. The heavenly sensation of warm sea foam lapping gently at her feet, and the wet sand squishing between her toes, made her smile. *Why have I waited for so many years to visit the beach again?* She wondered.

Inhaling the warm, salt air, she closed her eyes. She had Marie watching *Gemma*, and Haley's parents were with Haley. Since she'd cancelled her lavish vacation, now seemed like the perfect time to enjoy a peaceful, romantic interlude. Smiling, she relished the rare freedom to do as she pleased, with whomever she pleased.

Right on cue, Andrew stood behind her, wrapping his strong hands around her waist to support her petite frame against the powerful thrust of the hammering surf. As the next wave crashed on the shore, they stood together and simply watched, allowing the seawater to soak them up to their knees.

Strolling pleasantly down the warm sandy beach, they playfully dodged the pounding surf. Several times Andrew lifted Vanessa high into the air to save her from a punishing, massive rouge wave before it hit the shore. Holding her close in a tender embrace, he paused before slowly setting her back onto the wet sand. She deliberately lingered in his arms, her lips parted in breathless anticipation, waiting for the passionate kisses that never quite ensued.

Feeling relaxed, Vanessa watched the foamy water roll all the way up onto the warm sand, forming a shallow, scalloped-shaped finger, pausing briefly in the sunlight. Squatting down she noticed miniature air bubbles begin to surface in the shallow water, as tiny sea creatures beneath the sand became drenched. Then, without warning, the ocean demanded the waves' return, sucking the water back into its depths with amazing force. The receding water seemed to claw at the warm sandy beach, dragging seashells, small glistening rocks, and sand in its wake, before finally surrendering to the tides. Spying the skeleton of a pink starfish caught in the undertow, Vanessa reached down to rescue it. Turning her find over in her hands, she ran her finger over the rough texture on the starfish's back. Wrapping her arms impulsively around Andrew's neck, she initiated a fleeting kiss and proudly displayed her treasure. "Every time I look at this starfish, I'll remember being here with you today."

Carefully, she tucked it inside the wide pocket of her knee-length cotton skirt and kicked at the slimy green seaweed, now wrapped unpleasantly around her leg. He took her hand, guiding her further up the beach. He frowned, silently wondering if she had seriously just referred to today as a one-time event.

Walking up the warm, sandy shoreline, their beach combing eventually led them to a dock. Assorted boats bobbed in the water, tied securely to the dock by strong, coiled ropes. Andrew escorted her down the warm, rough, wooden planks, eventually halting in front of a boat slip where an imposing, fifty-foot sailboat was resting serenely in the water.

"Is this your boat?" Vanessa asked, stunned, as she intently scrutinized the magnificent sailboat.

"This is my *Sunset Seeker*." He shrugged modestly. "Allow me show you around." He stepped up and gallantly offered her his hand, which she readily accepted and cautiously stepped aboard.

The sailboat appeared to be brand new. It had a cozy cushioned lounging and eating area outside on the back deck, with three enormous masts towering overhead. The sails were closed, the riggings jangling rhythmically in the wind. He helped her carefully down three smoothly polished wooden steps leading inside, where she speechlessly gazed around the cabin.

"This is the galley," he said, talking casually, sounding as though he was conducting an exclusive, private tour just for her. "You'll note that it is conveniently located near the back deck. Here is the indoor dining area; note the mahogany dining table and benches. Then we have the reading, TV and living room, with a cubby for my desk. Now if you'll just follow me down the hall..."

Vanessa obediently followed him, pausing briefly to admire the polished, intricately carved, lightly stained wood, spread tastefully throughout the inside of the ship.

".... As you can see, there are two staterooms with one bathroom separating them." He opened the doors to each room. The décor was impressive with furnishings that appeared new, extraordinarily plush, and very alluring. After she'd poked her head in to inspect the rooms, she turned to face him with awe.

"What do you think?" he asked.

"I love it! Did you use a decorator for this too?" she asked, dazed by the simplistic glamor inside the staterooms.

"No, this, I did myself," he boasted. "Would you care for something to drink?" He politely guided her back toward the galley and stood behind the counter in bartender fashion.

She couldn't believe the complexities of this man, who not only had an incredible home, but also owned a magnificent sailboat. *Yet, he seems so remarkably humble and unassuming*, she thought.

"What are you offering?" She perched on the nearest bar stool, smiling at him expectantly.

Andrew sent her a wolfish smile full of suggestive heat, before he turned to open his full-sized refrigerator. "I have beer, wine, lemonade, and iced tea. What can I get you?" he asked, in his host voice.

"I'd love some white wine."

Grabbing the chilled bottle of wine, he poured her a glass before pouring himself an iced tea. She realized he was still on duty, which made her feel slightly guilty for indulging in wine. But she really needed something to take the edge off her day, so forgetting about Andrew, she sipped her white wine with unbridled pleasure.

Stepping back outside into the blinding sunshine, they sat down. The towering masts shaded them, as they settled on the lushly padded deck seat. The ocean view, warm sunshine, and gentle rocking of the boat created a delightfully hypnotic ambiance.

"I could get used to this." She sipped her wine, purring with pure contentment. Noting his quiet smile of smug satisfaction, she decided it was time for him to tell her his story. "All right, you promised you'd explain all of this, so let's hear it."

He preferred watching her relax with her wine, but he knew he couldn't hide his private life any more; it was time for him to tell her the truth.

"Hmm... as you know, I was married. My wife, the woman you saw in the photo, died five years ago of ovarian cancer. She grew up as an only child, and her parents are, let's just say they're *well off*. Before we were married, they'd set up a hefty annual fund for her. It was hers, to use as she saw fit. I never cared or knew much about it. But after she died, I discovered that I was named the sole beneficiary of her ten million dollar a year trust fund." He raised his eyebrows, tipped his head back, quickly gulping his iced tea, while watching covertly for her reaction.

Far too modest, he'd failed to mention that he donated most of the money to a foundation in Grace's name. One that specifically supported women diagnosed with ovarian cancer and their families, as his tribute to the memory of his late wife.

Remaining silent, she sensed his suffering when he'd referred to his wife's untimely demise. Self-conscious about his wealth, it seems he had remained a hard-working detective. She found his obvious work ethic admirable.

"The more I get to know you, the more astonished I am by you," she whispered.

He set his iced tea and her empty wine glass on the table beside him, and pulled her easily onto his lap. Once she settled comfortably within his arms, he kissed her with an intense yearning, partly fueled by his raw emotions, and partly by his potent desire for her.

An eager and willing recipient, Vanessa savored his deep, overdue kisses. The uninhibited passion of his kisses instantly ignited her previously dormant sensuality. The thrilling vibrations he stimulated within her traveled clear down to the tips of her toes, causing her entire body to tingle excitedly. The erotic, electric sensations continued well after they'd pulled apart, both gasping for air. Andrew held her close, cuddling her in his protective embrace, while he proceeded to sprinkle feathery kisses over her cheeks, nibble on her inviting earlobe, and tenderly nuzzle the back of her delectable neck.

Vanessa was stunned. She couldn't believe how quickly Andrew had managed to finish his somber conversation, before he effortlessly transported her into a mystical state of burning desire and arousal. It had been years since Vanessa had been intimately involved with, or even touched by a man. But even then, no man's kisses had ever triggered such an instantaneous, passionate response within her before. Even at their first glimpse on her doorstep, there had been an undeniable, magnetic chemistry between them. She tried to clear her mind, to think rationally. She paused, briefly considering the consequences of their reckless actions. If they crossed the imaginary line between friends to lovers too soon, it could result in messy, emotional complications for them in the near future.

But Andrew remained relentless; his caresses continued to fan the flames of her desire, driving her senses wild with his intimate touch. Her suppressed sexuality sprung to life, consuming her mind and overriding all rational thought. Sliding her hand slowly down below his belt, she lightly felt for evidence that he might be equally affected. His expanding, firm bulge confirmed her suspicions, and she instantly released the last threads of her fears and inhibitions. Unbelievable physical pleasure, combined with the intimate knowledge of his arousal, made her act impulsively. She ceased to consider the consequences, and began intimately fondling him. Innocent young girl no more, Vanessa responded to Andrew as the passionate, experienced woman she had become, and she wanted him!

Meanwhile, Andrew's hazy mind told him he should stop, but he was already well past the limits of his control. Now that he'd tasted her, felt her undeniable response, he wanted more, much more. As she boldly touched him, he struggled helplessly to control the wild, erotic hunger boiling deep within him.

Vanessa began to tug away, and Andrew feared he'd gone too far. But, when she leaned back toward him, he felt her brazenly nibble on his ear, shocking him into utter stillness. "I think its naptime. I noticed that you have a luxurious looking bed in the other room," she whispered, suggestively.

Andrew pulled back slightly, searching deep into Vanessa's eyes to be sure she'd meant what he thought she'd meant. Stunned, he saw the pupils of her eyes were fully dilated, radiating with unrestrained desire. Her gaze and sensual smile gave him was all the encouragement he needed. Lifting her reverently up into his arms, he stood in one fluid motion and carried her inside the boat, down the darkened hall, before he kicked open the stateroom door, and tossed her gently onto the high bed. He stood momentarily at the foot, their eyes locked in breathless suspense. Then a mischievous grin crossed his face, and a predatory gleam glowed in his narrowed eyes. He placed one hand on the bed and proceeded to crawl toward her with cougar-like stealth, until their eager bodies lay side by side.

The outside world faded away as Vanessa and Andrew lay beside each other, panting softly, eyes locked in anticipation. Facing each other, they lay perfectly still on the bed, without the slightest physical contact, a mere whispered breath apart, both in a suspended state of aroused expectation, waiting to see who would bravely take the next step.

Chapter 12
Hearts Aligning

*K*ate's mouth fell open. Glimpsing the five o'clock news, she watched in horror as her company picture flashed across the screen. Thank goodness she'd tucked all of her wild, red hair under a shorthaired, blond wig. Painstakingly, she'd removed her bright red nail polish and scrubbed off her garish makeup. Clipping her nails short and removing all of her jewelry, she'd dressed in the frumpiest pantsuit she could find. Even her own mother wouldn't recognize her today.

Hunching down impatiently, Kate waited, her face buried behind the pages of a fashion magazine, endeavoring to fade into the background of the lively Los Angeles airport. Even though she used a false identity, Kate toyed nervously with the stray strands of her red hair popping out from under her wig, growing more and more anxious for her departure on her long overdue flight.

Every minute seemed like an eternity. Kate stared blankly at the same page in her magazine, while her queasy stomach flipped summersaults. Oh Marvin! She thought about how they'd carefully planned this escape route together. The pictures on the page suddenly blurred; inconspicuously, she dashed away the tears gathering in her eyes. Now he's dead, damn it Marvin! His inconvenient demise had forced her to escape all alone. Without the bank money he'd promised, she'd barely scraped together enough cash to survive for a month or two. After that, she'd have to get a job, or find a rich boyfriend. But at least she wouldn't be spending her life in prison.

Skillfully avoiding the airport cameras, Kate finally boarded her plane. Once safely in the air, she pulled out the crumpled piece of paper itemizing her detailed travel instructions written in Marvin's scribbled handwriting. Turning the worn piece of paper over in her hand, she found the name and address of the man who would give her a new identity.

Once she was sure the plane was safely out of the U.S., Kate put in her earphones, hoping her music would prove a soothing distraction to calm her frayed nerves. She tilted her seat back and exhaled some of the pent up tension she'd amassed. The stress and exhaustion of the past few days had proven to be overwhelming, and eventually, Kate drifted off.

Andrew and Vanessa stared at each other, their eyes locked in giddy anticipation, both hungry for the long awaited intimate touch of a lover.

Nervous grins of delight crossed their faces. His seductive clowning had offered just the right touch of comic relief to ease the awkward sexual tension they shared. Reaching for Vanessa, Andrew resumed his deep, probing kisses, rapidly returning her to her previously dazed state of arousal. Regretfully, he discovered that his radio and gun, always firmly attached to his belt, created a painful obstacle between them. He reluctantly detached himself from her embrace to stand by the bedside and removed his heavy-laden belt, stowing it safely inside the mahogany cubby at the head of the bed.

The temporary break in their close proximity gave Andrew the perfect opportunity to unfasten his pants and loosen his shirt. Taking a step away from the bed, he roguishly motioned with his pointer finger, beckoning Vanessa to come to him. Riveted by the sight of his tuft of downy, salt-and-pepper chest hair peeking out of his opened shirt, Vanessa momentarily failed to recognize his quiet gesture. He cleared his throat to capture her attention, causing her to appreciate his unspoken request. Silently, she moved toward him in a trance-like state of arousal.

Vanessa's heart pounded loudly in her ears as she stood in front of him. Pulling her gently into his arms, Andrew resumed his deep, seductively probing kisses immediately stirring her blood and causing her knees to weaken, as an involuntary moan of pleasure escaped her lips. Distracted by his luscious, sweet tasting mouth, and the vibrating warmth his kisses stimulated, she barely noticed him masterfully removing her clothes.

Andrew slid the last article of Vanessa's clothing around her ankles, and lifting her petite, naked frame up in the air in front of him during an especially deep kiss, while his big toe thrust her panties to the floor. Vanessa's arms tightened around his neck, and instinctively she wound her freed legs around his waist, without breaking the intensity of their kiss. Lowering her gently back onto the bed, he broke their embrace and stood again, rapidly striping off his own clothes, before carelessly tossing them in a heap on the floor and eagerly returning to her.

Andrew trembled with mounting excitement, but he wanted to savor his unexpected liaison with Vanessa. He cared deeply for Vanessa, and he was acutely aware of her vulnerabilities, especially the fact that neither of them had been with a partner in a very long time. Feeling protective of her, he desperately wanted to give her an experience that was both satisfying, and pleasantly unforgettable.

Taking his time, Andrew leisurely ran his warm hands over her quivering exposed body. Vanessa's sensitive skin tingled with desire under his gentle touch, her sensitive nipples hardening in response. Elated by her receptive temperament, he began intimately exploring the sensitive curves and crevices of her body, traveling unhurriedly with a series of tender kisses, sensual nibbling, and gentle suckling. The sound of her soft whimpering along with her deep, throaty moans, her back arching in response to his touch, thrilled him. Andrew beamed, reveling in masculine pride and satisfaction.

Vanessa, whirling out of control in an erotic sea of sensations, trembled with excitement, while her mind spiraled wildly. Andrew had triggered a uniquely pleasurable, stimulating flow of electricity, now pulsating intensely throughout her body. She squirmed under his warm touch, moaning under his sensually tender caresses. When his tongue plundered her mouth, she sighed, deeply inhaling his tantalizingly clean, male scent.

Despite her rapidly growing excitement, Andrew didn't let up, but continued to stroke her even higher, awakening all of her previously latent sexual desires. The sensation of hot, molten lava simmered deep within her. She dug her fingernails into his shoulder, clutching wildly at the blanket beneath her, silently begging for relief from the unbearable, mounting pressure.

Wonderment filled Andrew's eyes. He'd waited for over five years for this perfect woman. Vanessa's swift response to his slightest touch astonished him. She'd captured his heart with her beautiful, expressive face years ago, the same face he'd now caused to flush and distort in pleasure. He felt, for the first time in his life, like a sexually charged, virile stud.

But all too soon, he feared his own tightly held control would falter, having almost reached his own point of inevitable eruption. Suspending himself over her, he nibbled on her sweet, parted lips, and eased slowly into her moist, welcoming body. He watched, captivated, as a look of pure ecstasy crossed her lovely face.

Andrew and Vanessa's flushed, moist bodies entwined in perfect harmony. They feverishly embraced each other, both teetering on the pinnacle of their arousal. Hearts beating in unison, they climaxed exquisitely in conjoined bliss. Wave after wave of pulsating heat surged through them, and spontaneously they cried out in unrestrained pleasure, consumed by the pure intensity of their release.

Their satiated muscles quickly liquefied, and they collapsed onto the bed in breathless satisfaction. Lying side by side, limbs resting limply on the cool bed, they struggled to regain control over their panting breath, while beads of fresh perspiration trickled down their faces. The sound of their ragged breathing filled the cabin as they stared up at the knotty wood ceiling in disbelief. Both had experienced a physical pleasure unlike any they'd ever experienced before.

Vanessa turned on her side, resting her head comfortably on Andrew's shoulder. She placed the palm of her hand on his damp, furry chest, resting it lightly over his rapidly beating heart. He pulled her close against his bare body. Possessively, he covered her hand with his own, while his other hand idly meandered up and down her spine.

Vanessa sighed. *This must be what it feels like to be cherished,* she thought. She'd certainly never felt this way before! Although she hardly knew Andrew, she knew how he made her feel. A single teardrop slipped out of the corner of her eye, not from sadness, but from the unsettling emotions that suddenly overwhelmed her.

Meanwhile, Andrew quietly wrestled with his own feelings. The unexpected pleasure he'd just experienced with Vanessa felt like a betrayal to the memory of his late wife. He'd loved Grace with all his heart, but she'd seldom connected with him sexually, and certainly not on this level. He pushed away his guilty memories, reached over and tenderly pulled the cool sheet over Vanessa's naked form, kissing the top of her head with speechless admiration and appreciation.

Vanessa felt his tender kiss as her body floated, drained of all tension and stress. The dim cabin lighting and the gently rocking of the boat began to lull her into an after-sex, euphoric sleep. Safely tucked within Andrew's warm embrace, she listened to his breathing eventually slow. Listening to the sound of his soft snoring caused the corners of her mouth to lift. She lay contented, snuggled in his arms, and smiled in peaceful satisfaction, just before she too, slept.

The crackling of the radio woke Andrew. At first his foggy mind didn't recognize the sound. He reached behind him to grab the squawking radio and his movements disturbed Vanessa's slumber. Stretching, she sat up, kissed his cheek, and climbed out of bed to leave him to his work. Andrew smiled wickedly to himself, watching her boldly walk away from him in all her splendid nudity. Appreciating the erotic sight, his mind preoccupied, the radio signaled him once again. Clearing his throat, he struggled to sound official. "This is Detective Kelly."

It was the guard posted outside of Haley's room. "Haley's family went back to the hotel. She's wondering when Vanessa might be coming back."

"Tell her she'll be there in approximately forty-five minutes. Out," he said, maintaining his official tone.

The radio crackled. "Okay. Out."

Walking in the buff to the galley, Andrew proceeded to make them some fresh coffee. The length of their nap surprised him, and he found the rapidly dimming daylight outside momentarily disorienting.

Vanessa joined him in the galley. Groaning in satisfaction, she sipped her much-appreciated cup of coffee.

"Better stop that, or we'll have to go again," Andrew laughed.

She cocked her head and grinned. "What's up? What was your call about?"

He flashed her a wolfish smile, then answered seriously, "Haley, wondering when you'd be back. I told Mike to let her know we'd be there in about forty-five minutes."

A twinge of guilt hit Vanessa. She should have been there to support Haley. "Do I have time for a quick shower?"

"Only if I can join you," he teased. Bending down he kissed her tenderly on her shoulder as he murmured, "I promise, I'll behave."

She grabbed a handful of hair from the back of his head, gently lifting his face, and kissed him deeply in response. "I guess we'll find out," she said, playfully.

Giving her a little love tap on her behind, he chased her into the bathroom. Laughing, they playfully lathered each other up under the cascading water, slowly washing their well-satisfied bodies. Vanessa had never laughed playfully with a lover before. It had always been just sex for her. The reason she could play with Andrew suddenly dawned on her. She trusted him.

Much too soon for either of them, they were dressed and en-route to the hospital. Once in his car, they rode in quiet contemplation, both wondering what would come next.

Vanessa's phone rang, interrupting the peaceful silence. It was Marie. She'd made her an appointment with a Hollywood stylist for her planned makeover, and was calling to confirm the date and time.

After she hung up, Andrew glanced at her and simply raised one eyebrow in curiosity.

"That was my assistant," she explained. "It seems I have an

appointment with a stylist on Wednesday morning for a makeover."

Andrew laughed and Vanessa bristled. "Thanks. You have no idea how hard it is for woman of a certain age to compete in my profession!"

"It's hard for all of us as we age," he said sympathetically, hearing the distress in her voice. "Unfortunately we live in a society that worships youth. Frankly, I don't care what the stylist does, you'll always be beautiful to me." He reached over to hold her hand.

Although she smiled, her thoughts strayed to her tenuous position at the magazine. Finally, she silently vowed to herself that she'd work as hard as she could to hold on to her position at *Gemma*, but if it didn't work out, she'd be fine with that too.

When they reached Haley's room, they found her staring blankly at the TV. Andrew could tell by the eager way she welcomed Vanessa that she needed to speak to her in private, and he excused himself to return to his office.

Haley remained quiet until she was certain Andrew was out of hearing range. Then she gave Vanessa a knowing look, and they both broke out laughing.

"You two did it!" Haley said, jubilantly.

Vanessa instantly blushed, attempting to shield her eyes from Haley's probing gaze. "I don't know what you're talking about," she said, evasively avoiding direct eye contact.

"Your middle button is still undone," Haley teased. Vanessa looked down frantically, only to discover that all of her buttons were properly fastened.

"See, I knew it." Haley chuckled. Noting Vanessa's discomfort, she mellowed her tone of voice. "That's great! I knew it was only a matter of time. You two have been making eyes at each other ever since you met. Trust me, I know all about these things."

"How was your visit with your family? I only left to give you some privacy."

"And to get it on with Baby Blue-Eyes," Haley said, smirking. "My parents were disappointed, they wanted to meet you." Her mood suddenly shifted. "They're at dinner now, but Mom said she'll be back later. She wants to talk to me privately." She rolled her eyes and began to fidget.

"I think it will be nice for you to talk to your mother," Vanessa said, noting her unease. "I'm sure she wants the opportunity to find out what's happened to you in the past few years."

"That's what I'm afraid of. I don't want to tell her about Jimmy. I'm not even sure I want to go home yet, or ever." Her petulant tone surprised Vanessa.

"I know how difficult it will be," she said, attempting to reason with Haley. "But you might be surprised by how understanding your mother is."

"Will you stay here while we talk?" Haley remained apprehensive, wanting Vanessa's support.

"I'll stay until your mother comes back." She felt this was one conversation Haley needed to have alone with her mother. "Then I need to go take care of Callie. You need to have this conversation in private. Just you and your mother."

"I know, I guess I'm just a coward." She looked down at her hands.

Vanessa stood and gave her a quick hug. "You my dear, are anything but a coward!"

Sitting down, Vanessa noticed her mood had altered again. Now there was a slight spark of mischief in Haley's eyes. "So, tell me, was he any good?"

Vanessa laughed, shaking her head at her audacity, just as Haley's mother stepped into the room. Her mother rushed to Haley's side, hugging her fiercely before she sat in the chair on the opposite side of the bed.

Haley formally introduced Vanessa and her mother. Haley's mother, June, had soft brown, shoulder length hair, gentle dark brown eyes, and she spoke with a soft mid-western accent. Her resemblance to Haley was remarkable. Vanessa could only imagine the torture this poor woman must have endured, not knowing if her daughter was dead or alive. June thanked Vanessa profusely for looking out for Haley.

"The detective told us on the phone that you even stood up to him, in order to protect Haley from being arrested," June said, nodding appreciatively.

"I have to say, that was my first run-in with the law," she said, guiltily.

June laughed melodically. "We appreciate it more than we can say." Her smile faded slightly. "I hate to ask, but I was hoping I could ask you for a favor." June quickly explained that Haley's surgery on her ankle was scheduled for the following morning, and her family needed to return home. Vanessa immediately agreed she'd watch over Haley, until they returned to take her home.

131

"I don't know how we can ever repay you for your kindness. Our family is forever in your debt," June exhaled, visibly relieved.

"Thanks, Vanessa," Haley said innocently, sending her a pseudo-angelic look.

Vanessa gathered her things, shared her contact information with June, and gave Haley a brief goodbye hug.

"For years I prayed we'd get our baby back. I can't thank you enough," June said, holding Vanessa in a smothering embrace.

"It was a pleasure meeting you, June. Haley, I'll see you after surgery tomorrow. Now, I need to go to attend to a very cranky cat."

Vanessa disengaged herself from June and turned to leave, sending Haley a thumbs-up sign behind her mother's back and mouthing a silent "good luck."

Vanessa stepped out of the room, nodded to the night guard, and walked down the hall. Striding out of the elevator into the empty lobby, she reached for her phone to call Andrew.

"Hey there, I'm ready to leave. Is there a handsome detective who could come escort me home?" she flirted.

He smiled. He'd missed her while he'd been sitting at his desk, working through Haley's case. "Can you give me a minute or two? I'm just finishing up here."

"Of course, I'll be in the cafeteria having coffee." Just the sound of his voice made her heart accelerate.

"I'll be there as quick as I can. Love you." His smile carried through the phone line.

Wow, he said the 'L word'. Her heart skipped a beat. Her husband was the last person she'd said I love you to, right after his return from the Middle East. Once she'd suffered through her heartbreaking divorce, she'd kept men at a safe distance, callously using sex to manipulate them. *But Andrew was different,* she thought. *Maybe it was time to trust someone again.*

"See you, love you too," she said, attempting to sound as casual as he had, but feeling an uncomfortable sensation of fear twisting within her gut.

She sat down in the cafeteria with a cup of coffee to wait, brooding over her ambiguous feelings for Andrew. *Do I actually love him, or is he merely a pleasant distraction from my stressful work issues? Is this simply my change-of-life fling?* She sighed deeply. What would happen to their relationship once she returned to the daily demands of her work? Would it die a natural death? She frowned in concentration as she attempted to sort through her feelings for him.

When Andrew walked into the cafeteria twenty minutes later, it was like he brought the sunshine with him. *How has this fascinating man managed to worm his way into my neatly organized world anyway?* Her silent questions remained unanswered.

"Sorry, it took longer than I expected," he said, nonchalantly sliding in to the seat across from her.

"No problem." She handed him a cup of coffee. "I was just sitting here daydreaming." He smiled affectionately. She had an uncanny way of making everything feel right in his world.

"There's a good reason why I was late. I reviewed some of the initial forensic tests that came back today," he explained. "We found the DNA of the two female tellers, and expected to find the DNA from the two male bank robbers as well, but discovered we only had one."

"Really? What does that mean?" she said, momentarily confused by his findings.

"It means that one of the bank robbers got away."

"Oh great!" She instantly became alarmed. "Haley's still in danger?"

"I'm sorry, but there's more." He reached over to hold her hand. "Apparently, there were two explosions. One in the main bank lobby, and a second blast inside the vault."

"What do you make of that?"

"I believe the second bank robber was safely inside the vault during the first explosion," he speculated. "Then he set off the second explosion after he robbed the bank. Initially, everyone assumed that all of the paper money had been destroyed. Now I'm not so sure."

"Who do you think survived? Where do you think he is? Do you think he'll come after Haley?" Her eyes widened with panic.

"If he's smart..." Andrew shook his head thoughtfully. "He left the country long before we had a chance to discover that he's still alive. I don't think Haley's any threat to him now."

"I hope you're right." She felt calmer, but still concerned. "Do you think it was Haley's boyfriend, or his partner who escaped?" she asked, and began chewing on her lower lip.

"I have no idea. They're running the DNA now, maybe we'll get lucky."

They finished their coffee and Andrew tossed their cups into the garbage, casually reaching out his hand to help Vanessa up out of her seat.

"Well my princess, the ball is over, and your carriage awaits," he teased.

She laughed at his antics, cleverly designed to ease her worry. When they got to his car, she noticed Shep had joined them.

"Shep will be standing guard again tonight, in case I'm preoccupied," he explained with a wink.

"Oh really?" She raised her eyebrow mockingly.

"I picked up my favorite barbeque takeout for us tonight." The sweet-smoky aroma filled the vehicle. "I hope you're hungry."

Vanessa smiled, he'd thought of everything.

On the ride home, she informed Andrew of Haley's parents' plan to return home immediately following her surgery.

"I guess that makes sense. They dropped everything in their lives to come on a moment's notice," he reasoned.

"Her mother asked me to look out for her," she said. When he laughed at her, she lightly punching him on the shoulder.

"As if you weren't planning on doing that anyway," he said, gently teasing her.

"I think she just wanted to make sure that Haley wasn't left on her own again. When I left them, she and Haley were about to have a very deep mother-daughter conversation. I think Haley was going to open up and tell her mother everything." She gazed out the window thoughtfully.

"That will be a tough conversation for both of them," he said, frowning thoughtfully.

"I know. She told me she was scared, but I know she can handle it."

When they pulled up into her driveway, Vanessa's house appeared deserted and pitch dark. Andrew used his flashlight to turn on the lights and see her safely inside, before he settled Shep on the front porch for guard duty. Meanwhile, she carried the take-out food into the kitchen, followed closely by Callie. She bestowed a little extra affection on her cat, hoping that she'd settle down peacefully.

Vanessa turned toward the counter, about to investigate the contents of the take-out bag, when Andrew walked up behind her. He wrapped his arms around her waist, and affectionately nuzzled the back of her neck, causing chills to run down her spine. Tiny Goosebumps instantly erupted on her arms. Turning around within his embrace, she reached up her arms, winding them around his neck. Their lips touched and she anticipated his passionate kisses, but before their kiss deepened,

Andrew quickly pulled away, distracted by the aroma of his favorite barbequed chicken.

"I could kiss you all day and all night, but right now, I'm starving, aren't you?" he murmured in her ear.

She laughed, not the slightest bit offended. "Okay, let's see what you brought." She began removing the contents of the take out bag. Surprised by the barbeque chicken salad he'd bought for her, she gave him a quick kiss of thanks on the cheek. "You got me exactly what I would have ordered."

He smiled at her enthusiasm. "Of course," he said offhandedly, secretly relieved that he'd guessed right.

They sat in the living room with their food to watch the news. He discovered that she made even the most mundane topics interesting, and he enjoyed their verbal sparring. After dinner, they cozied up on the couch together to watch a movie.

Always a gentleman, Andrew refrained from making any advances toward Vanessa while officially protecting her. He wanted her to feel safe inside her own home, and although he wanted to be intimate with her, he was determined that he would only go to her room tonight if she specifically invited him.

Vanessa frowned, confused by Andrew's sudden lack of romantic interest in her. They'd kissed in the kitchen, but there'd been no flirting or physical contact since. *Didn't their afternoon romp mean anything to him?* She sulked silently, wondering if she'd completely misread his intentions.

Losing interest in the movie they watched, Vanessa decided she'd explore Andrew's true feelings.

"I'm tired." She stood and reached toward his hand. "Let's go to bed and get some sleep."

He immediately responded with a slow, sexy smile. Reaching for the control, he clicked off the TV, stood, and pulled her into arms. "I thought you'd never ask." Andrew's low, husky voice, followed by his fiery hot kisses, instantly relieved any doubts Vanessa may have had regarding his interest or his intent.

Chapter 13
From the Grave

*K*ate arrived early in the morning. She'd spent the entire night in crowded airports or squished in her seat up in the air. Exhausted, she checked into her hotel as planned. She didn't unpack, but instead she immediately caught a cab to the address Marvin had given to her, anxious to obtain her new identity.

After her meeting with the creepy little man who'd forge her papers, she returned to her room. Barely able to stand, she kicked off her shoes and fell into bed. Still too anxious to fall asleep, she tossed and turned, and stared hopelessly at the ceiling. She knew she'd feel uneasy until she picked up her final papers the following morning. What she needed was a strong drink to take the edge off. Maybe then she'd relax and stop tossing in bed, or pacing her room like a caged mountain lion.

She found herself ambling down the quaint cobblestone streets toward the local cantina. The advanced age and blemishes of the stone buildings were evident in the glaring, unforgiving afternoon sun. When she entered the cantina, only a few patrons sat at the bar, so Kate slipped into a seat at a table in the corner of the dusty room. With her back up against the cool, stone wall, she quietly surveyed the men in the room.

An enormous margarita before her, she sipped peacefully, until an extremely boisterous, intoxicated American captured her attention. She remained detached, observing the scene from a safe distance. He looked rough, as though he'd been drinking all night. He alternated between ranting at the bartender and flopping his head theatrically, dropping it heavily onto the rustic wooden bar. At first she remained disinterested, only mildly annoyed by the obnoxious man. But he caught her attention when she overheard the bartender making a feeble attempt to reason with the drunk American.

"Please señor, enough tequila," he said, endeavoring to pull the bottle out of the man's tight grasp.

"My name's not señor, my name's Jimmy, and don't you forget it, mister!" The intoxicated man had lifted his head just long enough to slur out his protest, before he hugged the bottle to his chest and passed out again.

Jimmy had started drinking late last night in his room. He'd met with the man forging his ID, and had quickly emptied the contents of his hotel mini-bar. Still craving alcohol, he'd staggered out of the lobby, down the *street, and into a local all-night cantina. Too drunk to remember his ID papers were ready and waiting, he'd continued his drinking binge well into the afternoon.*

Kate choked on her drink, taking a closer look at the inebriated American. How could this be? Although she'd never met Jimmy, she knew this couldn't be a coincidence. Who knows, maybe all was not lost after all! Maybe Marvin was alive too! She sat back in her chair, waiting patiently for the opportunity to follow Jimmy. Meanwhile, Jimmy drifted in and out of his nasty, intoxicated, hazy state of awareness.

Andrew woke with Vanessa resting peacefully in his arms. They hadn't really slept much during the night, yet he felt surprisingly refreshed. Looking over at her clock, he realized it was nearly ten a.m. He gently kissed the top of her head. "Honey?"

"Umm?" Vanessa murmured, stretching like a lazy feline. She looked up at him and gave him a sleepy, satisfied smile. Waking to his smiling face had to be the best birthday present she could ask for.

He couldn't resist. He bent down and kissed her forehead, reminding her gently, "It's almost ten. Haley's surgery should be over by now and she might be in her room."

"Umm okay, her parents should be there for her," she said, too cozy to get out of bed. "But I guess we need to get up."

Andrew laughed as Callie jumped up onto the bed. First, she placed her wet nose on Vanessa's nose, and then she turned herself around so that her indignant tail lifted straight into the air, directly in Vanessa's face.

"For heaven's sake, Callie, I'll get your food in a minute," she said, burying her head under her pillow.

"Why don't I feed her?" He bent down and kissed Vanessa's exposed shoulder. "I suspect she's a little upset with me this morning. After all, I took her place on the bed last night." He climbed out of bed and motioned to the cat.

Murmuring brief feeding instructions to him, Vanessa snuggled back into her warm bed. She should try to get up, but she felt so dreamy and relaxed, and had no desire to face her day yet. Last night she'd delighted Andrew with every trick she knew, as well as some moves she'd only read about. Now, every part of Vanessa's body screamed for mercy.

All too soon, he returned from the kitchen, giving her a quick update on Haley's condition. Then he gallantly served Vanessa breakfast in bed.

"You're spoiling me," she complained half-heartedly, examining the eggs, toast, and coffee. Vanessa could see she had no choice and pushed herself into a sitting position.

"It's my pleasure. Besides, you spoiled me last night," Andrew said, sending her a wicked smile, showing he was definitely a very satisfied, appreciative man.

Vanessa finished her breakfast and set the tray aside. She stood up to stretch, while Andrew nibbled on an untouched piece of toast she'd left on her tray. They quickly showered and dressed together. Maneuvering within the close quarters of her bathroom, they moved around each other with the acquired skills of an old married couple.

Arriving at the hospital a short time later, they walked through the lobby comfortably holding hands. Approaching Haley's room, Andrew and Vanessa overheard a rowdy commotion. Haley's entire family had crowded into the tiny waiting room at the end of the hall.

Haley remained asleep since her morning surgery. Her parents stepped out of the cramped waiting room and approached them, asking to speak with them in private. Andrew suggested the cafeteria, and they left their children in the waiting room after giving strict instructions to the older children.

Once in the cafeteria, the four of them sat down at the table with fresh coffee. "First of all, I want to thank you both for looking after our Haley," her father began. "Unfortunately, my wife got a little taste of Haley's nightmarish life last night. Even the thought of it breaks our hearts." He reached out for his wife's hand to comfort her.

"We take full responsibility for Haley's disappearance," he said. "We know that we counted too heavily on her. I'm afraid we didn't appreciate all of the sacrifices we'd asked her to make." He sent his wife an embarrassed look, and swallowed hard. He paused for a moment, struggling to find the words to continue. He stared down at his hand joined with his wife's, while he contemplated. Everyone waited silently for him to finish.

"Haley's surgery went well and the doctor thinks she can leave the hospital on Friday," he said, looking up again. "He wants her to stay in town for at least another week after that." He smiled at Vanessa, then his gaze shifted toward Andrew. "The DA informed us that Haley must stay in town until he gives his consent for her to leave. But we both need to get back to our jobs." He shook his head regretfully. "We hate leaving her."

Vanessa and Andrew looked at each other and nodded slightly. Andrew spoke first. "I'll work on the DA I'll make sure that Haley can go home as soon as she's ready."

"Don't worry about Haley, I'm on vacation for the next two weeks," Vanessa said. "She's welcome to stay with me. You can return to get her as soon as she's ready to go home."

Haley's parents smiled at each other, visibly relieved.

June reached for Vanessa's hand, tears glistening in her deep brown eyes. "You two were heaven-sent. You'll both be in our prayers, forever."

"We can't thank you enough." Haley's father nodded in agreement.

Once that was settled, the atmosphere between the four of them lightened considerably. June disclosed that immediately following Haley's disappearance, she'd quit her job at the cleaners, and that Haley's father had temporarily become their sole provider. He'd quickly secured a higher paying office job, while June completed an online degree in design. Currently, she successfully designed clothes from home. They'd creatively found a way to spend more time with their family, while still comfortably providing for their children and their financial future.

Vanessa and Andrew found Haley's parents fascinating, and their resourcefulness impressive. However, the tone of the conversation became uncomfortably personal, when June inquired about their upcoming wedding plans.

"Who, us?" Vanessa blushed, squirming in her seat.

"We've only been together for a few days," Andrew explained, obviously embarrassed by the subject.

"Well, keep us posted," Haley's father said, sending them a wink and a perceptively confident smile.

Vanessa said her goodbyes to Haley's parents in the lobby. She asked them to inform Haley that she'd check in with her later, aware that Haley's parents wanted to spend more time with Haley before they left for home.

Andrew dropped Vanessa off at her home, planning to return immediately to his office. But before he left her, he walked her to the door and kissed her tenderly on the mouth.

"Vanessa?" he asked, formally. "Would you do me the honor of allowing me to escort you to dinner tonight?" This would be their first official date.

"I would be delighted." The formality of his request tickled Vanessa, and she smiled with pleasure, keeping the significance of the day to herself. She refused to celebrate her unwanted fifty-fifth birthday!

He lifted her in his arms and twirled her around, giving her another quick kiss. "I'll call you later," he said, then jumped into his car and sped out of her circular driveway, kicking up the dirt and gravel in his wake. She shook her head and smiled as she watched him drive away.

Later as she sat peacefully at her kitchen table, Vanessa sighed contentedly, absently stirring her fresh cup of coffee. Excited to have Haley staying with her, she wanted to make everything perfect, and began concentrating on her shopping list. Haley was long overdue for some extreme pampering, and she planned to see to it, at least for the next week or two.

Finally satisfied with her list, she picked up her keys and was about to leave, when her phone rang. It was Marie, which gave her the opportunity to catch up with the latest office drama.

Marie informed her that she and Max's assistant, Jane, were enjoying an extra long lunch today. Vanessa smiled to herself, thinking of the old saying, *when the cat's away...* But she frowned when she discovered that Mindy had apparently been a no-show at work this morning, and that Max had been suddenly called away to an urgent meeting with his father. Vanessa reacted with detached concern to both unusual events.

"So, how's your birthday going?" Marie asked, attempting to lighten Vanessa's mood.

"Nothing too exciting for me today, except I'm on vacation." Vanessa had tried hard not to think about her age today, planning to ignore this year's birthday altogether.

"Do you have any instructions for the two of us?" Vanessa heard wine glasses clinking in the background.

"No instructions from me, except enjoy your lunch, and keep me posted."

"Will do. Enjoy your vacation. I think it may be your last," Marie warned. "I'll give you your present when you return."

"Thanks, Marie. I think I'm beginning to like the idea of having two weeks off every month," Vanessa admitted, her contented, mellow voice transmitting through the phone to Marie.

"Oh my gosh, did you meet someone?" Marie had sensed a change in

Vanessa's tone immediately.

"Maybe…" Vanessa hinted. She wasn't ready to define her relationship with Andrew, not right now.

"You did!" Marie couldn't contain her excitement. Vanessa had been alone for too many years; not counting the occasional, loveless dates she'd had with her clients. There'd been no excitement or sparkle in Vanessa during those relationships, but she could hear the energy in Vanessa's voice now. "Tell me everything!" Marie demanded.

"It's complicated. I'll tell you all about it when I get back." Vanessa evaded the sensitive subject, quickly ending their conversation.

Vanessa had almost made it out her front door, when her phone rang again. She could tell by the personalized ringtone, that it was her mother, calling from France. She walked back to the kitchen to make another cup of coffee. And an hour later, after hearing all about her mother's health problems, receiving birthday wishes, and discussing her next visit to France, Vanessa finally made it out of her house.

Wanting to spoil Haley, she bought everything she thought a teenage girl might want, including a new TV for the guest bedroom and a laptop. Considering Haley's over-sized, splinted leg, she selected an assortment of comfortable, loose clothes for her to wear. Feeling satisfied with her purchases, she reassured herself that Haley could pick out her own clothes once she was mobile and able to go shopping.

Andrew called Vanessa while she was putting Haley's new clothes away in the guest bedroom. "How's your day going?" he asked sweetly. She got the sense that he missed her, almost as much as she missed him.

"I've been busy shopping, how about you, Detective?" She smiled to herself, casually hanging up more clothes.

"We got lucky. The DNA in the bank was positively identified as Marvin's." Andrew had pushed and prodded the forensic team all day, just to get this information for her.

"That means that scum Jimmy is still out there somewhere!" Horrified by the news, she sat down hard on the guest bed, letting the clothes fall haphazardly to the floor. "We can't tell Haley," she whispered. "She'll never be able to sleep knowing he's still alive." She glanced fleetingly around the room as she spoke.

"I know how you feel." He rubbed at the mounting tension on the back of his neck, knowing she'd predicted Haley's reaction correctly. "I'm afraid it's worse, the press is about to release his identity. Wanted photos for Jimmy will be displayed everywhere. We'll simply have to convince Haley that we can keep her safe. She'll have twenty-four hour police protection, including Shep and I every night."

Vanessa smiled briefly at his certainty that he'd be spending his nights in her bed.

"Do you think he knows Haley came to my house? Or that she's in the hospital now?" This new development caused her to shiver involuntarily. Hearing her unease, Andrew wished he'd waited and delivered the news to her in person.

"No, so far I've been able to keep both of your names out of all the press releases," he said, hoping the situation hadn't changed. "Keep your doors locked, and turn on your alarm. I'll be there in thirty minutes. Will you be ready to go see Haley by then?"

Vanessa knew she'd exposed her feelings of vulnerability. *I'm probably overreacting*, she thought. She tried to control her voice, making it sound confident and steady. "I'll be fine. I have the best watch cat in the city." She laughed at the absurdity.

Andrew laughed. *Always the little toughie*, he thought. "I'm well aware of Callie's protection skills, but humor me. Lock the doors and set the alarm until I get there." He tried to downplay his own concerns.

"Fine, I'll see you soon." Callie appeared in the doorway, rubbing against Vanessa's legs as if to ask, *Are you talking about me?*

The trembling in her voice worried him. He could tell she'd tried to hide her unease, and had put up a brave front for him. "See you soon. Love you." He hung up, and dropping everything, he dashed out to his car.

Vanessa locked up the house as instructed. She began getting ready for her big dinner date, as a diversion from her mounting anxiety. Hair and makeup done, she'd just slipped into her favorite, slinky red dress, when the doorbell rang. Barefoot, with her zipper still hanging open in the back, she swung the door open to greet Andrew.

He looked positively charming, leaning against her doorjamb with a crooked smile and a bunch of her wild daisies in his hand.

"How did you know? I adore daisies," she smiled, accepting the flowers from him.

"I didn't know. I just saw all those daisies on the side of your yard, and I thought they might cheer you up." He gave her a sheepish, guilty grin.

Burying her face in the bouquet of perfect white and yellow daisies, she dreamily responded, "Thank you."

With the flowers held in one hand, she slowly walked into his waiting arms. After a brief hug, she pulled back to look at him, squinting her eyes in the bright sun. She crinkled her nose and cocked her head to one side. "You know, I sort of missed you today."

"That's nice to hear. I missed you too," he murmured, kissing her softly on the forehead.

He followed her back to her room, casually zipping up her dress, and sat down on her bed to watch her primp.

"You know...if Jimmy did get out of the bank in one piece, he's long gone by now. There's no reason for him to stick around," he said, attempting to soothe her nerves.

She turned to face him, wanting to check his expression, to see if he actually believed what he was telling her. "I hope you're right. But what about that woman?"

"No sign of her either. She's probably long gone, too."

He stood and walked toward her seductively, instantly causing the atmosphere between them to sizzle with electricity. He stood so close to her, that when she closed her eyes, she could feel the intensity of his heat radiating from his body into hers. He didn't touch her, but instead he simply leaned in close, whispering softly into her ear, "You look ravishing."

Vanessa stood completely still, her eyes shut tight, waiting in breathless anticipation. She felt his intense, sensual warmth slowly fade as he stepped away. Opening her eyes, she felt captured and totally mesmerized by his sensual, blue eyes. He maintained an almost hypnotic control over her with his penetrating gaze. Holding her rapt attention, he leisurely reached for her hand, brought it up to his lips, and pressed a very gentle, erotic kiss in the middle of her palm.

"I think if we're going, we should leave now," he whispered, wisely.

Vanessa wasn't sure if she wanted to go anywhere at that particular moment. But she slowly broke the spell by reluctantly removing her hand from his. Tearing herself from his possessive gaze, she pivoted away from him to reach for her purse.

"You're right." She struggled to make her breathy voice sound normal. "We'd better get going." Changing the subject, she added, "I'm not sure what kind of mood Haley will be in tonight, but I doubt she'll want to be alone after her parents leave."

144

They arrived at Haley's room to find her propped up like royalty with pillows surrounding her.

"Hey you guys." Wide-awake, she cheerfully smiled at their arrival. "I'm glad you're here. My mom tells me I get to stay in town for the next week or so. Thanks for putting me up." She beamed her brightly lit smile at Vanessa.

"It's my pleasure." Vanessa shrugged, handing Haley a bag full of assorted chocolates, gummy bears, and teen magazines. "I think it'll be fun. It's been years since I've had a roommate."

"Thanks." Haley looked into the bag and gleefully popped a gummy bear into her mouth. "Hmm...I've been craving these for years!" Looking up, she suddenly gawked, noticing Vanessa's classy red dress. "Wow, look at you! What's the occasion?"

"This pretty lady has agreed to go on a date with me tonight," Andrew said, smoothly answering for Vanessa.

"It seems to me...that you two have been *dating* already," she teased, and enjoyed watching Vanessa's instant blush. Glancing toward Andrew, Haley set the bag of goodies aside and frowned. "Why is there still a guard outside my door?" she asked, suspiciously.

Vanessa and Andrew exchanged quick glances.

"The woman who came into your room is still unaccounted for, and there's also been a new development in the case that I should tell you about." Andrew pulled a chair up next to Haley and sat down. "Apparently the DNA found in the bank accounted for only one of the two bank robbers. We believe the other one got away."

"Jimmy's alive, isn't he?" Haley whispered, turning pale.

"It indeed looks that way. That's why you'll have round the clock security until we're absolutely certain that he's left town."

Haley nodded solemnly. Her earnest gaze traveled from Andrew to Vanessa. She believed they cared for her, and she trusted them both to keep her safe. Vanessa noticed Haley's reaction and quickly changed the subject to distract her.

"How's your leg? Are you hurting much?" She walked closer to inspect the splint on her elevated leg.

"No, not much." The distraction wasn't working. Vanessa saw Haley begin twisting her fingers, attempting to cope with the news that Jimmy was still alive.

"If Jimmy's alive—I'm sure he's left town," she said, trying to convince

Andrew and herself. "He and Marvin cooked up an escape plan to someplace far away, where they wouldn't send them back."

"Did they tell you their plan?" he asked, immediately interested.

"No. I just overheard little bits and pieces. It was really nice for a while, thinking he was dead and could never hurt me again." She slumped down in her bed hopelessly.

"I know what you mean," Vanessa said, commiserating with her. "I felt the same way when my husband got locked up." She sat on the bed next to her, resting a reassuring hand on Haley's arm.

Haley threw her arms around Vanessa's neck. "Thank you, for understanding." She buried her face against Vanessa's shoulder.

Andrew silently watched while Vanessa consoled Haley. They shared an empathetic bond over the horrendous violence they'd each suffered. Neither would forget their injuries, or the two rotten men who'd inflicted them. Andrew felt his blood boil with rage. He hated the men who had physically and emotionally damaged them both. In times such as these, he had to remind himself that life wasn't always just, or fair.

Andrew stood and walked toward the door. He awkwardly excused himself to return to his office. He needed to change clothes for his dinner date, and suspected that Haley and Vanessa needed the opportunity to talk in private.

Vanessa absently waved a brief goodbye. She gave Haley a quick hug, and then she pulled Haley in front of her, tactfully changing the topic of conversation. She began describing the new laptop, and some of the clothes she'd bought earlier. Haley dried her eyes and slowly her wary look turned into one of delight, smiling appreciatively at Vanessa. Pleased by her response, Vanessa began jotting down a few new ideas of things to bring Haley in the morning.

Haley, touched by Vanessa's generosity, could hardly wait to tell her parents. She excitedly rambled on about her family's visit, anxious to share their stories with Vanessa. Glowing with enthusiasm, she began relating some of the details of the sensitive conversation she had with her mother the night before.

"You know what? My mom was great! I told her lots of horrible things. Things I thought I'd never talk about. But she wasn't upset with me at all."

"I'm glad you had a chance to see how much your mother loves you," Vanessa smiled, popping one of Haley's chocolates into her mouth.

"It's been great seeing everyone again. But they've all grown and changed so much since I left," Haley said, regretfully. "I wish I'd been home when J.J. was born. He doesn't even know who I am!"

"He'll get to know you when you go home," Vanessa said reassuringly.

"I'm not sure I want to go home. What if I don't fit in?" Tears of uncertainty suddenly filled her eyes, and she looked down at her lap.

Vanessa lifted her chin so she could look into Haley's wet eyes. "I know it will be hard, but you can make it work if you want to."

"I promise I'll try." Haley hugged her, and then popped another gummy bear into her mouth.

Andrew heard happy chatting when he reappeared a short time later. Now freshly showered, he stood in the doorway looking stylish, like he'd just stepped out of a men's fashion magazine, dressed in a fitted dark blue suit with a contrasting tie.

"I'm glad you're feeling better," he said, smiling appreciatively at Haley. "Now may I steal my date? I'm starving."

"Of course, I have plenty to keep me busy tonight." Haley lifted her bag of goodies back onto the bed. "You guys look great. Go have fun, I'll see you tomorrow." Vanessa gave her a brief hug before she joined Andrew at the door.

"Don't be mean to the nurses, and try to get some sleep. I'll see you in the morning." Vanessa admonished her, waving goodbye.

"Yes, Mommy," Haley responded in a fake, overly sweet tone.

Vanessa chuckled, and thought, *Haley certainly brings out the mothering in me.* Andrew offered his arm gallantly to Vanessa, and together they walked out of the hospital, into the balmy night air. Secretly, they both felt a little awkward and anxious anticipating their first official date together. Vanessa smiled up at him, happily welcoming Andrew's charming company, especially on this particular night. *Tonight's date with him, she thought, will be the perfect distraction from my miserably pathetic, and definitely unwelcomed birthday*

Chapter 14
Quarrels and Overtures

*K*ate ached, feeling tired, bored, and hungry. Jimmy hadn't moved a muscle in hours. His head remained nestled on the bar, where he dozed fitfully, and alternated between snoring and snorting. Rather than fight with him, the bartender had elected to ignore Jimmy, and occupied himself at the opposite end of the bar. The margarita did its job, now Kate struggled to hold her eyes open. She ordered two bottled iced teas, with some spicy bar nibbles, wanting to stay alert and ready to move fast, if and when Jimmy stirred to leave.

Kate peered outside the cantina door, marveling at the splendid pinks and yellows of the lingering twilight. As night fell, the crowd in the cantina grew, until the tiny bar had nothing but standing room left. Kate unobtrusively leaned back against the wall, separating herself from the regulars, while she kept a watchful eye on Jimmy.

As the cramped, local patrons drank, they became increasingly more intoxicated and rowdier. A ruckus broke out, and a heavyset man toppled directly into the inebriated Jimmy. Growling, Jimmy rose up off the bar and began swinging his fists wildly at the unruly men. His uncontrolled punches landed on several of the brawlers, before someone struck him squarely on the jaw, knocking him clumsily into some nearby tables and chairs. Jimmy's head hit the corner of one of the tables with a sickening thud as he fell, landing facedown on the dirty concrete floor.

Kate watched in horror, but the rest of the crowd ignored Jimmy, his now lifeless form lying inert under the table. Instead they continued their frenzied fighting above him. The agitated bartender ran out into the street, intent on summoning the local police to elicit help in restoring order to his bar.

Kate decided it was now or never. She moved cautiously through the bar and quickly bent over Jimmy, rolling him onto his back. She was startled to discover his eyes open, staring blankly back at her, a trickle of dark red blood slowly oozing out of his nose. She instinctively felt his neck for a pulse, but found none! Recovering from her initial shock, she reached inside his upper shirt pocket, quickly locating a small envelope with his hotel room number neatly printed on the outside. She felt the envelope to confirm it contained his metal keys. Apparently, he'd been staying in the same hotel as she, in fact just a few floors above her.

Kate hastily stuffed the envelope in her purse and scooted around the *edge of the room, smoothly avoiding the scuffling drunks. Slipping out the front door, she'd managed to slide past them undetected and untouched. Preoccupied by his anxious search for the police, the bartender failed to see her leave, and Kate disappeared safely into the shelter of the shadowy night.*

When she returned to her hotel, Kate pulled up a picture of Marvin on her cell phone, displaying his photo to the front desk staff and the bellhops. No one recognized him. Defeated and discouraged, Kate returned to her room. Back to square one, she thought. Jimmy's dead and Marvin's nowhere to be found. Perhaps he's dead as well.

Pulling the small envelope out of her purse, Kate dumped the contents onto her bed. The envelope contained not only Jimmy's room key, but also two smaller metallic keys. She instantly recognized them as belonging to the room safes, and wondered what valuables Jimmy had locked up. He'd miraculously escaped the explosion at the bank, she thought. Maybe he'd also managed to grab some of the money.

Some time later, Kate ventured out of her room, freshly showered, wearing a colorful local sundress and a wide-brimmed hat. The hall cameras failed to deter her, as she expertly averted her gaze.

Chills of excitement tingled up Kate's spine. She envisioned the workings of the regrettably botched bank robbery, and felt exhilarated by the real possibility that she'd find some stolen money hidden within Jimmy's safe.

Andrew pulled up in front of one of Vanessa's favorite seafood restaurants, and escorted her inside. The dim candlelight and fireplace made the room feel cozy and warm, while a small string quartet played dreamy classical music in the corner. The tables in the room were small, many of them occupied by couples engaging in intimate conversations. They were shown to a secluded, quiet corner table.

Vanessa considered ordering her usual dinner, but changed her mind. In honor of her special, secret birthday, she'd be bold, and try something new. Once the waiter left, Andrew leaned forward and reached across the table to hold her hand. "Thank you, for being my date tonight."

She smiled, but before she could respond, the wine arrived, and they pulled apart. The fragrance of the white wine stirred fond memories of a sunny vineyard Vanessa had once visited in France.

"My pleasure," she said, taking her first sip of the aromatic wine. She closed her eyes, delighting in the subtle combination of the sweet, fruity taste mixed with a dry overtone, savoring the individual flavors. She complimented his selection of wine. He smiled, and they began to discuss other personal preferences, both happily discovering that they shared many similar tastes. They both enjoyed classical music and beautiful landscapes, and rarely watched movies, but preferred to read books instead.

After dinner, during a conversational pause, Andrew leaned back, slowly sipping his wine as he thoughtfully studied Vanessa's face. He had become very attached to her, and he wondered if his feelings were reciprocated. *Could she envision her future with me?*

"Did I mention, I'm retiring in a few weeks?" he asked, abruptly changing the subject from the one they'd previously been discussing.

Initially surprised by the topic, she shook her head no, although she thought he might have mentioned it once before. Feeling mellow, she appreciated her wine, gazing thoughtfully into her glass, before she probed for more information about his upcoming retirement plans. "So, how will you spend your time, once you're no longer chasing bad guys?"

"I'd originally planned to spend it on my sailboat." Her inquiry pleased him, and he sent her a tentative smile. "I've been planning for some long trips at sea. There are so many exciting places I'd like to visit."

"Sounds adventurous." Seeing the spark of wanderlust in his eyes, she could sense his anticipation and excitement.

"But now, I'm not sure I still want to be gone, I mean for such long periods of time." He paused for a moment, searching her eyes. "Originally, I'd planned to sail for months at a time. Now I'm thinking I might want to stay a little closer to home." He looked at her expectantly, placing his warm hand over hers, and running his thumb absently across the pulse of her wrist.

His plans aroused mixed feelings. She knew by his tone that he'd just referred to her as his reason for sticking close to home. "Why would you want to do that?" She became distracted by the erotic sensations he casually created on her wrist.

"Originally, I thought it would be fun, spending day after day alone on my boat. Now, I'm thinking I might be lonely." He searched her face for a reaction.

"How would you feel about going on shorter trips, with a first mate to keep you company?" She'd instantly thought the exact same thing, hating the idea of him leaving, just when they were getting to know each other. "I've been promised two weeks off every month for the next year. What do you think? Will you sign me up as your first mate?" She sent him a seductive, inviting smile, turning her hand over to squeeze his intimately.

"Nothing would make me happier." He took a sip of his wine for courage then added, "I think I fell for you...the first time I met you in the hospital all those years ago. Being with you now has been a dream come true for me. When my wife died, I was prepared to live alone for the remainder of my life. I'd never expected to feel this way about anyone." He raised her hand to his lips and placed a soft warm kiss on top of her fingers.

"I don't think I've ever really been in love." Her eyes moistened with regret. "All I know is, I've felt things with you that I didn't think I was capable of. Every time I think of you, I feel warm and peaceful. I've never felt this way with anyone else. You make me feel special. Cherished."

Andrew smiled, pleased that she could feel his love, even in the midst of all her emotional bewilderment. He knew that no one had ever loved her as much as he did. Feeling the comforting, warm glow radiated between them, he gave her a decisive nod. "Welcome aboard, First Mate." Her offer to sail with him touched him, more than he could possibly say.

"I have to warn you, I know absolutely nothing about sailing," she said, laughing nervously.

"Not to worry, I'm an excellent teacher." Confidently, he sent her a smoldering look of desire.

Andrew's confession of love, anticipation of their romantic sailing adventures, and the burning look he sent her, not to mention the wine, caused a fiery need to burn deep inside Vanessa. "I think you'd better take me home now. If you keep looking at me like that, I might just spontaneously combust right here in this chair," Vanessa said, squirming a bit, the longing gaze she sent Andrew clearly betraying her desire.

"By all means, let's go. I'd rather watch you combust in private," he said, and signaled the waiter for their bill.

Consumed with desire for each other, they barely made it through Vanessa's front door before they both began peeling off each other's clothes in her entryway. Their kisses, short and sweet while they undressed each other, soon transformed into deeper, longer caresses, until Andrew lifted Vanessa and carried her impatiently into her bedroom.

Once in bed, the sudden coolness of the room and the sheets beneath them caused Vanessa's excited body to shudder. Feeling her tremble, he pulled the comforter up over them. He held her close, his overheated body radiating warmth into hers. Hot kisses filled her mouth, and he exhaled his warm breath onto the back of her neck, adding to her mounting excitement and external heat. Finally, Vanessa had to shove the blanket away, her smoldering body sizzling passionately from the erotic heat burning from within.

Andrew's gaze fixed on hers, and he tenderly ran his fingers across her cheek, outlining her jaw, down the curve of her neck, and finally cupping her ample breast with his large, warm hand. His thumb made lazy circles around her sensitive, erect nipple. He covered it, sucking her breast inside his fiery hot mouth, and began lashing it with his tongue. Vanessa threw the back of her hand across her face and thrust her breast toward him.

Tonight, Andrew thought, *I want her to know this means more to me than sex.* He'd already located Vanessa's many erogenous zones, but he wanted her to feel more. He wanted her to feel the deep connection between them. His kisses became unhurried and tender, stroking her delicate skin patiently, slowly igniting her flaming core. Vanessa felt the change in his tempo and began to match it. Instead of frantically seeking sexual release, like a pair of teenagers, they intentionally cherished and aroused one another, demonstrating an unselfish expression of their love and devotion. Each one caring more about the other's gratification, than they did their own.

Ultimately both climaxed, and feeling completely spent and satisfied, they collapsed limply into each other's arms, where they remained perfectly entwined and comforted by their serene embrace. Each had spent years sleeping in solitude, but tonight they slept skin to skin, wrapped together in blissful unity.

The morning sun was pouring brightly through the window when Callie pounced on top of Andrew and Vanessa, startling them awake. The cranky cat had been up for hours, and now not only was this man once again in her place, but her breakfast was late as well.

Fully awake, Andrew looked over at Vanessa's sleepy form. He kissed her tenderly on the back of her neck, glancing cautiously over the covers at her grumpy cat. "It looks like I'm in trouble again."

Callie climbed up next to Vanessa and began purring insistently.

"Don't take it personally," she said, apologetically. "I'm afraid she's a bit spoiled. She's used to having everything on her own schedule."

Andrew climbed out of bed. "Come on cat, I have a peace offering for you." He motioned and walked toward the kitchen, stark naked.

Vanessa got up to take advantage of a few private moments of bathroom time. They'd slept in late again; she wondered briefly why Andrew hadn't rushed off to his office.

Stepping into the heavenly shower, Vanessa closed her eyes, luxuriating under the warm sensation of the water cascading over her body. She smiled privately, thinking about her secret birthday dinner last night. Even though she'd dreaded turning the age of fifty-five, she hadn't become a pumpkin. In fact she'd discovered that she had a real chance at the life she'd always dreamed of. A pair of extremely male hands suddenly reached up from behind her and fondled her breasts intimately; she shrieked before recognizing them. Then she relaxed back against Andrew's firm, naked body.

"You frightened me. You came in so quietly," she smiled, half-heartedly protesting his unannounced arrival.

"I wanted to surprise you," he murmured, nuzzling the back of her neck, turning her relaxing shower into something a little more exciting.

Giddy from his attention, she rotated around in his arms to give him a proper good-morning kiss. Lingering much longer than anticipated in the shower, they enjoyed washing, kissing, and teasing each other's bodies, until the water turned cool.

While he shaved, she towel-dried her unruly hair and frowned. "Don't you have to show up at work at any certain time?"

Andrew playfully placed a dab of shaving cream on the tip of her nose. "Actually, if you must know, I'm at work right now." He seemed amused by her question.

"What do you mean?" She cocked her head to one side.

"I'm the head of your protection team." Returning to shave, he watched her reaction in the mirror, as a wide array of emotions crossed her expressive face. She slowly wiped the shaving cream off her nose and angrily threw her towel at him.

"You mean I'm just an assignment? I'm work?"

He could see that the emotion that had settled on her face was outrage. He turned to face her, attempting to hold her arms gently at her sides, even though she fought to release herself. "You know that's not true," he soothed. "I assigned myself, because I couldn't trust anyone else to protect the one person who means the world to me." He kissed her forehead tenderly.

Vanessa stopped struggling and reluctantly rested her head on his chest. She could hear his heart beating and believed him. "I'm sorry. It's just that this thing between us seems so surreal," she whispered.

"I know sweetheart, but please trust me when I tell you, what I feel for you is real." He held her closer, gently rubbing her back until she relaxed in his arms.

Andrew had discovered that Vanessa's kitchen cupboards were noticeably bare, so after they finished dressing, they went out for brunch. He dropped her off at the hospital before he returned to his office, promising he'd cook her a spectacular dinner later. They quickly made plans to do a little grocery shopping. And, since she wasn't much of a cook, his offer to make dinner sounded delightful.

Swinging down the hall on crutches, with her physical therapist, Nikki, and a watchful officer in tow, Haley grinned when Vanessa stepped out of the elevator toting a large bag. "Hi. Did you bring me something?" Vanessa laughed at her unrestrained exuberance.

"I'll show you after you're finished. I'm impressed. Look at you, you're doing great with those crutches."

"Thanks, Nikki says I'm a natural. I haven't fallen once. The doctor says I'm doing so well he might let me go home a day earlier. Will that work for you?" Haley beamed her stunning, hopeful smile at Vanessa.

"It's fine by me. But only if the doctor says it's all right." *She'd make it work*, Vanessa thought, knowing how much Haley needed to leave the confines of the hospital.

Following close behind Haley as she walked the halls, Vanessa chatted amiably with Haley and her therapist. The physical therapist asked Vanessa if she was Haley's mother.

"I guess you missed the large invasion of my family yesterday," Haley said, laughing. "Vanessa's my friend. I'll be staying with her until I'm able to fly home."

Vanessa simply smiled, allowing Haley to explain the complicated situation.

Once Haley had returned to her bed, with her leg propped up on pillows, Vanessa presented her with her new laptop. Thrilled by the unexpected diversion, she thanked Vanessa profusely. A few hours of going over basic computer skills revealed that Haley possessed only limited experience with the technology. Finally, Vanessa helped her to video chat with her family.

They caught the entire family during dinner, including her baby brother in his high chair, all comfortably seated around a large dining room table. Haley smiled, talking in a bubbly, animated voice to each member of her family. But, as soon as she signed off and closed her laptop, her mood rapidly changed. She sat quietly, deep in thought, almost melancholy.

"Is everything all right?" Vanessa asked.

"It's nothing." She lay back in her bed and closed her eyes. "It's just..." she continued. "When I lived there, my parents never had time to have dinner with us. I always fixed dinner and fed the kids by myself. The only time we all ate together was on Sundays."

"Your parents' lives changed dramatically after you left," Vanessa said, gently attempting to explain. "They have a different life now. The only thing they're missing is you. They love you, and they desperately want you to come home with them." She reached over to gently touch Haley's shoulder, attempting to reassure her.

"I know, but it still hurts."

Vanessa hated to see her struggling with her family dynamics. She wanted her to be happy. She didn't want her to dwell on the negative, so she gave her a quick hug and changed the subject. "How would you like me to show you some fun things you can do with your computer?"

"Okay. I guess so." She didn't want to, but she felt obligated to agree.

Soon, Haley sat giggling with delight, playing computer games and exploring a variety of Internet searches that Vanessa had demonstrated. Her traumatic, impending return home was temporarily forgotten.

Andrew walked calmly into Haley's room hours later. Amused, he watched them giggle over articles they'd found on the Internet. They both seemed happy, like a couple of carefree teenagers. He remained in the doorway, quietly observing them, until Haley's face suddenly turned ashen. Frowning, she leaned closer to the computer screen. She'd inadvertently pulled up a news release regarding the bank robbery. Her startled gaze fell on a photo of Jimmy. The caption read, *Dangerous Robber Still on the Loose.* Her eyes glued to the screen, she sat transfixed by his terrifying mug shot.

Vanessa finally noticed Andrew standing in the doorway, and her panicked expression clearly said, *Help me with this.* Message received, he walked casually over toward Haley.

"Hi, I see you've been busy today." He slowly closed the computer, and seated himself in the chair next to her. "I have some news for you regarding Jimmy," he said, using a calm, reassuring tone.

Haley looked up expectantly but remained silent.

"It seems the FBI tracked Jimmy to the airport. Apparently, he left the country under an assumed name." He looked into her eyes, gauging her reaction.

"He's gone?" Haley exhaled the breath she'd been holding. "I'm safe now?"

"Yes, and yes." He smiled paternally at the young woman.

Haley stared quietly at her hands, taking a minute to process her feelings about Jimmy's disappearance. When she looked back at Andrew, her voice conveyed poise and invincible strength. "Thank you, I feel so much better knowing he won't pop into my room at any minute." She paused, processing her emotional relief. "The article I just read says the security guard is in serious condition. Can you tell me how he's doing?"

"I'm not telling the press, but he is recovering well. I understand the doctors plan to release him on Monday."

"I'm up on crutches now, could I go see him?" she asked, anxiously grabbing his arm.

"You're on crutches already?"

"Yes, I am, but I won't feel right until I see him." Haley continued to plead her case. "I need to tell him how sorry I am. He didn't deserve to be blown up by Jimmy."

Andrew hesitated to grant her request. John's face and arms were covered with burns and cuts, not a pretty sight for a young girl to see. He persuaded Haley to wait one more day. Vanessa admired how calm and cool he'd remained, even when faced with a distraught teenage girl.

"Okay Haley, will you be all right?" Vanessa touched Haley's shoulder gently. "We need to run a few errands. Would you like us to come back after dinner?"

"I'm fine. You two have a nice evening." Haley enjoyed playing matchmaker, especially since she believed they were both very lonesome people. It made her feel good to think she'd brought them together. "Thanks for the computer, Vanessa. I know it will keep me busy tonight." She opened her laptop and turned to Andrew. "Please don't forget about tomorrow. I really want to see him."

"I won't forget." He realized that she'd keep asking him, until he actually took her to see John. "I'll check on him first thing tomorrow."

They all said their goodnights, and Haley quickly returned to searching the Internet. Curious, she wanted to see what else she could find on Jimmy and the bank robbery.

Andrew and Vanessa strolled into the local supermarket, planning to fill her cupboards with sustenance. She pulled out a long list, which included a wide variety of teen-type snacks for Haley. Intent on shopping for the ingredients of the dinner he'd promised to prepare for Vanessa tonight, Andrew had his own list. He instantly took command of the cart, which left Vanessa free to search the aisles for food products she normally never consumed.

Shopping with him had been great fun, until they reached the checkout line. Vanessa knew Andrew would insist on paying for the groceries, but she refused to allow it. It was a matter of principal for her. *This food is going into my house, and I'm paying,* she thought. But of course, he remained adamant, rationalizing that since he'd been staying with her, he should pay. They seemed to be at an impasse over the issue, and neither one would budge.

"I'll make a deal with you," she said. "I'll let you pay, if you let me drive your car home."

"You know I can't legally do that." He glanced up in the air, shaking his head in frustration.

"All right then." She smiled triumphantly, sliding past him to step up to the credit card reader, and swiped her card.

Andrew wanted to be mad at her, but her little victory seemed to give her so much pleasure, he decided to let it go. *I may have lost the battle*, he thought, *but I plan to win the war.*

Once they'd arrived at Vanessa's house, Andrew insisted that she relax on the back patio with a cool glass of wine, while he unpacked the groceries and prepared dinner. She resisted half-heartedly, but eventually she kicked off her shoes, sat down on a padded chair, and propped her feet up onto the empty chair beside it.

Their little tiff over and forgotten, he handed her a glass of cold, white wine and gave her a quick kiss. Heading back to the kitchen, he finished unloading the groceries and concentrated on preparing his famous shrimp creole.

Vanessa discovered she enjoyed the unexpected solitude. Relaxing her head back on her chair, she sighed contentedly. Andrew eventually joined her on the patio, allowing them a few moments of quiet conversation while dinner baked in the oven.

Even after the final remaining rays of sunlight slowly vanished, the evening remained comfortably balmy. Feeling warm and lethargic, Vanessa decided she had no desire to move inside. Andrew readily agreed, and lighting the candle in the middle of the table, he set it for a romantic patio dinner.

"Dinner will be ready shortly," he murmured, bending down to kiss her before disappearing inside.

Sitting idly, a handsome man catering to her, felt so unnatural to Vanessa. Serenely sipping her wine, she thought, *This is nice, but I prefer being the one in charge.* Depending on others made her feel a little *too* vulnerable.

Andrew reappeared with two freshly made green salads, and set one on each of their placemats. "I'll be back in a jiffy," he said, rushing back to the kitchen. He returned shortly, carrying two plates of steaming shrimp creole smothered with melted cheese, placing them onto the table with flourish. "Voilà," he said, standing back to gloat momentarily, before sitting down beside her.

"It looks incredible," she gushed, impressed by how he'd arranged the presentation on the plate. Leaning forward, she inhaled the tantalizing aroma of tomato mixed with fragrant spices, and sampled a small bite. The perfect blend of flavors and spices caused her to exhale a moan of pleasure.

"I take it you approve?" A wide grin of relief instantly spread across his face.

Vanessa nodded with her mouth full. Smiling in pleasure, she attacked her meal with gusto. Once she'd consumed half of her plate of the savory creole, she paused to sip her wine, silently watching Andrew enjoy his meal.

Surveying the scrumptious meal he'd just prepared, Vanessa felt guilty for the childish way she'd manipulated Andrew in the store. Sitting quietly she contemplated the night, her mind mentally rehearsing a variety of unique sexual moves she could perform on him later to make amends. She pictured his riveted response to her flexibility and creativity. She felt confident, that after her performance tonight, all would be forgiven.

Chapter 15
Secret Pain

*K*ate *yawned, exhausted after staying up past two am last night. Easing back in her chair, she relaxed while her newly treated light strawberry-blond hair flowed in the gentle, late afternoon breeze. She watched with fascination as seagulls dove into the warm water beyond her secluded veranda. The last twenty-four hours had been grueling. Sipping her tropical rum drink, she sighed, silently congratulating herself on her keen intuition and flawless timing.*

She'd managed to get in and out of Jimmy's room the night before, without running into another soul. His room had been a mess. His suit and new clothes were scattered across his bed, his shaving kit strewn around the bathroom, old food and empty liquor bottles had been thrown carelessly on the floor next to his bed, and his sheets were hopelessly tangled, sagging halfway off the bed. Initially ignoring the room, she'd walked directly to the wall safe, slipped on her gloves, and opened it on the first try. She found two satchels tucked safely inside, both unlocked, their tops carelessly left open. Both were stuffed to the brim with hundred dollar bills! The bills appeared used, and looked untraceable, just as they had planned!

Knowing Jimmy wouldn't be returning, she'd cleverly staged his room to look as if he'd checked out, and removed his personal items. When she checked out later in the morning, she'd simply dropped Jimmy's keys in the drop box along with her own. No questions asked.

Kate stirred her drink and smiled, recalling how she'd cleverly contacted the realtor that Marvin had placed on her list. Last week, Marvin had informed her that he'd secured a local property to buy. The house he'd located was a hundred miles south, situated on a tiny island inhabited by only two hundred residents, many of whom were Americans. By four, she'd managed to charter a plane to the island, meet with the realtor, pay cash for the fully furnished house on the beach, and get an invitation to a local party.

Kate sighed wistfully. She wished Marvin were here, but other than that, life was good. She loved her secret new life. Savoring another sip of her mixed drink on her new veranda, she blissfully watched the sun's slow descent over the watery horizon of her new life.

Andrew fussed in the kitchen. He'd insisted that Vanessa remain seated while he cleared the table, taking complete charge of cleaning up. She sat alone in the pleasant evening air while she contemplated Andrew. Attractive, smart, kind and considerate, he was a wonderful lover, an excellent cook, and apparently loaded. *What more could any girl ask for?* She silently amused herself with his attributes, but she frowned. *He did seem a bit hardheaded at times,* she thought, but so far, *that was his only discernable flaw.* And, if she were perfectly honest, she'd have to admit people have said the same thing about her.

Andrew, up to his elbows in soapy water, could tell by the way she'd purred during dinner that he'd scored big points with Vanessa. And, after he'd slipped a few shrimps to Callie while he'd cooked, he'd also scored some bonus points with her cranky cat.

Contentedly sipping her wine, Vanessa sat in her backyard, watching the pink glow as the sun slowly set. *How wonderful it was to be pampered,* she thought. She couldn't remember the last time someone had actually taken care of her. In fact, she hadn't felt this cared for since she'd moved out of her mother's house.

Andrew seemed perfect. But something about him nagged at the back of her mind. *Why hadn't she been able to talk to him about her issues at work? Or share her birthday with him?* Instead, she'd been embarrassed, brushing off her work as a minor problem with HR. She'd been secretive, reluctant to confide in him. Her work, always her first priority, was her whole life, but she'd scarcely mentioned it. Nor had he asked.

Her thoughts faded when Andrew returned to sit with her. After a quick kiss, they quietly enjoyed the sunset and the relaxing, warm evening, sitting in companionable silence. He brought out the wine bottle and quietly refilled their wine glasses.

Curious to know more about Andrew, Vanessa set her glass down, raised one eyebrow, and asked, "Where did you grow up? Would you say you had a happy childhood?"

"I grew up in San Francisco." He didn't mind her question; in fact he thought his childhood experiences reflected an aspect of his character that would be important to share with her. "My father was a neurosurgeon, and my mother managed the house, and me of course."

He sipped his wine for fortitude before he continued. "I also had a brother, Peter, who was eight years younger. Mother spent her days on charity events, and catering to the three of us. Although my father worked long hours and rarely came home, when he was home, my mother made sure we behaved. She insisted we remained well mannered, and perfectly quiet, especially in his presence. All in all, I would have to say, I had a happy childhood."

Obviously, he had grown up privileged. *No wonder money meant so little to him*, Vanessa thought. "Where is everyone now?"

Andrew hesitated. He hated this part of his family story. "My little brother had autism. He was diagnosed when he was two—he killed himself when he turned fifteen." Vanessa gasped, immediately regretting that she'd drudged such a painful memory up for Andrew. "I'm so sorry," she whispered.

Andrew gulped down another swig of his wine. Darkness had fallen. His gaze wandered over her yard, focusing on the few solar lights Vanessa's gardeners had recently placed near the fences. He calmly deflected her pity. "It happened a long time ago." His voice sounded flat and distant. "For most of my life I've been an only child. I'd always pictured myself as having a large family of my own, sort of like Haley's." He smiled at the irony of his statement.

"My parents still live in the same house in San Francisco. Both are in their late eighties." He realized, shamefully, that he hadn't spoken with them recently. "Dad developed severe dementia," he explained. "And Mother continues to fuss and care for him. Of course, she has an extensive staff to assist with his care, allowing him to remain safely at home."

Vanessa sat quietly, afraid that anything she might say at this point might sound too trite. A dog barking somewhere off in the distance distracted her. She remembered Shep, quietly guarding the front of her house.

Andrew also knew very little of Vanessa's early years. She was such a complex, fascinating woman, he wanted to know everything about her. "What about your childhood? Were you happy?" he asked, searching her eyes for clues.

Vanessa knew none of her petty childhood tragedies compared to what he'd experienced, but she felt relieved to change the subject. "I'm an only child. My early childhood was perfect. My parents loved each other then, and they doted on me constantly." Vanessa smiled to herself, remembering how happy life had been.

"Then what happened?" He watched the wrinkles slowly form on her forehead.

"They began to argue all the time, and my dad moved to the city to stay closer to his work. I never saw him," she said, painfully. "Then one day, I discovered that he'd moved in with his secretary. They married, and had three children together. I've never met any of them." Her gaze became distant as she focused on the twinkling lights reflecting from the bottom of the pool. "He died at sixty from a massive heart attack. I never forgave him for leaving us." Tears glistened in her eyes. Andrew reached out to take her hand, offering his silent support. She gazed down at their hands interlocked on the table, feeling the full intensity of her pain, and her shameful remorse.

"What about your mother?" he asked softly.

Vanessa looked up into Andrew's sympathetic eyes "The first year after my dad left, she did nothing. She just stayed home and cried a lot. Then she got a job as a travel agent, and began dating. She tried to make my life happy, but it was never the same after Dad left us."

"Where is she now?" Andrew was curious about her relationship with her surviving parent.

"She lives with her boyfriend in the South of France." Vanessa's smile didn't reach her eyes. "She doesn't travel anymore, so I try to visit her at least once a year."

Vanessa decided, as long as they were talking about their pasts, she'd risk broaching another painful subject. "How did you meet your wife?"

Andrew knew she needed to hear about Grace, but it still hurt to talk about her. He leaned back in his chair, gathering his painful, haunting memories.

"I met my wife in San Francisco, at a fundraiser for autism. Our parents had known each other for years. It was my father who first suggested that I dance with Grace. She was so sweet and funny, and she danced as if she were dancing on a cloud, so incredibly light on her feet, almost as if she floated on air. She reminded me of the actress." He paused, lost in his memories of Grace. "After that night, we dated for several months, then with our parents' blessing, I proposed to her the following year. I officially made her Grace Kelly." Andrew smiled, remembering the inside joke they'd shared.

"We tried to begin our family right away." His smile faded, tension creased his face, and his mouth turned down into a frown. "Her father insisted that he needed a blood heir. But, after years of trying, we finally consulted an infertility specialist. Looking back, I wish I'd pushed harder for us to adopt." He sounded angry with himself. His face couldn't hide his regret and pain.

Andrew attempted to pour more wine into her glass, but she waved him off. He filled his own glass to the brim and guzzled it down. Vanessa noticed Callie pawing at the sliding door and stood to let her out. The cat immediately disappeared, hiding in the dark corners of the yard. Returning to sit with Andrew, Vanessa observed his wine glass, now sitting empty in front of him on the table.

"When you and I met for the first time, Grace had been receiving hormone injections for almost a year." She could hear the strain in his voice. "I have to say, my emotions were completely out of control. I loved my wife with all my heart, but I still had an instant, uncontrollable attraction to you. I felt guilty and confused by my unwanted feelings for you. I would never dream of hurting Grace, so I immediately handed your case off to another detective." He began to pour himself more wine, but stopped, glancing over at her instead. She saw his torment evident in his glistening, crystal blue eyes.

Vanessa thought back to that day. The only thing she remembered about Andrew, was how gentle and kind he had been to her. She'd barely escaped her husband's beating with her life, and her baby had died. She'd felt nothing except emotionally drained and numb during his routine questioning.

"What happened next?" she gently prodded.

He took a deep breath, knowing this next part was going to hurt unbearably. He struggled to put into words, for the first time, the most agonizing years of his life.

"Grace continued with those painful injections for nearly two years. I can't even begin to tell you how awful it was to stand by, watching helplessly as she suffered in dignified silence. Although she'd always smile and tried to make light of her treatments, a couple of times I caught her weeping miserably. So I arranged to take time off to be with her. I started taking her to her doctor's appointment. Afterword, I'd lead her into the rolling hills for a picnic. We'd lie together on a blanket after lunch, and I'd read to her. She loved old novels, like *Gone With The Wind* and *Wuthering Heights*." His lips curved up slightly as he remembered their bittersweet picnics amongst the wildflowers and tall grass.

"Then Grace was diagnosed with ovarian cancer." His voice changed. Vanessa could hear his thinly veiled anger as he continued, "The first course of treatment was a hysterectomy, like yours. Ending any hopes she had for a family. She was devastated. Again, I stood by and watched helplessly, as my beautiful, fragile wife suffered through multiple courses of chemo and radiation therapy. For years, we would celebrate the cure of one site of her cancer, only to have another site appear somewhere else." He ran his hand through his hair in agonized frustration.

"She tried to fight, to stay optimistic and strong, mostly for my sake." He hated how she had tried to hide her suffering. "But all the makeup in the world couldn't hide the fact that she'd been crying all day. Finally, weak and discouraged, Grace took to her bed. She insisted that I continue to work. She couldn't control the cancer, so she tried to control everything else, including her medical care, and me." He heaved a regretful sigh.

A sudden gust of wind blew a napkin off the table and Vanessa bent down to retrieve it. Andrew sat still, his eyes closed in pain, remembering how she had suffered pointlessly. Grace had been such a good person. He was the one who'd deserved to suffer, not her.

"The last ten years of her life, she lived in constant pain." His voice changed, sounding oddly distant and detached. "The cancer we thought the chemotherapy had under control, eventually spread everywhere. She chose to suffer, hating the feeling of being drugged up with pain medications all the time, so I could only kiss her lightly, on her lips." He reached up to demonstrate, gently placing his finger to his lips. "Touching her anywhere else caused her excruciating pain. I would sit next to her bed, with the back of my hand resting close to the back of her hand. She would struggle to lift her hand and place it on mine. I knew if I reached out to help, I would only hurt her." He ran his agitated hands through his hair, barely holding himself together. "In the end, she didn't even recognize me, but everything went as she'd planned. She slipped into a coma, and I never left her side."

Vanessa sat still, absorbing the pain from his tortured memories. Neither of them spoke; they sat together in silence within the dark shadows of the warm night. Vanessa waited patiently, and wondered if he would, or even could continue talking about Grace.

"I remember the night she died." Andrew stared out into the darkness, struggling to control his quivering voice. "Her breathing would stop, and her breaths became farther and farther apart. So I wrapped her in a comforter, scooped her frail, ravaged body up off the bed, and held her gently on my lap. We sat in an overstuffed rocking chair, with her head resting on my chest. I hummed the first waltz we ever danced to while I rocked her. Grace always claimed it was our song." He smiled, recalling her steadfast assertion.

Vanessa cringed as Andrew relived the ghastly details of Grace's death. He appeared to be relating them in a trance, unable to stop, unaware of her presence, or her horrified reaction.

"Her breathing became a mere wisp of air. I kissed the top of her head and told her it was all right, I would always love her, but she should go. She exhaled once, and never inhaled again." Vanessa placed both her hands on her chest, covering her breaking heart. Andrew looked so pale; his drawn-out misery seemed so intolerable.

"She was gone, but I held her tight, the first time I'd been able to do that in years. Her agony had finally ended. Selfishly, I knew mine had as well. I wouldn't have to sit and watch her suffer anymore." Andrew paused. Vanessa, stunned by the depth of his grief, remained wide-eyed and silent.

"I don't know how long I sat there." His voice became a ghostly whispery. "I just kept rocking her. Eventually, the nurse talked me into returning Grace to her bed. I left her room completely dazed. I don't know how I made it to my own room, but I slept for two days straight."

Andrew sat quietly, trying to sort through his feelings and rein in the intensity of his emotional heartache. He hadn't heard Vanessa get up, but he welcomed her sweet touch. She cradled his head against her warm body and ran her fingers lightly through his hair. He looked up at her, teary-eyed, and saw that her face dripped with her own unrestrained tears. Wrapping his arms around her body, he wept.

Andrew held on tight to Vanessa, realizing that he finally thought of his marriage in the past tense. Although he would always love Grace, he had finally achieved a long-awaited sense of peace, freeing him to look forward to his future. He stood up, kissed Vanessa, and led her silently to a nearby hammock. Resting on his back in the hammock, Vanessa lying in his arms, they listened serenely to the crickets and bullfrogs chanting in the night. The air remained warm and still. Andrew inhaled the sweet fragrance of the honeysuckle hanging from the overhead trellis, exhaling the remaining echoes of his overshadowing grief.

Andrew's emotional release had come as a direct result of confiding in Vanessa about his feelings for Grace. Now he remembered his first encounter with Vanessa without any of his previous feelings of shame. He played with her hair and wondered what could have attracted Vanessa to her abusive husband. "I know how your marriage ended, Vanessa, but how did your relationship begin?"

Caught off guard, Vanessa wasn't prepared to talk about her ex-husband. "We met in college—", she began and hesitated. "We studied for our first midterm together and then remained friends," she recalled vaguely. "We dated our senior year and moved into a house together, along with a couple of my girlfriends. We're both only children, raised primarily by single mothers. When his mother had a terrible stroke, and was placed into a rehabilitation center to convalesce, he became distraught. She rapidly deteriorated, and by the time we'd graduated, she didn't even remember who he was."

"Umm," Andrew murmured passively in her ear. He had a hard time working up any sympathy for the bastard who'd destroyed Vanessa's life.

"After graduation, we both had big plans. I'd been working as an intern at *Gemma* magazine, and was asked to officially join their advertising team. He'd graduated with a degree in civil engineering, and accepted a two-year commitment to work in the Middle East. Besides his generous salary, they agreed to pay off all his student loans. It seemed like a good deal at the time." Vanessa's acrid voice added sarcastically.

"On graduation day, I think he suddenly panicked. He realized he had nothing to return home to, and asked me to marry him. Since I believed we were in love, I agreed. We were married right away, and then we both went our separate ways to start our careers."

Andrew puzzled over the casual way she talked about newlyweds having such a long separation. "And you were okay? I mean, not seeing each other again for two years?"

"We were both very busy." Vanessa suddenly realized how callous it all sounded. "We video chatted every Sunday, and wrote when we could." She went on, attempting to justify her decision. "But I know what you mean; the answer is, we didn't see it as a problem." Vanessa listened to herself trying to rationalize her thinking. Maybe she had loved the idea of being married more than she'd loved the person she had actually married.

"Anyway," she continued. "My career progressed right on track. I got noticed for my accomplishments, which put me in line for a major promotion. I enjoyed living on my own." She smiled to herself.

"His mother died the week before he came home. When he finally arrived, I immediately noticed how much he'd changed. I'd arranged for a couple weeks of vacation time to spend with him, to reconnect."

Vanessa gazed across her yard to where her favorite maple tree had once stood. She'd placed her baby's ashes at the base of that tree when she'd planted it as a sapling. For years she'd watched the leaves change colors with the seasons. She'd sat on the bench next to her tree and spent hours talking to her only child. Bitterness swelled in her heart when she thought about her ex-husband.

"The trouble began when I went back to work and he didn't have a job." She'd just realized the correlation and frowned. "Drunk all day long, he'd rant and accuse me of having affairs with the men I worked with. At first, he was just verbally abusive, but then it turned physical. I begged him to get help. I even set up appointments for him, but he never went." Her angry tears soaked through the front of Andrew's shirt.

"His physical abuse escalated," she sobbed, and Andrew silently fumed. "The day I found out I was pregnant, I went to a lawyer to file a restraining order and divorce him." She shivered in his arms. "I planned to raise my child alone. But I returned home to find him in a drunken, jealous rage. I didn't hesitate. As soon as I could escape from him, I locked myself in the bathroom and called 911. I guess you already know how that ended." She buried her face in his shoulder to hide from her bitter memories.

Andrew pulled her close and tenderly kissed her. "I'm so sorry you felt you had to deal with your husband alone," he whispered.

"I felt ashamed." Vanessa took a strengthening breath. "In fact, I did everything within my power to hide what was going on. The lawyer was the only person I told." She squeezed her eyes closed, trying to forget her nasty history, focusing on Andrew's warm, comforting embrace instead.

"Even now, you and Haley are the only people in my life who know the whole story." She laughed at the absurdity of the lie she'd used on her mother during her recovery. "My mother thinks I fell down a flight of stairs."

He smiled, hearing her return to her tough self. He wanted to know more. He hugged her close against him to help her feel safe enough to finish.

"I testified at his hearing, primarily because I wanted everyone to know how he'd killed our baby, and destroyed my future." He could hear the injustice in her voice. "He received one year in a minimum-security facility, and had court-ordered treatments for his post traumatic stress disorder. I have no idea why he had it, and frankly I don't care." She seethed with anger at the light sentence he'd received for killing her baby.

"Where is he now?"

"I've never spoken to him, but believe it or not," she snorted. "I heard he runs an alcohol and drug rehab center for teens. Our friends tell me he's happily remarried and raising four perfect children."

Andrew held his tongue. There seemed to be nothing left for him to say. Astounded by the ease with which she'd opened up about her violent marriage, Vanessa realized that all these years of keeping it a secret had allowed it to eat away at her insides, making her feel unworthy. Talking to Andrew made it seem more like a tragic episode in her past. Neither Haley nor Andrew had judged her. In fact, once she'd openly talked about it, the violent story of her past seemed to have lost its power. It no longer controlled or humiliated her.

Andrew wrapped his arms around her, snuggling her close to him as they relaxed together in the hammock. She could smell the Old Spice deodorant he used and it reminded her nostalgically of happy times spent with her father as a child. They lay snuggled in each other's arms, silently accepting their painful pasts. The honest, emotional release they experienced, quietly opening their hearts to the possibility of sharing a new love.

Completely cocooned together inside the hammock, Vanessa and Andrew lay spent and emotionally drained. The warm night air covered them like a comforting blanket and lulled them into a peaceful sleep. Slumbering in each other's arms, they discovered the strength of their reassuring love had finally allowed the painful ghosts from their past to depart, and rest in peace at last.

Chapter 16
Pretty Butterfly

S lowly awakening, Vanessa sat up, struggling awkwardly with the unsteady hammock beneath her. Shielding her eyes from the sunlight, she looked down at Andrew asleep beside her. *Had they actually slept the entire night outside?* Hearing Shep's insistent barking from the front yard, she instantly identified the sound that had aroused her. Andrew felt the hammock rock and reached up blindly, pulling her back against him for a sleepy good-morning kiss. Distracted by Andrew's caress, it took Vanessa a few minutes to clear her head enough to realize why Shep continued to bark.

"Oh no, what time is it?" she asked frantically.

Andrew rubbed his blurry eyes, attempting to focus on his watch. "Wow, it's nine thirty."

Vanessa scrambled to get up as gracefully as she could without falling head long out of the hammock. Instinctively, Andrew reached out his hand to steady her for a safe descent.

"My car must be here," she panicked. "Remember? My makeover is today."

"I think you're fine the way you are. Tell him to go away." Andrew laughed, stretching his arms lazily over his head.

"I'm sorry, but I really must go." Perturbed, she attempted to smooth her disheveled clothes, turning her head in the direction of Shep's agitated barking. "I'll just go tell him I'll be ready in a minute or two."

"I'll go," Andrew said, instantly rolling out of the hammock and standing nimbly on his feet. "You go get ready. How long should I say?"

"Give me fifteen minutes," Vanessa called over her shoulder, running toward the back door.

"Got it." Andrew placed his hands on his hips and stretched his low back; maneuvering to straighten out a few of the kinks he'd acquired sleeping in the hammock. Cautiously, he rounded the corner of Vanessa's house. Walking toward the front driveway, he approached an unknown black town-car with a middle-aged man leaning casually against the hood, curiously eyeing his agitated dog. *Vanessa was far too trusting*, Andrew thought.

"Can I help you?" Andrew inquired, advancing confidently toward him as he quieted Shep's barking with a single commanding glance.

"Hi, I'm Tom. I'm here to pick up Ms. Golden," he explained amiably, reaching out to shake Andrew's hand. The presence of both the barking dog and the imposing man confused Tom. He'd never encountered anyone at Vanessa's house before.

"Nice to meet you, Tom. Do you have any identification?" Andrew asked, reaching out suspiciously for his ID.

"Yes, of course, but I *am* Ms. Golden's regular driver." Tom quickly reached for his ID, flustered by Andrew's abrupt interrogation.

"I'm Detective Kelly," he said, using his official tone in a mild attempt to intimidate Tom. "I'm sure everything's fine, but it's my job to make sure."

Andrew was carefully examining Tom's driver's license, when Vanessa appeared in the doorway. She laughed at the absurdity of the scene.

"Andrew, please stop harassing Tom, or we'll be late for my appointment."

Tom's face relaxed when he saw Vanessa. His discomfort caused by the imposing man's overbearing presence instantly subsided at the sight of her. Tom assumed he was her security guard, but wondered why she needed one.

Andrew turned away and smiled, noticing how pretty and fresh she looked, and went to her side. Helping her into the waiting car, he gave her a quick, proprietary kiss on the cheek.

"Don't let them change you too much. Love you," he whispered.

Still smiling, Vanessa waved Andrew away, feeling awkward under Tom's covert scrutiny. *That man was definitely not her security guard*, Tom thought, as he glanced at them in his rearview mirror. Amused, Andrew sensed Vanessa's embarrassment with his flagrant display of affection, and flashed her a wicked grin while he slowly closed her door.

After he watched the car pull leisurely out of the driveway, Andrew returned inside to settle into Vanessa's cozy kitchen with an invigorating cup of coffee. His secretary had called to inform him that he'd missed several calls, including one from the FBI. Thinking of the full day he had ahead of him, he remembered his promise to Vanessa, and silently vowed to spend some quality time with Haley in her absence. He worried that the minute he visited with Haley, she'd demand an audience with John. He felt protective of her innocent sensitivities. John's face had been hideously burnt in the explosion, and he wasn't sure how she'd handle seeing him. But he realized he couldn't postpone granting her request forever.

171

Callie and Shep had fallen back to sleep. The house was quiet and felt peaceful. Andrew finished his coffee in solitude before he headed down the hall. A few more private moments of hygiene, and he'd be passable for the office.

In the warm late-morning sun, surprisingly excited and ahead of schedule, Vanessa arrived in downtown LA. The car pulled up to the curb in front of a busy, well-known Rodeo Drive department store, not too far from her office. The formally dressed security guard at the front door directed her to a receptionist tucked in the back corner of the swanky store.

The elegant, stylishly dressed receptionist escorted Vanessa to a private elevator. Stepping into the confined space, soft piano music drifted pleasantly to her ears. Inhaling deeply, she noticed a subtle fragrance, easily identified as expensive perfume and rug shampoo, filling the lavish, red-carpeted elevator. The tall, blond receptionist inserted a key card and they rose to the top floor. When they arrived, she personally escorted Vanessa to René's secluded, tastefully decorated office.

René waltzed into the room and introduced himself as *the* stylist to the stars. An older man, he wore a dark, pinstriped suit, with a contrasting, pale lavender silk shirt left open at the neck. A matching lavender silk scarf, tied loosely around his throat, completed his chic look. He had neatly trimmed graying hair with a crop of tight brown curls nestled on top of his head, and a ponytail hanging down his back.

René bent at the waist to briefly air-kiss her hand. Vanessa watched him with fascination. René's flamboyant personality and mannerisms made his diminutive size seem larger than life to her. She found him utterly charming.

René straightened and immediately proceeded to inspect her. Walking slowly around her as she stood, he occasionally hummed as he carefully scrutinized every aspect of her body. Examining her from each and every angle, he studied her as if she were a priceless piece of art. Feeling intensely self-conscious during his close analysis, Vanessa began involuntarily fussing with her hair and pulling at her dress. She'd worn a casual sundress with minimal makeup. René clucked his tongue as he lifted a strand of her dyed, dark auburn hair. Finally, he clasped his hands together and began to review aloud his plans for her makeover.

"First, we will work on a new look for your hair and makeup." He tapped a finger on his lips. "Next you'll have a mani-pedi. I plan to develop a new style of clothing just for you. You'll need something to wear for every occasion. I hope you have cleared your schedule for the entire day." It was more of a command than a question.

"Yes. Actually I'm officially on vacation." Vanessa gulped at his elaborate plans. *What have I done?*

"Excellent. All right, let's get going." René swept his perfectly manicured, ringed hands up before him, clasping them together in front of his chin. "I promise you, Vanessa, you will not regret coming to René for your transformation."

"Marie recommended you, so I'll place my complete trust in you." Amused by his confidence, she found his exuberance and enthusiasm positively contagious.

René escorted her into a private salon with only a single barber-style chair positioned in the middle of the room. She searched the walls and quickly noticed the lack of mirrors. "Is there a reason you don't have any mirrors in this room?" Vanessa couldn't resist asking.

"Don't worry, my dear." René smiled. "Sometimes it's very difficult for our clients to embrace their new look while it's developing. We've found it's much easier for them to wait and see the finished product. All will be revealed to you in good time, but not until after your hair and makeup are complete." As he spoke, he gestured with his hands. The passion he demonstrated reminded Vanessa of a dramatic orchestra conductor, which she found slightly unnerving. Following his sweeping arm direction, she sat cautiously down in the chair. René quickly sensed her apprehension and hesitance to relinquish control over the current situation.

"You must trust me." He walked up behind her, placing his hands lightly on her shoulders and bent around to gaze at her face. "No one has ever left here unhappy."

Vanessa smiled and nodded. *What's the worst that can happen?* she thought.

Returning the call from the FBI, Andrew sat at his desk clicking his pen. A gruff FBI agent briefly informed him that both Jimmy and Kate had been traced to the same South American town. In addition, Jimmy, having engaged in a bar fight shortly after his arrival, was now deceased. As for Kate, an undercover agent currently had her under close observation, shadowing her every move. They couldn't extradite her, but they could watch her. Andrew thanked the agent for keeping him in the loop. Leaning back in his chair, Andrew sighed. Now he could relax and release Haley's protection detail. Any imminent threat from Jimmy or Kate was over.

Next on his agenda, Andrew met with the DA. Considering the current circumstances of the case, he readily agreed to drop all charges against Haley, and she was free to go home as soon as she wanted. Andrew called Haley's mother to give her the good news. June once again thanked him profusely.

Winding things up at his office, Andrew prepared to head to the hospital, but delayed, waiting for a call from John's doctor.

"Detective, I just wanted to let you know that John has developed a severe case of pneumonia as a result of the charring in his lungs during the explosion. We've had to put him back on the respirator, and truthfully, given his age, I'm not sure he's going to recover." His voice conveyed his discouragement. "I wanted to let you know, in case you had any more questions for him. Right now, he's alert enough to respond, but his condition is rapidly deteriorating," the doctor warned.

Andrew thanked him for the information and hurried to the hospital. He had no further questions for John, but he knew he had to keep his promise to Haley while he still could.

Andrew approached Haley's room and immediately re-assigned her protection detail to another case before entering.

"Where have you been?" she demanded. "I've been waiting all day for you to take me to see John!"

"Look, I'm sorry." Andrew smiled at Haley's pouty face, holding his hands up in surrender. "I promise, I came as soon as I could." He walked closer to the bedside. "Actually," he said, his tone becoming serious, "I just stopped by to tell you that John has taken a turn for the worse. He's back in the ICU. I'll have to go check on him first. They may not let you in to see him. Usually they limit ICU visitors to immediate family only."

"It's all my fault," Haley wailed, instantly bursting into tears. "I have to see him. I have to tell him how sorry I am," she pleaded.

"I'll see what I can do." Andrew struggled with her sudden emotional shift from anger to despair. He paused, overwhelmed by her emotional outburst, then turned on his heels and left Haley's room, desperate to grant her urgent emotional plea before it was too late.

Andrew arrived in the ICU to find John awake and responsive, but breathing tubes connected him to a respirator, leaving him unable to speak. His granddaughter sat close beside him, solemnly holding his hand. Andrew felt intrusive as he approached them and waited awkwardly on the other side of the bed. He leaned over the bedrail to speak to John directly.

"I'm so sorry you've had to return to the ICU." Andrew had known the kindly old man for many years and his sympathetic gaze expressed his true remorse. "And, I'm also sorry that I need to ask you for a favor." The man's eyes encouraged him to continue. "The young lady you met in the bank, Haley? She would like very much to see you."

John smiled with recognition and nodded his consent. His granddaughter silently motioned for Andrew to step out into the hall with her.

"Please tell Haley she's welcome." Smiling, she continued emphatically. "If my grandfather hadn't been following her, I'm sure he would have died in that explosion."

Andrew, relieved by their reception, returned to Haley. He stood just inside her door and watched helplessly as Haley sat sobbing in her bed. She covered her face with her hands and refused to look at up him when he spoke.

"It's all set. They agreed to have you come to the ICU for a visit." When she failed to respond, he quietly walked over to her bed and patted her back in a feeble effort to console her.

"Oh Andrew, they must hate me," she wept, keeping her face covered by her hands and refusing to look at him.

"Actually, they don't." Andrew withdrew his hand while he attempted to reason with her. "They want to thank you. John's granddaughter credits the fact that he was following you out the door as saving him from the full impact of the explosion. Now dry your tears, let's go now, before he falls asleep," he said pragmatically, handing her a tissue.

Haley lifted her head, sniffled, and quickly wiped her face. Andrew helped her into the wheelchair and checked out with her nurse. Once they were alone in the elevator, he prepared her for all of John's tubes, and warned her about the nasty, reddened burn marks on his face. Haley promised she'd stay calm and keep her visit short. Looking up with sad, watery eyes, she thanked Andrew for making the visit possible.

Tears of shame silently flowed down Haley's face when Andrew wheeled her beside John's bed. Reaching out timidly, she gently lifted his frail, red, blistered hand, placing it gently within her own. Although Andrew had warned her, the elderly man's blistering burns, along with the ominous sound of the intermittent hissing of his respirator, alarmed her.

"I'm so, so sorry, I know this is all my fault. I should have called the police, I should have saved everyone in the bank." Remorsefully, she bowed her head in humiliation and regret.

John sadly watched her tears fall for a moment, and then reaching his hand out, he gently raised her chin to look into her eyes. Unable to speak, the respirator periodically swishing in the background, he beseeched her with his eyes while he slowly shook his head. His granddaughter spoke up on his behalf.

"My grandfather knows about your situation." She smiled kindly. "He doesn't blame you at all. He knows you were doing the best you could. It would hurt him deeply if he thought you might be suffering because of what happened to him. We're both extremely grateful for you, Haley. You saved his life!" She turned and smiled affectionately at her grandfather, who nodded his agreement.

"I'm so sorry. Please forgive me," Haley whispered. She reached up and softly captured his hand cradling her chin, turned it over and kissed the back of John's frail, burnt hand. Humbled by their kindness, she smiled weakly toward his granddaughter.

John squeezed her hand, and then Andrew slowly backed her wheelchair out of the ICU. He waited quietly while Haley processed the fact that she'd just been forgiven.

When they reached her room, Haley frowned, noticing an immediate change. "Where's my guard? Even his chair's gone!"

"You don't need him any more." Andrew calmly pushed her into her room. "Let's get you settled in bed. I have a lot to tell you."

She'd barely climbed in, when her nurse brought in her medications. Andrew stood by the window to wait. After the nurse left, Haley sent Andrew a very appreciative look.

"Thank you for taking me to John." She had watched Andrew pace the room waiting to talk. "I feel a little better now. I really hope he makes it." She paused, placing her hands together on her lap. "Now tell me, what's changed? How come I don't need my guard?"

"Primarily, the level of imminent danger has changed," he explained, pulling his chair next to the bed. "The FBI discovered that both Jimmy and Kate have fled the country. So you see, they're no longer of any threat to you."

Haley considered this new information briefly. "So, where are they?"

Andrew reached up to rub the back of his stiff neck, considering how to approach the next delicate subject. He wished Vanessa could be here for this next part. She'd know how to handle Haley's unpredictable, emotional response.

"Jimmy and Kate both ended up in a small town in South America," he continued cautiously. "And...apparently Jimmy died in a bar fight the day after he arrived." He studied her face, watching intently for her response.

Haley sat quietly while she methodically wrung her hands together in her lap. He gently placed his hand over hers, in an attempt to soothe her mounting unease. "Haley? Are you okay?"

"Of course. What about that woman?" Her voice sounded listless and distant.

"She's being followed by an FBI agent." He exhaled the breath he hadn't been aware he'd been holding; he really didn't want to discuss Jimmy, or explore Haley's feelings about his death. "Neither of them can hurt you now," he added reassuringly. "You're safe. That's why I let your guard leave."

Haley hunched her shoulders with relief. It was difficult for her to believe that she could finally feel safe. Trancelike, she remained absolutely still, staring down at her lap, until Andrew began to wonder if she had slipped into a mild state of shock.

"Haley?" he asked cautiously.

"Is there anything else I should know?" She snapped out of her daze almost as quickly as she'd lapsed, but failed to lift her head or make eye contact with him.

"The DA won't be pressing any charges against you." Andrew said calmly, relieved that she seemed to be responding to him again. "He says you're free to go home to your family. I called your mom this morning. She'll make arrangements with Vanessa for your return home. She seemed extremely pleased by the news."

"Umm, home." Haley's hands began fidgeting again.

Andrew really wished Vanessa were here! Haley seemed to lapse back into deep thought. She stared down at her hands silently, making no further effort to converse with him.

When Vanessa was finally allowed to look in a mirror, she didn't recognize the person who looked back at her. Her hair was now fashioned in a short, perky style. Her previously dark auburn hair now shimmered several shades lighter with glowing highlights. *René is a genius.* There's no way she could have watched them cutting off her hair. But, she had to admit the results were absolutely unbelievable.

The makeup artist had spent a lot of time teaching her how to apply both her daytime and nighttime looks. She glanced in complete awe at her new makeup case, stocked full of every cream, blush, lipstick, or shadow she'd ever need or want. She couldn't believe how much effort it took to create such a subtle look. Leaning closer to the mirror to inspect her face, she tried to discern any sign that makeup had actually been applied. She swore she looked fifteen years younger!

The day had flown by, even though they'd explored clothing designs for hours. René loved the way his fresh, unique styles flattered her well-toned, petite figure. He'd carefully coached her on her new professional style, and even discussed the importance of projecting a mature, experienced image with just the right attitude of confidence.

When René had finished with her, he pronounced her 'a beautiful butterfly.' He insisted she toss out her shabby sundress. Instead, he dressed her in sleek daytime glamour to match her new stylish flair. He insisted that she toss out all of her old clothes once she arrived home. Tomorrow a truckload of freshly designed clothes, shoes and accessories would be delivered to her home, completing her total transformation.

Smoothing down her new soft, linen, tapered pants, Vanessa turned from the mirror and placed a quick kiss of gratitude on his cheek. She left René feeling rejuvenated both inside and out. Incredibly, he'd helped her rediscover the confidence she'd felt when was she was much younger.

Bursting with enthusiasm and excitement, she couldn't wait tell someone, so she called Marie on her chauffeured drive home. "I cannot thank you enough!"

"I take it you enjoyed your day with René?" Marie chuckled, thrilled by the zest and exuberance expressed by her conservative boss.

"I swear," Vanessa exclaimed, looking down at her new shoes, "I think he gave me some kind of magic tonic! I look and feel fifteen years younger. In fact, I didn't look this young back then!"

"Well, I'm glad he met your expectations." Marie smiled to herself, quickly deciding not to spoil Vanessa's good mood by filling her in on the recent office turmoil.

"Frankly, I thought I would hate such a drastic makeover. But honestly, I can't remember when I've felt this good about myself. I still can't believe the way he made me look. Can you sneak out of the office to meet me?"

"Actually... now is not such a good time for me." Marie hesitated uncharacteristically. "Stay beautiful, I promise I'll see you when you return, if not sooner."

"All right." Vanessa sensed something was wrong, but she didn't want to know right now, and forced herself to curb her natural curiosity. "Call me if you need me, otherwise, I'll see you when I get back. Thanks again, I owe you."

"You're welcome. Have fun with your new hunk." Marie couldn't resist teasing her. After she hung up, Marie shook her head with regret. She should have told Vanessa everything!

Andrew sat quietly next to Haley. Unsure of what to say or do, he remained awkwardly silent. After a few moments, Haley asked him to hand her the laptop, explaining she wanted to video chat with her mother. After he complied, he took the hint and excused himself from her room. When he reached the door, he heard her unusually subdued voice.

"Thank you, Andrew, for everything you've done for me. I've always felt safe when you've been around."

Andrew nodded to her and walked out the door. Something about her voice felt off to him. It felt like she'd just said her final goodbye. Frustrated by his inability to read her emotions, he decided to stay close to her room, at least until Vanessa arrived.

Andrew had been sitting across from Haley's room, keeping watch and waiting impatiently for Vanessa's return, for what seemed like hours. Glancing down the hall, he noticed a beautiful, exuberant woman stepping off the elevator, rushing down the hall, directly toward him. He quickly did a double take. "Vanessa?"

"Oh, hi, what do you think?" She twirled in front of him.

He'd been reluctant for her to change, fearing she'd be unhappy with the results. But she looked gorgeous! She wore cream-colored linen pants with a sophisticated, pale peach lace blouse and a creamy, light linen jacket. The subtle shades flattered her petite figure, and highlighted the peach color of her lip-gloss and fingernails. Her high

179

heels, sassy short hair, and the polished glow on her face made her irresistible. He walked closer to her, without physically touching her.

"You look stunning!" His voice dropped to a low, sensual tone. "Lady, you take my breath away."

"Sweet talk will get you everywhere," she said, her sexy voice mimicking his low, husky tone. His overtly masculine response to her appearance made her feel feminine and desirable. Glancing around them, she noticed they were conspicuously located in a very public space, but she reached up to him anyway, placing her hands intimately on his warm, expansive chest.

Andrew smiled seductively. Stepping back, he grabbed her by the hand and led her into the nearest empty room. He pulled her into his arms, consumed with wanting her, and kissed her parted lips with all of the pent-up passion he'd been harboring since their abrupt parting from the hammock this morning. Drawing her close, his hands resting protectively on the small of her back, he pulled her tightly against him. Their kiss deepened. Tenderly he ran his warm hands up her tingling spine until her soft, feminine sigh had him shivering with need, instantly melting him into a mindless pool of yearning desire.

Lingering emotions they'd shared the night before weighed heavily on his mind. Long after they broke off their kiss, Andrew held her close, burying his face into her newly styled hair, savoring the sweet, feminine perfume of her recent makeover. Momentarily lost in a sea of pleasure, her body nestled against his, he'd temporarily forgotten all about his concern for Haley. Suddenly remembering Haley's unusual behavior, he cleared his throat, while attempting to clear his mind.

"Listen," he whispered in her ear. "I could take you right here, right now." Andrew noted the telltale flush of arousal on her beautiful face and forced himself to avert his gaze. "But we need to talk about Haley." Reluctantly he broke their embrace and took a step away from Vanessa.

She could tell he was serious, so she sat down and silently waited for him to explain. Andrew's concern for Haley caused him to pace as he reviewed the events of the day with her, including Jimmy's untimely demise.

She listened carefully, saddened and concerned about John's condition, but silently relieved by his response to Haley. But she quickly understood why Andrew was worried about Haley. Her boyfriend was dead, she clearly didn't know if she wanted to go home, and they both knew Haley didn't always make the best decisions. When he'd finished, she moved back into his embrace, wrapping her arms around him appreciatively. "You're such an incredibly good and decent person. I'm glad you stayed close to watch over Haley. I think I know what's going on with her. I'll try to talk to her, and see if I can't talk her off her emotional ledge."

"Thank you, I knew you'd know how to handle the situation." He sighed in relief and pressed his lips softly against hers. Hesitantly forcing themselves apart, they walked toward Haley's room together.

Haley's door was propped open when they arrived, and one quick glance at the empty bed confirmed their worst fear.

Haley had disappeared!

Chapter 17
Sorrows Run Deep

V anessa rapidly searched the adjoining bathroom for Haley. Fortunately, a nurse's aide came in to make the bed and casually informed them that Haley was downstairs in Physical therapy. They immediately went to check on her.

Seeing Haley through the glass window, they heaved a huge sigh of relief in unison. Silently they watched, as Haley walked between two parallel bars, squinting her eyes while she concentrated on her balance.

"How about I let you spend some quality time with Haley?" he suggested after a minute or two, deciding it was time for him to return to his office.

"Of course. Can you pick me up later? I had Tom drop me off." Vanessa sympathized and understood his need to get away. He looked haggard and he'd obviously had enough teenage drama for one day.

Andrew smiled as he stepped closer to her, placing his hands intimately on her hips. "What time would madam be wanting to return to her mansion?"

"I'll be ready when you are." She swatted him lightly on the shoulder for teasing her.

"It seems I'm always ready, when you're around." He wrapped her in a loving embrace. "Tonight, will be our last night alone together for a while. I plan to make it memorable. Call me when you're ready to leave." He kissed her, sending her a deep, soulful look, his eyes drinking in her distinctive beauty.

"I'll call you later." She pushed him away lightly.

Andrew walked to the elevator. Stopping, he pushed the button and waited, glancing back at her in adoring appreciation before disappearing through the sliding doors.

Vanessa sat in a chair outside the therapy room to wait. She tried to remember herself at seventeen, as she thought about things she could say to persuade Haley that everything would be okay. She cared about her, but Haley needed to go home to her family and resolve her issues with her parents. Only then would she be able to enter into her adult life guilt free, without any lingering regrets. Vanessa struggled to formulate the right approach to use. She needed one that would make it seem like Haley had made up her own mind. Vanessa shook her head, feeling out of her element. She knew plenty of strategies for manipulating her clients, but this was different, this was far more personal.

Still reflecting on her approach, Haley interrupted when she walked out into the hallway, demonstrating how quickly she'd become an expert with her crutches. Beaming with pride, she confidently approached Vanessa's chair. Her eyes lit up and she smiled appreciatively at the sight of the "new" Vanessa.

"How did your therapy go?" Vanessa asked.

"I hardly recognized you. You look incredible!"

"Do you really like it? Tell the truth." Vanessa laughed at Haley's response to her new look. Hamming it up for her, she pumped up her hair like a movie star.

"Are you kidding? I love it! Has Andrew seen you yet?" Haley laughed.

"Yes, he was very flattering." She tried to downplay Andrew's smoldering reaction. "But I really wanted *your* honest opinion."

"It makes you look younger and fiery hot! In fact, I'm surprised Andrew let you out of his sight." Haley smiled, touched that her opinion seemed to matter so much to Vanessa. "Did he tell you everything? You know about Jimmy and the security guard?" she asked. Haley's mood went from jazzed to miserable in record time. Vanessa knew how emotionally torn she was by Jimmy's untimely death, and her guilt regarding the security guard's critical condition.

"Yes, he told me." She decided to ignore Haley's fluctuating emotional reaction for the moment, and tried to keep her in a positive mindset. "It looks like you'll be able leave the hospital by tomorrow. You're doing great on those crutches."

"I can concur with that," Haley's physical therapist said, walking up behind them. "She's mastered everything she needs to go home. I'm sure the doctor will discharge her later this evening, or first thing tomorrow morning."

"Vanessa? Can you handle having me invade your space a day sooner than you'd planned?" Haley smiled, reveling in the prospect of leaving the hospital.

"Are you kidding?" Vanessa was thrilled. "All my new outfits will be arriving tomorrow. I could really use a female point of view. That man had me under some kind of spell. I still can't believe I agreed with everything he suggested. Now, I'm not so sure. Will you help me? I need someone to be completely truthful and help me decide how much of it to keep."

"I can hardly wait," Haley laughed, caught up in Vanessa's excitement. "I love what you're wearing now, those cream-colored slacks with heels make you look taller, and I'm sure the rest of your outfits will be just as spectacular."

Haley chatted nonstop as they traveled the halls to her room. The physical therapist said goodbye to them as soon as they stepped off the elevator on Haley's floor.

"You know? I'm really looking forward to having you as a roommate for the next week," Vanessa confessed. "I hope it will be as much fun for you as it will be for me."

"You're the best! I can't believe you're willing to take me in like this. After all, we're practically strangers." Haley sensed the ease of her sincere hospitality. She had a sudden insight regarding Vanessa's lonely life. After all, Callie wasn't much of a talker.

Vanessa thought about Haley's comment as she helped her into bed. "You know, it's hard to explain, but since we first met, I've felt a deep connection to you. Maybe I see a little of my younger self in you, but every time I do something nice for you, it feels like I'm doing it for myself. Just being with you makes me feel happy, and hopeful again. I've been traveling down the wrong path, mostly out of sheer fear, for a very long time now. Your strength has given me the courage and inspiration I needed to make some very difficult changes in my life."

"You mean like your fabulous new look?" Haley frowned, confused by Vanessa's confession.

Vanessa remained thoughtfully quiet before she replied. "Yes, but it's more about the changes in who I am inside, than my outward appearance. I've been in the same rut for a long time, constantly taking the easy path. Every day has been exactly like the day before. For years and years, I've been the same. I haven't vacationed, spent time with my friends, developed any close relationships, or really taken any pleasure in my life. I've been completely focused on my work. I've always done exactly what I thought I should do, instead of what I wanted, or desired. In fact, I've never given a single thought to what I actually wanted or needed."

Haley considered Vanessa's confession, and decided she might be able to help her. "Fine, I'll help you with your radical transformation, and you can help me to feel normal again."

"Believe me, you're already perfectly normal. You've just had a rough couple of years." Vanessa felt a familiar, sympathetic pull towards Haley. "Being home with your family will make the past few years fade away."

"I'm not sure I can go home," she said, softly. "Their lives are so different from mine. We've grown too far apart. In many ways, they're total strangers to me now."

"That's because you only saw them briefly." Vanessa tried to reassure her. "While you're at my house, you can spend hours talking to all of them. Then, when you get home, they won't seem like strangers to you any more, they'll feel like your family."

"I'm scared." Haley shook her head in doubt. "I don't see how I can ever fit into their way of life again." Painful tears gathered in her eyes.

"I know you're scared." Vanessa sat on the edge of the bed next to her. "But you've been given a chance to fix your past mistakes, and rejoin your family. Those are the people who will be your support for many years to come. Don't let fear get in the way of re-establishing your bond with your family. They love you. They'll always love you no matter what direction your life takes you. Promise me you won't let fear stop you from going home, or becoming part of your family again."

"Okay, I promise. I'll go home." Haley nodded sadly.

"I know this is going to be hard. But I believe it will be worth the risk. I'll do everything I can to make this easier for you." Haley threw her arms around Vanessa and hugged her close.

"Thank you. I'm so glad it was your door I knocked on."

Vanessa eased Haley back into bed, and changed the subject. She lifted a ragged lock of Haley's light brown hair. "What do you say to a new look for you, too? Something to match your return home and your new life."

"What? You don't like this look?" Haley laughed through her tears.

"Um, what did your hair look like three years ago?" Vanessa asked diplomatically.

"Believe it or not, I had long, straight hair."

"Well, given your hair's current length, we'll have to see what a real professional can do. Okay?"

"Okay, I think I'm ready for a change. You'll be surprised by how fast my hair grows." Haley smiled, already thinking about repairing the damage Jimmy had done to her hair.

They spent the next couple of hours chatting about clothes, men, and their plans for the future. Before Vanessa realized how long they'd been talking, she looked up and saw Andrew leaning nonchalantly against the doorframe. His brilliant, blue eyes sparkled with appreciation, and the corners of his mouth turned up slightly under his mustache.

"Excuse me for interrupting, ladies, but I'm hungry. I'm looking for my gorgeous dinner date."

"I'm so sorry." Vanessa glanced at the clock, shocked by the time. "I guess the day just got away from us."

"That's all right. But do you think we can go now? My stomach thinks my throat's been cut." Andrew crossed his arms, giving them both a good-natured smile.

"Call me. Let me know what time to pick you up tomorrow," Vanessa said, giving Haley a quick hug goodbye.

"I will. And, I'm really looking forward to hanging out with you this week," Haley smiled, shyly.

"Me too. See you tomorrow."

Andrew waved goodbye, and placing his hand in the small of Vanessa's back, he steered her out the door. Once they reached the elevator, he stood behind her, whispering softly in her ear. "Finally, I have you all to myself. Even if it's for only one more night."

"Just think about how much work you'll get done next week, while Haley and I are enjoying girl-time." Vanessa smiled. "After all, we don't need your protection any more. Although, there still might be some alone time for us in the near future."

"My world no longer revolves around my work," he said, shaking his head, and pulling her possessively into his arms. "You have become my world. I plan to hold you to that alone time."

Vanessa smiled, but suddenly felt a little claustrophobic, smothered by the overwhelming intensity of Andrew's affection.

After Andrew helped her into his car, he turned on his ignition switch and the angry voice from a far right, news-talk radio station filled the enclosed space. He left the rant on as he navigated toward the restaurant. He seemed not to notice the constant bickering as he drove. Vanessa assumed he normally listened to this news station when he was in his car alone, but she found the constant arguing of extreme viewpoints disturbing. It surprised her when Vanessa heard him occasionally comment aloud on the topics being discussed. She wondered if he was so used to being alone, or with just Shep, that he'd forgotten that she sat next to him in the car.

"Here we are." He stopped the car and the news station died into peaceful silence as he opened his door, and then ran around the car to gallantly help her out.

Vanessa waited until after they'd ordered to bring up the subject of the radio channel. "Do you always listen to that news channel while you're driving?"

"Yes, I guess I do." Andrew seemed surprised by the question. "I'm sorry I continued to listen, but I wanted to hear the rest of the story about the captured Christians in the Middle East. I can't believe how our government just sits idly by while innocent Americans are being slaughtered for their religious beliefs."

"I'm sure it's not as simple as all that." Vanessa rarely followed politics; instead she trusted her elected government officials to handle the country's international affairs. "I think they simply want to avoid another war."

"People are getting their heads chopped off in the name of religion." He sat stunned by her bland response. "How can we watch and not intervene?" he insisted.

"I'm sure they're well aware of what's going on." Vanessa said, shocked by his passion. "The Middle East has always been such a powder keg. They have to act with careful consideration. Anything they do today could have serious repercussions for years to come."

Andrew leaned back and studied Vanessa with astonishment. "So, you're all right with them sitting back while thousands of people are murdered?"

"Of course not." Vanessa wished they'd never started this conversation, and she hoped it would end soon. "I believe that sometimes you need to look at all the facts, before you make any rash decisions that could possibly make things worse."

Andrew frowned, quietly seething over her apparent apathy and fearful of what she would say next. He decided to end the conversation as the waiter served their dinners. Vanessa gradually began to relax and enjoy her meal, relieved that Andrew had stopped talking politics while they ate. But then suddenly, out of the blue, he inquired about another sensitive subject, "Which church do you attend? I'd be happy to escort you and Haley this Sunday," he offered politely.

"I'm sorry, I don't attend church." *Here we go again,* she thought.

He remained thoughtfully silent for a moment. "Don't you believe in God?"

Vanessa knew her answer would upset Andrew, but at this point, she dared him to comment further. "Actually, no I do not." She hoped her sharp answer would put him off, ending the whole disturbing discussion.

He ate quietly for a moment. "Did you attend church as a child?"

"Yes, my mother and I attended the Methodist Church every Sunday," Vanessa answered his inquiry quietly, having no idea why he cared, or why he persisted in this line of conversation, one in which she was obviously uncomfortable.

Andrew leaned back in his chair, calmly sipping his wine. He'd failed to notice the deepening flush of anger on her face before he asked, "When did you stop believing?"

"After God let my husband beat me, and murder my only child!" She responded through her clenched teeth, seething with uncontrolled fury. She stood up nearly toppling her chair, threw her napkin on her plate, and grabbed her purse. Incensed, by how he'd carelessly open her deepest wound, she stormed off toward the ladies' room without explanation.

Andrew kicked himself for upsetting Vanessa so callously. They obviously looked at the world through different eyes and experiences. He remembered being angry with God himself during the really bad years. But he also remembered how his faith had helped him to survive. It broke his heart to see how Vanessa had blamed God. She'd struggled to survive her physical and emotionally abusive battle, without her faith.

They'd talked openly about so many topics, but they'd never discussed politics or religion. Andrew wondered if they had reached an impasse in their relationship. Could they learn to agree to disagree? Or, would they constantly fight?

He finished his dinner in thoughtful solitude and paid the bill. Glancing at his watch, he grew concerned when Vanessa still had not returned to the table after quite some time. Undecided, he sat wondering if he should go look for her, when his phone rang. It was Vanessa.

"Hi, I took a cab home. I'm tired. I really just want to be alone tonight. Please, don't come over. I'll call you tomorrow after I get Haley settled in."

"I'm sorry I upset you," Andrew apologized, stunned that she had left him sitting alone in the restaurant. "I don't think you should be alone tonight. Please let me come over for a little while. I think we need to talk."

"If you care about me, you'll respect my wishes and let me work through this by myself," she said, firmly. Vanessa had a will of iron, and she'd clearly made up her mind.

"Very well, if that's what you want." Andrew knew he had no choice.

"Will you call me tomorrow?"

"Of course. Goodnight." Her voice sounded flat, lacking any expression or pleasantries.

"Goodnight, Vanessa. Call me if you change your mind and decide you want to talk."

Vanessa hung up.

Andrew looked at his phone in amazement before placing it back in his pocket. Confused by her detached reaction, he suddenly realized just how little he knew her.

Pulling slowly out of the restaurant parking lot, Andrew remained bewildered by Vanessa's cold dismissal. He imagined her sitting at home alone and suffering, while she painfully relived her tortured past in solitude. It ate at his gut that she'd turned away from him. He admired her independent spirit, but he couldn't stand to think of her handling such intense feelings of grief on her own.

He pulled up to an intersection, where the light had turned red. Looking both ways, he thought, if I turn right, I'll go home, and if I turn left, it will take me to Vanessa's house. He sat contemplating his next action when the light turned green. The car behind him honked, impatient for him to move, and he impulsively turned left.

Andrew's car rolled quietly into Vanessa's driveway. He switched off the engine. Pitch dark outside, he noticed that no lights shone from inside the desolate-looking house. He knew she wasn't asleep, so he sat in his car, trying to decide what to do next. He hesitated to go inside, but instead decided he'd secure the outside of her property. After securing the front yard, he walked toward the back. He paused, hearing the eerie sound of heartrending sobbing coming from the patio.

A black, wrought-iron fence separated Vanessa's pool from the rest of the yard. Andrew peered through it cautiously, barely able to make out Vanessa's silhouette in the darkness. She sat in a chair, her feet tucked under her, and her forehead resting on her knees. Essentially, she'd balled herself up into a fetal position, and was sobbing uncontrollably. Ashamed that he had pushed her to this point of agony, he leaned over the barrier of her fence and called to her softly.

"Vanessa?"

Startled by his voice, she looked up at him, pain etched across her face. The dim light glistened on the tears streaking down her cheeks. Her look of gaunt pain tore at his conscious. But she quickly replaced it with wide-eyed, frowning fury.

"I told you to leave me alone!" she screamed. "Take your gun-toting, right-winged, bible-thumping ass and get the hell out of here!" She pointed at him accusingly, sweeping her finger dramatically toward the front of the house.

The corners of Andrew's mouth lifted slightly at her colorful description. She had to be the first person to ever call him that! Her head had already fallen back onto her knees, and she resumed her pitiful sobbing. He took note of the bottle of wine and the empty glass on the table in front of her.

Andrew remained outside the gate, but called to her again in a calm, reasoning voice. "I can't leave you like this. If you don't want me to come in, I'll just wait here until you stop crying, then I'll go home."

"Go...away." She didn't lift her head. Instead she weakly pleaded with him. Her crying continued, but her tone had changed. She sounded utterly hopeless and heartbroken.

Andrew felt his heart twist in his chest. The sound of her despondent crying was more than he could stand. He slowly opened the gate and swiftly walked determinedly toward her. In one move, he scooped her out of the chair, lifting her up into his arms. She never looked at him, but simply snuggled her head into the crook of his neck, wrapping her arms around his shoulders. Without a word, he carried her into the house, down the hall to her room, and laid her softly on her bed.

Carefully, he placed her under the covers and knelt down beside her. He pushed the damp hair out of her face as she lay, eyes swollen and closed.

"I'll just sit here until you fall asleep, then I'll lock up and go home," he murmured.

"No, please don't go," she whispered, without opening her eyes, she reached out desperately to grab at his arm.

"Okay—I'll sleep on the couch then," he said, unsure of her mood. He tucked her arms securely beneath the covers, but she shook her head no, pleading with him softly. "Please—stay with me."

"All right sweetheart, if that's what you want." He kissed her forehead lightly.

Vanessa nodded. Seconds later she fell fast asleep.

Andrew kissed her sleeping lips tenderly before he walked outside to pick up her glass and the empty bottle of wine. After locking the back door, he entered the kitchen and noticed the bottle opener with the new cork still attached. He simply shook his head sadly, proceeding to secure the rest of the house.

When he returned to Vanessa's room, he found her peacefully snoring. He quietly undressed and slipped in beside her. She immediately rolled over and snuggled into his arms. Andrew held her close, cherishing the feel of her warm, pliant body in his arms. Disturbed and unable to sleep, he lay awake while he held her close, wondering what to expect from her in the morning? *Will she resent me? Or, will she find it within her heart to forgive me?*

Chapter 18
Reconciliation

Vanessa woke the next morning to the sound of her cell phone ringing. She untangled herself from Andrew's arms to reach for it. Holding the top of her pounding head, she lifted it gingerly off the pillow.

"The doctor came about an hour ago." Haley's bubbling voice exploded in her ear. "We video chatted with my mom and he went over everything I have to do until my ankle heals. He said I could go home today. I can leave anytime."

Vanessa's head ached. Squinting painfully in the morning light, she struggled to clearly see her clock. "I'm sorry. I just woke up. What time is it now?"

"It's eleven thirty. Rough night?" Haley giggled.

"I guess you could say that. What time do you want me to pick you up?" Vanessa groaned inwardly.

"Whenever." Haley tried to sound cheerful although Vanessa's unenthusiastic response hurt.

Vanessa looked over at Andrew. The wary look on his face reminded her that she owed him one huge apology for her behavior last night. "Can I pick you up at two?"

"That's great, I'll let them know. Will you please ask Andrew how John is doing?"

"What makes you think Andrew's here?" Vanessa sat up on the side of the bed clearing her parched, unpleasant tasting throat.

"Well, is he?" Haley teased.

"Yes," Vanessa answered, softly.

"Please just ask him for me," Haley implored. "I'll see you later."

"I'll ask him. And I'll see you at two." She struggled to clear the cobwebs out of her fuzzy mind.

Vanessa staggered into the bathroom and nearly screamed at her reflection. Her hair was standing on end, and her makeup had hideously smeared all over her face. The eyes staring back at her were puffy and red, with huge dark bags under them. *What have I done to myself? How will I ever look as good as René made me look yesterday?* She groaned at her reflection and began scrubbing her face aggressively with cold water.

When she returned to the bedroom, she found a steaming cup of coffee and a bottle of aspirin on her nightstand, but no sign of Andrew.

She sipped her coffee, silently blessing him. Coffee had never smelled, tasted, or felt so good. Swallowing hard, she thought, *I might just live after all.* She noticed Andrew's clothes resting on the back of her chair and exhaled in relief. Embarrassed by her behavior last night, she didn't want him to leave before she had a chance to apologize. She downed her aspirin and went in search of Andrew.

He stood in the kitchen with his back to her, totally naked, talking insistently on his phone. She admired his firm, toned body with his beautifully rounded backside. He wasn't twenty any more, but she stared anyway, captivated by his masculine form. Andrew sounded stressed.

"Look, please explain to them that I got tied up this morning and try to reschedule for later this afternoon. Thanks, I owe you one." He hung up and Vanessa cozied up behind him. She placed her arms around his chest, laying her head against the warm skin of his exposed back.

"I'm so sorry. I know last night wasn't the romantic night you had planned."

"I'm sorry too." He turned in her arms so they were face to face, still embracing, his exposed maleness pressing against her waist. "I should never have talked to you that way. How are you feeling today? Are we still friends?" he asked, hopefully.

"I hope we're a lot more than friends," she whispered in his ear, pulling his head toward her and kissing him deeply.

Andrew withdrew just enough to search her eyes. Her passionate kiss and the seductive smile on her face were all the reassurance and encouragement he needed. He reached for her hand and led her willingly back to bed.

An hour later Andrew and Vanessa continued to happily enjoy each other's bodies in the shower. Glowing in the aftermath of his sensual touch, she no longer felt smothered by Andrew. They'd reached a new level of trust and intimacy in their relationship. She'd opened up, shared her innermost demons with him and he hadn't run, he'd stayed by her side.

Suddenly, her laughter ceased and she moved closer to him, resting her head on his soapy chest and winding her arms around him. Andrew didn't question her sudden change of mood, but simply hunched over to hold her in a sheltering embrace.

"You know? I think you may have done me a favor last night." Vanessa closed her eyes, listening to the steady beat of his heart, feeling the warmth of the showering droplets on her back, and sighing contentedly.

"How's that?" Andrew asked, thinking she had something amusing to say.

"I just realized that I'd never cried when my baby girl died. Instead I've been clinging to my anger for years." Andrew stopped smiling and listened quietly. "I think grieving was too painful for me. I believed, if I really let myself feel all of the pain at once, my heart would shatter, and I would simply cease to exist."

Andrew held her closer, feeling the wet warmth of her tears on his chest, waiting silently for her to continue.

"But I didn't die..." she sighed. "In fact, today I feel as if a great weight has been lifted off my heart. It's hard to explain, but I feel free. I will always love my baby, but for the first time, I think I can move on with my life. My baby's dead. I can say that out loud now and accept it as a fact. So, thank you," Vanessa whispered and looked up at Andrew with teary appreciation.

The soapy film between their bodies glided sensually against their skin and the warm water enveloped them in a comforting cocoon. Secreted away from the outside world, sheltered in a loving embrace, they merged intimately together. No need for words, their bodies communicated the depth of their growing emotional bond.

Later, Andrew puzzled over the events of the past day while he dried off and hastily dressed. Explaining that he needed to rush to his office, he kissed her and held her close, searching her expression for any indication of her true feelings for him. Last night had shaken him, and despite their emotional recovery this morning, he still felt insecure and vulnerable. Vanessa meant everything to him, so he decided it was best to give her some space today, hoping she might miss him.

"I'll call you later." He reassured her. "But I'm planning to go home to sleep tonight. I have a full day tomorrow, and I won't be able to see you 'til tomorrow night. Okay?"

Vanessa, unlike Andrew, felt secure about his feelings for her. She readily agreed with their brief separation, knowing it would allow her undivided time to devote to Haley. "Sounds good, I'll talk to you later." She walked into his arms again, for a lingering goodbye kiss.

Andrew held Vanessa close, savoring the soft feel and tantalizing scent of her freshly washed hair. He nuzzled her briefly, regretting his hasty departure, anxiously hoping he'd be missed.

After Vanessa heard Andrew pull out of her driveway, she dashed back to her room, mindful of Haley waiting at the hospital for her. She searched for her makeup kit and wondered in a panic, where are those instructions? Looking at her puffy reflection in the mirror, she lamented aloud, "Looks like I'm going to need a considerable amount of repair work!"

Her makeup applied, she was just about to tackle her hair, when the doorbell rang. Tying the sash on her robe, she rushed down the hall to answer. Two young men in overalls informed her they had a large delivery for her from René. All of her very expensive, new clothes and accessories had arrived! The deliverymen literally packed her entire living room with oversized boxes filled with racks and racks of clothes. She tipped them generously, and the minute they left, she searched through the racks to find something pretty to wear.

Once fully dressed, Vanessa made a final check of herself in the mirror. She wore a light, flowing, colorfully printed dress, with new off-white, medium-heeled shoes and a matching purse. Her hair and makeup appeared surprisingly close to the way it had looked the day before. She made one final twirl in front of the mirror, and thought, *Not too bad for an old girl.*

Gathering the clothes and shoes for Haley to wear home, she hurried out the door. She was halfway to the hospital before she realized she hadn't taken the time to eat today. Later, she thought dismissively.

Vanessa rushed into Haley's room with her arms loaded with clothes. Haley had sat, patiently waiting in a wheelchair near the window, and her face lit up at Vanessa's harried arrival.

"You're early." Her eyes danced with pleasure. "Thanks for coming to get me."

Vanessa efficiently laid out the clothes she'd brought for Haley on the bed. "I hope you like these. We can shop for more later."

"Thanks, they look great!" Haley gawked at the tags on them, realizing she hadn't had any new clothes in years.

"What did Andrew find out about John?" Haley inquired, while Vanessa helped her dress.

"I'm so sorry. I forgot to ask him," she said. Haley shrugged, but Vanessa felt bad, knowing how it was important to her. "I could try asking at the nurse's station?" Vanessa suggested.

"I already tried." Haley focused on her shoes. "They said they couldn't tell me anything because it was against the law or something." Haley secretly worried that John had died and no one wanted to tell her. It would be all her fault if he had.

Vanessa noted the dejected look on Haley's face, and she felt guilty. "Let *me* try." *I usually manage to get my way*, she thought resolutely, She marched down the hall with determination, requesting to speak with Haley's nurse. "Hi, my name is Vanessa Golden, I'm here to pick up Haley."

The nurse knew all about Vanessa, and her affair with the handsome detective on Haley's case. The nurse's cousin had been one of the bank tellers who'd died in the explosion.

"Yes, of course, Ms. Golden." She struggled to answer respectfully. "Haley is all set to go. You just need to sign her discharge papers." She handed Vanessa a clipboard and watched as Vanessa carelessly dashed off her signature.

"Do you have any further questions about Haley's care?"

"No," Vanessa said, offended by her question. "I think I've got it, but can you tell me about John's condition? You know, the security guard from the bank?"

"I'm sorry," the nurse said, formally. "I can't give out any patient information. I can connect you to his room. If his granddaughter is there, maybe she'll talk to you?"

"Thank you. I'd appreciate it if you would." Vanessa resented being stonewalled and returned reluctantly to Haley to await the answer.

A few minutes later the nurse returned. "I talked with his granddaughter. She asked me to tell you to bring Haley upstairs. They're in ICU 2." She walked over to address Haley. "You're all discharged. Please take care of yourself."

"Thank you." Vanessa promptly collected all of Haley's belongings as Haley said goodbye to her nurse, and steered her wheelchair toward the ICU.

"Do you think he'll be all right?" Haley asked, anxious about seeing John and fearing the worst.

"I'm sorry, I wish I could say yes. Let's just wait and see how he's doing."

Haley remained quiet except to give Vanessa directions to his room. His granddaughter watched them as they approached and stepped out into the hall to talk to Haley.

"It's nice to see you again, Haley. It looks like you're going home today." She indicated Haley's attire and the bags.

"Yes, I'm going to my friend Vanessa's house." Haley feared she was about to get bad news, and asked warily, "How is he doing?"

"He's sedated, so he sleeps most of the time." His granddaughter didn't want to alarm Haley, knowing how her grandfather felt about her. "We'll just have to wait a few more days to see if his lungs will heal. He's comfortable for now. He's not suffering or having any pain."

"If he wakes up, will you tell him I was here?" Haley asked, peeking apprehensively through the door at the pale, sleeping man. She shuddered, observing the countless lines and hoses attached him. He appeared very old and close to death.

"Of course I will. Please take care of yourself, and feel free to call me if you'd like." She handed Haley a card with her cell number on the back.

"Thank you. You're very kind."

Vanessa wished her well and pushed Haley back to the elevator. The doors closed and Haley slumped down in her wheelchair, she hung her head, and whispered softly, "It's all my fault."

Vanessa considered reassuring her that it wasn't, but instead she rested her hand lightly on Haley's shoulder in silent support.

When the elevator doors opened, Vanessa could see a large crowd of people had formed outside the hospital entrance doors.

"You may want to go out the back door," a young volunteer walking by holding a vase full of flowers quietly suggested.

"Why? What's going on?" Vanessa asked, stunned by the idea they'd need to escape out the back of the hospital.

"Those are reporters, and they're waiting for both of you." The volunteer pointed to the crowd.

"I don't understand. Why are they waiting for us?"

"It's about the bank robbery." The volunteer signaled Vanessa to follow her. "Someone must have let them know of Haley's involvement. Those reporters have been outside waiting for the past hour."

"Thanks for the heads up." Vanessa followed the helpful girl without question and managed to get Haley out the back way without any confrontations with the persistent media. She only hoped the reporters and photo hounds would not be waiting for them when they reached her house. Personally, she didn't care, but she could see by the solemn expression on Haley's face, that she was extremely upset by the

197

unwanted attention.

"I'm so sorry. Maybe I shouldn't go to your house," Haley said, quietly.

"Don't be ridiculous, we're in this together."

No vigilant reporters stood guard outside her home when they pulled into the driveway. They even maneuvered the tricky entrance into her house without any harassment from the persistent press. "See, no problem. I don't know about you, but I'm starving."

"I could definitely eat." Haley laughed and the tight-lipped expression on her face began to relax a little.

"Wow, Vanessa!" Haley gazed around Vanessa's living room at all of the racks of clothes. "It looks like you bought the whole store!"

"See what I mean? René talked me into buying everything!" Exasperated, Vanessa surveyed the crowded room, shaking her head in dismay. "I swear, that man had me under a spell. I can't believe I agreed to all of this! See why I desperately need your help?"

Haley laughed as Vanessa helped stow her crutches and settle comfortably into the living room recliner, before heading to the kitchen to fix a late lunch.

Vanessa returned with two glasses of iced tea and a store bought Cob salad artfully arranged on two plates.

"Thanks. I hope I'm not going to be too much bother for you."

"Don't be silly. Look at this room!" Vanessa motioned to the clothes scattered around her living room. "I really need you to help me decide what to send back."

"Thanks." Haley smiled, appreciating the extent with which Vanessa had welcomed her into her home. She'd missed feeling welcome and secure during the uncertain, traumatic years she'd lived with Jimmy.

After they ate, they spent hours laughing, while sorting through the racks of clothes consuming Vanessa's living room. One by one, the clothes moved from the crowded living room into Vanessa's closet. Once the very last pair of new shoes made it into her closet, Vanessa heaved a heavy sigh of relief. Admiring her tidy space, Vanessa's gaze landed on Haley's pale face. She noticed the gaunt look of exhaustion on her face, and guessed that she might be in pain. "I'm sorry Haley, is your ankle hurting you?"

"I'm fine. Well, maybe my ankle hurts a little."

"Thank you *so much* for all of your help! But it looks like I'm keeping everything after all. Okay now; let's get you to your room. Then later I'll call for some pizza for dinner."

"That sounds good."

Vanessa settled Haley into the guest bedroom, and then returned to tidy up her kitchen. The muffled voices emanating from Haley's TV drifted into the kitchen, and Vanessa bent down to cuddle Callie. "Nice to have someone else in the house, isn't it?"

Restoring her kitchen to its spotless condition, she went to check on Haley. She'd fallen asleep, the remote resting a few inches away from her hand. Vanessa switched off the TV, but left the remote where Haley could easily reach it.

Returning to the living room, she called and ordered pizza. Resting quietly on her couch, she read the paper while she waited. Her cell phone rudely interrupted her peace and quiet. Andrew's photo she'd snapped earlier and his name popped up on her screen. "Hi there, handsome."

"Hi yourself. I just called to see how you two were getting along." Andrew's voice sounded listless and tired.

"We're doing great. But I'm afraid I wore Haley out." Vanessa glanced around her living room. "I had her help me sort through my entire new wardrobe. You sound tired."

"I'm all right, how about you? How are things going?"

"Haley agreed with René." Vanessa sighed. "She had me keep it all. And, I had to throw out all of my old things to make room."

"That was brave of you." Andrew knew how hard such a drastic change could be.

"Not really," she hedged. "I actually just put them in the garage for now."

"I see. What are you doing now?" He missed her, even though he wanted to give her some space.

"Nothing much, just sitting here reading my left-wing newspaper."

"I said I was sorry!" Andrew groaned, the sting of her calling him a right-winged, gun toting, bible-thumper still fresh in his mind.

"Just playing with you." His overreaction amused her. "Better develop a sense of humor, if we're ever going to survive our differences."

"Hmmm." Relieved by her light-hearted response to a sticky situation, he relaxed back in his office chair.

"I'll miss you tonight." She liked having him around.

"I'll miss you too. Be sure you lock up and set the alarms tonight. I have to go into the city first thing tomorrow morning, and I'm not sure what time I'll be back. Call me if you have any issues, otherwise I'll call you when I'm done."

Vanessa didn't like the idea of sleeping alone tonight. "Thanks for checking in, don't work too hard tomorrow. And Andrew?"

"Yes?" Andrew wanted her to keep talking. He missed the sound of her voice.

But before she could answer, the doorbell interrupted, and she bid him a hasty goodbye.

"Did you know there's a bunch of news station trucks down the street?" The pizza delivery boy informed her in a high-pitched voice. "There are people in your bushes, and lots more down the street!"

"I know." Vanessa expected this. "Do me a favor... don't talk to any of them." Wide-eyed, he shook his head no. Vanessa smiled at his trepidation, tipping him generously.

Haley still slept soundly, so Vanessa placed the pizza in the refrigerator for later. Carrying her newspaper and glass of wine down the hall, Vanessa settled thoughtfully into bed.

She'd deal with the annoying paparazzi tomorrow.

Chapter 19
Corruption of the Night

Despite the flocks of reporters surrounding her house, Vanessa had eventually fallen into a deep sleep. At least she *had* been sleeping, until a strange rattling noise, emanating from the kitchen, suddenly woke her. Glancing at the clock, she saw that it was only five in the morning. Remaining quietly in bed she strained to listen for the noise to repeat itself. She couldn't imagine who or what had caused the mysterious sound. Finally, Vanessa decided it must have been Haley, so she shrugged off her alarm, put on her robe, and got up.

But, as she passed by Haley's room, Vanessa saw she was still sound asleep in her bed. Standing outside of Haley's door Vanessa heard the noise again and froze, silently cursing. She belatedly remembered that she had neglected to lock the back door or set the alarm. Anyone could have gotten in. Returning to her room, she retrieved her cell phone and dialed 911. Holding her phone tightly in her hand, finger poised over the send button, she crept toward the sound. She paused by her front door to retrieve the baseball bat she kept in the corner, and quietly moved closer to the unidentified sound. The kitchen door stood open, but she kept her body hidden off to one side and peered cautiously into the dimly lit room.

A dark figure hunched over her opened purse resting on the counter. Vanessa immediately recognized her intruder as Juan's older brother and exhaled the breath she'd been holding. He startled when she boldly entered the room, and looked up at her with wild, red-rimmed eyes, a large knife dangling from his left hand. He hesitantly flashed the knife at her, the tremor in his hand noticeable. "Please forgive me. I must have money, or they will kill me," he pleaded in his heavy accent.

Confused by his behavior, she recalled her first impression of him. He'd seemed troubled and sullen when he was here before. She wished she could remember his name. "Who are you afraid of?" Vanessa asked, trying to calm him.

"I can't tell you." His hands shook uncontrollably and he dropped the knife onto the counter. "I don't know their names, but I know they will kill me!"

"Did you ask your brother to help you?" Vanessa asked, still confused why he had broken into her house.

"If my brother knew I was using drugs again, he would send me back home." Sweat dripped from his forehead. "Please, I beg you, do not tell him."

Vanessa didn't care about the money in her purse, but she was concerned for Haley's safety.

"Very well, just take what you need, and please go."

"Please forgive me, señora." He snatched up the knife, pulled a handful of bills out of her purse, and disappeared out the back door.

Vanessa watched Juan's brother push out of the back gate, and disappear through the bushes. She immediately locked her back door and set her alarm. Lowering herself into the kitchen chair, she placed her phone on the table to consider her next action. She sat stunned, looking at her phone, with 911 ready to call. *Juan would be mortified by his brother's behavior*, she thought. But his brother was apparently in mortal danger. Deciding to break her word, she immediately called Juan. He thanked her, and confessed that his brother, Roberto, had previously struggled with a drug problem, and assured her that he'd been clean for years.

"I'm so sorry, Ms. Golden. I can't believe he'd do this again. It took him such a long time to recover from his addiction before."

Vanessa had heard vivid stories about the drug cartel, including the gruesome ways they tortured and killed the people who double-crossed them. "Please, this isn't your fault." His brother's actions didn't affect how she felt about Juan. "I really don't care about the money. I called you because I'm worried about your brother. He seemed terrified of the people he owes money to. I hope you can find him before it's too late. I'm afraid he's going to get hurt, or worse."

"Thank you. You're a good woman." Juan was relieved that his brother's actions hadn't affected his employment. "I think I know where to find him. My brother and I will go look for him. After we find him, I'll send him back to Mexico where he'll be safe. I know I have no right to ask, but would you please not report this to the police?"

Vanessa thought it over briefly before she responded. "All right, I won't report it tonight, if you promise to let me know as soon as he's safe."

"I promise. I owe you everything." Juan exhaled in relief. "Thank you, señora."

Vanessa ended her call with Juan. Still feeling a little shocked, she sat down with a fresh cup of coffee. Hoards of reporters surrounded her home, yet he'd somehow managed to get in. She wondered if she'd made a mistake by not calling the police immediately and worried how she'd feel if Juan's brother were killed.

Her home phone suddenly rang, her frayed nerves jumping at the unexpectedly loud noise. She knew Juan would call her cell phone, but decided to answer anyway since she was awake, and lifted the receiver.

"Get Haley!" a deep, gravely male voice demanded. She instantly disliked his unsettling tone and arrogant command.

"I'm sorry? Who is this? Haley's asleep. May I take a message?" Vanessa asked in her haughty, formal tone.

"Yeah." He cleared his throat, coughed, and his voice became deeper, and challenging for her to hear. "Tell her if she doesn't give me back my money, I'll make her wish she were dead." He abruptly hung up.

Vanessa listened briefly to the dial tone and set the receiver down. An apprehensive chill ran up her spine. She immediately reached over and switched off the ringer, setting the answering machine to answer all incoming calls silently. She had no idea who the caller had been, but she hoped it was just a prank call. She would definitely discuss the call with Andrew later. For now, she'd keep it to herself. Haley didn't need to worry about some other creepy man threatening her life.

The house tightly locked and secured, Vanessa made another quick cup of coffee to take back to her room. As she passed Haley's room, she felt reassured that she'd slept peacefully through the break-in. Vanessa looked down at her angelic face, realizing just how young and vulnerable she was. She silently vowed to do everything within her power to make sure that no one ever hurt Haley again.

Tired, but too unhinged to sleep, she settled into bed to read the rest of yesterday's newspaper, until she finally fell into a fitful, unsatisfying sleep. She woke to the sound of the guest bathroom toilet flushing. *Haley must be awake and starving*, she thought. The screen on her cell phone showed she'd had no message yet from Juan, even though it was all ready after eight. *Maybe I should have called the police*, she thought. Her cup sat full of cold coffee at her bedside. Taking a swig for fortification, she grimaced and got up to make herself presentable.

Vanessa found Haley in the kitchen leaning on her crutches, making fresh coffee and munching on a piece of cold pizza. Vanessa glanced at the answering machine and saw that there had been over sixty messages since she set it just a couple of hours ago. Ignoring the machine, she gratefully sipped the fresh cup of coffee that Haley handed her. After her fragmented, interrupted sleep, hot coffee was a welcomed sustenance.

"Thanks, this is just what I need."

"You're welcome." Haley smiled. "Sorry I conked out so early last night. Those pain pills always make me sleepy." She carelessly licked some pizza sauce off of her finger.

"That's okay. Did you sleep well?" Vanessa asked, thinking how resilient Haley seemed, as if she didn't have a care in the world. None of the abuse she'd suffered had destroyed her ability to appreciate the simple pleasures of life. Vanessa smiled, watching as she devoured another slice of pizza.

"I can't remember when I've slept so well." Haley stretched her arms out to her side and sat down at the table, balancing her crutches against the edge. "It was kind of hard to sleep at the hospital. Someone always woke me up, just to ask me if I was okay. But last night, nothing woke me."

"I'm glad you slept." Relieved, Vanessa was grateful she'd slept through both Roberto's break-in, and the unsettling phone call. "Today however, I have some news that might disturb you."

"Oh? What is it?"

"Well, we're sort of prisoners here," Vanessa tilted her head toward the front of the house. 'The streets around the house are covered with reporters and photographers. Also, judging by the number of messages on the answering machine, I think they've discovered my phone number as well."

"How did they find out?" Haley's face wrinkled in confusion. "What do they want? What should we do?"

"I have no idea how they found out." Vanessa tried to appear nonchalant about the whole situation. "But I'm pretty sure they want a story and our pictures. We'll just have to stay put for now. I'll ask Andrew what he thinks we should do when he calls later."

Vanessa stood, sliding the kitchen curtains closed, then turned back to Haley. "In the meantime, what would you like to do?" she asked. "Did you get enough to eat?" She'd watched Haley gobble down her fourth piece of pizza. "Would you like me to make you something else for breakfast?"

"No thanks. I'm fine." Haley laughed, rubbing her flat belly.

"Why don't I help you take a shower, and then I'll show you the clothes I bought you." Vanessa suggested, wanting to keep Haley busy and distracted from the activity outside. "You can video chat with your mother later if you want."

"Okay." Haley shrugged without enthusiasm.

Vanessa helped her cover her leg splint in plastic wrap, and went to get a metal end table from the patio for Haley to sit on while she showered.

While Haley showered, Vanessa returned to the kitchen to consume her usual morning protein bar. The sight of the greasy pizza on the counter made her stomach turn, but she wrapped it for Haley to eat later. Returning to her room, she intended to quickly change, but her cell phone began to ring. Marie's name appeared on the screen.

"What's going on?" Marie asked insistently. "I saw a video of you and some young girl with a cast sneaking out of the hospital. Did that innocent looking child really help to rob your local bank?"

"I didn't know anyone was videotaping us." *Oh great,* Vanessa thought.

"Really? That's all you have to say about it?" Marie could tell Vanessa was being evasive.

"Look, it's a very long story. I'll explain everything to you later. How are things at the magazine? How's Max doing?" Vanessa asked, trying to avoid going into details about her relationship with Haley.

"That's a long, complicated story too. I wasn't sure you wanted your vacation interrupted by everything that's happening here." Vanessa thought for a minute. *Do I really want to know?*

"Can it wait until right before I'm scheduled to return?"

"Actually, yes it can." *If there's anything to return to,* Marie thought. Vanessa couldn't change the ultimate outcome, so why worry her. "I do think we should get together before your first day back. We can exchange stories, and I'll get you up to speed on everything here. That way you're not blind-sided when you first walk through the door."

"Thanks. No matter what happens, I know you'll always have my back." Vanessa said, relieved not to have to deal with her work problems today.

"I do, so don't hesitate to call me if you need anything." Marie bit her lip to keep from blurting out the whole sordid mess to her boss. She had no idea what Vanessa was mixed up in, but apparently *Gemma's* crisis would have to wait.

Relieved that Marie seemed to understand, Vanessa was glad to end the conversation.

Knowing there was bad news coming about *Gemma* didn't thrill Vanessa. But her mind remained preoccupied with Andrew and Haley.

Any worries about *Gemma* would just have to wait. Max and his father were perfectly capable of solving their problems without her assistance.

Vanessa heard the shower water stop, and called to Haley to see if she needed any help. Independent soul that Haley was, she hobbled out of the bathroom a minute later. She hopped across the floor to her bed with a towel tightly wrapped around her wet head. Sitting gingerly on the edge of the bed, she peeled off the plastic from her splint and watched excitedly as Vanessa began to display the many outfits she'd recently purchased for her. Haley had expected maybe one or two outfits, but not dozens. She became speechless, overwhelmed by the sheer volume of clothes Vanessa removed from the closet.

"I'm sorry, don't you like anything I bought?" Vanessa noticed the stunned look on Haley's face. "We could shop online for something you might like better?"

"They're wonderful," Haley whispered. She could see by the frown on Vanessa's face that she had misinterpreted her silence. "Everything you've done for me has been over-the-top incredible. I don't deserve any of it."

"Of course, you deserve it." Vanessa squatted in front of Haley to look into her face, reaching out to touch her hand. "You're an amazingly kind, considerate girl!"

"No, I'm not." Haley shook her head stubbornly. "I ran away from home because I'm a spoiled brat. I became a prostitute, I stole, I cheated, I lied, and now I've killed two innocent people, maybe three. I'm not a good person at all!"

Vanessa put down the clothes to sit beside her on the bed. "You made one bad decision," she said calmly. "You trusted and believed in the wrong person. Jimmy was responsible for all those horrible things, not you." Vanessa stood to retrieve a box of tissues from the bathroom.

"Now, dry your eyes, I want you to pick out an outfit. You don't want to look sad and shabby when you talk to you mother, do you?"

"Do I have to talk to her?" Haley protested, dabbing at her soggy eyes, and sniffling. She wasn't in the mood to divulge any more information about her sorted past to her mother.

Vanessa believed it was important for Haley to make her own decisions, after having been abused and bullied for years by Jimmy. He'd forced her to bend to his will and perform unspeakable acts for far too long.

"No, of course you don't have to, but I think these are the types of conversations you should be having with her. She knows you better than you think. I'll bet she's the one person whose forgiveness will mean the most to you."

"Okay, can I call her later?" Haley perked up, once it was clear Vanessa wasn't going to force her to call against her will. "I'd like to wear the green shorts and top."

"Whenever you want," Vanessa laughed, handing her the selected outfit. "But it's time to be really honest with her. Tell her what you did and how you feel about it. Trust me, you have nothing to lose, she loves you very much."

"Okay, I'll try." Haley wanted to please Vanessa, but appreciated that she had a choice.

Vanessa gave her some privacy while she dressed. In the meantime, she sat down in the kitchen to listen briefly to the messages on her answering machine. She tediously skipped through the messages from reporters wanting interviews. A few of the calls were from her neighbors, complaining about the blocked streets. She hoped they were calling the police to complain as well.

Haley entered the kitchen supported by her crutches, her eyes sparkling with excitement. "I peeked out the window. I can't believe how many people are outside in the street!"

"Don't worry about them." Vanessa tried to make light of it. "Just keep in mind that every time they see you, they'll be snapping your picture."

"I don't care about that." Haley frowned. "I'll be in another state pretty soon. I'm worried about you. Will this affect your job or anything?"

"No, I doubt it. Did you call your mother yet?" Vanessa couldn't resist nagging her.

"No, I thought I might watch a movie or something. And, I think it's time for my pills." Haley wasn't in any hurry to have a deep conversation with her mother.

Vanessa talked her into a pain pill when she noticed the toes on the foot with the splint appeared swollen. "I think you should lay down for a while, you need to get the swelling out of your toes."

Obediently swallowing her pills, Haley returned to rest in bed with her leg elevated. Vanessa set her up with snacks and drinks at her bedside, then left Haley to watch a movie in peace, while she made some calls in private.

Vanessa decided to call Juan first, and then Andrew. She kicked herself for not having Roberto picked up by the police, at least then she'd know he was safe. Juan answered on the first ring. He'd found his brother after he'd been badly beaten, but he'd survived. Juan said he'd taken him to the hospital, and the police were questioning him now. She silently hoped Roberto would identify his attackers.

"I'm glad Roberto's going to be all right."

"Thank you for your help. You saved his life, and for that I am very grateful," Juan answered quietly. "I will call you soon, and I promise I will pay you back."

"Just keep him safe."

Vanessa let out a big sigh of relief. She definitely would not tell Andrew about Roberto, at least not right away. She doubted he'd understand her actions in the matter. The thought barely crossed her mind, when the phone rang in her hand, and of course it was Andrew.

"Hi there." Her false cheerfulness covered her distress over last night's events.

"Hi yourself, is everything all right?" Andrew asked, carefully.

"What do you mean?" she asked. "Oh, you mean the reporters and photographers outside my house?" She chuckled nervously.

"I want you to know I tried very hard to keep both of your names out of the press."

"I know, apparently the leak came from someone at the hospital."

"That's great!" he said, frustrated that he hadn't been able to protect their identities. "I can wrap things up here in an hour or two. What would you say, to me smuggling you out of there? I can take you both to my beach house," he offered, fearing again for her security.

"I'll check with Haley, but it sounds good to me." Vanessa hated feeling like she was in a fish bowl. She'd feel a lot safer staying with Andrew, plus she missed him.

"Okay, pack up everything you need." Andrew smiled, wanting an excuse to have her close to him. "I'll call you with the plan shortly before I arrive."

"That's a ten-four, good buddy." Vanessa teased.

"Very funny, I didn't know you talked CB?"

"What do mean? That was my best cop talk."

"All right, very nice," Andrew smiled, relieved that she'd maintained her sense of humor given the current circumstances. "I'm going to send some officers over to disperse the crowds. Apparently, your neighbors have been complaining since last night. Call me if you have any problems. Love you."

"Love you too, bye." Vanessa answered without thinking. She ended all her phone conversations with her mother exactly the same way.

Haley squealed with joy when she heard they were moving to Andrew's beach house. And, true to his word, the police arrived to disperse most of the lingering reporters on the street.

Vanessa convinced Haley to video chat with her mom, while she packed for their move to the beach. Her mother was obviously concerned. She'd heard about them on the national news, and had watched the video of them leaving the hospital. Vanessa overheard her while she packed Haley's clothes, explaining they were moving to Andrew's, and assuring her that Haley would continue to stay in touch.

Haley seemed happier after she talked with her mom. Then again, they hadn't had enough time to talk about anything deep or troubling. All her mother knew were the basics. The difficult conversations were yet to come.

When Andrew called back, Vanessa had piled everything they needed in the middle of the living room.

"How are you both doing?" Andrew asked, officially, sounding very police-like.

"We're fine, Detective," she teased. "We're all packed and ready to go. Haley can't wait to see your beach house."

"Okay, here's the plan," Andrew continued seriously. "I'll borrow another detective's car with tinted windows and pull up behind the garage. I'll open the car door right next to the back gate. You two will get in while I load all of your things into the trunk. We'll then proceed to the police station where I'll park the car in the underground parking garage and we'll switch vehicles. Once we're in my car, you'll both have to crouch down until we get to my place. Any questions?"

"That sounds very complicated to me, I'll trust you to handle the details. We'll be ready to come out the back door when you arrive," Vanessa said, looking forward to escaping.

"Great, I'll be there in about ten minutes."

"Great. Oh, and Andrew?"

"Yes?"

"Do you have internet access? Haley needs to be able to video chat with her mother."

"Yes I do. I'll see you soon." He still had a lot to accomplish before he arrived.

"Thanks, see you soon." She felt giddy and excited to see him again, but nervous about moving into his home.

The black limo with tinted windows pulled up by the back gate and Andrew hopped out to open the rear door. Vanessa and Haley quickly climbed into the back seat, while Andrew gathered all of their belongings from the living room, which included Callie's carrier, and a giant bag of kitty litter. He laughed and left the litter behind. She'd have one giant sand box where she was going.

Everything went into the trunk, except for the howling cat, which he handed to Vanessa in the back seat.

"Sorry, hope you don't mind." Vanessa smiled at him apologetically. "I didn't have time to make other arrangements for her."

"Doesn't bother me..." He smiled back at her. "Shep might be another story," he warned playfully.

Andrew made sure the house was secured. Additional officers had arrived around the front to create a diversion, covering their clandestine escape. He cautiously drove the long, black limo smoothly out of the driveway, with his anxious passengers safely protected behind the tinted, bulletproof windows.

Chapter 20
Beach Party

$\mathcal{A}$ ndrew turned into his carport with his usual finesse. After taking an entirely different route home, along with the other privacy measures he had in place, he felt confident about his decision to move Vanessa and Haley to his home. Smiling with self-satisfaction, he thought, *The media will never find them here!*

"All right ladies, you can both get up now."

Andrew watched in the rearview mirror as both of their heads popped up from the back seat. They'd crouched uncomfortably since switching from the spacious limo into Andrew's cramped car. Relieved to sit up straight again, they struggled to get out of the restrictive space and alleviate their aching muscles.

Callie's incessant moaning and yowling had thankfully ceased, once Andrew switched off the engine. Shep, on the other hand, woke amiably from his undisturbed slumber.

Vanessa reached inside the car, releasing Callie from her confinement. "I'm sorry girl, I know how you hate riding in the car," she said, cuddling and soothing her tense, disgruntled cat. Callie continued glaring angry accusatory daggers at her.

Andrew helped Haley maneuver her crutches inside his house and returned to unpack the car. Vanessa gave her a quick tour, carefully escorting Haley through the living and dining rooms. While she walked through the house, she held Callie securely in her arms attempting to comfort her. But the nervous cat's muscles remained taught and her eyes darted suspiciously around the unfamiliar dwelling. Shep, ignoring everyone including Callie, meandered toward the kitchen and carelessly dropped onto his pillow-bed to finish his nap.

Opening the door to the only downstairs bedroom, Vanessa informed Haley, "This will be your room."

Haley nodded quietly, noting the neatly made bed covered with a fluffy, cream duvet, perfectly centered in the middle of a clean, minimally decorated, generic-looking room.

They turned, taking a few more steps toward the back of the house where Vanessa opened the sliding glass door that led outside.

"Wow!" Haley said. The bedroom was simply a bedroom, but Haley instantly fell in love with the sparkling blue pool and the sandy beach below. She stood motionless; she'd never actually seen the ocean in person before. Mesmerized, she stared out at the beautiful azure water covered with sporadic frothy white caps that stretched out as far as her eyes could see.

Giggling with pure joy, Haley eagerly swung out of the sliding glass door on her crutches into the bright sunshine. Closing her eyes, she turned her face upward, accepting a warm kiss from the sun. Inhaling the warm moist air, she savored a hint of salty taste in the back of her throat. A flock of chattering, scolding seagulls on their journey out to sea instantly caught her attention. Shielding her eyes with her hand, she silently watched as the noisy birds flew effortlessly across the sapphire colored sky.

Stepping down onto the flat patio embellished by various rocks and shells, she suddenly wished she were barefoot, wanting to feel the heat radiating from the concrete. She spied an inviting chaise lounge with an appealing thick, navy blue cushion sitting beside to the sparkling pool, and made her way toward it.

Balancing on one foot, Haley kicked off her shoes, set her crutches aside, and lowered herself gracefully onto the hot, soft cushion. She scooted back to recline, absorbing the warmth that radiated from her sun-heated seat, soaking gloriously into her stiff, tired muscles. Closing her eyes, she sighed contentedly. *This feels heavenly,* she thought.

Vanessa waited by the door, happy to watch Haley settle in beside the pool, before she returned inside to Andrew. Lingering indecisively at the bottom of the stairs, she waited for Andrew to finish unloading the luggage and direct her to a bedroom. Once he'd carried in the last suitcase, he noticed Vanessa standing uncertainly at the bottom of his staircase. Turning toward her, he saw the way she held her cat in front of her, shielding herself with the fluffy ball of fur like a security blanket.

"I can take the couch, or sleep on the boat if you'd prefer," he offered, thoughtfully.

Vanessa blushed, embarrassed by her apprehension. After all, they'd already slept together, more than once. She lifted her cat to her face, nuzzling against her soft fur.

"I'm not sure—what I should do about Callie." Her blushed deepened and her voice faltered.

The corners of Andrew's mouth barely lifted. Walking slowly toward her, he began calmly scratching Callie behind her ears, talking softly, fearful of spooking either one of them. "It's a big bed, Vanessa. She could sleep with us if you'd like."

Callie purred under Andrew's soothing touch, while Vanessa hesitated. She hadn't lived under the same roof with a man since her doomed marriage.

"What about Haley?" she asked, cradling the cat like a baby, safely keeping Andrew at bay.

He smiled, knowing he would get his way. Gently tucking a stray lock behind Vanessa's ear, he leaned forward, and whispered, "I think she already knows we're sleeping together." Then, leaning further across the relaxed cat, he placed an affectionate kiss on the back of Vanessa's neck. She bent her head toward him, nuzzling him with her cheek, instantly aware of the light tingling sensation traveling down her spine. Once again, he'd mystified her by the ease with which his simple kiss on her neck had sent pulsating vibrations throughout her body, awakening sleeping embers of desire, throwing her off balance, and causing her to tremble again with unanticipated arousal.

"You're right, she does," Vanessa agreed demurely, licking her suddenly dry lips, her voice sounding soft and airy.

Looking at her exquisitely flushed face, all he wanted was to carry her upstairs. There, he knew he could convince her that staying with him had countless benefits. But he had other obligations as the host. With regret, he wisely broke their close contact, but remained close enough to watch as she struggled to recover her equilibrium. Seeing her reaction, he reached out gently to steady her, his hands resting lightly on her shoulders as she wobbled slightly.

"Okay." He said, judging her to be balanced enough to walk back into the living room, and the recently created chaos. "What goes in Haley's room, and what goes upstairs?" he asked, businesslike.

Vanessa instantly snapped out of her daze, helping him sort through the jumble of bags to form two separate piles. She left him to finish distributing them on his own, carrying Callie up the stairs to check out his spacious master bedroom. She glanced around the sandy colored room, then closed the door behind them, permitting herself a quick, private look around to explore Andrew's intimate space. With the door closed, Callie roamed the room freely, sniffing cautiously in all of the corners and under the king-sized bed.

Juggling her luggage, Andrew opened the door unexpectedly, and Callie scooted past him, ran down the stairs and out through the open patio door. Vanessa followed her in a panic, worrying that she would run off. But she instantly relaxed when she located Callie cuddled on Haley's lap, contentedly curled up in the pleasant afternoon sun.

"Callie, you little traitor," Vanessa said, playfully scolding her unfaithful cat.

"I think I've made a friend," Haley smiled, nestling the cat on her chest.

"Would you mind keeping an eye on her while I go unpack?" Vanessa asked. Haley's healthy pink glow and the relaxed expression on her face pleased her. She decided it was safe to leave her disloyal cat to keep her company.

"Sure, no problem." She snuggled Callie back down on her lap.

"Can I get you something to drink before I go?" Vanessa asked, moving an umbrella across the patio to shade them.

"Ice water is fine," Haley said, leaning back and closing her eyes. She felt like a pampered queen, lounging back, slowly stroking the purring cat stretched across her lap.

Andrew, following Vanessa downstairs, had watched them from the doorway. He overheard their conversation and promptly went into the kitchen to grant Haley's wish.

Walking toward Haley's little oasis, he handed her the requested glass of ice water, and sat down. Conversationally, he began telling her about a few of the famous residents living close by, pointing out his boat docked down the beach, and the lighthouse on the jetty. Vanessa watched them briefly before returning inside to unpack Haley's room.

Finished with organizing Haley's belongings, she returned outside to discover that both Haley and Callie had fallen fast asleep in the shade. Since Andrew had disappeared, she climbed the stairs to his room.

Vanessa entered the master bedroom, interrupting Andrew while he meticulously hung her clothes in his closet. She stood approvingly in the doorway to watch.

"I'm sorry, I just wanted to put some of your things away for you. I hope you don't mind. How's Haley?"

"She's asleep. I don't know how to thank you for rescuing us from those hounding reporters. I felt so claustrophobic."

Noting her appreciative gaze, he set down the dress he was holding and moved toward her. He placed a brief, tender kiss on her luscious, inviting lips, and murmured, "It's truly my pleasure." Sighing, Vanessa rested her head against his chest.

"I think I need to tell you about a couple of unusual things that happened during the night." The wary tone of her voice gave her uneasiness away, although she hadn't intended to.

Andrew raised his head, just enough to look at her face. The look of apprehension he saw in her eyes caused him momentary concern. "Okay. Tell me," he said, and the calm tenor of his voice lulled Vanessa into elaborating.

"First of all, I want you to know that I've gotten so used to having you and Shep around...that I completely forgot to lock the back door or set the alarm last night." She crinkled up her nose, ducking her head. Shrugging, she suddenly felt foolish about her omission.

Drawing back from her, he inhaled deeply. She watched as his jaw muscles contracted and he began abruptly pacing away from her, running his hand through his hair in frustration. But he didn't dare scold her because he wanted to know everything. "And? Did something happen?"

Vanessa hesitated after this dramatic display of disapproval. "Sometime around five this morning I had an intruder."

"Did you or Haley get hurt?" Troubled, he returned to her, visually scanning her body, checking her for any sign of injury.

"No, I actually knew him. He's my gardener's brother," Vanessa said, and chuckled nervously.

"What did he want?"

"He needed money." Vanessa raised her eyebrows, attempting to plead his case. "He'd gotten into a bit of trouble with some drug people. He looked terrified and he told me they'd kill him. I let him take all the money I had in my purse, then he left," she said rapidly, not looking at him for fear of the condemnation she'd see on his face.

Andrew, furious by Vanessa's cavalier attitude and her defense of a criminal who could have easily murdered her, frowned, sending her a seriously stern, paternal look. "Did you lock the door and set the alarm after he left?" he asked, between clenched teeth.

"Yes," she answered contritely.

"Did you call the police?"

"No." *Oh oh, now I'm in big trouble.*

"Vanessa, why not?" he exhaled, feeling frustrated.

"I called my gardener, Juan, instead." She tried to justify her actions. "I couldn't bear the thought of those people hurting his brother. I've known Juan forever, he assured me he'd take care of it personally, and he asked me not to call the police."

Andrew patiently looked her into her pleading eyes, taking both of her hands gently in his. He attempted to reason with her. "Don't you think he might have been safer with the police?"

215

"I thought about it," Vanessa admitted, knowing he was probably right, especially since Roberto was nearly killed. "But as it turns out, everything's fine. I called Juan right before you called me this morning. His brother was badly beaten, but he made it safely to the hospital. The police were there when I called."

"Why didn't you call me right away, as soon as he left this morning?" Andrew sighed, placing the palm of his hand tenderly on her cheek, disappointed by her lack of faith in him.

"Because I wanted to talk to Juan first. Which brings me to the second thing that happened this morning." She moved, turning away from his probing gaze, needing some space between them. He'd disapproved of the way she'd handled Roberto's break-in, and she feared he'd overact even more to her response to the next incident as well.

"What else happened?" he asked suspiciously. He respected her, but decided she clearly lacked self-preservation skills, and it frightened him.

"I almost called you about this, but decided to talk to you in person instead."

"All right, I'm here now," he said patiently. He didn't touch her, but remained close, a little too close for her liking.

"After I hung up with Juan, my home phone rang." Vanessa launched into her story about her early morning, creepy phone call. "A scary sounding man with a low, gravely voice threatened Haley."

"What did he say, exactly?" Andrew asked, suddenly on high alert. He'd switched automatically into his calm, detached, detective mode.

"He said something about her taking his money, and if she didn't give it back, he'd make her wish she were dead." Vanessa struggled to remember everything he said clearly. "I honestly thought it was just a prank call," she said defensively.

"Do you have any idea who he was?" Andrew frowned, taking the threat to Haley seriously.

"No. That's all he said. Then he hung up on me."

He flipped out his pad, probing her for more information. "What time was the call?"

"I don't know, about five thirty this morning," she said vaguely, knowing their emotionally charged conversation had turned into a police investigation.

He reached for his cell phone. "This is Detective Kelly. Ms. Golden received a threatening phone call on her home phone, at approximately 0530 this morning. Could you please trace the call and get back to me?"

He turned back to Vanessa. "Did you ask Haley about the caller?"

Vanessa shook her head. "No. I didn't want to scare her unnecessarily. I planned to discuss it with you first."

Andrew tucked his pad back in his pocket. He gathered her in his arms, holding her close while he calmed his own erratic heartbeat. "That's all right. I'll find out who he is. Then I'll talk with Haley about it if I need to. Don't worry, I'll take care of this." He held her tight, running his hands rhythmically up and down her back. "I'm glad you told me, and now I'm especially glad that I moved you both to a safer location. It would kill me if anything happened to either one of you." He swept back her hair, his hands resting possessively on the sides of her cheeks, and kissed her reverently on the forehead. Lowering his gaze back to her lovely face, he confessed, "I've grown rather attached to you."

Vanessa rested her head on his chest.

"Now, I want you to promise me that you'll always confide in me. Don't ever keep me in the dark about things that upset or frighten you. You have to trust me!" he commanded, authoritatively.

Vanessa nodded without lifting her head.

He held her tighter. She lifted her head to search the expression on his face just as he lowered his head, kissing her aggressively on the lips, quietly seething inwardly with anger and desperation. His possessive, emotional kiss made Vanessa squirm uncomfortably within his confining embrace. The quietness of the house suddenly felt oddly disturbing, and she turned her head away to listen. "I think I'd better check on Haley and Callie. I'm afraid Callie may have run off." She pushed him forcefully away from her, rushing toward the door. Although Andrew had meant well, she needed to escape his possessive grasp. She resented his overbearing attitude, and his arrogant need to control her. She thought belligerently as she reached the door, *I've managed pretty well without you for years!*

"Takeout for dinner?" he called lamely after her.

"Sounds good to me." Vanessa dashed out of the room and down the stairs.

Andrew lowered himself onto the edge of the bed, leaned forward to rest his elbows on his thighs and sunk his head into his hands. Frustrated, he scrubbed his hands across his face, listening to the clip-clop of her rapidly retreating footsteps down the stairs. He knew she'd used her cat as an excuse to bolt from him. His panic had made him act pushy and overprotective, and he cursed himself for his insecurity, and his thoughtless insensitivity.

Vanessa rushed outside to find Haley still asleep where she'd left her, but no sign of Callie. She quickly scanned the yard. Shep lay in the sunshine on the opposite side of the pool with his back to her. As she walked closer, she discovered that Callie had curled up between Shep's legs. They both slept peacefully on the sun-warmed patio together. Amused, she shook her head; never could she have imagined her cat sleeping with a dog.

The sun dipped down over the edge of the ocean. Pinks and oranges cascaded from the horizon, sending flaming rays streaking across the sky. Vanessa exhaled, relieved to be standing alone, silently captivated by the stunning view. Breathing in the ocean air, she felt her worries and stress drain away. Drawn to the edge of the patio, she watched the peaceful ocean foam rolling gently onto the sand below her, and she listened to nature's contrast, hearing the violent waves slapping harshly against the rocks. Her thoughts were interrupted by the shrill sound of the seagulls, loudly crying out while scavenging for food.

Standing motionless, spellbound by the gradually disappearing sun, Vanessa sensed Andrew's presence close behind her. He moved nearer, cautiously circling her waist with his hands. Leaning back, she rested comfortably against his firm body.

"Spectacular, isn't it!" he whispered in her ear. Not a question, but merely a statement of fact. Her annoyance with him instantly melted away. His close presence didn't break the magical spell for her; it enhanced it.

"Yes, this is incredible."

"Wow you guys, look at that sunset!" Haley's exuberant voice broke through their short-lived serenity, and they turned as one to look back at her.

"Are you hungry?" Vanessa asked.

"Yeah, I could eat." Haley responded with her typical response to that particular question, and Vanessa laughed.

"I have a bunch of takeout menus. Select what you want, and I'll go pick it up. Would you like to move inside?" Andrew offered.

"No, if you don't mind, I'd like to stay outside. Can we eat out here?" Haley loved relaxing by the pool, especially after being cooped up all week. She relished the warm, fresh sea air.

"Sounds good," Vanessa and Andrew answered in unison, and then

Full-Sailed Surrender

chuckled.

"Thanks, it's really nice out here."

It took a few minutes, but finally, everyone agreed on something from the same restaurant. Andrew showed Vanessa around his kitchen and left to pick up dinner.

Vanessa brought Haley's laptop outside and she happily talked with both of her parents, while she sat outdoors, basking in the soft glow of the evening sunset. Because of the time difference, her siblings had already gone to bed. Haley seemed more relaxed with her parents then she'd been in the past. They didn't ask her anything difficult, but simply talked about routine day-to-day life, as if she'd never left home. Before her mother said goodbye, she asked to speak with Vanessa in private. Vanessa shrugged silently at Haley and carried the laptop inside to the kitchen.

"I need you to be honest with me. How is Haley doing? Do you think she'll be all right?" June asked anxiously.

"She seems to be healing up nicely."

"I've already heard a little bit about what she did when she arrived there in California. You know—how she had sex with men to support her horrid boyfriend?"

"Yes..." Vanessa encouraged, knowing that June had trouble asking for favors.

"We were wondering—that is, if it's not too much of an imposition—if you'd take Haley to Mass on Sunday? We believe that it's important for her to attend confession as soon as she can."

"Very well, I'll see what I can do." Vanessa understood. June clearly thought Haley's salvation hinged on her ability to confess her sins.

"I'm sorry for imposing on you this way, but I know it will help her to make peace with her past."

"I understand." Although Vanessa was a Methodist, who no longer participated in any religious practices, she acknowledged and respected June's religious beliefs. "I'll do my best to get her to church."

After saying their goodbyes, Vanessa closed the computer and returned to Haley deep in thought.

"What did my mom want to ask you in secret?" Haley asked, suspiciously.

"Your parents think you need to go to church on Sunday. They want you to go to confession." Vanessa watched for her response, having no idea how Haley felt about the ritual.

Haley looked down at her hands resting in her lap. She didn't fidget, but remained perfectly still. Vanessa sat down next to her, reluctant to disturb her obvious reflections; she simply watched Haley, waiting patiently for her reply.

"I'm afraid," she whispered, without looking at Vanessa. "I've done so many bad things, I might be struck dead if I walk into a church."

"I'm certainly no expert." Vanessa smiled to herself. "But I thought everyone was a sinner. Isn't that why people go to church? To confess their sins?"

"Do you go to church?" Haley asked.

"I did when I was your age." Vanessa evaded her question, unwilling to discuss her personal beliefs.

"You don't anymore?"

"No, but I'll go with you if you want me to." Vanessa preferred not to reveal the painful reasons she no longer attended church, or influence Haley's decision one way or the other.

"Thank you," Haley said, relieved by Vanessa's support, and thrilled that she'd agreed to attend with her. "I guess I should go. I know it will make my parents happy, and I owe them a lot."

"Think about it." Vanessa believed Haley should decide for herself, not simply attend out of guilt or obligation. "I'll ask Andrew if there's a church nearby, somewhere safe. Then, if you want to go, I'll make sure it happens."

"Thank you," Haley answered somberly.

They both sat in quiet contemplation, lost in their own thoughts, watching the last few remaining rays of the sunset disappear.

"You two look very serious, everything all right?" Andrew asked, setting the takeout dinner on the table.

"Everything's fine," Vanessa responded, following Andrew back inside to the kitchen to talk privately.

"Okay, tell me the truth," he said, searching Vanessa's face for clues once they were alone in the kitchen. "I know something happened while I was gone, spill it."

"Nothing happened. Haley talked to her parents, that's all."

"Yes, and...?"

"They want her to go to church on Sunday. They believe if she goes to confession, it will help Haley heal her soul, or something like that," she said, rolling her eyes.

"And...?" Andrew sent her a cautious look.

"I offered to go with her," she said, looking away and shifting her weight on her feet, carefully avoiding his questioning gaze. "She's scared and hasn't been to church in years. Do you know of one close by?"

Andrew squelched his amusement at her obvious discomfort over appearing in a church. He remembered how she'd accused him of being a *bible-thumper* not too long ago. It astonished him that she'd even contemplate going to church, even for Haley's sake.

"There's a small Catholic Church about twelve miles up the coast. The church is secluded and safe, and I know the priest well. Let me know what you decide, and I'll escort you."

The subject closed, he flipped on the outside lights, including the ones shining from the bottom of the pool, and carried the dishes, utensils, and a bottle of wine outside. The illuminated pool shimmered an enchanting turquoise blue while the three of them laughed and talked companionably during their enjoyable meal.

Vanessa and Andrew quietly sipped wine, entertained by Haley, who candidly confessed to several of her childhood transgressions. Most of them were harmless, including the time she'd spray-painted her dog green for St. Patrick's Day.

After dinner, Andrew brought out a very decadent mud pie for dessert and Haley clapped her hands in delight. Closing her eyes, she savored every bite of sweet, dark chocolate crust, filled with smooth coffee ice cream, and smothered in chocolate sauce.

The shrill ring of Andrew's cell phone interrupted their cozy party. Setting his dish aside, he answered and immediately began jotting down notes as he listened intently. After he hung up, he glanced at the pad in his hand. "Do either of you know a man named Scott Grant?"

Shocked to hear Scott's name, Haley shivered involuntarily and set her dish down on the table with noticeably unsteady hands, giving Andrew her full attention.

"Yes. I do," she whispered.

Andrew could see the startled look of surprise and the sudden paleness of Haley's face. As a detective, he sensed a difficult conversation ensuing, and wondered if she'd be candid enough to answer his questions.

Vanessa also noticed the look of dread on Haley's face. She wanted to jump in to protect her, but Andrew gave her a warning glance, shaking his head slightly in her direction.

"There's a reason I'm asking about him," he said, sounding more like *Detective* Kelly, than easy-going Andrew, that he'd been just a moment ago. "I've been informed that he's the suspect who called Vanessa's house earlier this morning. It seems—he made a direct threat toward you, Haley. Apparently, he's upset that you took his money? Do you have any information that might help me to understand his accusation?"

She didn't want to talk about the horrid man who'd brutally abused her. A minute ago, she'd been happier than she'd been in years. Now, just thinking about Scott, and how she'd robbed him, made her stomach heave. *Would Andrew really send her to jail?*

"Yes," Haley answered sheepishly, not wanting to elaborate.

"His rap sheet says he has two prior felony convictions for possession of narcotics. What's your connection to him? And why does he think you have his money?" Seeing the pale, shocked look on her face, he softened his tone and reached for her hand. "I promise, I'll do everything I can to protect you."

She struggled with her composure, and a few enormous tears rolled down her face. She wanted to hide, but instead she looked him straight in the eyes and confessed. "I did take his money. Jimmy made me go to his place the night before the bank robbery. He beat me! And he raped me! He was really high—so when he fell asleep, I stole all of the money he had hidden in a coffee can. I was going to use it to get away from Jimmy. But, when I tried to count it, Jimmy caught me. He grabbed all of it. I don't even know how much money I stole."

A sob escaped her lips, Vanessa quickly enveloped her in a supportive embrace, and Andrew leapt from his seat and began pacing. Jimmy and his friends had used her in such a cruel, ruthless way. He cursed silently to himself while he struggled to appear calm.

"Thank you." Andrew finally sat back down in front of Haley, placing his hand gently on her arm. "I appreciate how difficult it must be to talk about this. I promise, that man will never hurt you again!"

"Are you going to kill him?" Haley asked, her eyes large with anticipation.

"No." Andrew dropped his hand and laughed at her innocence. "But tomorrow I'll have a little chat with him. Once I remind him of your age, and the three strikes law, he'll never bother you again. Trust me, tomorrow I'll take care of this for you." Haley hugged Andrew appreciatively and Vanessa exhaled a sigh of relief.

"Now finish your mud pie," Andrew smiled, handing her the

remainder of her rapidly melting desert. Haley smiled timidly before she resumed devouring her thawed mud pie with relish.

Andrew returned her smile, then picked up the remainder of his own melted mud pie and walked into the house. Vanessa gave Haley a quick hug and followed him inside.

"Thank you, I thought for a moment I might have to intervene on Haley's behalf. I guess I should have trusted you." Vanessa's voice became silky soft and appreciative as she moved closer, standing directly in front of him. Reaching for his hand, she sent him a grateful smile of relief.

Their close, intimate proximity caused Andrew's emotions to shift rapidly from passionate anger, to passionate arousal. He locked eyes with Vanessa and squeezed her hand gently. Maintaining eye contact, he raised her hand to his lips for a tender kiss. His warm lips caressed her knuckles, and he slowly drew her finger into his mouth. Her eyes dilated as he scorched her with his sensual, burning gaze, bursting with erotic hunger and promise. Vanessa's breath caught in her chest, her heart skipped a beat, and her strained nerves quivered.

She inhaled deeply, his musty, clean scent tantalizing her heightened senses. She forcefully exhaled, as he blew lightly across the moisture on her knuckles, causing her nipples to ache with need. There was no awkward shyness between them. Suddenly, she eagerly anticipated the approaching night nestled within his intimate embrace, with both smoldering impatience and uninhibited desire.

Chapter 21
Painful Sting

$\mathcal{H}$aley feigned exhaustion and Vanessa helped her to bed. She made a big show of placing her headphones on and turning up her music. She'd watched the secretive, sexually charged glances smoldering between Andrew and Vanessa ever since they'd returned from the kitchen. *They need their privacy tonight*, she thought. So, saying a quick goodnight, she headed for bed and shooed them away.

After climbing the stairs to Andrew's bedroom, he surprised Vanessa, leading her by the hand through a previously unnoticed set of french doors in his room. Stepping through the unnoticed doors, she sighed with enchantment, discovering they opened up onto a large balcony overlooking the ocean.

Two comfortable looking, high-backed wicker chairs separated by a small white table caught her eye. The seat cushion of one chair was well worn, while the other one appeared brand new. A sad vision of Andrew sitting alone on his balcony, staring blankly out over the ocean, vividly flashed through Vanessa's mind.

Andrew didn't speak. He simply rearranged the chairs so they sat side by side, and helped her into the one with the pristine cushion, before seating himself. Resting his elbows on the armrests of his chair, he reclined back, silently listening to the familiar rhyme of the surf crashing onto the rocks below. Looking up, Vanessa saw twinkling celestial bodies whimsically dotting the dark sky above them.

Vanessa didn't know what to expect next, and then the full moon slowly began to rise, reflecting shimmering light across the water's dark surface, causing the ocean to magically sparkle and glitter in the night. Sitting in complete awe, she felt the warm, moist ocean air wrap around her like a soft, gentle hug. Wordlessly they sat beside each other, enjoying the timeless, mystical rising of the full moon.

Beneath the moon's soft glow, joy and wonderment filled Vanessa's heart, and the muscles in her body liquefied. She had no worries or regrets about her past, and no fears for her future. She simply existed in this one moment in time, never having felt so content or safe before in her life. Recognition of her emerging love for Andrew filled her heart, and she couldn't imagine a life that didn't include sharing quiet, serene moments like this one with him.

Stifling a yawn, Vanessa felt the long, stressful day suddenly overwhelm her. Andrew noticed, rose to stand in front of her, and gently pulled her up onto her feet into his waiting arms. He cradled her close and softly began to hum the classic tune *Moon River* in her ear. Swaying within his tender embrace, she began slow dancing with him under the moonlight. Then he whispered softly in her ear, endeavoring to prolong the magical, fairylike mood. "I think a good night's sleep is long overdue for you."

"You could be right about that." She rested her head on his shoulder and closed her eyes.

Andrew led Vanessa back inside, leaving one side of the french doors standing ajar. Bedtime rituals complete, she quietly snuggled into his bed, marveling at the pale moonlight filtering into the room, and the light brush across her cheek, as the warm, gentle ocean breezes swirled around them.

Vanessa nuzzled next to Andrew, her head resting on his shoulder with her hand comfortably over his heart. He gently hugged her toward him. Although Vanessa had never slept in a room open to the outside before, she felt completely at ease and safe with Andrew beside her. Within minutes she fell into a sound sleep. Andrew smiled at the sound of her low, rhythmic breathing, before he too succumbed, and joined her in a deep, contented slumber.

The next morning, Vanessa woke cradled in Andrew's strong arms. She couldn't remember when she'd slept so soundly. *Maybe it's the salty sea air*, she thought. But in her heart, she knew it had been the feeling of complete safety, for perhaps the first time that she could recall, which had allowed her to sleep so deeply. She felt Callie curled up on the other side of her and smiled, feeling totally contented. The sensation of the gentle rise and fall of her head resting on Andrew's chest while he slept comforted her. *Life is good*, she thought. Closing her gritty eyes, she drifted back into a tranquil slumber.

When Vanessa awoke the second time, Andrew had gotten up and stood barefoot at the end of the bed, reaching into the closet with his hair tousled and wet from his shower. Wearing only a pair of casual shorts, he smiled instantly when he caught her covertly watching him.

"Good morning. How'd you sleep?"

"Umm..." Vanessa stretched her arms out to her sides. "I think that was the best night's sleep I've ever had." He crawled across the bed to kiss her, a wolfish smile spread across his face.

"I heard Haley downstairs, so I thought I'd better go down and help her," he said, kissing her good morning. "You take your time. I'll fix breakfast, and if you're not down, I'll bring it upstairs to you."

"You're going to make me fat and lazy," Vanessa laughed.

"I'm not worried about that." Andrew smiled, gently swatting her behind playfully, before climbing off the bed and pulling at his waistband to fasten his shorts. "I mean it, take your time. I've got everything under control."

"Aye aye, Captain, trust me, I will." Vanessa rolled over and closed her heavy eyelids.

Andrew shook his head in delight as he headed out the door, Callie quickly scooting out ahead of him. Vanessa heard him whistling an unrecognizable tune as he ran down the stairs, amused by his good nature.

Once Andrew reached the kitchen, he noticed Haley sitting alone outside with her laptop open through the closed sliding glass door. Callie began to rub against his legs, loudly demanding her breakfast. He found some milk and a can of tuna fish for her. She swished her tail, sending him a dirty look, but made do with her makeshift breakfast. Andrew left her to it, and went outside to see what he could get for Haley.

"Good morning, how'd you sleep last night?"

"Oh, good morning. I slept great." She paused the movie she was watching, removing her headphones to talk.

"What would you like for breakfast?"

"Whatever you have is fine. I hope you don't mind, but I already helped myself to a cup of your coffee."

"Please feel free to help yourself to anything you can find." He sat down in the chair next to her. "All right, what do you usually eat in the morning?"

"Well, I never had breakfast when I lived with Jimmy." Haley shrugged and considered. "But in the hospital I ate pancakes."

"Okay, pancakes it is." Andrew leapt up, rubbing his hands together. "I'll go see if I can whip some up."

Haley smiled at his enthusiasm. She loved that he always seemed to be in such a good mood. Watching Andrew walk toward the kitchen on a mission, she returned to her movie.

Vanessa heard the clattering of dishes downstairs in the kitchen, and guilt got the better of her. She jumped in the shower and slipped into a simple cotton sundress, deliberately omitting her underwear.

When Vanessa entered the kitchen, she laughed. Andrew had flour all over him. Meanwhile, Shep, hunched on the floor next to him, was busily eating burnt pancakes. A charred aroma filled the room.

"I see you're fixing pancakes for breakfast. Are you just fixing burnt ones for Shep? Or were you planning on making some edible ones for the humans?"

Andrew looked a little bewildered and she instantly regretted teasing him.

"Would you like some help?" she offered.

"I guess I haven't made pancakes for a few years." He smiled good-naturedly. "I did manage to make one good batch for Haley."

The two of them proceeded to spend the next hour working together in the kitchen. They made a great team, and eventually they enjoyed an edible breakfast outside, family-style with Haley. She gobbled down her second helping just as enthusiastically as she had the first.

Returning inside, with Haley once again occupied by her movie outside, Andrew and Vanessa began to clean up. Soon, their playful teasing turned cleaning drudgery into a thoroughly sensual event. They tossed soapsuds at each other, and Andrew water-soaked Vanessa's thin sundress with the kitchen sink sprayer, leaving nothing beneath her soaked cotton dress to the imagination. Staring at her exquisite female form, Andrew found he couldn't resist and pulled Vanessa into his arms for a kiss.

"You're not wearing anything under this little dress, are you?" he whispered.

She shook her head in silent response, feeling his arousal pressed against her belly. She sent him a deliberately wicked smile as she danced away from him.

"Go make an excuse to Haley," he groaned. "I'm going upstairs to change. Please—don't be too long."

"I won't be."

Taking a few moments to regain her poise, Vanessa stepped outside to talk to Haley.

"Can I get you anything?" Vanessa asked, standing behind Haley's chair to cover her soaked, indecent appearance.

"No, I'm stuffed, but thanks anyway." She smiled angelically without removing her headphones or glancing back. "I think I'll just relax out here for awhile. I'd like to finish watching the rest of this movie, that is, if you don't need me for anything."

Haley had heard their playful laughter in the kitchen, followed by Andrew's pounding steps up the stairs, and had been waiting curiously to hear the excuse Vanessa would give her, before she followed him.

"No, no, in fact, I thought I might go up and change into my swimsuit. I think I'd like to swim a few laps."

"Don't you think you'd better hurry up? You don't want to keep Andrew waiting," Haley giggled.

"I'm sure I don't know what you're talking about." Vanessa smiled, feigning indignation.

They both laughed at the pretense. Then, Vanessa turned and ran inside, rushing breathlessly upstairs in anticipation of a pleasurable interlude with Andrew.

Vanessa burst into Andrew's room, only to find him sitting alone outside on the balcony. He'd washed off the flour, and now wore only his shorts. Unaware of the view, he seemed far away, absorbed in deep thought. She stood in front of him to gain his attention and he regarded her with a serious frown.

"You must think—all I ever want to do is get you into the sack. I can't explain why I'm so insatiable. I've never felt this strong of an attraction to anyone before in my life. I just can't seem to get enough of you," he apologized, but then his gaze dropped automatically from her face to her chest, and he groaned inwardly, squirming uncomfortably in his chair. Her nipples, stretching the thin, wet, cotton fabric of her dress, stood fully erect, begging for his attention.

Vanessa watched the expression on his tortured, guilty face, then smiling she reached out her hand to him. Andrew took it, and stood before her. She whispered to him, as if they were involved in a secret conspiracy. "Don't worry, I understand completely. And trust me, the feeling is mutual."

She led him by the hand back into the bedroom where they hastily undressed, feeling as eager and free as a couple of teenagers. Confessions of mutual love and attraction had fueled their intimate fire. Accepting their unfulfilled sexual excitement and desires, they fell into bed. Once they'd embraced the truth of their lust for each other, they rapidly reached a new pinnacle of sexual ecstasy and satisfaction.

Lying together, Vanessa curled against Andrew in the warm afterglow of their lovemaking. He toyed affectionately with a strand of her hair and thought aloud. "You know… I bought all new furniture when I moved in here. You're the first woman to ever share my bed." He cuddled her closer against him, knowing they'd christened his virgin bed once and for all.

Vanessa gazed affectionately up at him. *And I plan to be the last,* she answered inside her satiated, love-drunk mind.

Nearly an hour later, Andrew descended the steps and returned to sit beside Haley for a quick conversation. Although it was Saturday, he'd dressed in his usual work clothes, long brown trousers and a light shirt and brown jacket, preparing to leave for LA and his "chat" with Scott.

"I thought this was your day off? You're not going to see Scott today, are you?" Haley asked, noting his attire.

"I want to take care of this right away. I'll just have a little talk with him, and then I'll be back. Here's a menu for a restaurant that will deliver. You two can order lunch after you've recovered from your scrumptious breakfast." He chuckled and sent her an apologetic smile.

"I wish you wouldn't go," Haley said, suddenly wanting him to spend a carefree day with her and Vanessa, instead of revisiting her sleazy past. "Please don't talk to him, he's a really nasty man."

"I can handle the likes of Scott." Andrew sent her a patronizing smile. "Please try not to worry. I'll be back before you know it. Trust me, he'll never hurt or threaten you again." With that, he gave her a reassuring pat on her shoulder and turned to leave.

"Please be careful, he takes drugs and drinks a lot and he can be sort of unpredictable," she warned, squinting up at him, a frown creasing her forehead, painfully recalling her last violent night with Scott.

"I'll be fine, but thanks for the heads up."

Andrew looked toward the door. Vanessa had appeared wearing a stunning, dark red swimsuit. He admired her athletic shape, remembering the sensual, smooth sensation of caressing every one of her scrumptious curves, and moved toward her. She wore a similar look of concern on her face. Holding her loosely at arms length, he kissed her softly.

"I'll call you as soon as I get this little matter wrapped up," he said, confidently reassuring her.

"Be careful." She moved into his arms and clung to him.

"I'll be fine, you two." He untangled himself, laughing. "This is my job.

I do it all the time."

Andrew unlocked his car and sat alone for a moment in his carport. He'd left Shep at home to guard the girls. Suddenly he had a feeling that he'd forgotten something important. He patted the front of his shirt, realizing he'd forgotten his bulletproof vest upstairs. He briefly considered running upstairs to get it, but Scott was a low level thug with no record of violence. He'd frequently interviewed suspects without one, so he decided it was too hot and too much bother for today's simple, informal chat. With a quick reassuring pat of the gun resting on his hip, he backed out, and turned his car toward LA.

As soon as she heard Andrew's car, Vanessa jumped into the pool. She swam hard, lap after lap without counting, trying to work off an unshakable feeling of unease she felt in the pit of her stomach. Haley had set aside her computer, fixated on Vanessa's tortuous workout. Finally exhausted, Vanessa climbed out of the pool, and vigorously towel-dried her dripping hair.

"Wow, Vanessa, you really take your workout seriously."

Vanessa's quick smile didn't reach her eyes.

"Don't worry about Andrew," Haley said. Her guilt had increased with each strenuous lap she'd watched Vanessa swim. She feebly tried to reassure her. "Scott's usually passed out drunk by this time of the day."

"I hope you're right," Vanessa said, as she sat in the adjoining chaise lounge. Leaning back, she continued to silently air dry in the warmth of sun.

Haley watched Vanessa glance at her cell phone resting on the table next to her, before she closed her eyes. Sensing Vanessa didn't wish to discuss Andrew any longer, Haley reached for her laptop and placed her headphones over her ears, allowing Vanessa temporary peace, and solitude.

Andrew arrived in LA and checked in with his buddy, Mike, an LAPD detective. Mike had been the one who'd previously informed him of the details of Scott's rap sheet, and his current address.

When Andrew pulled up to the seedy-looking apartment building, his detective senses switched into high alert. He realized he wasn't just warning off a drug-taking sex offender, he was about to enter a potentially hazardous location. The graffiti, broken windows, and peeling paint were all dangerous red flags of probable gang activity. He cursed himself, and wished he'd worn his protective vest.

Andrew sat cautiously in his car as he carefully surveyed the area outside of Scott's apartment. Almost immediately, he spotted two shifty-eyed characters, both wearing jackets despite the sweltering heat, loitering near the entrance to the apartment building. He pulled out a map, pretending to be a lost tourist, and covertly snapped photos of them with his cell phone. These he sent to Mike, before dialing Mike's number at the station.

"You know that address I asked you about? The one you gave me for Scott Grant? I'm sitting outside his apartment now. There are a couple of suspicious-looking characters hanging around. I could be wrong, but it looks to me like something's about to go down. I just sent you a couple of photos, maybe you'll recognize them."

"What do you think?" Andrew asked after a brief pause.

Mike instantly recognized the two men. They were both street thugs, known to be working for one of the most dangerous drug operators in town.

"Whatever you do, do not get out of the car," Mike's excited voice warned. "Stay right where you are. I'm on my way, and I'm sending in reinforcements. I think you might have accidently stumbled across the drug buy we've been attempting to locate. Our sources have had nothing. In fact, you've just given us our first good lead. Stay put!"

"All right, but I think you'd better hurry. It looks like something's going down right now."

"We're on our way. Sit tight."

Andrew kept his gaze down on the map, avoiding eye contact with the two shifty-eyed men. But they kept glancing over towards him, and Andrew considered moving his car farther down the street. He didn't want to be in the middle of a shootout, especially without his vest.

One of the men stared directly at him as he talked on his cell phone. Andrew knew he'd been made and started his car. But before he could pull out, two other men came running out of the building. They ignored him and walked briskly up the street. He switched off his engine and watched them through his rearview mirror. The SWAT team materialized out of nowhere, rapidly surrounding the four suspects before they reached the first corner. The dangerous group was arrested, without so much as a single shot fired!

Relieved that the big bust was over, Andrew got out of his car and watched Mike, his slightly younger counterpart, ambling down the street toward him.

"Thanks for your help Andrew. I was beginning to think we'd never get these guys," Mike said. He shook Andrew's hand and patted him on the shoulder.

"No problem, happy to assist. As far as I'm concerned, drug suppliers are the scum of the earth."

"I couldn't agree with you more," Mike nodded. "Now..." he said, looking up at the five-story dilapidated apartment building. "We just have to find out who in this building just received a very large drug shipment, before it gets out onto the streets. Although, my guess is that who ever he is, he's long gone by now."

"What about my guy?" Andrew asked. "You suppose I could still go in and take care of the little matter that brought me here in the first place?"

"Unfortunately, as you know, this is a crime scene now." Mike hesitated. "It'll take hours to thoroughly investigate each apartment and search for the drugs. But I'll go in with you, confronting your guy shouldn't be too much of a problem."

As they were talking, Andrew watched swarms of SWAT members dressed in full tactical gear filing up the stairs into the building.

"Thanks Mike, this should just take a minute. You don't suspect Scott in this do you?" he asked.

"Nah, he's too small-time for these guys." Mike considered Scott to be more of nuisance than a threat. "According to his rap sheet, he's been convicted for several counts of possession, but nothing big like this. Those guys we just arrested were carrying over a million dollars. Someone in this building bought a truck-load of cocaine, so watch your back."

"Got it." Andrew felt his adrenaline rushing. It had been quite a few years since he'd been involved in anything more than a small-town investigation, or a little paper pushing from his desk.

"Thanks again for your assist," Mike said, socking Andrew's shoulder playfully. "This city owes you big time. Those were some very nasty drug suppliers you got off the street!"

Mike gave him a nod and they entered the building together. Scott's apartment was on the third floor, and of course the elevator was out of order. Andrew unsnapped his gun, his adrenaline pumping overtime, keeping him on high alert for whoever had recently received a substantial amount of cocaine. He followed Mike up the filthy stairway.

The walls were scribbled with gang symbols, the stairs strewn with old garbage, and the landings reeked of stale urine. The steady stream of SWAT officers tromped up the stairs in front and behind them, peeling off on each floor to conduct their search.

Arriving on the third floor, the SWAT team fanned out to search the adjacent apartments, while Andrew and Mike walked down the hall toward Scott's place. Loud heavy-metal music blasted from inside the apartment, loudly filling the dingy hallway. Mike knocked on the door of Scott's next-door neighbor, and Andrew stepped up to knock on Scott's door.

Andrew drew back his hand, preparing to knock with enough force to be heard over the blaring music. But before his knuckles even hit the solid wooden door, it suddenly splintered and shattered, and he instantly felt an intense burning deep within his chest. Blood spattered across the walls as Andrew catapulted across the hallway, hitting the opposite wall like a rag doll, landing in a crumpled heap on the floor.

Nearby members of the SWAT team swarmed on the scene within seconds of the shotgun blast. Scott didn't have a chance. Panicking, he aimed at the officers, but they gunned him down before he made it to his door.

Mike rushed to Andrew's side, tore open his shirt, and exploded with a string of profanities. No vest! Andrew gushed blood from the gaping wounds on his bare chest, the direct result of the shotgun blast. Mike used Andrew's torn shirt in an attempt to stem the bleeding, and yelled for an ambulance.

Andrew remained conscious, but dazed. *This can't be happening to me, not now*, he thought. He felt the blackness slowly overtake him, and used his remaining strength to grab Mike's arm and pull him close.

"Tell Vanessa... I'll love her forever," Andrew whispered, passing out where he lay, in the warm, sticky, red pool of his own blood.

Mike frowned; he had no idea who Andrew had just referred to. But he was going to make damn sure that Andrew would be around to tell her himself.

The paramedics arrived within minutes, finding Andrew's limp, unconscious form scarcely breathing. They quickly bandaged him, began intravenous fluids, and whisked him off with lights and sirens to the nearest hospital.

A rapid search of Scott's apartment revealed a stack of newly acquired cocaine bricks sitting carelessly on his kitchen table.

Mike left a SWAT officer in charge of wrapping up the scene and then contacted Andrew's precinct, asking them to locate Vanessa. Mike rushed to his car to follow the ambulance. He wasn't sure if Andrew would survive, but he knew he had to contact Vanessa immediately. They patched him through to her cell phone just as he got into his vehicle.

"Hello?" Vanessa answered on the first ring, hoping it was Andrew.

"My name is Mike. I am an LAPD detective and I'm a friend of Andrew's. Is this Vanessa?" Mike hated to be the one to contact loved ones after an incident such as this.

"Is Andrew all right?" Something in this man's voice told her he did not have good news.

Mike tried to soften his voice as he continued. "I'm sorry to tell you, but Andrew's been shot."

"Shot! Is he dead?" Vanessa asked, her heart stopping.

"I'm not sure, he's been taken to the University Hospital. They'll do everything they can." Mike really had no information to give her yet.

"Mike?" She held her breath. "Are you telling me that Andrew's going to die?"

"No, Vanessa..." Mike thought, *I'm doing a very poor job of this.* "I'm telling you, I just don't know. He mentioned your name before he passed out, that's why I'm calling you."

Vanessa felt as if all the blood had left her body. She could faintly hear Haley crying somewhere in the distance. She took a deep breath to pull herself together. *I need to stay strong now! I can fall apart later.*

"Of course, Mike." Vanessa mustered up her best version of her controlled, composed self. "I'll go to the hospital immediately. Thank you for letting me know, and please keep me informed of any updates you may receive."

"I will, and Vanessa? I'm so sorry this happened. Andrew was the kindest, most decent person I've ever known." *And he certainly has excellent taste in women,* he thought, impressed by Vanessa's poise.

"Thank you, Mike." Vanessa couldn't help the tear that suddenly rolled down her cheek. Mike had just referred to Andrew in the past tense.

"I won't have you driving. I'm sending a squad car for you now." Mike knew her falsely calm voice covered her fear. "Where should I send it?"

"Have you ever been to Andrew's beach house?"

"Yes, they'll be there shortly," he said, wondering how long they'd lived together.

"Thank you." Vanessa continued to cry silently, but felt grateful to Mike for contacting her.

They hung up, and Haley, who'd been balancing on her crutches close by to listen, collapsed into Vanessa's lap, wailing like a tiny child.

"This is all my fault. God is punishing me!"

"Hush now, Haley, don't you dare blame yourself." Vanessa tried to calm her. "Andrew is a grown man, and he knew what he was doing. They're picking us up, so let's get ready to go to the hospital. We have to go see for ourselves how he is, okay?" Vanessa gently pushed her out of her lap, took a deep breath, and stood on her own shaky legs, handing a slightly subdued Haley her crutches.

Vanessa didn't have the luxury of becoming hysterical, at least not yet!

Chapter 22
Bleak Anticipation

*T*he police cruiser pulled swiftly up in front of Andrew's beach house. Officer Miles stepped out and briefly introduced himself, while assisting Haley to adjust her crutches as they hurried into the back seat, anxious to get to Andrew.

"My name is Audrey." A pretty, uniformed woman with light blond, shoulder-length hair smiled tentatively from the front seat. "I'm with the victims support team."

"Do either of you know what's happening with Andrew? Is he alive?" Vanessa asked anxiously, leaning forward to grip the back of the front seat, attempting to control the panicked tone of her request.

"I believe—he's in surgery," Officer Miles answered from the driver's seat. His soft, sympathetic, brown eyes reflected in the rearview mirror as he spoke, "He took a blast from a shotgun—they're going in after the BBs," he said, struggling with his emotions, as he had to say the words aloud.

"Well, that's encouraging isn't it?" Vanessa asked. "They wouldn't be doing that if he was dying, would they?"

"I agree, but the full extent of his injuries may not be revealed—until after surgery."

Haley had been quietly staring out the window until his cautionary comment, and then her uncontrollable sobbing began again. Haley's shoulders shook with guilt and grief. Vanessa sighed, pulling the distraught child close to comfort her distractedly. Scenery flew by in a blur; all the while she mentally urged the police car faster, needing to get to Andrew.

Vanessa imagined the worst-case scenario as she sat, numbly patting Haley's back. She'd never blame her if Andrew died; he would never have been in her life at all, if not for Haley. She would always be grateful for the time she'd spent with Andrew, no matter how brief it turned out to be.

The police car screamed up to the hospital emergency entrance. Vanessa and Haley rapidly scrambled out and rushed anxiously to the surgery waiting room. The room was completely occupied by solemn looking police officers. A worried looking plain-clothed officer of about forty, stood from his seat and approached her. His hair was dirty blond, cut military-style, and he was dressed in light brown khakis with the sleeves of his white shirt rolled up to his elbows.

"You must be Vanessa. My name is Mike, we spoke on the phone?" Mike was about six foot tall, muscular, with a kind, sympathetic face. Although he was younger, he resembled her childhood memory of her father, making her instantly relax and trust him.

"Yes, I am, is there any news yet?"

"Not really," Mike said, offering her his chair. "Andrew seemed better after the blood transfusions and the chest tube. Although he still hadn't regained consciousness before they took him into surgery. They're going in now to remove the small BBs imbedded in his chest, it could take hours."

Vanessa suddenly felt her stomach contract, and instantly became alarmed that she might gag or faint. *I'll be fine in a moment*, she insisted to herself, clutching her abdomen.

Vanessa searched the room for Haley. She sat in a chair across the room, soberly dabbing at her soggy eyes with a tissue; she was well attended, surrounded by a large group of young, concerned officers.

"Here, take a sip of this. It'll help." Vanessa didn't look up at Audrey, but simply sipped the offered water and reigned in her fear.

Audrey sat, remaining quietly in the seat beside her, while Mike continued to stand by, shifting his weight between his feet, feeling helpless. He couldn't leave Vanessa's side, but he'd just met her, and had no idea what comforting words to say. He hoped he could count on Audrey to handle the emotional fallout, if the news about Andrew turned out bad.

After waiting for nearly an hour, Vanessa became impatient. *Why was it taking so long?* She suddenly couldn't sit any longer and began pacing the room.

Audrey watched as the troubled furrow of Vanessa's brow deepened each time she paced past her chair. But she sat silently. She knew Vanessa's type. Needing to being in complete control at all times, waiting helplessly for news about Andrew's condition was driving her crazy. Audrey also knew Vanessa would eventually give up on trying to manage the situation, and then she'd need someone to talk to. The men in the room watched Vanessa with growing apprehension. But Audrey sat patiently sipping her coffee, seemingly undisturbed by Vanessa's agitated state.

Vanessa had paced the halls and the waiting room for quite some time before she noticed the nervous expressions on the faces of the men in the room. No one had dared say a word to her, but she could see they were uneasy. Vanessa forced herself to sit back down next to Audrey, who'd patiently been waiting for Vanessa to make the first move.

"I hate waiting like this!" Vanessa's eyes focused on the surgery doors and sighed. "I hate not knowing." Audrey seized her opportunity.

"Andrew must be very important to you."

Vanessa realized that Andrew had become everything to her. She'd allowed him to get under her skin, and inside her heart. He represented all of her possibilities and her dreams for the future. The idea of a life without him seemed flat, empty and very lonely.

"That would be a fair statement," Vanessa said.

"Have you two been together very long?" Audrey gently probed.

"Not long enough," Vanessa sighed. She didn't want to talk. She wanted action. Vanessa walked to the information desk. "Excuse me? What information do you have on Detective Kelly?" She needed to know something, anything.

"I'm sorry, but Detective Kelly has not been moved to the recovery room yet," the elderly volunteer responded calmly.

"I understand, thank you." Vanessa knew that the grey haired woman behind the desk couldn't help her, but she silently cursed, frustrated with her lack of information and control over the situation. She walked back toward Haley. "I'm going for a walk outside, please call me as soon as there's any news."

Vanessa didn't wait for an answer from the stunned Haley, whose mouth fell open in surprise, but simply turned around and marched out of the gloomy waiting room. Mike observed her departure and sat down next to Audrey.

"Do you think she's going to be okay?" he asked.

"Hard to say, she's a very tough lady," Audrey said, and shook her head. "My guess would be that she's suffered many losses in her life, ones that she couldn't control, and still hasn't come to terms with."

"Do you think you'll be able to help her, I mean if Andrew dies?" Mike asked quietly.

"Only if she wants me to." But Audrey doubted Vanessa would.

Mike sipped his coffee and beat himself up; *Why hadn't he asked Andrew if he had his vest on? Why had he just assumed?* They hadn't had a chance to catch up before the shooting, and he wondered about Andrew's relationship with Vanessa. He could see how devoted she was to Andrew. And, when Andrew thought he was dying, his last words had been about his love for her. *Come on Andrew, don't make me tell her what you said*!

Vanessa wandered around the hospital grounds. She wished she could go for a run. She felt as if she would explode from all the pent up anxiety and frustration. Once she knew Andrew's fate, she'd deal with it, no matter what the outcome. She simply couldn't stand not knowing. Vanessa found a path that led around a large pond and followed it. She walked slowly at first, then faster and faster, around and around. She had no idea how long she'd walked before her phone rang.

"Vanessa, Andrew's in the recovery room and the doctor will be out any minute."

"Thanks Haley, I'm on my way now." Vanessa ran back to the waiting room. She arrived breathlessly just as the doctor entered. He looked at her, puzzled by her gasping state, but continued to report on the results of Andrew's surgery and gave his guarded prognosis.

"First of all, are there any family members here?"

"His parents live in San Francisco. They're both elderly and in poor health," Mike explained then looked toward Vanessa. "This is Vanessa, his girlfriend."

Vanessa had a hard time hearing herself referred to as a girlfriend, but anxiously stepped forward, unconcerned by the title.

"Very well." He walked towards Vanessa, addressing her directly. "Andrew suffered what could have been a fatal wound. Thanks to the first aid provided by the officers on the scene, he has a chance of pulling through, but he has a long recovery in front of him. His right lung collapsed; the impact scarcely missed his heart. There's extensive damage to his right shoulder, but eventually he should recover full function of his arm. He owes his life to the angle of the blast, and the prompt response of the officers on scene."

"Thank you, Doctor." Vanessa eyes swam with tears of relief. *Andrew would live!*

The room was full of subdued merriment and animated talking. Haley balanced on her crutches, smiling through a steady stream of tears. Vanessa dabbed at her own wet eyes with the tissue Mike had discreetly handed her.

"When will I be able to see him?" Vanessa asked.

"He'll need an hour or two in the recovery room." The doctor smiled.

"You'll be able to see him once he's moved to the ICU. I'm afraid all other visitors will have to wait until he's stable enough to be moved out of the ICU." Vanessa nodded. She was acutely aware Andrew was still in critical condition.

"Thank you, Doctor."

After he left, she turned to Mike to shake his hand. "Thank you for saving Andrew's life."

"He would have done the same for me." Mike blushed.

"I'm sure he would." Vanessa nodded in agreement. "But this time it was you. Thank you, I'll never forget you."

Mike simply smiled and nodded.

The police officers began to file past Vanessa and out of the waiting room. They each briefly introduced themselves and wished Andrew a speedy recovery. The number of officers who had close ties to Andrew impressed her. It seemed he was well respected and loved. Mike was the last to leave.

"I'll check in with you daily to see how Andrew's doing. Please call me if there's any change in his condition or if you need anything. Here's my office, cell, and home phone numbers." Vanessa was impressed by Mike's bond with Andrew.

"Thank you, Mike. I'll keep in touch. I'll be sure to contact you if he changes or I think of something I need."

Vanessa was finally all alone with Haley, and a politely lingering Audrey.

"Thank you for your support, Audrey." Vanessa reached out to shake her hand. "If you have a card, I promise either I or Andrew will contact you if we need anything." Audrey knew a very controlled, efficient businesswoman had just dismissed her. Vanessa had no use for her, and no intention of confiding in her at this point.

"Very well, here's my card. Please call me, even if you just need someone to talk to," Audrey smiled, secretly impressed by Vanessa's coping skills.

Vanessa flashed her a professional smile, using the friendly tone of voice she frequently used when she was in her office. "I'll do that. Thank you again."

Audrey left, and now it was just Haley. What was she going to do with Haley? Vanessa had no intention of leaving the hospital, at least not until she was sure Andrew was going to survive. Haley needed to keep her ankle elevated. And, she needed to recover from her own surgery. She helped Haley back to a chair, giving her a brief hug and handing her a box of tissues.

"I'm going to step outside to make a few calls. Will you be okay?"

Haley simply nodded and blew her nose.

It was late afternoon and she hoped Marie would be available. Vanessa knew she could count on Marie; she always came up with the perfect solutions whenever Vanessa was too tired or stressed to think of one.

"I'm fine," Haley reassured her. "I'll call you if they decide to move Andrew to the ICU." Haley had a good idea what Vanessa was up to. She'd already decided that she'd comply with whatever Vanessa wanted her to do.

Vanessa smiled, nodded back at her and walked toward the door.

Vanessa wandered back to the path around the pond to call Marie, who was surprised to hear from Vanessa so soon. Hearing Marie's voice caused Vanessa to break down.

"You know that man—I'm seeing?" Her voice cracked as she swallowed her tears of self-pity.

"Yes, how is he?" Marie heard the uncharacteristic break in Vanessa's voice.

"Well, he managed to get himself shot." Vanessa's voice quivered.

"Oh my God, Vanessa! How is he doing?" Marie quickly made the sign of the cross.

"He's critical, but alive. The reason I called you is I need a favor." Vanessa didn't want to take the time it would require to explain the situation in great detail.

"Anything, you just name it." Marie heard Vanessa struggling to speak.

"I have a houseguest." Vanessa didn't have time to explain everything, but she wanted to give Marie a clear idea of what she needed. "We're both staying at my friend's beach house, along with my cat and his dog. Haley, my guest, is recovering from ankle surgery and she's still on crutches. I need someone to stay with her and maybe take her to church tomorrow. She'll be here until she flies home on Friday. I'm in a real bind Marie, do you know of anyone?"

Marie knew full well who her houseguest was. She'd watched Vanessa and Haley on the news, along with the handsome man who'd smuggled them away from Vanessa's house. She assumed he was the one who had been shot.

"Diane's home from school." Marie referred to her daughter, a freshman in college home for the summer. "She could stay with her if you think they'd be safe?"

"Absolutely, even though the media is hounding Haley because of the bank robbery, no one knows we're staying at Andrew's house." Vanessa understood her concern. "Even if it were discovered, the only threat now is from the paparazzi. I just don't want to leave Haley alone while she's still on crutches."

"I agree and I trust you, Vanessa. Where are you now?" Marie decided if it didn't work out for Diane, she'd stay with the girl herself.

"We're at the University Hospital," Vanessa sighed. "I'm waiting for Andrew to be moved to the ICU."

"I'm close. I could pick Haley up."

"That would be great, if it's not too much to ask?"

"We live only a few blocks from there." Marie would make it happen. "I'll be there soon."

Vanessa walked around the pond a few more times, contemplating how to juggle her time between Andrew and Haley. Vanessa felt guilty. Feeling frazzled, she deliberately stalled her uncomfortable conversation with Haley about returning to stay at Andrew's with strangers.

When she returned to the waiting room, she found Haley sitting alone. She looked like an abandoned child in her crumpled green shorts and striped yellow t-shirt, watching TV in the now empty waiting room. Vanessa's guilty heart ached as she sat down beside her. "I'm sorry, Haley, but I need to stay here until I'm sure Andrew's going to be alright. Unfortunately, this isn't such a great place for you to hang out."

"It's okay, I don't mind." Haley slumped down in her chair, knowing she was about to get dumped.

"I'll need someone to look after Callie and Shep while I'm here." Vanessa tried to appeal to Haley's kindhearted nature. "If you weren't on crutches, I'd just have you look after everything by yourself."

"I can get around just fine," Haley answered defensively.

"I know, you're a pro." Vanessa found Haley's vehement response sadly amusing, and gently patted her good leg, trying to proceed delicately. "I invited a friend's daughter to come hang out with you. Will that be okay?"

Haley began to do that thing where she focused her gaze on her lap, twisting her hands together. Vanessa placed a calming hand over her hands.

"Haley? Look at me. I wish I could be with you, but please try to understand, I can't leave Andrew."

"I know. I've ruined everything." Haley looked up, and her lower lip began to quiver. She quickly lowered her head, feeling ashamed. She knew Vanessa must be angry with her. After all, she got Andrew shot!

"No you haven't!" Vanessa wouldn't allow Haley to take the blame for any of it. She jumped up from her chair and began pacing angrily across the floor in front of Haley's chair. "He did this! He's the one who was careless. He got himself shot!" Vanessa vented her pent up fear and anger toward Andrew before she sat back down dejectedly, and placed her arm around Haley. "I'm not upset with you in any way. Understand?" She regained control, softly asking, "Please tell me you're all right spending the next few days with my friend's daughter."

"You know I'll do anything for you." Haley threw her arms around Vanessa's neck. "Don't even think about me, I'll be fine. Please, tell Andrew how sorry I am that he got shot, the very minute he's awake. Promise?"

"I promise." Vanessa smiled, hugging her, impressed by how rapidly Haley had adjusted to the idea of having someone staying with her.

They both sat back to wait for Marie and hopefully Diane, or for any word of Andrew's condition. Vanessa occupied her troubled mind by writing out detailed instructions for Callie's feeding schedule and Haley's medications. Meanwhile Haley watched TV, silently stressing over her upcoming meeting with Diane.

Less than an hour had passed when Marie and Diane appeared in the waiting room. No word on Andrew as yet. Vanessa quickly pulled Marie aside, huddling quietly together, and allowing the girls a chance to meet. Diane, a vivacious, outgoing, dark-haired, brown-eyed beauty, and a very shy Haley eyed one another. Diane promptly sat down next to Haley. Although Vanessa couldn't make out their conversation, she heard Haley's laughter. They chattered together excitedly, like a pair of old friends. The girls were only a few years apart in age. Vanessa's guilt eased considerably once she observed the relaxed way Haley smiled and joked with Diane. While they got acquainted, Vanessa relayed the list of detailed instructions to Marie, handing her the keys to Andrew's house.

Vanessa walked over to Haley, suddenly feeling sad to part with her. She stood, propped up by her crutches to give Vanessa a long hug goodbye, making her promise she'd call with any news. Vanessa thanked both Marie and Diane profusely. The three of them departed the waiting room in a flurry, anxious to get settled at Andrew's beach house for the night.

Once alone, Vanessa tried to wait as long as she could tolerate before walking back to the information desk to inquire about Andrew's condition.

"I'm sorry." The elderly lady squinted at her computer screen. "It seems he's still in the recovery room."

Vanessa chewed on her lower lip. He'd been in recovery for over two hours. She was sure something was wrong. Currently, she was the only person left in the entire waiting room. All of the others had left. Their loved ones had been moved to other rooms or discharged. She looked at the older woman with an air of determination. "I need to see Andrew Kelly now! I will not wait here another second. Please inform the recovery room nurses that I'm coming in."

With that, she turned away from the elderly lady whose mouth gaped with shock, and walked toward the entrance to the recovery room. She had just pushed through the doors marked Do Not Enter, when she noticed that the recovery room was completely empty. Only two doctors and a couple of nurses crowded around a single patient connected to a noisy, hissing breathing apparatus in the far corner of the room. The phone was ringing, but no one moved to answer it. As she got closer, she saw Andrew, still unconscious and still needing assistance to breathe. He appeared pale and lifeless. She gasped at the horrific sight, which instantly drew the attention of one of the nurses.

"I'm sorry, you can't be in here."

"I'm not leaving," Vanessa bristled.

All eyes turned toward Vanessa. An older doctor in blue scrubs moved from the head of Andrew's bed and stated calmly, "You must be Vanessa." He waved the barricading nurse aside.

Vanessa silently nodded. Unhindered, she slowly moved past him to Andrew's side. She lifted his hand, which felt limp and cold in her own hand, and she cradled it. Multiple intravenous drips infused into his veins. She heard the periodic hissing of the machine pumping air into his lungs, and noticed the blood soaked bandages on his chest and right shoulder. No obvious signs of life seemed visible, and she wondered if she'd been lied to about his prognosis.

"Is he dead?"

"I know this all looks very frightening." A different doctor other than the surgeon stepped toward her. "I'm Dr. Fuller. I was called in because Mr. Kelly has sustained a severe shock to his system. We've decided to keep him in a cooled state, sedated, and on the respirator for a period of time. This will allow his body time to heal."

"Is that normal?"

"No, but we've had success treating individuals with similar injuries as his."

"Will he survive?"

"We'll know more in a day or two."

"Does he know I'm here? Can he hear me?" she whispered. Her throat constricted, suddenly so dry she could hardly swallow.

"No one really knows the answer to that question, but I believe it's possible."

Vanessa brushed the hair off his cold brow, leaned forward, kissed his cheek, and then whispered softly into Andrew's ear. "Please... don't leave me."

Chapter 23
The Church on the Bluff

$\mathcal{M}$ arie returned to the hospital to find Vanessa sitting zombie-like in the ICU waiting room. It was heartbreaking for Marie to see her resilient boss sitting alone in such a state. She sat down close to her, waiting silently for Vanessa to notice her. It was a few minutes before Vanessa spoke in a flat, exhausted tone of voice. "Did the girls get settled in at the house?"

"They're fine," Marie answered calmly, resting her hand on top of Vanessa's. "Diane said she doesn't think she can take your money for staying in such a fabulous place. She feels like she's on an extravagant vacation instead of house sitting."

"How can I ever thank you for coming to my rescue?" Vanessa said, sending her a weak smile of appreciation.

"How's Andrew?" Marie shrugged off her gratitude.

"They're keeping him sedated." Vanessa's voice quivered. "They want him in a coma for a while so he can heal."

"Have you eaten anything today?" Marie noticed how sunken Vanessa's eyes looked.

"I'm not hungry."

"Vanessa, look at me!" Marie couldn't stand how defeated she sounded. "You're coming home with me. I'll make you dinner and you can sleep in Diane's room. We're only a few blocks away if anything happens."

Vanessa shook her head adamantly. "Thank you for the offer, but I can't leave him. Besides, I've imposed on you too much already."

"He doesn't even know you're here!" Marie snorted. "You're sitting in the waiting room. What difference will it make if you sit here or at my house. Andrew doesn't want or need you to make yourself sick. You can return anytime of the day or night. Now, I won't hear another word, let's go."

Vanessa stood up in a daze. "Let me go kiss him goodbye."

Marie watched as Vanessa walked into his glassed-in room, jam-packed with beeping machines and drips, to place a tender kiss on Andrew's forehead. Marie quickly crossed herself, saying a prayer for Andrew and another one for Vanessa. When Vanessa came out of the room, she spoke with the nurse caring for Andrew and wrote down her number. Marie could see the nurse nodding. She obviously approved of Vanessa's plan to leave the hospital for a while.

As soon as Marie walked into her house, she sat Vanessa down at the kitchen table and fixed her a cup of hot tea. Then she left her sitting silently, while she went to straighten Diane's room and change the sheets. She hoped she might get Vanessa to lie down. Finishing up, she heard her husband's car pull into the drive. She suddenly remembered he was bringing her mother-in-law home for dinner and quickly went out to meet him in the driveway. She briefly explained the situation to Vanessa before they entered. Vanessa looked up from her cup of tea to greet them, and then excused herself to go rest.

Marie showed her to her room, apologizing. "I'm sorry, I forgot my mother-in-law was coming for dinner tonight. Would you like me to bring your dinner plate in here?"

"No thank you." Vanessa suddenly felt exhausted. "If you don't mind, I think I'd like to rest for a while."

"Alright, why don't you lie down?" Marie knew it was going to be a challenge to get any food into Vanessa. "I'll save a plate for you in the refrigerator. Please try to eat when you feel up to it."

"Thank you for everything." Vanessa sent her a weak smile. "I promise I'll try to eat later."

Marie closed her door softly. She understood why Vanessa would be upset, but the depth of her despair confused her, especially for a man she'd just met.

Several hours passed, and Vanessa woke in a dark, strange room. She had no idea what time it was. She felt groggy, as if she'd slept fitfully off and on for hours. Unsure of the time, she urgently needed to see Andrew. Quietly opening the bedroom door, she discovered the house bathed in darkness, except for one light thoughtfully left on over the kitchen sink. The plate Marie had left her in the massive refrigerator had been thoughtfully marked with her name. Warming it in the microwave, it smelled savory. Vanessa forced herself to eat some of it, if only to appease Marie. When she'd finished, she cleaned up, put on her sweater, dashed off a note of thanks, and proceeded to walk back to the hospital. Back to Andrew.

Checking with the nurse, she discovered there'd been no change in Andrew's condition. Pulling up a chair next to him, she talked softly, as if he could hear her. She talked about normal things. Haley's parents, the Chinese food she ate for dinner, Marie's daughter, anything that popped into her mind. She kept thinking that any minute now, Andrew would respond to something she said. But soon she realized how deeply drugged the medication kept him; well beyond the reach of her voice.

She spent the rest of the night dozing in the chair beside him. At some point in the morning, Marie arrived and stood quietly in the doorway of the ICU. Her gaze traveled from Andrew's lifeless form, back to Vanessa dozing in an uncomfortable-looking position in the hard chair.

Vanessa startled awake and caught Marie silently observing them. "How long have you been here?"

Flustered a little at being caught watching her sleep, Marie quickly replied. "I just arrived. I'm on my way to meet with Haley and Diane. We're all going to the church up the road from Andrew's house. I believed you'd originally planned to go with Haley."

"Before..." Vanessa looked at Andrew. "When I thought Andrew was going with us."

"Has there been any change?" Marie knew it would be hard for Vanessa to leave.

"No," Vanessa answered despondently.

"Do you think he'd mind if you went to church with Haley?" Marie said, thinking Vanessa needed a break.

"Actually, I'm sure he'd be thrilled," Vanessa chuckled, rubbing her sandy, gritty eyes.

"Well?" Marie thought there might be a chance.

Vanessa sighed and looked at Andrew as she debated with herself for a minute. "Oh all right, I'm coming." She stood, pushing the chair away from the bed. Then she leaned over Andrew; kissing him lightly on the forehead. She bent lower, whispering pleadingly in his ear, "Please... don't leave me."

As she stood, Marie could see the painful tears glistening in Vanessa's eyes. Wiping at her tears, Vanessa walked to the nurse's station to inform Andrew's nurse she planned to leave. Her watchful gaze through the glass window never left Andrew as she spoke. When she finished, Marie wrapped her arm around Vanessa's waist and whisked her away from the depressing ICU.

Once Vanessa and Marie arrived at Andrew's house, they found Haley and Diane dressed and ready to go. Vanessa hugged Haley, giving her the latest news regarding Andrew's condition, trying to conceal the tears forming in her eyes as she spoke of him. Then she hastily ran up the stairs to get ready for church.

She walked into his room to find the french doors still standing wide open, drawing her outside onto the balcony. She stood looking out over the roaring ocean, and the cloudy skies above, in a daze.

"We're not done yet," she whispered, pleading with the universe.

Marie pulled her car into the parking lot of a small chapel-sized church overlooking the ocean. The old bell hanging in the tower fascinated Vanessa, as did the beautifully tinted stained-glass windows on both sides of the building. An elderly priest stood at the entrance cheerfully greeting everyone as they arrived for Mass.

When she stepped up to greet him, he embraced Vanessa's hands, as if they were long, lost friends, who'd finally met again. "Welcome my dear, my name is Father Patrick, what brings you to visit our church this morning?"

His question surprised Vanessa. "My name is Vanessa, I'm a friend of Andrew Kelly."

"And how is Andrew?" The priest smiled in recognition. "I don't see him with you this morning."

"He's in the hospital." Vanessa felt a twinge of guilt; she should be at Andrew's side. "I'm afraid he was shot yesterday. He's in critical condition."

"Thank you for sharing with me." He absorbed this information with calm concern. "I'll notify our prayer group immediately, and I'll be by to see him later today. Which hospital is he in?"

"He's in the ICU at University Hospital." Vanessa relayed the information as tears filled her eyes.

Father Patrick held her hands in his and offered her some unusual words of comfort. "Whatever happens now is in God's hands. Sometimes it's not exactly the way we'd want it, but rest assured, Andrew will be just fine."

She nodded and walked somberly into the church. Shaking her head silently, she thought, *That kindly old man doesn't understand how badly God has let me down in the past, or how much He hates me.*

Haley approached the priest reluctantly. He quickly noted the look of apprehension and fear shining in her eyes. He surrounded her hands with both of his in gentle, warm support. "And who might you be?"

"I'm Haley." She tried to force a smile. "I'm also a friend of Andrew's."

"Andrew's a lucky man to have such wonderful people as his friends. Welcome, Haley."

There was something about this kind man. Haley felt safe. She felt welcomed into his tiny church. Walking through the doors, she slowly gazed around, sliding into a seat next to Vanessa. The soft, colored light shining through the stained-glass windows, along with the familiar scent of burning candles, gave the church a warm, mystical aura. Haley somehow felt everything in her life was about to return to its normal path. The path she'd been on before she'd met Jimmy.

The service was shorter than Vanessa expected, and surprisingly, all in English. Father Patrick gave an inspiring sermon about forgiveness. He stressed that forgiveness wasn't only for the other people in our lives; it was equally important that we forgive ourselves. Vanessa stole a glance at Haley who sat on the edge of her seat, gazing in rapt attention at Father Patrick, hanging on his every word. Vanessa was glad Haley had come to church at this particular place and time. She desperately needed a way to find forgiveness for herself.

After the service, Haley remained inside, while Father Patrick listened to her confession. Vanessa watched Marie light a candle for Andrew. Observing Marie, Vanessa did the same, without any expectations. Wandering outside toward the cliffs overlooking the churning ocean, Vanessa contemplated her life without Andrew. She stood gazing at the dark moss covered rocks below, watching the waves crash dramatically against them. The warm sea air blew her hair across her watery eyes and she impatiently turned away from the wind.

Meanwhile, Marie and Diane strolled through the graveyard, reading the inscriptions on the headstones. Many of them dated back over a century ago.

They all waited patiently for Haley. Vanessa, because she knew how important confession was in Haley's family, and the other two, because confession was a big part of their own faith. It was tradition they both respected and understood.

Appearing in the doorway, Haley balanced on her crutches with Father Patrick at her side. She emerged from the church with a serene smile on her face.

"Thank you, Father, I'll be going home on Friday, but I will always remember your kind words. I hope to return someday, and I'll be sure to come back to see you again."

"Please remember to call me anytime. I would be delighted to see you again, Haley."

"Thank you, Father."

Vanessa, having regained her composure, shook his hand. "I can see Haley is coping better already."

"Happy to be of service." He smiled fondly at her. "Will I see you at the hospital later today?"

"Yes, I'll be there."

"Wonderful, I'll look forward to seeing you later then."

The others had already said their goodbyes and piled into Marie's car. Vanessa waved to Father Patrick and hurried to join them.

Once back at Andrew's house, Marie insisted on fixing lunch. Vanessa changed her clothes again. She'd slipped into a comfortable skirt with a loose fitting t-shirt, thinking she'd be comfortable in Andrew's bedside chair. She looked around Andrew's room for some personal item to take to him and finally settled on a large seashell. She hoped, he would hear the soothing ocean when she held it next to his ear.

Marie dropped Vanessa off at the hospital entrance. When Vanessa arrived in the ICU, Andrew still remained in a coma, but she noticed his face had maybe a little pinker coloring. There also seemed to be less blood draining out of his chest tube. She placed the shell on the pillow beside his left ear, kissing him softly on his forehead. Then she sat next to him, holding his hand, as she related everything that had happened that morning with Father Patrick. She paused her monologue as his doctor quietly stepped into the room. She cleared her throat when she noticed him looking closely at her with mild curiosity. "Just in case he can hear me," she said, blushing.

"And the shell on his pillow?" The doctor smiled indulgently.

She felt silly, but responded, "So he can hear the ocean. You know he lives at the beach."

"No, I wasn't aware that he did." The doctor raised his right eyebrow. "I just reviewed Andrew's chart and I have some good news for you."

"That's great, what is it?"

"All of his tests show that he's stabilizing." He continued. "He's recovering much faster than we'd anticipated. Tomorrow morning we'll start warming him and we'll slowly decrease his sedation."

"Does that mean he'll wake up tomorrow?" Vanessa asked, unable to bear watching Andrew in his current unconscious state.

"I can't tell you that he'll definitely wake up tomorrow." He looked down guardedly. "But all of his test results indicate that he should. We'll all just have to wait and see."

She could feel the doctor hedging. What was he not telling her?

"Mike mentioned that Andrew was still unconscious right before surgery, even though he'd had treatments in the emergency room. Does that make it less likely that he'll wake up?"

He walked around to her side of the bed. Sitting on the bed's edge he talked softly. "I'm not sure I should legally be giving you this information. Andrew's parents didn't even know you two were dating. But, according to Mike, Andrew mentioned your name right before he lost consciousness, so I'm willing to take a chance." Vanessa knew he was going to say something she didn't want to hear.

"What is it?"

"Andrew had lost a lot of blood before he'd arrived in the emergency room." His voice took on a somber tone. "His heart stopped, and the paramedics had to start CPR. He received multiple units of blood as soon as he arrived in the ER, which caused his heart to resume beating on its own again. But Andrew remained unresponsive. His brain scan shows normal function, but we don't really know if he'll wake up, ever."

Agonizing tears began to fall, and she whispered, "He'll wake up, I know he will!"

The doctor admired Vanessa's determination, but didn't share her conviction that Andrew would regain consciousness. He awkwardly patted her back in a clumsy attempt to reassure her, while she covered her face to weep.

Vanessa suddenly dashed her tears aside and lifted her face, surprised to find Father Patrick silently watching them from the doorway. The doctor followed her gaze to the priest. He quickly stood to greet him, immense relief noticeable in his smile.

"It seems you've arrived at a very opportune time, Father Patrick." He shook the Father's hand enthusiastically and made a hasty escape from Andrew's room, and away from the emotionally distraught Vanessa.

"Seems I have indeed. May I come in Vanessa?"

Vanessa and Father Patrick stood next to Andrew's bed and talked for a while. She told him of the possibility that Andrew might wake up as soon as tomorrow.

"What would you say to a walk outside? I think the fresh air would do us both a world of good."

She agreed, but took her cell phone, informing the nurse that she'd be back shortly. They headed outside to the path around the pond. Vanessa was getting very familiar with this particular path, but today was the first time she'd noticed the full, green trees with the delicate flowers planted along the sidewalk. She inanely commented on how much work must have gone into such intricate landscaping. Father Patrick waited patiently for Vanessa to come to a point where she might consider confiding in him.

Vanessa noticed a rock bench she hadn't seen before. Perky, white daisies completely surrounded it. Once they got closer, Vanessa noticed a dedication plaque on the bench that read:

Dedicated to our beloved daughter Cassie
Born Oct.12th 2010-Died Oct.12th 2010

Vanessa sat down on the bench, placed her face in her hands, and burst into uncontrollable sobbing.

"There, there, my dear, now what's this all about?" Father Patrick said, and sat down beside her.

"Oh Father, I don't know what I ever did to make God hate me so much," Vanessa sobbed.

"Why on earth would you think such a thing?"

"First, he made my father leave me, then he let my husband beat me, and then he killed my unborn baby. Now he's taking Andrew away from me. I can't survive one more heartbreak in my life, I just can't!"

Father Patrick had been a priest for many years, but there was a time in his own life when he'd railed at God the very same way. He too had endured a multitude of senseless tragedies, and felt sure that his own experiences would help him to address Vanessa's anger and bewilderment. Looking deep into her tear-filled, tormented eyes, he spoke with certainty, "Listen to me, child. God does not hate you, or anyone on this earth. I understand that you've grieved and you're angry because you can't make sense of it all. But know this, it was your suffering that has made you the wonderfully strong, compassionate woman you are today. Because of who you are, you've reached out and utterly transformed poor little Haley's tortured life. Don't write Andrew off yet; he's another person whose life you've touched. He won't leave this earth without putting up one hell of a fight."

Something about the way he spoke, soothed her, and a spark of hope flickered within her for the first time in many years. There might be a chance she wouldn't lose Andrew after all. Slowly, Vanessa wiped her eyes, trying to subdue her sobbing hiccups.

"Thank you, Father."

"My pleasure," he said, briefly patting her knee. "Now let's say a little prayer for Andrew, just to cover all of our bases. You know prayer is a powerful thing. In fact, right now there are over a thousand members of the church praying for Andrew. Please, feel free to join me." He bowed his head and began to say a prayer aloud. Vanessa bowed her head, calmly listening to the peaceful, low tone of his voice, and added "Amen" when he'd finished.

"Please believe me when I tell you, you are very loved and blessed. Try to remember your many blessings each day; soon you'll notice how your heart has healed itself, and your life is filled with abundance and joy."

"I will Father, thank you." She knew she'd been ungrateful for many of the blessings in her life. She'd spent most of her time focusing on her shortcomings.

"Now shall we walk a ways and enjoy this glorious day?" He slowly stood up, reaching his hands up to his sides to inhale the sweet fragrance of the flowers.

"Alright, Father," she said, wiping her tears, managing to produce a weak smile. They strolled down the familiar path, but today everything seemed different to her. A tiny sliver of faith had found its way into her heart.

Long after Father Patrick's visit, Vanessa sat next to Andrew. She'd decided to read aloud to him and pulled up a book on her phone about sailing. She read quietly to him over the constant noise of the ICU contraptions. Ignoring the doctor's words of caution, she assumed that Andrew would wake up tomorrow, instead of the heartbreaking alternative.

Vanessa's phone rang, interrupting her story and she stepped out of the room to answer. It was Haley. "How's it going, Haley?"

"We're doing great here, how's Andrew?" Haley's voice sounded surprisingly cheerful. "Did Father Patrick come see him today?"

"Yes, he stopped by. He said a very nice prayer for Andrew. Andrew's still asleep, but the doctor says he's doing better. He may wake up as soon as tomorrow. How's Callie?"

"She's great, she loves Shep's dog walker." Haley bubbled on feeling relieved.

"You're not spoiling her too much are you?" Vanessa admonished.

"I'm not, but Diane is. She let her sleep with her," she laughed, tattling on her new best friend.

"That's all right." *Callie is in good hands.* "Thanks for looking out for her. Are you two getting along okay? Are you getting enough to eat?" Food was a favorite subject of Haley's.

"Yep, Diane's mom brought us dinner last night. She also fixed us lunch today. Andrew's maid came by later and she made us a killer lasagna. She even put it in the oven for us before she left. So, we're doing great. What about you? Are you eating?" She knew Vanessa wasn't eating. Marie had already voiced her concerns on the subject.

"I'm fine, Marie's been watching over me."

Haley could tell Vanessa fibbed. She'd watched her pick at her lunch earlier today, but she didn't want to push the subject.

"I like Marie, and Diane's been great. Thanks Vanessa, for asking her to come hang with me."

"You're welcome, I'm glad it's working out. I wish I could spend more time with you before you have to leave."

"Don't worry about me. Andrew needs you now, and we can always video chat after I go home."

"Thanks for understanding." Vanessa still felt guilty for deserting her. "I'll try to spend some time with you after Andrew wakes up." Impressed by Haley's optimistic nature, she smiled. She was about to return to Andrew's room when Marie appeared in the waiting room with bags of take-out food from one of Vanessa's favorite lunch places.

"How are the girls doing?" She'd overheard the tail end of her conversation with Haley.

"They seem to be getting along great. Apparently, both you and Andrew's housekeeper are keeping them well fed."

"Diane is really enjoying spending time with Haley. You didn't eat much at lunch, so I brought you something else. I noticed a picnic table outside, why don't we sit out there and we can talk while you eat." As Vanessa's assistant, she was used to feeding her.

"Let me just tell the nurse, then we can go." Vanessa could tell Marie would not take no for an answer, and she appreciated her steadfast determination. "Thank you again, I can't tell you how much you mean to me. You're always the one person I can count on."

Marie waved her off, waiting for her to return.

As they sat together outside, Marie struggled with her conscience in relationship to something she hadn't let Vanessa know. Something critical had been happening at *Gemma.* So, she thought she'd try.

"I know this isn't the time or place, but there are some things happening at *Gemma,* things I really need to tell you about. Please let me know when you feel ready to discuss work."

Vanessa knew there was something major happening at *Gemma,* and normally she'd be dying to have all the details, but not today. Today, all she could think about was whether or not Andrew would wake up tomorrow. "Thanks. I know I asked you before I left for vacation to keep me informed, but I'm afraid my priorities have changed. Let's table any talk of *Gemma* for a future conversation, okay?"

Marie quietly sighed, releasing a tiny shred of guilt regarding *Gemma.* She'd tried to tell Vanessa. But, she clearly understood and respected Vanessa's current priorities, and refrained from elaborating.

Vanessa would find out, soon enough.

Chapter 24
Patience, Faith, Reward

*A*fter enjoying a momentary break for lunch with Marie, Vanessa excused herself. "Thanks again for everything," she said, wearily. "I need to get back. I'm not leaving Andrew's bedside again until he's awake." The determined, firm set of her lower jaw left little room for argument.

Marie studied Vanessa's exhausted face, while she reluctantly gathered the half-emptied food containers. Before she turned to leave, she insisted that Vanessa take a copy of her house key, making her promise to eat regularly, rest, and call her if she needed anything. Vanessa thanked her hastily, rushing back inside the hospital to sit beside Andrew to wait. Although he'd shown no signs of improvement, and the doctors had warned her not to get her hopes up, she planned to remain by his side and hold an unwavering vigil. Andrew *would* come back to her!

Vanessa spent the evening reading aloud to Andrew, pausing briefly only when his respiratory therapist entered the small confines of his cubicle-sized room. The short, middle-aged, heavyset woman introduced herself as Beth. Beth tried to offer Vanessa a little friendly reassurance, familiar with the uneasiness of loved ones in the ICU.

"Hi, you must be Vanessa?"

"Yes... how did you know my name?"

"I overheard the nurses talking about you. They're awestruck. It seems when you're in the room, Andrew's heart rate and blood pressure return to normal. But, as soon as you leave, his heart slows and he requires medication to keep him stable. It means a lot more work for them, so they appreciate that you're staying the night with him. I noticed his breathing wasn't this relaxed earlier," Beth casually commented, noting the ease of Andrew's chest movement as she spoke. "I had some trouble keeping his oxygen levels stable last night."

Vanessa had been feeling in the way, a bother to the staff. She'd assumed Andrew had no idea whether she was there or not. Now she wondered. "You can let them know that I plan on staying right here until he wakes up for good."

"Thanks, he seems to be resting quietly now," Beth smiled, convinced that Vanessa's presence helped her patient's condition improve. "I'll let you know if there are any changes throughout the night." Beth jotted down the settings from his breathing machine, smiled briefly at Vanessa, and left the room.

"Thank you, Beth," Vanessa whispered.

The ICU remained quiet except for the constant beeping and occasional alarms of the life support machines. The nurses came in and out of the rooms, frequently adjusting drips and closely observing their patients. The rest of the time they remained at a central nurses' station with the hall lights turned low, carefully watching the flashing lights and illuminated screens, which replicated the data from the bedside monitors.

Andrew's nurse had brought Vanessa a pillow and a blanket, pushing a comfortable reclining chair into the cramped space. Resting next to Andrew, Vanessa lapsed into a restless sleep, her hand safely tucked in his, believing she'd awaken the instant he stirred. She tossed and turned, frequently waking to the sound of shrill mechanical alarms, making the disturbing night seem endless.

The hall lights shone brightly when Vanessa finally roused. Day shift had arrived along with echoes of boisterous talking and laughing. Doctors had also commenced their morning rounds. Andrew's day nurse arrived, the same young, bubbly one he'd had the day before.

"It seems Andrew had a good night. The doctor will be in to talk to you in just a moment, but it looks like we'll be warming him up today."

Struggling awake, Vanessa rubbed her gritty eyes. Everything seemed to be proceeding as the doctor had previously explained. *Coffee, I need coffee.* She kissed Andrew's pale, cool cheek and made a quick trip down the hall to the waiting room. Using the facilities, she splashed cold water on her gaunt-appearing face, and grabbed a cup of lukewarm, stale coffee. The doctor stood patiently beside Andrew's bed when she returned.

"There you are." The doctor looked up from Andrew's chart as she entered. "I just wanted to let you know that all of Andrew's lab tests are good this morning. I've ordered the cooling blanket adjustments, so he should gradually warm up to a normal temperature by sometime this evening. I've also ordered his sedation medication be titrated down. But remember, this is a very slow process, so don't expect him to respond to you anytime soon."

"I understand. I'll be patient," Vanessa promised, appearing calm and understanding, but secretly resenting his implied warning that Andrew might not respond.

"Very well, now take care of yourself, this is going to be a very long day." He closed the chart briskly. "Please remember what we discussed yesterday. There's no guarantee that he'll wake up."

"Thank you, Doctor. But he's going to wake up!"

The doctor nodded, smiling ever so slightly at the very determined, brave lady before him. He only hoped his patient wouldn't let her down.

Marie didn't have time to check in on Vanessa. Running late for work, her desk phone began ringing the minute she stepped through her office door, and she grabbed it on the seventh ring.

"Marie, it's Jane, I'm having a horrible day already." Jane's normally composed voice sounded flustered. Marie relaxed, setting her jacket and purse down on her desk while they talked.

"Is the old geezer giving you a bad time already today?"

"I'll say." Jane sounded exasperated. "He's already fired and rehired me three times so far this morning. When is Vanessa getting back?"

"I told you, not until next Monday."

"How can she stay away?" Jane moaned. "Given what's going on around here?" She let out a sigh of frustration. "If she doesn't come back soon, there may be nothing for her to return to, and we'll all be unemployed!"

"I know, believe me, but there's nothing I can do." Marie hated letting Jane and the rest of the staff down. "I can't tell her about everything right now. We'll just have to get through this week somehow."

"I can't believe you haven't told her." Jane's mouth fell open, shocked by Marie's confession. "Vanessa will flip when she finds out!"

"Vanessa's dealing with a very serious personal crisis right now," Marie explained, but wondered if she should have tried a little harder to get Vanessa to listen to her yesterday. "And I'm afraid that it trumps anything happening in this company."

"I'm sorry. Please give Vanessa my best," Jane said, suddenly feeling a twinge of selfish, petty guilt. "You and I will simply have to hold down the fort until she returns," she said. Jane stopped talking and Marie could hear the elderly Mr. Edward's loud, demanding voice over the intercom. "I've got to go now," Jane said, and Marie heard her inhale sharply, searching for her last shred of patience.

"Good luck," Marie smiled, thankful she had no one bellowing at her.

The hospital ICU remained a flurry of activity all day. New patients arrived, while others were moved elsewhere. Vanessa had gone to breakfast in the cafeteria, but only after Andrew's nurse had insisted that she wanted privacy to clean him up. Later, she went to grab a tasteless lunch while his nurse changed his bandages. Vanessa knew she wouldn't stomach the gruesome sight of his unwrapped gaping wounds, currently concealed under the bandages on his chest.

Throughout the day, Andrew's nurse raised the cooling blanket temperature and lowered his sedation drip. Andrew remained unresponsive through it all. Vanessa sat by his side for hours, no longer reading, but instead listening anxiously to the constant swish of the mechanical respirator, rhythmically pumping air into his lifeless lungs, prolonging his life.

Later in the afternoon, Father Patrick stopped in to check on Andrew. Although his coma remained unchanged, Andrew's skin felt slightly warmer to Vanessa's touch. But his body remained deathly pale and lifeless, only his chest movements gave her hope, even if they were a direct result of the air pumping through his respirator. Vanessa looked like she felt. Fatigue had created dark circles under her eyes, uncombed hair had matted and tangled beyond repair on the back of her head, and her clothes, mercilessly crumpled, clung limply to her petite frame.

The persistent priest used all his powers of persuasion to talk Vanessa into taking a walk outside with him. Finally, unable to resist, she found herself mindlessly walking around the pond at his side.

Vanessa's exhausted mind began to doubt that Andrew would ever regain consciousness. And, unlike their previously inspiring walks, she felt her faith teetering, her optimistic resolve on the brink of vanishing.

"It's far too early in the game for you to give up hope, you know," Father Patrick said, sensing her exhaustion and dwindling fortitude. "I believe you still have the strength within you to keep going."

She smiled weakly, admiring his ability to cut straight through the fluff to the truth of the matter. Whatever Andrew's fate, she knew she could always count on Father Patrick to be her unwavering friend. Slowly, she began to notice her surroundings. She focused her attention on a pair of pure white geese, swimming effortlessly side by side in the still water of the pond. "Do you honestly believe he'll wake up?" Vanessa asked, her voice flat and emotionless.

"If it's God's will," he sighed. "Maybe we should pray to Him, and ask

Him?"

"All right, Father." Vanessa grasped Father Patrick's hand in quiet desperation. *It won't hurt to ask God to send Andrew back to me.* "Will you please say the prayer for me?"

"Of course, my dear."

They paused, seating themselves on the familiar cement bench, the one dedicated to the baby who'd died on the day of her birth. Father Patrick prayed aloud solemnly, asking God for Andrew's swift recovery. Vanessa sat mutely, listening dispiritedly to his prayer.

"Amen. Thank you, Father," she added, lifting her eyes to him.

He looked at her thoughtfully. "Have you forgiven God for all of your previous sorrows, the ones you described to me yesterday?"

"I want to say yes, Father, but the truth is, I'm not sure I ever will." Vanessa couldn't lie to a priest, whether she truly believed in God or not.

"You need to look deep within yourself, search your heart. Try to find forgiveness," he said, nodding sadly, and understanding her dilemma. "Only after you do, will you be able to freely ask Him for what your heart desires."

Vanessa gazed down at the baby's plaque, nodding silently. Forgiveness had always eluded her. She'd blamed God for every painful episode in her life. Father Patrick's unfaltering support and prayers gave her confidence. She silently vowed to remain optimistic about Andrew, to find the strength to forgive, to let go of her painful past, and begin focusing on her future.

Returning to the ICU with revived hope, Vanessa paused in Andrew's doorway with Father Patrick following close behind her. Andrew lay in bed, pale and deathly still, covered with only a white sheet to his waist. He remained unconscious, his condition unchanged. *Without these detestable machines, he'd be dead*, she thought, as she felt her new found assurance wane.

The night nurse stood over his bed fussing with his multiple drips. She smiled, heaving a sigh of relief when Vanessa walked through the door. "I'm glad you're back. I know it might be superstitious, but he seems better when you're here."

"Thank you for watching over him while I was outside with Father Patrick." Vanessa nodded in recognition at the nurse, taking a seat disappointedly, her furrowed face the picture of sorrow.

"It's my pleasure." The nurse smiled, sensing her melancholy. "Your friend dropped off some dinner for you. I put it in the staff refrigerator. Let me know when you want it. I'm happy to heat it up and bring it in to you," she offered graciously, moving toward the door.

"Thank you, for everything." Vanessa sent her a tired smile of appreciation.

"You're welcome."

The nurse left, acknowledging Father Patrick as he walked past her toward the head of the bed. He took out a small bottle, reverently dabbing his finger into its clear liquid contents. He made the sign of the cross on Andrew's forehead while he said a prayer in Latin.

Vanessa, unfamiliar with this particular practice, simply added: "Amen."

"Now, try to hold onto your faith." Father Patrick turned to her, reaching out to hold her hands in his. Sympathy creased his wizened eyes. "Promise to take care of yourself and get some rest tonight. Remember what we talked about on our walk today. I'll return tomorrow. If you should need me, feel free to call me anytime of the day or night."

Vanessa thanked him with a quick hug and sat back down in her chair. She reached out for Andrew's hand, and although it remained pale and limp, it felt slightly warmer. Glancing toward the nurses' station, she watched Father Patrick greet the nurses. They returned his jovial smile with familiarity, and several of the nurses hugged him.

"You're such a kind darling, would you please take Vanessa her food in about an hour? We both know she'll forget to eat if left to her own devices," he said to Andrew's nurse with a twinkle in his eyes. She returned his smile, a big fan of the kind, elderly man. A frequent visitor in the ICU, he'd often arrived unannounced, during times of insurmountable grief. Her experiences as a nurse had convinced her how much Vanessa needed his kindhearted solace. "Of course, Father, anything for you."

Vanessa read aloud to Andrew for hours, until her throat became parched and dry. His color slowly improved, and his skin felt closer to his normal temperature, but he remained unresponsive. His nurse had brought Vanessa dinner, but although it was one of her favorite dishes, she barely tasted it.

When she'd finished, she walked to the waiting room to use the restroom and call Marie. She thanked her for dinner, requesting that she check in on Haley. Vanessa knew Haley would be upset by Andrew's unchanged condition. In her fragile state of mind, she couldn't bear hearing the disappointment in Haley's voice.

A young couple had entered the tiny waiting room while she was on the phone, causing Vanessa to abruptly end her conversation with Marie. The young man had his arm around his obviously distraught, weeping wife. Watching her mourn, listening to the tormented sound of her sobbing, unnerved Vanessa, and she urgently felt she had to escape from the cramped room.

Vanessa, spooked by the precarious state of each of the ICU patients, rushed out of the waiting room and down the hall, needing to see for herself that Andrew was still alive. When she drew closer to his room, she saw both his nurse and the respiratory therapist standing at the head of his bed checking his respirator, and she imagined the worst.

"Is he all right? Beth, is everything okay?" she asked, dreading her answer.

"Everything's just the same." Beth calmly turned toward her. "He's stable. They called me because his sedation drip has been turned off. It doesn't appear I need to adjust anything now, but I'll be checking him more frequently tonight as a precaution."

Vanessa forced herself to relax. Dropping despondently into her chair, she slowly allowed her pumping adrenaline to dissipate, and struggled to slow her rapid breathing. "Beth?" she asked cautiously. "Do you think he's going to wake up?"

"I'm sorry, I wish I could tell you." It saddened Beth to hear the despair in Vanessa's voice. "No one knows the answer with certainty. I'm afraid it's still too early to tell."

Vanessa thanked them both as they left the room. The hall lights dimmed, she pushed her chair closer to the bed, and eventually fell into a troubled, fitful sleep, anxiously clinging to Andrew's lifeless hand. Most nights she'd simply toss and turn, suffering dreamlessly until morning. But tonight, Vanessa dreamed of her baby girl.

Hazy, misty, dormant memories floated within wistfully soft, fluffy clouds. Her baby's pale, feather-light, tiny body wrapped snuggly inside a doll-sized, pink, flannel blanket, mystically materialized in her arms. This time, instead of the old feelings of remorse and pain, she drifted weightlessly in serene fascination, studying the tiny baby she held. Vanessa's heart swelled as she lovingly outlined her baby's angelic face with her fingers. Her child radiated beauty, looking as if she were only asleep, resting safely, at peace.

Her baby faded away into the mist, and her ex-husband's face floated before her. She watched him curiously, noting the devastated look of remorse that crossed his face as he fearfully sat in the courtroom. She witnessed him realizing he'd caused the death of his unborn child and his face crumpled. His body slumped forward, wilting pathetically in a sobbing heap onto the table in front of him. Instead of feeling callous and incensed, as she previously had, her heart broke at the sight of his immense grief, and she felt nothing but compassion for this tormented man. He slowly dissolved into the dense fog.

Her cloud-like dream took her back even further, to when she was seven, the day she discovered her parents were divorcing. She traveled through the dreamy mist, materializing on the other side of the kitchen door. And, although she'd only heard her parent's exchange through a closed door before, she could now observe the father she'd always trusted and loved, as he paced across the floor. She saw the painful remorse and shame on her father's strained face, powerless to look into her mother's eyes, as he begged her for a divorce. Her fragile mother, consumed with grief, sat at the kitchen table weeping pitifully. Previously, her mother's pain and disillusionment had also reflected Vanessa's. Watching her mother now, Vanessa felt her mother's deep sorrow and betrayal, entirely separate from her own. Resentment and anger melted away, replaced by endearing, sympathetic regret for her beloved parents.

The ghosts from her past slowly disappeared into white, wispy clouds. Vanessa felt her anger and disappointment vanishing along with the glimmering apparitions. Humbled and regretful for the pain she'd caused her loved ones, she felt the hateful, painful anger she'd been harboring for so long slowly float toward the heavens, dissipating mystically amongst the feathery clouds.

Vanessa woke from her dream with a start in the semi-darkness of the hospital room. Beads of damp sweat dripped from her forehead, and remorseful tears rolled freely down her cheeks. Gradually she became aware of the constant beeping of the machines in the room, and she stretched her arms overhead, recalling comforting bits and pieces of her dream. Sadness filled her heart, as she realized she'd shut out those closest and dearest to her. Trapped within her own, unremitting pain, she'd caused untold suffering for the people she supposedly loved.

Vanessa bowed her head repentantly, and for the first time since before her parents' divorce, she silently prayed. *Please, forgive me, I promise I have forgiven those whom I've held in contempt all these years. If you return Andrew to me, I promise not to treat him so shamefully.*

Vanessa nestled back in her chair, feeling stronger than she had in years. The burden of carrying such intense anger and grief floated off her shoulders. Standing, she bent down to Andrew, gently smoothing his hair back from his face before placing a tender kiss on his forehead. She gazed down at him and smiled, feeling uplifted with revitalized faith for his recovery. Turning away from his bed, she quietly stepped through the open door, out into shadowy, hushed hallway. Only the constant beeping of the ICU monitors filled the empty space.

Returning from her brief break, Vanessa felt a renewed sense of optimism. She gazed down at Andrew and frowned. *He needs more strength*, she thought. *He needs my strength, and my determination to help him survive.* The only way she could think of transferring her strength into him, was body to body. Carefully she lifted his sheet and climbed into his bed, positioning herself close beside him. All of his wires and tubes remained undisturbed by her actions, safely situated on the opposite side of the bed. She snuggled closer to his moderately warmed body and gently rested her cheek on his uninjured shoulder.

Placing his seashell next to his ear, she recalled the soft sound of the constantly rolling surf drumming against the sandy beach. She closed her eyes and imagined they were back in his bed, the gentle ocean breezes dancing around them in the pale moonlight. Relaxing against him, his limp, lifeless arms resting at his sides, she blocked out some of the hissing respirator noise and focused on the sound of his heart beating. Lulled by its steady rhythm and the gentle rise and fall of his chest, she closed her eyes and drifted into a deep, peaceful sleep. *Please wake up, Andrew. I need you to hold me close again.*

The distant misty mountains glowed. The sun shimmered as it slowly rose, reflecting its image on the glassy pond surrounded by brightly, blooming flowers. The pair of geese glided gracefully across the still water, while Andrew walked beside her, smiling and holding her hand. He lifted her easily into the air and twirled her in circles as they laughed. But all too soon, Andrew and the sparkling pond faded away, and Vanessa woke, instantly aware that she'd been dreaming again. Resting on Andrew's shoulder, her body was suddenly jolted as he began violently coughing and gagging. In a panic, Vanessa reached for the call light, but before she could locate it, his nurse appeared at the head of the bed with his RT, Beth, close behind.

Frightened by Andrew's unexpected choking, Vanessa struggled to climb off the bed, but she felt Andrew's arm, wrapped loosely around her body, preventing her frantic escape. She looked up at his face with alarm. For days he'd had the same, serene, unexpressive look on his face. Now, although his eyes were still closed, his face contorted in agony.

The RT's face appeared out of thin air above them and she quickly removed Andrew's breathing tube. Vanessa held her fist to her mouth and sobbed as Andrew gasped his first unassisted breath. The nurse stepped away and paged the doctor. Andrew remained mute, his eyes clenched closed, struggling to clear his throat with a guttural sound. The nurse returned and began carefully spooning a few drops of water into his parched mouth. Vanessa felt Andrew's arm tightening slightly around her. He finally swallowed, and after a moment, he tilted his head down toward her, croaking out the first words he'd said in days.

"I—love—you."

"I love you, too," Vanessa laughed. "Welcome back."

Beth turned off the hissing respirator and the nurse checked his vital signs. Then they left, giving them a few moments of privacy.

Andrew frowned as he fought to open his heavy, matted eyelids, eager to see Vanessa's lovely face. Finally, his eyes opened to two tiny slits, and his brilliant blue eyes beheld Vanessa as she lay beside him, tears of joy streaming down her beautiful face.

"I know you do," he whispered.

Vanessa burst out in delighted laughter, and Andrew pulled her closer, a hint of a smile stretching across his ragged, chapped lips.

Chapter 25
The Gemma Dilemma

A peaceful, serene smile rested on her face as Vanessa sat in the chair next to Andrew. The doctor had arrived early this morning, declaring Andrew's recovery miraculous. He was lucky to be alive! Let alone on the path to a full recovery. Andrew tired easily, required oxygen, and his chest tube would stay in for now, but he no longer needed the breathing machine. Soon, the doctor said he expected him to graduate out of the ICU. Vanessa gazed at him happily, unable to contain the joyous smile that spread across her face every time their eyes met.

Stretching her arms overhead, Vanessa realized she'd spent a long, tedious morning on the phone. His parents had been the first to be notified of his awakening and rapid recovery. His mother had cried when she heard his voice, relieved that he'd survived his shooting ordeal. His eyes lit up as he'd listened to her enthusiastic response, smiling fondly. But, even after talking to his mother only briefly, breathlessness and fatigue assailed him. His mother encouraged him to rest, and assured him she'd convey the message of his recovery to his father, as soon as he had a *good* moment.

Andrew had slept for most of the morning while Vanessa sat in the waiting room making calls. She relaxed and checked in on him frequently, but only after the nurses had promised her they'd call her right away if he needed her.

Vanessa called Haley, who'd screamed ecstatically when she informed her that Andrew was awake and doing well.

"When can I see him?" Haley asked, excitedly.

"I'm sorry, not until after he's moved out of the ICU," Vanessa patiently explained.

"I get it." Hearing the disappointment in her voice, Vanessa imagined Haley felt left out.

"When Andrew moves, I'll try to come get you. I really need to clean myself up, now that he's awake. I want to get a little more presentable. René would be absolutely horrified if he saw me looking like this." Vanessa pulled on her tangled hair, groaning at her pathetic reflection in the waiting room window.

"I'm sure Andrew is just glad to see you, no matter what you look like, but it would be great if you could come here. Then, maybe I can go back to the hospital with you?" she asked hopefully.

"I don't see why not. We'll have to play it by ear, okay?"

Vanessa returned to the task of calling everyone on Andrew's long list. Halfway through, she grabbed a quick bite to eat, feeling ravenous for the first time in days.

Once she'd finished with the calls, she returned to Andrew's bedside. Hypnotized by his effortless breathing while he slumbered serenely, she suddenly realized how emotionally drained she felt. She curled up in the chair beside him and allowed her eyes to close, listening to the reassuring sound of his soft, peaceful snoring.

Some time later, Father Patrick stood silently in the doorway to Andrew's room, smiling fondly at the devoted, sleeping couple. Andrew's color had turned a nice shade of pink, and he breathed easily on his own. Vanessa had curled up in the chair and slept beside him. He noticed with a smile, how their hands intertwined with each other, as if they couldn't bear to be separated. The doctor had already updated him on Andrew's unbelievable awakening. *Good for you, Vanessa*, he thought. He silently thanked God, murmuring a quick blessing for the exhausted, slumbering lovers. As he turned to leave them undisturbed, Andrew's nurse walked by, and he quietly left the message that he'd return tomorrow.

Father Patrick left the hospital, delighted by the current turn of events. He began humming a cheerful tune as he turned his old Ford station wagon toward his ocean-side church. Impulsively, he decided he'd stop by Andrew's house first. Something told him, with Vanessa preoccupied with Andrew, Haley might possibly need him.

His intuition paid off. He found Haley home alone. She dropped her crutches and fell into his arms the minute she opened the door to him, sobbing buckets of tears.

"Now, now, Haley, what's all this about?" Father Patrick patted her back, attempting to calm her.

"Oh Father, Vanessa hates me." She straightened up to look into the priest's eyes. Foolishly, as soon as she hung up with Vanessa, she'd worked herself into a complete crying jag. "It's all my fault that Andrew almost died. I don't think she'll ever be able to forgive me."

"I know for a fact that Vanessa does not hate you." Father Patrick steadied her as she balanced on one foot in front of him, holding her shoulders, and smiling at her sympathetically. "I believe she's rather fond of you. Now let me help you with those crutches and let's see if we can find somewhere for you to sit. You need to calm down and tell me all about it."

He picked up Haley's crutches and handed them to her, following close behind her as she hobbled back toward where she'd been sitting outside. He stepped out of the door and gazed reverently upward, watching as the fluffy white clouds passed leisurely overhead in the pristine, clear blue sky.

"Father? If it weren't for something I did, which was totally sinful, Andrew wouldn't even be in the hospital!"

"I see..." Father Patrick turned toward Haley, slowly returning his undivided attention to the distraught child. "Tell me, what exactly was this sinful act that you committed?"

"I stole some money. From a very bad man," Haley confessed, looking at her lap, shamefaced. She began anxiously twisting her fingers together. "He called Vanessa's house and left a threatening message with her. He wanted me to give his money back, money that I don't even have anymore! But, Andrew traced the call back to him and then went to talk to the guy. And he shot him! You see? It's all my fault!"

"Ah, and you believe that Vanessa blames you." Father Patrick nodded, deep in thought for a moment, a concerned look settling on his face.

"Well, she says she doesn't, but I know she does. She won't even let me go see Andrew." Haley squirmed a little, tears streaming down her checks again.

"First of all..." Father Patrick sat next to Haley and leaned toward her as he spoke in a soothing, reasoning voice. "I've spoken with Vanessa on multiple occasions. She's never once mentioned that you were to blame for Andrew's condition. Secondly, Andrew is a trained detective, who accidently stumbled upon a drug transaction. Unfortunately he arrived unprepared for the whole situation. That is why he was shot. In all the talk about how Andrew was injured, no one has even brought up your name. Now tell me, are you truly sorry for stealing the money?"

"Yes Father, I'm very sorry. I know it's wrong to steal," she whispered shamefully, after having sat transfixed, listening to the father's logical explanation of the situation. She'd stopped crying, although she continued fidgeting with her fingers. She looked at the priest, dreading his reaction to her next confession. "You know, that guy Scott? I saw him on the news. The police shot him, and now he's dead. That's my fault too!"

"Now then, Haley." Father Patrick shook his head patiently and sighed. "You know he's dead because he shot Andrew, and then tried to shoot the other officers attempting to arrest him." He patted her leg affectionately. "Would it make you feel better if we said a prayer for absolution?"

Haley nodded her head.

"Very well, let's pray together, shall we?"

Haley's confession to Father Patrick, and his prayer, lessened her feelings of guilt, and her hands relaxed in her lap. Feeling braver, Haley smiled and hugged the elderly priest.

"Father?" she asked carefully. "Would you mind video chatting with my mother? It would mean the world to her."

"I would be delighted, although I have no idea what you're talking about." Father Patrick smiled at Haley's sudden change of subjects and mood.

Haley lifted the laptop from the table beside her and rapidly contacted her mom. Her mom became flustered, honored to be able to talk directly to Father Patrick. After some preliminary exchanges regarding Haley's spirit, she asked to speak to him privately. The Father, with Haley's directions, tactfully carried the laptop inside to Andrew's living room.

Father Patrick seated himself on Andrew's cozy couch, and was deep in serious conversation with Haley's mother, when Diane abruptly popped open the front door, her arms loaded down with groceries. Relieved, he realized that Haley now had Diane to entertain and visit with her while he continued his conversation.

Diane waved to him, briefly mouthing *hello* on her way to the kitchen. Dropping the bags onto the kitchen counter, she called to Haley. Sitting in the sunshine, Haley slipped on her dark glasses to hide her embarrassingly swollen, puffy eyes.

"I'm back," Diane announced, walking toward her. "Why's Father Patrick here? And why is he talking so seriously to your mom?"

"I don't know." Haley glanced toward the house. "I just thought he could calm her down a little. She wants to come out here to stay with us, since Vanessa's not here. I just thought Father Patrick could reassure her that we're fine on our own."

"She knows I'm here." Diane plopped down in a chair and pouted, insulted by Haley's mother's lack of faith in her. "I thought she seemed really nice when we chatted. Besides, we've both been on our own for a while now, she doesn't need to come."

"I agree." Haley shrugged. "Maybe she'll feel better knowing Father

Patrick is close by."

"Good thinking, Haley. Are you hungry? Do you think I should offer Father Patrick something to eat or drink?"

"I don't know about him, but I could eat." Haley suddenly realized how much she would miss Diane's easy-going nature, once she's home.

After an extensive conversation with Haley's mother, a weary Father Patrick carried Haley's laptop outside and seated himself. He declined any refreshments offered by Diane, except a glass of ice water.

"Your mother's a very fine woman." He handed Haley her laptop and smiled. "She's worried about you on so many levels. But I reassured her that you're a responsible young lady, and will be just fine here with Diane."

"Does she still think she needs to come here now?" Haley asked, setting her laptop aside, avoiding his probing eyes.

"No." His eyes danced with merriment, knowing Haley had manipulated him. "I convinced her that you need some time without her, in order to transition from your old life, to the one you'll be returning to."

"Thank you, Father. I'm not ready to have her fussing over me yet."

"Be that as it may, I did promise your mother I'd look in on you two from time to time."

"Thank you, Father, for everything." Haley appreciated his intervention with her mother. She wanted more time to hang out alone with Diane. She'd have her mother hovering over her, asking probing, uncomfortable questions, soon enough.

"Well, I'd best be on my way." He got up with a soft groan and guzzled the last sip of his water. "You girls stay out of trouble." He nodded toward them. "And, promise me you'll call me for anything. I'll check in with you tomorrow."

"We will, Father," both girls, answered sweetly in unison.

He chuckled to himself, returning his empty glass to the kitchen on his way out the door. He hadn't been fooled by their seemingly innocent response, and planned to pop in unannounced again tomorrow.

Hours later in the ICU, Vanessa woke to the sound of murmuring. Popping an eye open, Andrew came into focus, sitting propped up like a king, while a nurse spoon-fed him flavored gelatin. He noticed her watchful gaze and her slow smirk out of the corner of his eye.

"I'm sorry, did we wake you?" he asked, apologetically. "I never

271

thought I'd eat this junk and like it, but it tastes divine."

"Today he can only have clear liquids, we'll see about some real food tomorrow." The nurse spoke with authority while concentrating on filling Andrew's open mouth.

Andrew's right arm was out of commission, Vanessa realized, as she glanced at it hanging limply in a sling. She stood, stretched, and sat on the side of his bed, casually taking over the task of feeding him. After the nurse left the room, he grinned wickedly, licking his lips, and turning gelatin feeding into a sensual event. His exaggerated moans and sighs after each bite amused her. Vanessa sent him a teasing, warning look when he leaned forward to press his sweetened lips against hers.

"Don't get too used to this kind of service, mister. I expect you to get that arm of yours back in service pronto." Vanessa actually didn't mind feeding him. But, his lifeless arm hanging in the sling disturbed her. She worried he might have a difficult time adjusting to life without the use of both of his arms.

"Don't worry," Andrew said, watching the obvious concern cross her face, and hearing the false bravado of her teasing. "My arm's going to be just fine before you know it."

"Of course, it is."

Marie silently observed from the hall, watching the two of them surreptitiously through the glass window of Andrew's room. They were just talking and teasing each other, but she noted an aura of intimacy between them, and she suddenly felt like an intruding voyeur. Clearing her throat, she walked through the door to make her presence known. "Hi, Vanessa."

Vanessa jumped off the bed quickly, feeling like a young girl who'd been caught kissing her boyfriend at school. "Oh Marie, you startled me. I didn't see you come in."

Andrew sent Vanessa a curious look. He'd never had the opportunity to actually meet Marie, although he'd heard a lot about her.

"Marie, this is Andrew," Vanessa introduced them formally. "Andrew, this is my assistant, and dear friend, Marie."

Vanessa's mounting blush amused him. Since his right arm remained limp in a sling, he couldn't shake Marie's hand. But, charming as always, he accepted her hand with his good one, and brought it to his lips.

"It's a pleasure to meet you, Marie. Vanessa's told me so many wonderful things about you."

His gallant demeanor surprised Marie. Yesterday he lay in his bed, near death. Yet, today he'd become the charming host of the ICU. Vanessa's instant attraction to him seemed understandable, given her past disappointments.

"It's a pleasure to meet you, too." She secreted a glance toward Vanessa, noting her blush, and felt surprised by the sensation of her own face flushing. "I—just stopped by to see if Vanessa would like to come our house for dinner," she stammered. "And maybe freshen up a bit. We just live a few blocks away."

Andrew had previously noticed Vanessa's pale, exhausted state. He hated to part with her, but her haggard condition concerned him. *It's time she looked out for herself*, he thought.

"That's very generous of you. We're lucky to have your support." Andrew smiled at her, hoping she would help him to convince Vanessa to go with her. He couldn't stand to watch her suffer on his behalf.

"Vanessa?" He gazed lovingly into her rebellious face. "I need you to go with her," he said, patiently. "It's time to take care of you. I'm fine, and it's hard for me to watch you trying to rest here with the noise and constant interruptions. I promise, I'll just be sleeping the rest of the evening and through the night. Please go. Do it for me?"

Vanessa knew she must look a complete mess, and every inch of her body hurt from sleeping in the chair. *He does seem tired*, she thought. She leaned across the bed and kissed him lightly on the lips. With her face just inches from his, she whispered, "All right, I'll go, but promise me you'll call if you need me."

Andrew hid his victorious smile. He loved it when he won even the smallest of battles with this gorgeous, strong-willed woman. He placed his good hand over his heart. "I promise." He sunk back against his pillows. "Now scoot, so I can nap.

"I'd love the opportunity to freshen up and rest at your house," she said, turning her smile on Marie, who had just witnessed both their verbal and nonverbal sparring. "I guess I'm ready to go now."

"Thanks, Andrew." Marie nodded, saluting Andrew's finesse, knowing she'd never have convinced Vanessa by herself.

"And I thank you, for watching over Vanessa for me." Andrew sent her a winning smile, his engaging, blue eyes twinkling.

Vanessa rolled her eyes. *Just what I needed, both of them conspiring against me*. Following Marie to the door, she turned to wave goodbye to

Andrew, and on a whim, she blew him a kiss.

Andrew laughed at her antics, thinking, *I'm a very lucky man.*

Marie's husband wasn't expected home until later, so they had the house to themselves. After a meal and a long, hot shower, Vanessa settled in Marie's cozy living room with a glass of red wine for an informal chat. Vanessa felt drained, but reluctantly decided to let Marie explain the mysterious crisis at *Gemma.*

"Alright, I'm ready now. Tell me what's been going on at *Gemma,*" Vanessa sighed. Taking a fortifying sip of wine, she searched Marie's troubled face for clues.

"Umm," Marie paused, gulping down her wine. *Where should I begin,* she thought. "Remember how Mindy was assigned to watch your accounts while you were gone?"

Vanessa nodded, feeling a knot of fear in the pit of her stomach.

"Mindy disappeared the day after the fire sprinklers went off. Jane and I saw her that night, after our little dinner, arguing with the man you later identified as Stephen. Apparently, that's the last time anyone from *Gemma* saw her. She's simply vanished."

"Where is she?" Vanessa asked, stunned by the unanticipated news. "What happened to her?"

"I don't know. But, remember the account she worked on before you left? The one she and Stephen handled, after he'd been promoted to head the Blissful Hair Care account? Apparently, the police traced the link and discovered that he'd installed some sort of spyware during the sprinkler fiasco, while all of the computers were temporarily shut down. He siphoned millions of dollars from *Gemma,* and even more from our outside accounts, all within seconds during the rebooting of the servers."

"I don't believe this. What does that have to do with Mindy?" Vanessa stared at Marie with wide-eyed shock.

"Since both she and Stephen dropped out of sight on the same night..." Marie explained, and then frowned, feeling she was relaying the story poorly. "The police believe they were both involved in the computer theft as partners in the scheme. And so far, they've been unable to track either one of them."

"What about our accounts?" Vanessa placed her wine on the table unsteadily, covering her heart with her palm, stunned by the unexpected information. "Have they recovered *any* of the stolen money?"

"They traced the money to an offshore account, but it's totally protected." Marie shook her head sadly. "And out of U.S. jurisdiction. Unrecoverable."

"What is Max doing about all of this?"

"You're not going to like this either. Last week when Max was summoned to see his father, he never returned."

"Oh no, please don't tell me..."

"I'm afraid so, his father fired him!"

Vanessa and Max had worked together for years. *This can't be happening,* she thought. She forced herself take a deep breath, attempting to remain calm enough to wrap her mind around the entire dilemma.

"So, who is running *Gemma* now?"

Marie stalled by taking another sip of her wine to give herself courage. "Would you believe, Max's father?"

"What!" Vanessa leapt to her feet and began pacing the room in agitation. "That old man can hardly get around the office in his wheelchair. He's in his eighties, for heaven's sake! How's he planning to control our damaged image and repair *Gemma's* reputation? Exactly who is taking care of my accounts? *Are* there any accounts left? Marie? Talk to me!"

Marie sipped her wine with mixed feelings as she watched Vanessa pace and rant. Part of her was pleased to see her old boss in action; the other part of her realized the hopelessness of the situation.

"Your team really stepped up and saved some of the accounts," she reassured Vanessa, who'd stopped pacing, and stood glaring at Marie. "Mr. Edward's plan is to either put millions of his own money back into the magazine and make restitution to the companies who lost capital on our server. Or...to take the loss, and close down the magazine all together."

Vanessa tapped her fingers on her chin and slowly began walking across the room, her mind started shooting off in multiple directions all at once, while trying to imagine how much time, money, and work would actually be required to pull *Gemma* back from the brink of disaster. She finally halted in front of Marie.

"What's he waiting for?" she demanded. "Why hasn't he made his decision? The longer he waits, the harder it will be to bring *Gemma* back to life. Marie, tell me, what on earth is he waiting for?"

"He's waiting for you," she whispered.

"And why is he waiting for me?"

Kathleen L. Gregory

"He's waiting for *you* to return and take over *Gemma* Magazine!"

Chapter 26
Undecided Destiny

M arie sat, quietly waiting for Vanessa to say something, anything. But Vanessa seemed to be at a complete loss for words. Vanessa had expected a lot of things, but not this, not being asked to assume the most powerful role at *Gemma* Magazine! All the more ironic, since her last conversation with her editor, and long-time friend Max had been more about transitioning her out of her job. Recently, she'd been considering leaving *Gemma* all together. Pacing the room like a wild tiger, she reflected on the events that had led up to such an outrageous offer.

Max had escaped Mindy's sexual harassment charge threats, but not his father's retribution. Mr. Edwards clearly blamed Max for the destruction of *Gemma*! He'd fired Max from his job, furious about Max's estrangement from his wife and his naive vulnerability to Mindy's schemes.

Mindy, Vanessa thought with disgust, she'd never trusted that girl. Not only had she tried to take over her job, Mindy had used her relationship with one of Vanessa's trusted, long-term accounts, in order to swindle *Gemma* out of millions of dollars. *Stephen*, she thought angrily, he was another despicable person she'd never trusted. He'd known Mindy since college, and apparently together they'd managed to commit, what seemed to be on the surface, the perfect corporate crime. They'd both worked their way up the ladders in each agency, ruthlessly positioning themselves within the company to gain the exact security access they'd need to pull off their fiendish caper. Now, Mindy, and her accomplice Stephen, were nowhere to be found. They'd left town, leaving *Gemma's* reputation in tattered shreds.

Thank goodness her team had stepped up to provide some of the necessary damage control while Max was gone. Vanessa trusted them, although she knew without a doubt, they'd never be able to salvage the company without her help. Vanessa shook her head in disbelief. Just last week she'd been seriously considering retiring, convinced it was time to move on.

But Vanessa's life had changed considerably in the past week. She'd actually begun to look forward to the upcoming year of two-week vacations every month. She'd even planned a timetable to train one of her junior executives to take over her current position. The idea of taking on the full responsibility for *Gemma*, especially in its current condition, had never appeared on her radar.

Her calculator-sharp mind had analyzed everything she'd need to accomplish in order to save *Gemma*. In her opinion, Max's father had made a huge mistake firing Max. Only Max would know how to pull off the monumental task of saving the magazine. After all, he'd spent a lifetime building it.

Vanessa quickly calculated the logistics of her financial situation. Her house was completely paid for. Since she had no husband or children, she rarely spent money on vacations. Instead, she'd spent countless years putting most of her six-figure salary into an annuity, which had reached a substantial amount, one that could easily sustain her for the rest of her life in total luxury. Financially, Vanessa could retire anytime her heart desired.

And then there was Andrew. If she took on this kind of responsibility, she'd have no time to spend with him. No short sailing trips in the sun, no leisurely hours spent making love. Both her heart and her gut told her that Andrew was her destiny, her future. He'd need her love and support to get him through his grueling recovery. After all, he'd been shot protecting Haley.

What about Haley? She'd promised to continue to support her through her painful transition home. Haley had no close friends; she needed Vanessa. Could she simply put her on a plane, say good luck, have a good life, and return to her old life?

Feeling as though a tornado had been released inside her brain, a whirlwind of disjointed thoughts flooded her mind. She struggled with an internal battle between her professional ambitions and her personal desires.

Stopping suddenly in her tracks, Vanessa realized Marie hadn't said a word, but had silently watched her pace, waiting patiently for her decision. Reaching down for her glass to take a calming sip of wine, she composed herself enough to formulate a response to the bombshell Marie had launched at her.

"I'm sorry, I'll need more time to consider my options. Committing to taking over *Gemma* at this point will require a lot of careful deliberation. I'm afraid there are many factors and individuals I must consider before I make my final decision. I'm glad you warned me, but I doubt I'll have an answer for you before Monday morning, when I'm scheduled to return to the office."

Marie frowned in disappointment, but to her credit, she accepted

Vanessa's response gracefully. She didn't resort to persuasion or guilt to influence Vanessa. At least now Marie knew she would sleep tonight. She'd let Vanessa carry the fate of *Gemma* on her shoulders instead. "I understand completely. I won't tell anyone we spoke of this."

"Thank you," Vanessa nodded, but her unsmiling face appeared somber. "I think that would be best. Now if you'll excuse me, I'm very tired."

"Of course, thank you for listening tonight. I needed to get this off my chest. I've been wanting to tell you for a long time."

"I'm actually glad we were able to discuss this now," Vanessa said, attempting to smile, but the frown lines remained between her eyes. "It gives me the opportunity to be thoughtful. Now I'll be able to make an informed decision, in the event that I'm asked. Goodnight."

Marie stood, giving her boss a quick hug goodnight; she carried the empty wine glasses to the kitchen. Vanessa slowly turned to retire in Diane's room for the night.

Hours later, Vanessa kicked at her covers. Although she'd promised herself she would sleep, she had a tendency to allow big decisions keep her awake at night. Perhaps she should talk things over with Andrew; use him as her sounding board to determine if she really wanted to manage *Gemma*. But for tonight, she just needed some sleep. She forced all thoughts of *Gemma* into the darkness and finally slept.

Vanessa roused from a deep sleep the following morning. Even though the night had started off rough, she'd actually slept well, keeping all thoughts of *Gemma* and Andrew at bay during the night. Overhearing the soft, muffled voices of Marie and her husband in the kitchen, she felt guilty for imposing on them, and for her deep, dreamless sleep. She knew she should get up and hurry back to the hospital, but after checking her phone, seeing no urgent messages, she opted for a long, hot relaxing shower instead.

Carefully grooming herself, Vanessa took her time getting presentable. She even applied makeup. After all, Andrew wasn't in a coma any more, and he'd already seen her looking like a zombie. Finishing the last touches, she nodded appreciatively at herself in the mirror and walked into the kitchen in search of sustenance.

The deserted house felt refreshingly quiet after spending so much time in the noisy ICU. The constant beeping of the bedside monitors and alarms was enough to drive a sane person mad. Marie had left her an encouraging note along with her breakfast on a plate. Vanessa sat in the homey pale blue kitchen, quietly savoring her morning cup of coffee in peace, enjoying every drop of its rich aroma and soothing taste.

Eventually, she phoned the hospital. She could tell by the cheerful greeting that Andrew's animated day nurse was back on duty. She happily informed Vanessa that Andrew had had a good night. The doctor had been in to examine him a short time ago and had written orders to have Andrew moved out of the ICU. Vanessa thanked her for the care she gave Andrew, asking the young nurse to let him know she'd be there shortly.

Feeling more relaxed than she had in days, Vanessa looked around Marie's kitchen while she slowly ate breakfast. Marie's dishes displayed the classic Blue Willow pattern. The glass cupboards housed stacks of dishes in the same pattern. She noted the same pattern also edged the top of the pale blue walls. Her kitchen had a comfy feeling, capturing both modern and classical styles.

Vanessa's mind began to wander. She imagined what it would be like to be the editor-in-chief of *Gemma*. It seemed like it was just yesterday that Max and Mindy were trying to put her out to pasture. Age is all in the eyes of the beholder, she thought. Mr. Edwards didn't seem to think she was too old. The fact that she was fifty-five undoubtedly seemed very youthful to a man in his eighties. It would be poetic justice for her to return to *Gemma* and assume the highest position at the magazine.

Having taken her time with her appearance, and feeling especially lighthearted, Vanessa waltzed into the ICU. Surprised, she discovered the housekeepers busily stripping Andrew's now empty bed. Her face became ashen. Her heart skipped a beat as she began to panic, until Andrew's nurse spotted her and rushed over to explain.

"Andrew's gone for some x-rays, and he'll be in room 602 when he's done."

"Thanks," Vanessa exhaled, chiding herself for thinking the worst, even if it was only for a second. "I wanted to thank you in person. I appreciate that all the staff here has taken excellent care of Andrew."

The nurse smiled, hugging her briefly. Then she waved as she dashed off to respond to an alarming machine in one of the other rooms.

Andrew's new room was private. It seemed spacious without any of his previous medical equipment cluttering the area around his bed. A large window overlooked her special pond. She paused to gaze out at the path surrounding the shimmering pond below, lost in her own thoughts. Distractedly she heard someone clear his throat and instantly became aware that she was no longer alone. Turning, she gasped, "Oh, Father Patrick, you startled me."

"I'm sorry." He walked toward her, smiling broadly. "I didn't wish to disturb you while you were in such deep contemplation. How is Andrew today?"

Vanessa flushed. Not only had she been caught off guard, but she also hadn't seen Andrew yet. "He's out of the ICU," she answered vaguely.

"So I see. How are you today, Vanessa?" Father Patrick could see by her guilty expression that he'd made her uncomfortable.

"To tell the truth, Father, I've just arrived a few moments ago. I haven't seen Andrew today." Vanessa acknowledged. "I spent the night with my friend Marie, who lives just down the street."

"I can see that it did you a world of good." He took her hands and looked carefully at her face. "You're positively glowing this morning."

"Thank you." She blushed under his studious scrutiny. "Please, have a seat. Andrew should be back shortly." Vanessa sat on the wide window seat, leaving the chair next to the bed for Father Patrick. He tactfully changed the subject.

"You know, I stopped by Andrew's house yesterday. I had a little chat with little miss Haley. She's such a sensitive young lady. I'm afraid she's convinced herself that you blame her for Andrew's condition. She also believes you're keeping her from seeing him." Vanessa's mouth flew open in shock.

"I told her very clearly that I didn't blame her. And you know all about the hospital visiting policies. What can I do?" she pleaded, defensively.

"Don't worry. I had a nice long chat with her. I think she understands. She's a clever girl. In fact, she had me talk to her mother using her computer. Seems the little dickens tricked me into discouraging her mother from flying out to Andrew's, in order to look after the girls."

Again the sensation of guilt washed over Vanessa. She instantly felt the warmth of her face flushing. She'd promised Haley's mother she'd protect Haley. Instead, Haley had been exposed to hoards of paparazzi, an intruder invading her home, she'd received a threatening phone call, been moved to a new location, and now the two individuals who were charged with her care were spending day and night in a hospital miles away. *Why wouldn't her mother be concerned?* she thought sarcastically.

"Oh Father, I'm making a mess of everything. I know Haley needs me, but I've been too terrified to leave Andrew."

"Trust me, you're doing just fine." He engulfed her petite hands between his large, rough, warm palms. "Diane and Haley are having a wonderful time together. I predict they'll end up as lifelong friends. Besides, Andrew needs you. I predict the two of you will also end up as lifetime friends. You'll know when you feel it's safe enough to leave him. Besides, I told those girls I would be checking in on them daily," he chuckled.

"You've been an absolute godsend, Father." Vanessa smiled affectionately at the kindly priest.

"That's the job I signed up for," he smiled, goodheartedly. "Now tell me what else is troubling you. I sense you're struggling with something very important."

"Father, perhaps you can help me to prioritize," she said, astounded by his incredibly perceptive, inquisitive nature. Hesitantly she began, although she felt unconvinced that he could actually help her, given the specific details of her current dilemma. "I need to decide if I want to retire, or take on a new position at work. It's a position I've always dreamed of having, but one that would demand all of my time, energy, and concentration."

"I see, and what of your relationship with Andrew, or Haley?" Father Patrick asked, raising an eyebrow with innocent curiosity. "How would they fit in?"

"That's the thing, there'd be no time for either one of them," Vanessa confessed, chewing on her bottom lip.

"I see." Father Patrick leaned back in his chair and nodded. "I would love to help you, but this is a situation in which you're the only one who knows what's important to you. Only you know the answer to your question. But, let me tell you about a similar situation I once faced. I was offered a grand promotion. The church offered me a huge cathedral, with thousands of parishioners. But, it meant leaving my church and the congregation I loved. I'd baptized them, married them, and even buried some of them. The diocese planned to close my tiny church if I decided to leave. My entire congregation would be required to join another church several miles away. So you see, I could either have had a large beautiful church with thousand of parishioners, or I could stay in my tiny church overlooking the ocean, where the parishioners had become my family.

You know which one I selected. Now, it's up to you. You must choose."

"Thank you, Father," Vanessa smiled weakly. She understood what he was telling her. "I think you've helped me more than you know."

He responded with a wink and a quick smile, one that spoke volumes about his ability to share his wisdom effortlessly, and quietly provide solace and guidance.

Father Patrick had left briefly to get them each a glass of water when Andrew arrived in his new room. Although exhausted, his face lit up, and he smiled from ear to ear at the sight of Vanessa. Although he rode in a wheelchair, all of his tubes and wires had been removed. The only remaining signs that he'd suffered a severe, life threatening injury were his pale skin, the bandages on his chest, and his right arm hanging lifelessly in a sling.

"Hey, will you look at this room? I have a window!"

Vanessa had to laugh at his cheerful mood. He looked almost like his old self again. "You look great. Where are all of your tubes and wires?"

"They removed most of them before I left the ICU." Andrew adjusted his position in bed as he spoke. "And then they took out my chest tube while I was in x-ray. Apparently, I don't need them any more."

Father Patrick walked into the room holding a cup of water in each hand. Vanessa paused in mid-air as she bent toward Andrew for a kiss, and stepped toward the priest to relieve him of the cups he carried.

"Oh my, you're looking healthy, Andrew."

"Thanks, Father," he beamed. "I heard you stopped by yesterday while we were sleeping. Sorry I missed you."

"I could tell you both needed your rest." Father Patrick cleared his throat. "I can see you're still a little tired today. You've had quite a big day."

"You can say that again." Andrew smiled in acknowledgement. "I'm looking forward to a much quieter night tonight."

"I can't stay long, I need to check on your house on my way home."

"Is everything all right?" Andrew frowned, confused by his statement. "What's wrong at my house?"

"No, no, no, it's nothing to worry about." Father Patrick waved him off. "I simply promised Haley's mother I'd check in with Haley once a day."

"Okay then, thanks for watching out for the girls," Andrew said. He knew how June worried about Haley. "I'm not worried though, I have a patrol car staying in the neighborhood. The girls and the house are under constant close surveillance."

"Between the three of us, we have a babysitter in the house, a priest stopping by, and a patrol car in the neighborhood. I guess they'll be fine," Vanessa laughed. The three of them were greatly amused by their efforts to protect the two perfectly capable young women.

Father Patrick said a prayer, blessing them both with his usual flair, and then excused himself. As soon as he left the room, Andrew reached for Vanessa with his good arm. She came to him eagerly for a passionate, long overdue kiss. Climbing up into the bed with him, she snuggled close, relishing the feel of his warm skin under her fingertips.

"Father Patrick is a very good man," she observed, thoughtfully.

"I didn't realize you knew him all that well." Andrew pulled her closer, pleased by her statement.

"You might be surprised by what I've been up to, while you've been out of commission," she whispered playfully in his ear.

"Do tell. What have you been doing?" Andrew cuddled her against his side, enjoying her flirtatious mood.

"Haley and I attended your church on Sunday. That's where we met Father Patrick."

"That's nice, what else?" He nibbled her ear.

"Well, he's been here every day," she said, her heart fluttering. His playfully sensual attentions were making her feel giddy. "We've—spent time walking together, and we've—talked."

"That's nice..." Andrew yawned, his voice sounding tired and hushed.

"Let's rest," Vanessa said practically, realizing how exhausted he must be. "We can talk more later."

"Uh, huh."

Andrew fell asleep almost immediately. Vanessa listened to his regular breathing, making an instantaneous decision, thinking, *I don't need to talk over my work issues with him. I know what I want. It's exactly what I've always wanted.*

"Excuse me." Andrew's new nurse interrupted Vanessa's thoughts. "I'm sorry, but I need to assess Mr. Kelly and it's time for his medication." Vanessa peeled herself out of Andrew's embrace and waited awkwardly at the bedside. She moved toward the door, and Andrew stirred, searching for her beside him. Vanessa quickly explained, "I'll be back in a few moments, after your nurse finishes with you."

Andrew stretched, giving her a lazy smile that made his blue eyes dance mischievously. "See you in a few, beautiful."

Vanessa walked out into the warm sunshine, returning to her walkway around the pond. Cell phone reception was better outside, and it felt good to move around in the fresh air. She dialed Haley.

"How are you two doing?"

"We're great, Father Patrick's entertaining us with his stories." Haley voice sounded relaxed and cheery.

"I thought I might try to take you both out to dinner tonight. I want to spend the night there with you."

"What about Andrew?" Haley asked.

"He's doing much better. In fact, they moved him into a regular room today."

"I know, Father Patrick just told us. I'm so happy he's doing better." Vanessa noted her enthusiasm.

"Anyway, I thought we could all come back here tomorrow. You could visit with Andrew, and Diane might appreciate the opportunity to go home for more clothes and things. What do you think?" Vanessa heard Haley's muffled voice as she conferred with Diane.

"Diane says that would be great. We didn't know what we were doing for dinner tonight anyway."

"Fine, I'll spend the afternoon with Andrew," Vanessa said, pleased with her decision to make time for Haley. "Then I'll see you both around six."

"Thanks, Vanessa. It'll be good to spend some time with you. I can't wait to hear all about Andrew."

Vanessa felt better after having made a plan. She had an obligation to watch over Haley, besides, she really wanted to see her. She'd make sure Haley didn't add Andrew's incident to her long list of discredits.

Returning to Andrew, she found him sitting up, eating a modest portion of meat loaf and mashed potatoes with his good hand. He ate like a man who hadn't eaten in a week, thoroughly enjoying every bite. *A sure sign of his recovery*, she thought.

"Hi, did you miss me?"

"Of course." Andrew paused his eating long enough to answer her question. "Everything okay?"

"Yeah, I just needed to check in with Haley and Diane." Vanessa sat down next to him in the chair.

"Everything good at the house?"

"Father Patrick's there now." She sent him a reassuring smile. "It seems he's been keeping them entertained with his stories." She handed him a napkin to wipe the potatoes off his mustache whiskers. "I told Haley I'd have dinner with them tonight. I think I'll spend the night at your house tonight, then bring Haley back to visit you tomorrow, if that's all right with you?"

Andrew had finished eating while she talked. He wiped his mouth, and pushed his table to the side of the bed. He reached for Vanessa's hand and she leaned closer to him. He made small, sensual circles around the base of her thumb, while gazing at her face, and then he frowned slightly.

"You know, I'm going to be right as rain in no time. I know you feel guilty about abandoning Haley, so go. Spend some time with her. I'd really enjoy visiting with her tomorrow when you come back. She needs to see for herself that I'm perfectly fine. I don't want her worrying about me." Andrew always had such a calm, stabilizing effect on Vanessa.

"Thank you for understanding. I don't want to leave you, I just need to go calm Haley's fears in person."

"She blames herself for everything." Andrew shook his head regretfully. "I'll support you. I'll have a serious talk with her myself tomorrow."

"Thank you." Vanessa smiled at his sweet confidence. He truly believed he could solve any problem.

They spent the rest of the afternoon holding hands, laughing at each other's jokes, and occasionally flirting with a few serious topics, including the expected time period for his arm to fully recover. Vanessa snuggled alongside him in his bed and dozed, while Andrew napped off and on throughout the day. A few minutes before she needed to leave, Andrew revived, feeling refreshed and wide-awake, and wanted to discuss plans for after his discharge home. He mentioned casually the fact that Vanessa would soon be returning to work.

"I know you have to go back to work on Monday, but will you still be getting another two weeks off next month?"

"That all depends." The question caught Vanessa unprepared. She hadn't decided what to tell him, so she avoided giving him a direct answer.

"On what?" Andrew wondered at her reluctance to discuss her work schedule.

"On whether or not I take over at *Gemma* as editor-in-chief," Vanessa blurted, deciding she should just tell him, and face the music.

Andrew's heart sank; it was the last thing he'd expected Vanessa to say. Like Vanessa, he'd been unaware of the difficulties, or the drastic changes at *Gemma*. Speechless, he lay silently stunned next to the woman he loved, overwhelmed by the cruel heart-wrenching ache twisting deep within his chest.

Chapter 27
Sensual Surprise

*A*ndrew's silence spoke volumes to Vanessa. She realized that she'd revealed her prospect of the position at *Gemma,* as if it were fact. He took a few moments, struggling to acquire something resembling composure, before he spoke cautiously. "If you do 'take over' the magazine, what does that mean for us?"

Guilty over divulging her complicated work situation, especially since she hadn't actually talked with Mr. Edwards, Vanessa backtracked. After all, there'd been no official offer yet. "*If* it is offered and I decide to accept the position as editor-in-chief at *Gemma,* I doubt I would have any spare time to take vacations, or even date. The magazine is in big trouble, Andrew. It will take a minimum of a year to put it back on solid ground," she explained.

Andrew's brows furrowed. He had no idea how he should respond. She'd always been committed to the magazine, not to mention a consummate workaholic. *Gemma's* growth and success had been partly due to her perseverance and hard work. He wasn't sure if she'd appreciate any of his efforts to try to influence her one way or the other, considering their brief relationship. If he told her not to take the position, she'd resent him. If he supported her ambitions, they'd drift apart from lack of contact. Consequently, he said the only safe thing he could think of. "I'll support whatever you decide."

Vanessa surprised herself. Her initial reaction to Andrew's neutral answer was an intense feeling of disappointment. She'd assumed he'd try to encourage her *not* to take the new position at *Gemma.* That he'd try to cleverly convince her to stay with him, so they could sail away into the sunset together. She paused, considering his position for a minute. Ultimately, she decided she was relieved by his response, admiring his ability to respect her judgment. He trusted her to make up her mind, and choose her own destiny.

"Thank you. I'm pretty sure I know what I want to do, but I won't know for sure until I meet with Mr. Edwards on Monday."

Andrew exhaled a sigh of relief. Judging by Vanessa's calm reply, he knew he'd responded properly. Although he said she could decide for herself, he secretly planned to plot subtle ways to sway her decision toward staying with him. He motioned seductively for her to climb into bed with him. She willingly complied, having no desire to continue their conversation on the subject of her future at *Gemma.*

Andrew deliberately kissed her, nibbling seductively on her lower lip, plunging his tongue playfully into her mouth, adding a sufficient amount heat and passion to disarm her. He intentionally gave her just enough pleasure to remind her of exactly what she'd miss, should she choose the demanding position at *Gemma* over him. Vanessa pulled away, breathless after just a single kiss. He was the only man who'd ever made her feel so tingly, breathless, and excited by a mere kiss, or even the slightest touch of his hand. She snuggled up against him for a few more precious moments, treasuring the feel of his firm body, the warmth of his skin, and the faint sweet smell that was uniquely him. She regretted that Haley and Diane would be waiting for her to take them to dinner. All too soon, she forced herself to push out of his intimate one-armed embrace.

"Sorry sailor, but its time for me to go," she teased.

"Can't blame a guy for trying." He grinned affectionately down at her, giving her another potent kiss to remember him by. Andrew heard Vanessa quietly pant as she got off the bed, and smiled with masculine satisfaction. Futilely she fussed, endeavoring to right her disheveled clothes and smooth her wayward hair. Frustrated, it seemed that no matter how hard Vanessa tried, she couldn't hide the fact that she'd just been thoroughly kissed, as well as physically stimulated. Confidently amused, Andrew reclined back in bed, watching her feeble attempts to hide her firm nipples, which clearly revealed her level of arousal.

She blushed slightly under his close surveillance, mortified by her obviously aroused state. His direct gaze at her embarrassingly erect nipples, and his amused smile made her feel like a rebellious child, so she stuck out her tongue and blew him a kiss.

"Call me if you need anything, see you tomorrow."

"I will." Andrew laughed at her playful antics. "And Vanessa, remember me tonight in your dreams."

Vanessa's face flamed. She knew she'd do more than remember him, if she managed to get to sleep at all. *He'd obviously recovered from her unexpected news*, she thought, smiling back at him, pleased by the way he continued to arouse and tease her. Exhaling in relief, she laughed and tormented him, sending him a coy little bye-bye baby wave, as she exited his room.

Vanessa had previously arranged a car to take her to Andrew's house. Her usual driver, Tom, now stood patiently waiting for her when she stepped out of the hospital lobby. Completely preoccupied by her volatile emotions, struggling to control the multiple thoughts whirling around in her head, she flashed him a quick smile, extremely pleased to see him.

"Nice to see you again, Ms. Golden," he said, helping her into the car.

She greeted Tom fondly, requesting that he swing past her house. She wanted to grab more clothes before continuing on to Andrew's beach house.

Pulling up in her drive, she noticed how deserted her house appeared. Vanessa walked through her front door and immediately felt the cold, strange, unwelcoming sensation her house gave her. It seemed unusually unnerving to her today. *Maybe it's because Callie isn't here to greet me*, she thought. But, as she walked through her empty kitchen, she felt a chill of apprehension run up her spine. Standing at the doorway, she relived faint, ghostly memories of the beatings she'd received in this room, years ago. Glancing toward the counter, she recalled the more recent violation of her home, when she'd caught Juan's older brother rifling through her purse.

Carefully checking the entire house, Vanessa walked outside by the pool. She stared at the new, mature maple tree that Juan had planted to replace the one she'd lost during the windstorm. The tree appeared full and healthy, but it lacked the emotional attachment she'd felt for the one she'd planted for her daughter. This tree was simply a tree. Everything else seemed unchanged, in its usual place. So why did she still have such a strange, uneasy feeling? She hastily gathered what she needed, locked the house up tight, and set her alarms, before rushing back outside to Tom. Efficiently whisked away from her unsettling house in the back seat of the black sedan, she looked forward to the comfort of Andrew's sunny beach house. Vanessa watched from the back window as her house disappeared from view, feeling oddly relieved. She shook off her spooky feelings, and decided to distract herself, using the travel time to make a few calls.

Her first call was to Juan. She wanted to know if his brother had recovered. Juan sounded pleased to hear from her, gladly informing her that Roberto had returned to Mexico. He again thanked her for her help. He'd noticed her absence and offered to watch over her house. She appreciated his offer, satisfied that their relationship had returned to its previous status quo.

Next, she decided she should check for any news regarding John, the bank's security guard. She found his granddaughter's number and dialed it reluctantly, surprised when she answered on the first ring. The news was good. John had been taken off the ventilator, and his prognosis was better than originally expected. He was projected to make a slow, but full recovery. Vanessa knew how relieved Haley would be. She could hardly wait to share the good news.

Andrew's assistant was next. Vanessa asked her if there had been any news regarding Kate, the strange women who'd entered Haley's room posing as a nurse. Vanessa knew that an FBI agent currently kept a close eye on Kate, somewhere in South America. Andrew's assistant had no new information, but was thrilled to hear about Andrew's recovery. She promised to update Andrew as soon as she received any news.

The final call she made was to Mike, the detective who'd saved Andrew's life. She informed him of Andrew's condition and his new room number. Mike seemed extremely relieved by Andrew's recovery, promising to stop in to see him later tonight. Vanessa thanked him again for saving Andrew's life and promised to call again soon.

Satisfied by the results of her calls, Vanessa suddenly realized that Tom had already turned down Andrew's street. He helped her out of the car and carried her clothes to the doorstep. She thanked him, tipping him generously. Vanessa appreciated the security of having a familiar face drive her home.

Haley hobbled toward her with her crutches the minute Vanessa stepped through Andrew's front door. Diane rushed over to relieve Vanessa of the clothes she carried, while Haley threw her arms around Vanessa for a big hug.

"I've missed you!" Haley smiled broadly.

Delighted by her warm reception, Vanessa realized she'd missed Haley too. Stifling her own overly emotional response, she spoke practically. "I'm happy to see you too. Now if you two will give me just a minute, I'll run upstairs to change so we can all go out to dinner and catch up. Andrew told me how to get to a little place just down the road. He says the window tables have an incredible view." Vanessa finished the last sentence after she'd run halfway up the staircase, toting her bulky clothes effortlessly.

The two young girls watched in amazement as Vanessa jogged up the stairs. When she closed the bedroom door, they both giggled.

"Wow, Vanessa's a real whirlwind," Diane couldn't help noting. "She makes me feel like a slug. I camped out down here on the couch, because I didn't want to keep going up and down the stairs, and she acts like it's nothing."

"She's always like that," Haley agreed.

Diane drove, and on the way to the restaurant, Vanessa updated Haley on both Andrew's and John's conditions. Haley wept, overwhelmed with relief.

"Haley, it's all right, it seems they're both going to be fine." Diane attempted to comfort her, surprised by Haley's weepy reaction to such obviously good news.

"I know, but I've been so worried about them." Embarrassed, Haley quickly brushed her tears away. "Thank you, I can't tell you how much better that makes me feel."

Vanessa smiled affectionately, and observed the two girls' interactions with fascination. They chattered and giggled, gushing over Andrew's beach house, and agreeing how much they loved being right on the ocean. Later, they all laughed to the point of tears as Diane entertained them with stories of Shep and Callie's adventures. It seemed odd to Vanessa how quickly Callie had accepted Shep, but she wasn't about to complain. Thoughtfully she observed Haley, who seemed on the surface to be having a great time, although there were glimpses of sadness on her face, especially when she talked about leaving for home.

"I wish I could have hung out with you and Andrew more. I can't believe I have to leave on Friday."

"I know, I wish we could have too." Vanessa had forgotten Haley was leaving so soon. "But look on the bright side, you got to meet Diane and hang out with her." Diane and Haley looked at each other, and spontaneously giggled.

"That's true, it's been a blast, and with Father Patrick, too."

"You're right." Vanessa smiled at the thought of Father Patrick. "It's sort of remarkable, how he manages to get so close to people, in almost no time at all."

"Yes, in fact, I think I've decided to attend his church, that is, whenever I'm home from school," Diane said. She'd obviously become another one of Father Patrick's conquests.

"I hope I have a chance to come back. I'd like to go with you," Haley said, wistfully. "Do you think Andrew will be home before I have to leave?"

"I'm sorry." Vanessa sadly shook her head. She had no idea when he'd be home. "I'd be surprised if he came home that soon. I'm just hoping he'll be home before I have to go back to work."

"That's right, don't you go back on Monday? What about Andrew? Who's going to take care of him?"

"I don't know," Vanessa said, wondering the same thing. "I've actually been thinking about that myself. Do you think his housekeeper could handle it?" The girls looked at each other and smirked.

"Have you met his housekeeper?" Haley asked Vanessa, in a very innocent voice.

"No, why? Is she too old?" Vanessa puzzled over their response.

Haley stifled her laughter enough to answer Vanessa's question. "She's twenty-four, and she's a hot swimsuit model!"

"I guess I'll need to find someone more suitable before I go back to work." Now, Vanessa understood why they'd smirked. No way was that situation going to work for her.

"What about his dog walker?" Haley smiled innocently.

"No, I've seen his dog walker." Vanessa shook her head, frowning at the thought, as the girls laughed at Vanessa's jealous response.

"I might have to check in with an agency, maybe even interview a couple of people."

"I'm not a nurse, but if you get in a bind, I could watch over him next week," Diane offered shyly. "I won't be going back to school until the following week."

"Thanks for the offer." Vanessa smiled at Diane's kindness. "The truth is, I have no idea exactly what his care will entail. But thank you, I'll definitely keep you in mind."

Vanessa found she really enjoyed both Haley's and Diane's dinner conversation. Sitting at an outside table, they watched the lights of the boats in the harbor as they twinkled and bobbed, reflecting off the calm water. When it was time for dessert, all three of them decided to splurge on a very decadent molten chocolate lava cake. Vanessa realized distractedly that this was the first relaxing evening she'd had in a long, long time.

Later, arriving back at Andrew's house, Haley and Diane went outside by the pool to talk. Feeling exhausted, despite the girl's protests, Vanessa excused herself to go upstairs to bed. Vanessa hadn't had any alcohol during her dinner with the girls, but she carried a large glass of red wine upstairs with her now. Sitting alone in the dark on Andrew's bedroom balcony, she sipped her wine and listened to the comforting murmurs and occasional youthful laughter drifting up from Diane and Haley on the patio below.

Vanessa reflected on the uncanny, spooky feeling she'd felt earlier while at her own house, and compared it to how she felt being here. At her house today, she'd felt unusually anxious, like something was off, or a little out of place. Her cold, empty house seemed to represent memories of horrendous violence, enormous grief, and lonely isolation. She shivered at the thought.

In contrast, Andrew's house gave her a sense of warmth and peace. She felt like she belonged here. He'd tucked away the photo of his deceased wife after the first day he'd brought her home with him. And since Andrew's wife had never lived here, Vanessa never sensed any lingering spiritual imprints from her. In Andrew's house, she felt only love, acceptance, and physical pleasure. She couldn't explain why, but at some point, her emotions had shifted dramatically, and she no longer felt the appeal of returning to her own home.

Vanessa finished her wine, took a quick shower, and climbed into Andrew's bed with eager anticipation of a good night's sleep. She buried her face in his pillow, inhaling his musky, male scent. She assumed she'd fall right to sleep, but instead she tossed and turned, struggling to find a comfortable spot, and fighting viciously with the pillows. Haley and Diane had long since fallen asleep when Vanessa squinted irritably at the clock, noticing it was after two in the morning. Cursing aloud, she reached for her cell phone. Andrew answered on the second ring.

"I told you to dream about me, not stay up all night." He sounded alert and awake.

"Were you awake?"

"Yeah, the nurse just took my vital signs and gave me some medication. Is everything all right, Vanessa? You sound a little irritated."

"I'm so tired… I just can't seem to fall asleep," Vanessa sighed.

"Miss me, don't you?" he smiled.

"Maybe," she answered coyly. "Have you been sleeping?"

"Like a baby. Face it, you want me."

"You did this to me on purpose, didn't you?" Vanessa snorted in disgust.

"Well, I have to admit I tried." Andrew smiled to himself. "I didn't really think it would be so effective. I'm really sorry. I know how much you need sleep. Do you want me to tell you a bedtime story or something?"

"I'd prefer the *or something*," she smirked. "But it's a little difficult to accomplish, given we're miles apart from each other."

"Difficult, but not impossible," he laughed. "I'm game, if you are?"

"I'm not so sure that's such a good idea, you're recovering," She said, but she had to admit she found his suggestion intriguing. "You need your rest."

Andrew lowered his voice, attempting to sound seductive as he challenged her. "You're not afraid, are you?"

"All right, mister, bring it on." Vanessa snorted at his dare.

He smiled, astonished by her response. He suddenly felt a little self-conscious, and wasn't sure he could actually deliver on his threat. "Alright, are you willing to do everything I ask?"

"At this point, I'll do anything to get some sleep."

"First of all..." Andrew could hear the frustrated desperation in her voice. "I need you to stop talking. Just listen to me and do everything just the way I say. Can you do that?"

Vanessa shivered, vaguely uneasy about where this was heading, but since he wasn't actually in the room with her, she knew she could always fake whatever she felt uncomfortable doing. He'd have no way of knowing what she was actually doing. "Alright."

Andrew dropped the tone of his voice and spoke in a low whisper. His baritone voice vibrated through her body, and she immediately relaxed, trusting him completely. "Take everything off and lie on top of the bed naked."

She rebelled at first and didn't move, but somehow, he seemed to know.

"Vanessa?"

"Oh, okay." She pulled her sleep shirt over her head in nervous annoyance and threw it to the far corner of the room.

"Now, place the phone on speaker mode and set it on the pillow next to your head. Try to pretend I'm in bed with you. I want you to imagine my hands and lips are the ones touching you,

This time she complied without hesitation. He could tell she had, by the way things sounded on his end of the phone. He could hear the ocean waves outside, and smiled. She'd left the french doors open.

"Now, focus on the sound of the ocean," he continued in the same sensual voice as before. "Concentrate for a moment on the moonlight filtering into the room, then allow your eyes to slowly close. Take slow deep breaths, in through your nose and out through your mouth."

Andrew struggled to recall a self-hypnosis class he'd taken a few years ago for stress reduction. He thought if he could get her in the proper state of mind, she would respond easier to his suggestions.

"Just breathe in slowly through your nose, then out slowly through your mouth. As you exhale, let all thoughts of anything outside of the room drift away. Focus on the ocean sounds, on your breathing. Now feel the warm air in the room, as it tantalizes and floats across your exposed skin."

He could hear her deep breaths over the phone, so he continued slowly in the same deep, low tone. "Remember how you felt after we kissed today. Feel that same sensation in your body now. Imagine we're kissing, feel the pressure from my lips, starting with gentle pressure on yours, then feel the pressure slowly increasing as our kiss deepens. Now feel my lips as they caress the smooth, slender nape of your neck, behind your right ear, just a soft, tender nibble, just enough so you can feel tingling down your spine, then feel it traveling through your entire body." *What now,* he thought.

"I'm nibbling on your ear, slowly my lips are moving, placing feathery soft kisses across your shoulder. My kisses are slowly moving down the top of your arm. When I reach your hand, I gently turn it over, and place a tender kiss on the sensitive palm of your hand."

It surprised Vanessa how vividly she remembered these sensations from when they'd previously made love. She felt tiny Goosebumps rise on her arms as she imagined his tender, feathery, moist kisses. She recalled more and more of the intense sensations of his touch as she listened to Andrew's throaty voice guiding her through each movement, until she felt her body vibrating with anticipation.

"Now reach up with both hands, and gently place them on each side of your face." Andrew's voice grew husky as he went on. "These are my hands caressing you. Slowly trail my fingertips softly down your face to your neck. Now, slowly cup your breasts. Remember these are my hands caressing your breasts. Gradually move my hands lower... down your smooth waist... pausing to rest them on the top of your thighs." Vanessa became lost in a unique sea of sensations tantalizing her sensitive skin.

"Bend your knees, letting your beautiful legs fall apart." He could tell by Vanessa's sighs that she was with him. He also knew this next part was going to be especially tricky. "Breathe slowly in and out, while you make small circles with the tips of my fingers on your inner thighs."

She had stopped thinking, obediently following his every suggestion and command. Knowing where he was heading, she made circles with her fingertips on the delicate skin of her inner thighs, feeling the intense, stimulating sensation on her smooth skin from her light touch. She remembered how delicious it felt when Andrew kissed her there.

"Now move my fingers softly up your thighs, until they're close to, but not yet touching, the top of your soft, feminine mound between your legs."

How wickedly erotic this feels, she thought. She become thoroughly aroused just listening to Andrew's husky voice, drifting sensually to her from afar, even though she hadn't even touched her now throbbing feminine core.

"Remember, these hands are my hands. I'm now massaging your beautiful, soft mound with my fingertips, exploring with a gentle, circular motion, moving very slow, deeper and deeper between the folds until I locate your secret, sensitive pleasure point."

She could vividly imagine Andrew touching her, as she reached between her legs. Her raspy breathing became wilder. Her heartbeat beat faster and faster, echoing loudly in her ears.

Hearing her heavy breathing, he was convinced he'd almost aroused her to the point of her sweet release. "As I continue to pleasure you with my right hand, allow my left hand to find it's way back to your breast. I'm cupping your soft, smooth breast in the palm of my hand, slowly rolling your nipple between my thumb and forefinger, gently tugging, as I suckle it tenderly. Feel the kisses I'm trailing from your breast to your mouth."

He heard her quietly moan, as she grew closer to her release. "Now, I'm moving my other hand lower, plunging my fingers deep inside your feminine core. Plunging in and out of your soft, moist, mysterious womanly core."

Vanessa moaned loudly and cried out, "Andrew!" as wave after wave of intense electric pleasure coursed through her body. She arched her back with wild abandon, and the phone slid off the pillow, onto the bed beside her.

Andrew heard her call out his name, and discovered he could no longer speak. He'd managed to not only arouse Vanessa, but he also suddenly found himself preoccupied by his own unexpectedly imminent release. He saw stars before his eyes as he exploded with exquisite pleasure into the crisp white sheets of his hospital bed. His vision blurred and the room grew dark.

Vanessa's climax shocked her. The length and intensity of the rolling

297

waves of pleasure that pulsated through her body monopolized all of her senses. As she relaxed in the limp, warm aftermath of her release, she realized that Andrew had stopped talking. She grew even more concerned when she heard his soft, muffled groan, and his raspy, labored breathing in the distance. She grabbed her phone off the bed.

"Andrew? Are you alright?"

"More than alright," he said at last, having recovered his wits, and answering in an amused state of euphoria. "Although, I'm a tad embarrassed. I just had a wet dream. The kind teenage boys would kill for."

"Did you?" she smiled.

"Oh yeah, how about you? Did you?" He struggled to calm his breathing.

"Yeah," Vanessa sighed, stretching an arm over her head in languid triumph. They both remained quiet for a few moments longer, recovering from their unexpectedly erotic experience.

"So, where'd you learn phone sex?"

"Would you believe this was my first time?" he chuckled.

"Mine too," she laughed.

"Well I guess we were a couple of phone sex virgins, and I think I just took your virginity," Andrew smiled, sounding pleased with himself.

"I guess so, and since you were my first, thank you."

"My pleasure, my lady," he whispered, lightheartedly. "I guess I should try to rearrange my sheets and get some more sleep." He sounded tired, but thoroughly satisfied with his performance.

"Thanks, I have to admit, I'm feeling so relaxed, I can barely keep my eyes open."

"Get some sleep. I love you." Andrew's voice floated to her through the phone like a tender caress.

"Love you too, goodnight," she yawned.

Vanessa hung up and hugged Andrew's pillow to her chest. She buried her face in it and inhaled the rich, musky scent of sandalwood, uniquely Andrew's. She snuggled in his bed to sleep with her arms wound around his pillow. The last conscious thought that drifted through her mind: *I can't believe I just did that.*

Chapter 28
Mending Wounds

Vanessa woke to brilliant rays of sunshine streaming in through the open french doors, and the comforting sounds of Haley and Diane's voices filtering up the stairs. She listened carefully, recognizing the gentle cadence of a distinctive male voice as well. Evidently, Father Patrick had arrived for his routine daily visit.

Stretching her arms over her head, she quietly laughed, realizing she'd slept completely in the nude. Glancing at the corner of Andrew's room, she discovered her crumpled nightshirt, where she'd hastily thrown it, and smiled at her unprecedented wanton behavior. *No other man could have accomplished what Andrew did to me last night*, she thought happily. Frowning, she fleetingly thought about their future together. *What am I going to do about Andrew?*

Even though she really wanted to linger in bed, Vanessa reluctantly got up to shower. On impulse, instead of dressing, she changed into her bathing suit. *After so many days of sitting around in the hospital, a few strenuous laps in the pool is just what I need this morning*, she thought. She slipped on her matching cover-up in deference to Father Patrick. Grabbing a towel, she stepped out of the bedroom door, running lightly down the stairs to join them.

Haley and Diane relaxed lazily in chaise lounges next to the pool. There was no sign of Father Patrick, but an incredibly beautiful olive-complexioned, tall, thin woman stood beside them, serving omelets.

Haley looked up as Vanessa came through the door. "I'm surprised you slept so late. You must have really been tired. Did you sleep okay?"

"Not at first." Vanessa hesitated, hiding her blush. "I finally fell asleep sometime after two."

"Hello, you must be Vanessa?" The beautiful young woman smiled at her as she finished serving the two girls. "I'm Andrew's housekeeper, Jaszel."

Vanessa almost choked. The girls hadn't simply been teasing her last night, when they talked about Jaszel. She wore a sarong over her bathing suit and she *looked* like a model!

"Nice to meet you, Jaszel. I see you're spoiling these two," she said, nodding her head toward Haley and Diane as they sat gobbling down their omelets with delight.

"It's my pleasure. Can I get you some coffee, or an omelet?"

Jaszel was about a foot taller than Vanessa. Glancing up at her, Vanessa hesitantly removed her own cover-up, feeling physically inadequate next to Jaszel's towering, perfectly shaped figure. "No, thank you. I'll just swim some laps and help myself when I'm done."

Gracefully, Jaszel responded with a slight shrug and a smile. She'd seen the condemning look in Vanessa's eyes. She knew all about independent American women. She wasn't offended, but she wouldn't force the issue with Vanessa. "Please, let me know if I can get anything for you before I leave. Have a nice swim," she smiled pleasantly, returning into the house carrying an empty platter.

"Thank you," she called after her. "Did I hear Father Patrick this morning?" Vanessa changed the subject, facing Haley and Diane with a raised eyebrow.

"Yes, but he left a while ago," Haley answered, smiling angelically.

"I'm sorry I missed him. You two behave yourselves," she admonished, indicating they were shamefully taking advantage of Jaszel. Walking past them to the deep end, she dove smoothly into the pool in one fluid motion.

"I don't think Vanessa approves of us letting Jaszel wait on us," Diane giggled.

"I don't know about you, but I'm injured *and* on crutches," Haley smirked. "I think Vanessa might be a bit put out. After all, Jaszel's been Andrew's housekeeper for the past year."

"I know my mom would never allow Jaszel anywhere near my dad," Diane chuckled, shaking her head.

They both watched as Vanessa effortlessly swam lap after lap, smoothly navigating back and forth across the pool. Finally, Diane wondered aloud, "How long do you think she's going to swim? I think she's already swum about a hundred laps."

"I don't know," Haley said, shaking her head. "She has a pool at her house, so she's probably used to swimming lots of laps."

Vanessa loved to swim. Gliding sleekly through the cool water gave her a chance to clear her mind. When she swam, all she thought about was getting from one end of the pool to the other. She never counted her laps; she simply stopped whenever she felt finished.

Climbing out of the pool, Vanessa looked for Jaszel and assumed she had left, so she helped herself to a cup of coffee. Lowering herself into a chair next to Haley, she began air-drying in the warmth of the sun, feeling thoroughly relaxed, as she peacefully savored her morning cup of coffee.

"Oh my gosh Vanessa, how many laps did you swim?" Diane asked.

"I don't know. I never keep track," Vanessa responded offhandedly. Her body began to unwind, releasing her pent up frustration, along with some nagging residual anxiety she'd felt previous to her swim. It felt pleasantly cathartic, as the tension she'd held deep within her aching muscles gradually eased.

"Haley, how would you like to go visit Andrew as soon as I get dressed?"

Haley gave Vanessa a thumbs-up sign since her mouth was full. Diane spoke up instead. "I'll drop you two off while I go home. I need to get some more clothes and things, if that's okay?"

"That reminds me, I've been sleeping in your room. I need to clear my things out for you," Vanessa said, grateful for Diane on so many levels. She'd willingly stepped in and made a bad situation manageable.

"No problem, you can leave it if you want," Diane shrugged, unconcerned by the intrusion of her personal space. After all, she was staying here *in paradise*.

Vanessa didn't plan on staying as close to Andrew for the remainder of his hospitalization. He'd proven to her how fast he'd recovered last night. "Thanks for letting me sleep in your bed, Diane. Are you two finished, or are you still hungry?" she asked, picking up the girl's empty plates.

"I could eat, what do you have in mind?" Haley piped up.

Vanessa laughed at Haley's insatiable appetite. "I know a little place where we can have some lunch. It's right on the way to the hospital. Diane?"

"Sounds good," she shrugged.

Feeling calmer, with her long-overtaxed nerves under control again, she ran up the stairs to quickly shower off the chlorine and pool water, and primp for Andrew. Thinking about last night's phone sex made her feel a little self-conscious about seeing him today. She deliberately selected a conservative pair of navy-blue slacks with a matching striped blue and white blouse, and a light cotton, short-sleeved, white jacket to wear for the day. Standing in front of the mirror, she smoothed down her slacks in front and smiled. *This should cool his jets today,* she thought.

After a quick lunch, Diane dropped the two of them off at the hospital. Vanessa, slightly ahead of Haley, walked into Andrew's room and found

301

him sitting quietly in a wheelchair by the window. Remembering last night's erotic phone conversation, a secretive smile crossed her face, as she noticed the clean linens on his freshly made bed. Leaning down to give Andrew a quick hello kiss, she whispered, "I see you have clean sheets today." The wicked look in his eyes warned her that he was about to say something raunchy in response, so she hastily added, "Careful, Haley's right behind me."

"Later," he grinned, threatening her playfully.

"Hi there, you're looking pretty good. How have you been?" Andrew turned his wheelchair toward the door to give Haley his full attention while she cautiously entered his room on her crutches.

Beaming at him happily, Haley paused as she observed him closely. Instant relief engulfed her eyes at the sight of Andrew, casually reclining in the wheelchair in his shorts and t-shirt, his arm, resting in a sling, the only outward sign of his recent trauma. "I'm great. You're not looking too bad yourself. I'm glad to see you're up out of bed. I can't tell you how bad I feel about all of this." Andrew shook his head, watching the guilt reflecting in her suddenly misty eyes.

"I don't know why you feel bad, this was all my fault." He indicated his arm with a nod. "I know better. If I'd simply done what I've been trained to do, I wouldn't be here in this hospital right now." He saw the relief flooding into her eyes as she dashed away her tears, and he sent her a reassuring smile, before changing the subject. "I know what I've been doing recently, tell me about you. What have you been doing for the past few days?"

Haley sat and began waving her hands wildly as she rapidly filled Andrew in on her new relationships with Diane and Father Patrick. She chattered on and on about Shep and Callie's escapades, and finished her monologue by telling him all about her family. Vanessa stood behind Haley while she talked, smiling as she silently watched Andrew's reaction. She loved the way he always seemed to say just the right thing. He seemed to have the uncanny ability to quickly defuse any potentially emotionally volatile subject with ease.

Andrew and Haley chatted informally, clearly enjoying their visit, until Vanessa noticed Haley's tone of voice turn abruptly confidential, and serious. "I was wondering if I could ask you for some legal advice?"

Sensing Haley needed privacy for her conversation with Andrew, Vanessa excused herself. "If you two don't mind, I think I'll take a walk over to Marie's house. I need to pack up my things out of Diane's room.

Will you be alright?" Andrew smiled up at Vanessa and nodded. He admired how sensitive and perceptive she could be.

"Sure, take your time. We'll be fine." His statement portrayed considerably more confidence than he felt concerning his ability to handle Haley's unpredictable mood swings. His gaze returned to Haley and he smiled with a hint of a frown, cautiously wondering about the nature of the advice she needed from him.

Haley didn't want Vanessa to leave, but she couldn't help feeling relieved that she'd suggested going to Diane's for a while. She preferred that Vanessa remained unaware of how cowardly she'd behaved during the past couple of years.

"Can I get either of you something before I go?" Vanessa asked.

"I'll take a kiss." Andrew pointed to his cheek.

Vanessa smiled, gave him a quick peck, and whispered, "Good luck," in his ear before she casually strolled out the door, hopeful that Haley didn't have any serious legal tangles for him to deal with.

As soon as Vanessa left, Haley looked at Andrew intently and asked, "Am I considered guilty for all of the crimes that Jimmy committed? I mean if I was with him when they happened?"

Andrew thought quietly about what kinds of crimes she could be referring to. "Could you have reported his crimes?"

"Yes, but I thought if I did, he'd kill me."

Andrew thought for a minute. "Were you being held captive?"

"Honestly, not at first," Haley wrinkled her brow. "But later, I wasn't allowed to leave Jimmy's sight, except to have sex with his creepy friends."

Andrew wished he could have met Jimmy just once in a dark alley. He'd have loved sending him to prison for the way he'd destroyed this young girl's life. "Other than the bank robbery, were any of these crimes recent?" he asked.

"I guess so. Jimmy broke the law just about every day," Haley scoffed.

"I understand what you're telling me..." Andrew had always been a real law and order guy, but he didn't believe in punishing innocent young girls. "Here's my advice. You were underage, being intimidated by Jimmy while he was engaging in illegal activities. Jimmy is dead now, and no one is looking for any justice or restitution from him. No one has charged Jimmy with anything besides the robbery, therefore I don't believe there will be any charges brought against you as an accessory."

"Are you sure? He did a lot of very bad things to lots of people. Should

303

I tell you about them, just in case?" Haley had already lost countless nights of sleep, painfully reliving the horrible things that Jimmy had done to her, and to others.

"Did you witness him murder anyone?" Andrew decided it was best not knowing about any of Jimmy's law breaking activities, and prayed that Jimmy's victims had moved past whatever they'd suffered because of him.

"No!" she answered emphatically.

"Will anyone be helped if you confess to me now?" he asked, trying to ease his own conscience.

"No... I don't think so." Haley cocked her head to the side, gazing up at the ceiling for a minute while she considered his question.

"Alright then," Andrew said, making his mind up decisively. "I want you to forget the last few years and go home to your parents. Resume the life you were born to live. Let your mind bury all of Jimmy's evil deeds, along with him. Do you think you can do that?"

"I'll try, if you really think I should." Haley looked at her lap and began fidgeting with her fingers. Andrew knew he'd asked a lot of her.

"Look at me, Haley." He placed a comforting hand over hers. Slowly lifting her head, she quietly regarded Andrew. "I know it won't be easy. If it will make you feel better, go to church and light a candle for each person that Jimmy hurt, including yourself."

"I can do that." Haley smiled shyly. "Thank you," she whispered.

"Anything else?" Andrew said, wearily heaving a sigh of relief.

"What about the bank robbery?" Haley asked, tentatively.

"You're in the clear. The DA agreed not to prosecute you in exchange for the information you've already given him. You have nothing legally to worry about."

"I can't thank you enough for helping me." She smiled adoringly at Andrew. "I'm really going to miss you." Reaching over to him, she affectionately squeezed his good hand, resting casually on the arm of his wheelchair. Smiling at her impulsive show of affection, he realized he was going to miss her too.

"That's right, you're flying home tomorrow evening. I can't believe you're leaving us so soon. Can you manage those crutches on the plane?"

"I'm supposed to have an x-ray later today." Haley glanced at her crutches leaning against the wall next to her. "If it looks good, tomorrow I can ditch those horrible things. I'll only have to use a walking cast."

"I hope you'll be able to go home and spend some real quality time reconnecting with your family. You don't need to worry about anything that's happened to you since you left home. Instead, I want you to focus on your family, the people who love you, and begin to make plans for your future."

"I will," Haley smiled at the thought. "I hope we can all remain friends."

"If I know Vanessa..." Andrew laughed. "She'll never forget you. Neither will I. We'll always be here if you need us."

Andrew's physical therapist, Sheila knocked on the open door. Her unexpected arrival saved him from continuing his increasingly awkward conversation with Haley. "Mr. Kelly, are you up for a little rehabilitation of that arm?"

"Sorry, but its time for this beautiful lady to escort me to the dungeon and torture me," Andrew groaned, reaching over to protect his bad arm.

Haley laughed at his teasing, looking up at the very petite, harmless-looking Shelia. "I know all about it." Haley pointed to her splinted ankle.

Andrew waved cheerfully as Sheila wheeled him away.

"Be kind to him," Haley called after them.

Once they'd left, Haley positioned herself in the recliner next to his bed to watch TV while she patiently waited for everyone to return. Vanessa arrived some time later, and stood at the door to watch Haley dozing peacefully. After talking briefly to Andrew's nurse, Vanessa decided to sneak down to watch his physical therapy session. The minute she stepped off the elevator and began walking toward the PT room, she heard Andrew's agonizing cries.

"Next time, Mr. Kelly," the therapist gently scolded. "I strongly recommend you take some pain medication before we try to work out this arm."

"I'm fine, I don't need drugs," Andrew argued, displaying his stubborn, macho streak. "You just go ahead. Do whatever you need to do."

"Alright, but this is going to be painful," Sheila said, doubt evident in the warning tone of her voice.

"Just do it!" Andrew said, his voice uncharacteristically impatient and frustrated.

Vanessa couldn't stand listening to him suffer, and turned on her heels, deciding another stroll around the pond was in order. She shivered at the mere thought of Andrew's torturous suffering.

Sitting on her special bench, she attempted to console herself. *He's alive, and hopefully his arm will recover quickly. But what if it never fully recovers?* Vanessa shook her head, refusing to wallow in negative thoughts. She stood abruptly, and began walking at a swift pace around the pond to clear her mind. Soon, she lost all track of time. Her fast-paced walking and rapid breathing absorbed all of her attention and thoughts. Eventually, she realized that someone had joined her. Vanessa turned her head to find Diane smiling at her.

"Are you training for a triathlon or something?"

"I'm just clearing my head," Vanessa said, easing her rapid pace. "What time is it?"

"It's almost four. Andrew's been watching you from the window," she said, pointing toward it. "He asked me to come see if everything was all right. Are you okay, Vanessa? You seem a little upset."

"I am, a little." Vanessa knew she must look like a crazy person, and discovered she needed to confide in someone. "I'll tell you why, if you promise not to tell Andrew." Diane didn't like keeping secrets, but nodded her head.

"I heard Andrew during his physical therapy session earlier," Vanessa explained. "I heard him crying out, and I couldn't stand to hear him in pain. I guess it really upset me."

"I totally get it," Diane said, attempting to reassure her. "I wouldn't want to hear anyone in pain either, especially not someone I loved."

"Thanks. It's not that I want to baby him, but I never want to listen to another one of his therapy sessions again!"

Diane nodded her understanding. "I'm sure he won't expect you to, but right now he's really worried about you. You might want to think up an explanation for him, before we go back."

"Good thinking, any ideas?" Vanessa sighed.

"What about telling him you're worried about going back to work on Monday?" Diane smiled slyly.

"Well it's true..." Vanessa thought about it. "I am worried about that, good idea. Oh, oh you said it was almost four?"

"Yeah, why?"

"Haley has an appointment for her x-ray at four-fifty in Bitton." Vanessa rolled her eyes at her thoughtlessness. "We'd better get going!"

The two of them hurried back to Andrew's room, where they found him sitting up, resting on top of his bed. He'd been freshly showered and shaved, and wore a pair of loose shorts with a t-shirt. He appeared relaxed, and looked devilishly handsome as he smiled at her arrival. "There you are. I missed you."

"Sorry, I had a lot on my mind," Vanessa smiled, noting his concerned but casual demeanor. "I trust these ladies have kept you preoccupied." Vanessa's voice sounded calm, but Andrew wasn't buying it.

"Actually, I've been ignoring my guests. The nurses banded together and decided I needed to get cleaned up."

Vanessa couldn't stop herself. She walked over to his bed and placed a tender kiss on his lips, running her fingers leisurely across his smooth, freshly shaven face.

"You clean up pretty nice, sailor," she whispered. Before she could pull away, Andrew wrapped his good arm around her, pulling her close against him. "I'm going to be as good as new, I promise," he said, earnestly.

Vanessa pulled herself together, cleverly extricating herself from his tight arm hold. She moved to lean nonchalantly against the windowsill, well out of his reach. "I'm sorry, I'd like to stay longer, but Haley has an x-ray appointment. I'm afraid we have to go."

"So, soon? I've hardly seen you today," Andrew said. He frowned, clearly disappointed.

"I'm sorry, but she needs her x-ray."

"Will you come back afterward?" Andrew wondered why she seemed to be avoiding him.

"I don't think so." Vanessa felt torn; she could see both Andrew and Haley had dark circles under their eyes. "She needs to pack for her trip home. We'll try to come by tomorrow around noon, before we go to the airport."

"Alright, I understand, but before you go, I want to show you my new trick." Smiling, he grabbed a soft blue ball from his table. He had everyone's rapt attention as he picked up the ball with his good hand, and placed it into the center of his right hand. The fingers of his right hand slowly began to curl loosely around the ball.

A few tears of joy blurred Vanessa's vision. His right arm had been hanging lifelessly at his side since the shooting, and she feared it might be permanently paralyzed. The tiny, controlled movement of his fingers confirmed for her that he still had functioning nerves in his right arm.

Haley and Diane clapped enthusiastically.

"Andrew, that's fantastic! When did your fingers begin moving?" Vanessa asked.

"About an hour ago, during my physical therapy session," he said, laughing at the excited response from his audience.

"I'm so happy for you. I know this means a lot," she whispered, moving into his one-armed embrace, feeling an overwhelming sense of relief and optimism.

"Okay then." Exhaustion had caught up with Andrew and he yawned uncontrollably as he placed the blue ball back on the table beside him. "I guess I'll see you all tomorrow. It's my naptime now."

The girls said their goodbyes and left, while Vanessa lingered behind for a private farewell.

"Is everything okay?" Andrew asked, as Vanessa snuggled next to him in bed.

"Everything's fine, I'm just sorting things out in my mind. Are you going to be alright tonight?"

"Don't worry about me." He kissed the top of her head. "Take care of Haley. Make sure she gets home safe and sound." Andrew pulled her closer. "You know, I'm only concerned about you because I love you."

Vanessa turned her face up to Andrew's, their eyes met, and they kissed with time-stopping passion. *So much better in real life*, Vanessa thought, enjoying the pleasurable feeling of actually touching Andrew, instead of the elusive sensations she'd imagined during last night's fantasy call.

"I love you, too," she said, leisurely tracing the outline of his face with her fingertips, as if committing him to memory. Leaning forward, she caressed him tenderly before she reluctantly broke their intimate embrace, and slid off the bed.

"I'm fine," she said, squeezing his hand reassuringly. "I'll call you later."

Vanessa flashed Andrew a final, dazzling smile before she left the room. His good-natured laughter followed her out the door. She hoped that her soothing gestures and humor had been enough to alleviate any lingering worries he may have had regarding her enduring emotional strength and resilience.

Chapter 29
Entrances and Departures

*T*hanks to Diane's driving skills, they arrived at Haley's x-ray appointment with time to spare. Haley's ankle had healed enough to graduate to a walking cast, meaning that after tomorrow her crutches would become optional. Vanessa was pleased by the upgrade, suggesting that the three of them head for the closest mall to celebrate both the good news and Haley's birthday with a shopping spree.

Haley would require entertainment to pass the time on her long plane ride home tomorrow. The teen-scene had been out of Haley's realm for the past few years. She hadn't been to a movie, or even watched television since she'd left her home in Ohio. The current fashions, musicians, and movie stars were completely foreign to Haley, but fortunately for Vanessa, they were commonplace to Diane. She quickly gave them both a crash course. Diane gushed over the latest fashion trends and celebrity gossip, while helping Haley to select stylish new clothes and several popular magazines.

After they'd shopped, Vanessa asked if she could take them out to a fancy restaurant, wanting to celebrate Haley's birthday someplace elegant. But Diane and Haley wrinkled their noses, begging for pizza instead. Wanting to oblige them, they agreed on a popular pizza parlor. Unfortunately, walking into the one that Diane had chosen, they discovered the tables were overcrowded with rowdy, boisterous teens, and they quickly opted for take-out.

Arriving back at Andrew's house, Vanessa cautiously slowed her pace up his walkway, noticing his front door resting slightly ajar.

"I'm sure I locked the door," Diane said, her voice hushed.

In light of recent events, Vanessa didn't hesitate. She picked up her cell phone and called the police dispatch, asking if an officer could assist them.

The police cruiser had been parked only a block away and quickly pulled up in front of the house. A tall, young, uniformed officer with short, dark hair peeking out of his cap got out of the cruiser and approached them.

"Thank you for coming, Officer. I know I might be overreacting, but we're sure we locked the door before we left. Now, as you can see, it's clearly unlocked." Vanessa calmly stepped aside, allowing him to look inside the house.

"You must be Vanessa." He removed his hat politely. "And you must be—Haley." He nodded toward Haley's crutches. Turning toward Diane, an amused smile crossed his face when he caught her carefully studying him. "Are you Diane?" he asked, in a softer, vaguely curious tone. Diane's faced reddened as his eyes beheld hers, and their gaze lingered intently.

She continued to hold his gaze, responding breathlessly, "Yes I am, and your name is?" She smiled invitingly.

"Officer Todd Kinsley." His facial expression changed, his intensity softening slightly, returning her cordial smile, and revealing his deep-set dimples.

Vanessa cleared her throat to get Todd's attention. "Todd, the door?"

"Right." Todd straightened up and frowned, shifting his gaze back toward Vanessa. "I'll just go in and look around, to make sure the premises are secure. You wait out here." He placed his hat back on his head, and reached for his weapon, before moving past them to the entrance.

He unsnapped his holster, cautiously pushing the door wide open, while keeping one hand firmly planted on his gun. The three women huddled in the doorway, watching him move carefully from room to room. He disappeared from view several times, walking outside by the pool, and finally stealing his way up the staircase. They waited anxiously by the door, exhaling in relief when he casually lumbered down the stairway, his gun fastened securely on his belt, and his arms swinging freely.

"Everything seems secure. No sign of any trespassers or forced entry. Does anyone else have a key to the door? Or is it possible you left without locking it?" he asked.

"I'm sure Andrew's housekeeper and his dog walker both have keys. I don't know about his pool cleaner, but he might as well," Vanessa said, walking confidently into Andrew's house.

"That could explain the unlocked door. I'll file my report and stay close, just in case you need anything more," Todd said, as he helped Diane carry in the pizza.

He turned to leave, but Diane touched his arm to waylay him, looking uncertainly toward Vanessa. "I'm still not feeling very safe; don't you think Todd should stay for pizza? I know I'd feel safer if he did."

Vanessa didn't blame Diane. Todd was tall, dark and very attractive. She'd have to have been blind not to recognize the chemistry between the two of them.

"Please, we'd appreciate it if you'd stay. We have plenty of pizza,"

Vanessa offered graciously.

"Thank you," he said, shrugging his broad shoulders casually. "I am due for a dinner break about now. Please excuse me, I need to call in my report and sign out for dinner." Stepping out the front door to use his radio, he gave dispatch an *all clear* on his response to check the house, and the code indicating his break.

"Doesn't Detective Kelly have a police dog?" he asked, stepping back into the kitchen, looking perplexed.

All three women stopped what they were doing and froze. None of them had seen or heard Shep, or for that matter, Callie, since they'd arrived.

"Todd, there should be both a dog and a cat here somewhere. The dog walker may have Shep, but I doubt she took my cat for a walk too."

"I didn't see either one of them when I searched the house," Todd said, keeping his tone calm. "Would you happen to have the dog walker's phone number?"

"I'm sorry, I don't. In fact, I don't even remember her full name." Vanessa looked bewilderedly at Diane and Haley, who both shook their heads no. She grabbed her cell phone to call Andrew.

"Hi, beautiful, miss me already?" he answered cheerfully. Vanessa could tell he'd had his nap. He sounded rested and refreshed.

"Andrew, Shep and Callie are missing. Could you please talk to officer Todd Kinsley? He needs your dog walker's information."

"Wait—is everyone all right?" Andrew asked, immediately alarmed.

Vanessa didn't want to waste precious time filling him in. "Hang on, here's Todd."

"Tell me everything," Andrew's voice became serious and businesslike once Todd got on the phone. "Is there anything else suspicious there, other than the missing pets?"

Todd, intimidated by Andrew's impressive reputation, responded professionally to each of his questions. "I was originally called to the residence because the front door was found unlocked. I inspected the entire house and found no signs of a forced entry, robbery, or anyone on the premises."

"Thank you for being there," Andrew responded authoritatively, stomping down his own personal fears. "Please stay with them until the animals are located. The dog walker's name is Shelby Crandall. I'll forward her contact information to Vanessa's cell. Take care of them, Todd. I'll need you to stay there until you're absolutely sure there's no threat." His voice softened as he added, "These women mean a lot to me, understand?" Todd received his message loud and clear, glancing toward the women in question. Todd wasn't worried about their safety, but he'd be more than happy to lounge around the pool and enjoy pizza with them. "I understand, sir. I'll notify you the moment we find the animals. I plan to stay across the street and observe the premises for the remainder of the night."

"Thank you," Andrew sighed, relieved by Todd's presence, but wishing he was stronger himself, and home to keep them safe in person.

Shelby's information pinged on Vanessa's phone, just as they heard Shelby opening the back gate, carrying Shep's leash in one hand, while the docile dog walked calmly beside her and Callie trailed close behind. She immediately noticed the puzzled, concerned look on the officer's face. "Hi everyone, is there a problem?"

"Are you Shelby Crandall?" Todd asked officially, seemingly immune to Shelby's stunningly striking appearance.

"Yes," Shelby smiled; she found his serious, official tone mildly amusing.

"Did you happen to leave the front door unlocked?"

"Probably, why, is that a crime?" After dealing with easy-going Andrew, this young officer seemed ridiculously intense and formal.

"I'm sorry, Miss. I need to know if you definitely left the front door unlocked."

Shelby frowned; she didn't care much for his tedious inquiry, but answered patiently. "Let's see, I unlocked the front door when I arrived, and then I took Shep out the back gate. That means I didn't go back and lock the front door." She ignored Todd, "I'm sorry..." she turned to hastily to apologize to Vanessa. "But your cat insisted on following Shep. I hope you don't mind."

"No problem. But I think that's the first official walk she's ever been on," Vanessa chuckled. She stepped forward and gently removed her cell phone from Todd's sweaty palm. "Thanks for your help. I'll call Andrew and fill him in."

"Thank you, Miss Crandall, for your cooperation," he said, clearing his throat. "You're free to go."

Shelby laughed openly and Haley smothered a giggle. Diane remained thoughtful. She'd watched Todd's lack of response to Shelby's beauty with surprise. She'd assumed, by his earlier behavior, that Todd enjoyed flirting with all women. But he hadn't flinched when Shelby arrived. He remained totally disinterested in Shelby's sleek, tanned body, and completely oblivious to her feminine charms.

"Do you usually take Shep out this late?" Haley asked Shelby curiously, melting into the closest chaise lounge, sensing the crisis had passed.

"No, but I knew Andrew had company," Shelby smiled. "I also had a job interview in the city earlier today. So I came as soon as I could."

"Would you like to stay? Have some pizza with us?" Haley, curious about Shelby's glamorous life, wanted to hear more.

"Maybe some other time." She walked toward the house, waving off her offer with a friendly smile. "I'm already late for my dinner date. Got to run." She hung Shep's leash by the door, waved goodbye, and disappeared out the front door.

Vanessa ran upstairs, carting her cell phone so she could talk to Andrew in private. Haley rested comfortably beside the pool with the pizza, while Todd followed Diane into the kitchen to get plates and drinks.

"What can I get you to drink, Officer?" Diane asked, opening the cupboards to search for some glasses.

"Please, call me Todd." He stood so close to her, his quiet, rich, deep voice reverberated down her spine.

They stood only inches apart. She turned toward him, and the minute their eyes met, a faint smile of recognition appeared simultaneously on both of their faces. The sound of Vanessa's approaching footsteps echoed somewhere off in the distance.

"Diane, can I help you with anything?" Vanessa asked, walking into the kitchen. Instantly, the brief magical spell between the two of them was broken, and they stepped apart self-consciously. "Andrew wanted me to thank you. He asked me to tell you to park in the driveway tonight," she informed Todd. Feeling the heat and tension in the room when neither of them responded, she continued cheerfully, "Let's eat, and later, if you want, why don't you stay for awhile and keep Diane company, while I help Haley with her packing." Diane's face flamed, embarrassed by Vanessa's less than subtle matchmaking. She quickly handed Todd some plates to take outside.

"I appreciate what you're doing, but I already have a boyfriend," Diane said, once Todd was no longer in the kitchen.

"I don't know what you're talking about," Vanessa responded

innocently.

"Sure you do," Diane murmured under her breath, avoiding Vanessa's eyes. She lifted a heavy glass pitcher of iced tea and scooted past Vanessa, carrying it outside, and ending the whole embarrassing conversation.

Vanessa simply smiled at Diane's adamant protest, and followed her with the glasses.

Outside, the air remained calm and warm. The rhythmic crashing of ocean waves provided a relaxed setting for the four of them while they enjoyed chatting socially. They shared pieces of their individual backgrounds with each other while they casually dined on gourmet birthday pizza.

Haley tilted her head to the side and suddenly asked Todd why he had chosen to become a police officer.

"My father was a police officer. I guess I never considered doing anything else." He wiped his mouth and took a swig of his soda. "He worked with Detective Kelly once many years ago. My dad would brief me on Detective Kelly's cases every night, instead of telling me bedtime stories. Last year I received my bachelor's degree in criminology, and I just graduated from the police academy. My goal is to become a detective, like Detective Kelly." Hero worship lit up his eyes. "When the surveillance detail of his house came up, I jumped at the chance."

"What about your father?" Vanessa wondered why he hadn't wanted to follow in his footsteps instead. Todd immediately looked away and leaned back, physically withdrawing from the conversation. He seemed reluctant to talk about his relationship with his father, and deliberately paused, stalling for time while he swallowed a bite of his pizza, and washed it down with a swig of tea. "My father was let go from the police force after he became the focus of an internal investigation when I was twelve. He then worked as a security guard, until his death two years ago. He never saw me graduate from the academy and join the force."

"I'm sorry for your loss, Todd," Vanessa said quietly, after a sudden change of atmosphere, and an awkward silence.

"Thank you." Todd looked down at his plate pensively, his face expressionless. "Now, if you'll excuse me, I should go check in." He stood and walked away, leaving the three of them exchanging silent looks of curiosity, eyebrows raised in concern.

"I think you hit a nerve, Vanessa," Diane commented, as soon as he was out of earshot.

"Sorry about that," Vanessa sighed, busily picking up the plates. "I had no idea about his father." She stood uncertainly for a moment, but when Todd failed to return, she asked Haley, "Why don't we get you packed?" Haley nodded and stood with her crutches to walk into the house while Vanessa lingered briefly.

"Great—now you want to leave me alone with him?" Diane rolled her eyes.

"Don't worry, we'll be able to hear you if you need us," Vanessa whispered to Diane, seeing Todd returning through the glass door.

"Thanks." Dianne squirmed, suddenly feeling abandoned, socially uncomfortable.

Todd returned, passing Vanessa in the doorway, and approached Diane awkwardly.

"Thanks for dinner," Todd said, slowly walking toward her. "I'm sorry, but I need to go. I've been asked to do a drive-by down the street."

"Will you stop back later?" Diane could tell by the way he avoided eye contact with her that he'd hastily made up an excuse to leave.

"I'm not sure—maybe, if I have time." Todd looked broodily out over the dark ocean before he turned his attention back to her. "But you can call me if you have any problems. I'll come right back if you need me."

He walked closer to hand her his business card. Todd's cool fingers inadvertently brushed Diane's, causing an electric spark between them. Diane blushed, raising her gaze to look directly into his startled, dark, wide pupils. Their eyes locked, creating the same time-stopping sensation she'd felt when they were alone in the kitchen together. *What is it about him? I can't catch my breath*, she thought.

"It was nice—to meet you, Diane," he stammered, forcing himself to take a stumbling step away from her.

"It was nice meeting you, too." Diane smiled shyly, but her eyes sparkled with desire.

Todd wanted to leave, but his legs felt temporarily paralyzed. His feet stuck to the ground, like they were caught in quicksand.

"I hope you—enjoy college."

"I will, I hope you make detective soon," she said quietly, while her eyes remained fixed on his.

"Thank you." He still couldn't make his feet move. "Call me—anytime. My cell number is on the back of the card."

She glanced down to turn over the card he'd given her. Once their

315

eyes lost their connection, Todd took a deep breath, and he began rapidly backing up toward the door. "Good night, Diane."

"Good night, Todd," she whispered, though he had already disappeared through the sliding glass door.

Diane sat down hard in the chair, staring vacantly into the darkness beyond. She wondered what was it about Todd that made her feel so drawn to him. Hearing the murmuring voices of Vanessa and Haley inside packing, she chose to remain outside in solitude. Time had ceased to exist while her jumbled mind struggled with a multitude of inexplicably complicated emotions. Her judgment became cloudy, fuzzy-brained, as she struggled to justify her unwanted attraction toward Todd.

Currently, she already split her free time and attention between two boyfriends. One she'd known for years from high school, and the other one she'd recently met at college. Frustrated, she exhaled a sigh, confused by her strong emotional attraction toward Todd. Why Todd? He was several years older than both of her other boyfriends, and he'd already graduated. Todd, unlike her, lived the life of a grown-up. Mysterious and dark, Todd seemed moody and complex. Next week she'd return to school and realized she'd probably never see Todd again. Why did that thought make her feel sad? Leaning back, she allowed her unwelcome emotions to assail her in the shadowy silence.

Most of Haley's packing completed, she cheerfully video chatted with her excited mom, discussing her travel arrangements for the following day. Vanessa carried a final load of clothes to the laundry, noticing Diane through the glass door, sitting alone by the pool.

"Where's Todd?"

"He had to go." Diane lifted her head wearily in response, as Vanessa sat down beside her.

"I hope it wasn't anything I said."

"I don't think so," Diane shook her head. "I think he was uncomfortable being alone with me."

"He is on duty. Maybe he felt guilty about not doing his job."

"Maybe," Diane smiled faintly. "How's the packing going?" Vanessa could tell the subject of Todd was closed, at least as far as Diane was concerned.

"Almost done. Haley is checking in with her family now."

"I'm sure she'll be glad to get home," Diane smiled, genuinely happy for Haley.

"I hope so, I think she's still a little worried about fitting in with her family again."

"I know what she means," Diane frowned, she could relate to Haley's concerns. "I felt a little weird when I first came home from college. It's an adjustment to live with your parents again, once you've been out on your own. It's nice though, you really do feel protected and loved when you're home."

"I hope you're right." Her maturity impressed Vanessa. "She needs to feel safe, especially after the troubled life she's been living."

"Hey, what are you two talking about?" They both looked toward the door, watching Haley struggle toward them on her crutches.

"Diane was just saying how safe she felt when she returned home from school," Vanessa said. Haley laughed, noticing the furrowed eyebrows on Vanessa's troubled face.

"Don't worry about me. I'll be fine when I get home. I have to thank you for letting me use your computer to talk to my family. I feel like I know them a lot better than I did before."

"Haley, that's *your* computer, and there's a case for you to take it with you on the plane tomorrow."

"Thank you so much!" Tears filled Haley's eyes. She was touched by Vanessa's generosity. "I don't know how I can ever repay you."

"Just consider it a birthday present," Vanessa smiled. "After all, you'll need a computer to finish school."

Diane watched them embrace with a slight smile. Haley had turned out to be one of the nicest people she'd ever met. She marveled at her genuine sweetness, and her constant, kind consideration of others. With all the things that had happened to Haley since she'd run away from home, she could have easily turned cynical and bitter, but she hadn't.

Haley sat down, making herself comfortable, and the three of them began a conversation that lasted well into the night. Each woman was reluctant to say goodnight; fearing that tonight may be their last night together.

Hours later, Vanessa stood and stretched, the first to excuse herself to go to bed. The younger girls continued to talk; making extravagant plans for their future adventures. The soothing tones of their muffled voices beneath her on the patio continued long after Vanessa had snuggled into Andrew's comfortable bed to sleep.

Before Vanessa drifted off to sleep, she wondered where she should sleep tomorrow night. Here, by herself with Callie and Shep? Home, alone with Callie? Or should she stay with Andrew at the hospital? Pulling Andrew's pillow into her arms, she inhaled his sweet, sandalwood scent and sighed. *Oh Andrew, what are we going to do?*

The next day started with a flurry of activity. First, they squeezed all of Haley's luggage, plus Diane's, into Diane's tiny car. Their bags completely filled the little car to the roof. Then they rushed to Haley's final doctor's appointment where, much to her delight, she was fitted with a walking cast.

Last stop before heading to the airport, they stormed the hospital to visit with Andrew. This time Andrew sat fully dressed, seated in his recliner, laughing with delight at the sight of the three women bursting excitedly into his room.

"Hi everyone, look at what I can do today," Andrew boasted, smiling at his boisterous visitors. He supported his injured arm with his good hand, and reached out to pick up the soft rubber ball from the tabletop.

All three of his female visitors laughed and clapped in appreciative admiration. Vanessa walked to his side to sit on the arm of the chair. Draping her arm lightly across his shoulders, she bent down to place a quick, rewarding kiss on his lips. Haley watched them, beaming an appreciative smile. Wanting Andrew to observe her, she dramatically cleared her throat, commanding their undivided attention.

"Notice anything?" Haley asked Andrew, turning in a circle without her crutches, positively glowing.

"I see you got your walking cast today, very nice," he laughed, giving her a thumbs-up with his good hand.

Diane felt uncomfortable, not having known Andrew very long, and quietly excused herself. She wanted to drop off her things at home before they took Haley to the airport.

"I want to thank you, Diane, for all of your help," Andrew said, before the perky brunette disappeared, unsure when he would see her again. "I really appreciate that you stayed with Haley and watched out for the animals. Thank you again, for everything." His smiling, crystal-blue eyes shone brightly, displaying his sincerity and appreciation.

"It was my pleasure," Diane said, feeling her face blush unexpectedly. "I've met a wonderful friend." She regarded Haley with a smile. "Honestly, I feel like I've been on a luxurious vacation. I should be the one thanking you," she said, waving quickly as she left.

Once Diane had gone, Vanessa, Andrew, and Haley sat down to discuss communication strategies, promising to stay connected. She hugged Vanessa, expressing her gratitude for saving her from the hopeless life she'd shared with Jimmy, and giving her the best birthday of her life! Unaware of Haley's silent dark reflections, Vanessa busily scheduled weekly video chats and made plans for Haley to return for a visit as soon as she could. Andrew checked to make sure Haley didn't have any last minute legal questions. Then he shared his recent update regarding Kate, the bank robbery accomplice who had escaped to South America. Haley listened quietly, wishing she didn't have to leave so soon.

"The FBI has a new man watching Kate now. He's using his aunt, who lives on the same island where Kate is hiding out, as his cover. He'll continue to watch Kate to determine the extent of her involvement with the robbery, and then arrest her, if and when she ever tries to return to the U.S."

"Thank goodness," Vanessa exhaled. "It appears there's no one else lurking out there who'd be of any threat to you in the future." She hugged Haley affectionately. "Now, you can go home and start fresh, without any worries."

Haley smiled through her tears, hugging and thanking them both for their support and kindness. "I don't know what I would have done without both of you," she said, tears of appreciation streaming down her face. Vanessa's eyes watered in response to Haley's emotional outburst, and she held her close.

Haley's mood suddenly changed, her hug became stiff, her face devoid of expression. She hid her face, as she moved out of Vanessa's warm embrace, suddenly fearful of returning home, only to become a disappointment to her family once again. She believed deep in her heart, that despite all of Vanessa's reassurances, she'd have to pay for her shameful, lurid behaviors and poor choices, one way or another.

Haley walked quietly toward the window, where she stood, blankly staring out at the pond below. She listened to the quiet, soothing sounds of Andrew and Vanessa's voices as they conversed intimately, unaware of the sudden dark, emotional shift within Haley. Lost in her own black world, she gazed out of the window, consumed by her feelings of guilt and remorse.

I should have known better, Haley thought bleakly, resting her head against the cool glass, staring through it without seeing. *Why did I have to run off with that creep, Jimmy? Now he's dead, and I'll be reaping the consequences forever!*

Chapter 30
Love to Die For

*H*aley's send-off at the airport was an emotional display of hugs and tears. Haley promised to call both Vanessa and Diane once she'd arrived home safely. Vanessa had previously scheduled a weekly video chat with Haley on Saturdays. Texting was Diane's preferred method of keeping in touch, and they'd vowed to text each other daily.

After watching Haley board her plane, Diane and Vanessa walked back to the car in quiet contemplation. Having grown close to Haley, Diane knew she would miss her dearly. She'd enjoyed spending carefree days with her, lounging by Andrew's shimmering, crystal blue pool.

Vanessa imagined that saying goodbye to Haley was similar to the pain she'd have felt if she'd sent her own daughter away to school. Her heart ached, as her thoughts turned to all of the missed occasions and events she'd never known with her own daughter. Having Haley in her life had been the closest she'd ever come to being a mother. Sighing, Vanessa felt the deep ache, realizing just how much she'd miss Haley.

Diane dropped Vanessa off at the hospital. They hugged briefly, commiserating over Haley's departure.

"Thank you, for everything." Teary-eyed, Vanessa hesitated to let Diane leave. "I'd never have survived this week without you."

"Anytime." Diane's own eyes misted, but she shrugged carelessly, trying to act nonchalant.

"If I can't find anyone by Sunday, would you still be interested in watching out for Andrew during the daytime, while I'm at work?"

"Now I understand...why my mother has so much faith in your ability to control the world," Diane laughed. "Of course, I'd love to hang out by the pool with Andrew. Just call me."

"Thanks again. I'll be in touch."

Vanessa felt disheartened as she walked into the hospital. She was surprised by the intensity of her loss. Wrapped up with helping Haley, she'd made no arrangements for the remainder of her night. The thought of simply curling up beside Andrew for comfort during the long, lonely night quickly ended her dilemma, and she hastened her idle pace in anticipation.

So caught up and distracted by her own deep thoughts, she nearly collided with a casually dressed gentleman. "Vanessa?" he asked, reaching out to stabilize her. "I was hoping I'd have a chance to talk to you." She smiled, immediately recognizing the man as Mike, the detective who had saved Andrew's life. "I can't believe it, but Andrew looks great! You'd never know how close he came to dying."

"He's made an amazing recovery," Vanessa said, quickly regaining her composure.

He smiled, appreciating the enormous stress she'd been under. "I just stopped by to let Andrew know that the city plans to honor him with a ceremony, and a medal. After all, he's responsible for bringing down the worst drug ring this city has seen in years."

"How did he take the news?" Vanessa tilted her head and smiled, already guessing how he'd responded.

"He said he didn't deserve it. He claimed he'd only been there by accident." Mike shook his head. "Instead, he insisted that I deserved the glory, because I'd spent so many hours working on the case. But honestly, we weren't getting anywhere. We didn't even have any decent leads before he called to alert me. Please, try to convince Andrew to attend, and accept the medal that he clearly deserves. It would sure mean a lot to everyone. I'm counting on you, Vanessa."

"I'll do what I can." But she knew Andrew, and she doubted that she'd be able to change his mind. "But, in case you haven't noticed, he can be a very stubborn man."

"How long did you say you two have been together?" Mike laughed, shaking his head.

"Just a couple of weeks," she smiled.

"I don't think my own parents knew each other as well as you two seem to," He chuckled. His amusement died and he became thoughtfully quiet before he added confidentially, "I probably shouldn't tell you this, but when Andrew thought he was dying, he asked me to tell you, that he'd love you forever."

Vanessa felt a shiver travel down her spine at the thought of losing Andrew. "That's okay. The feeling's mutual," she whispered.

Mike told her he planned to call Andrew next week to set the date for the ceremony, before hastily kissing her on the cheek as he left.

Vanessa found Andrew tucked quietly into his bed watching TV, a slight frown plastered across his face.

"Hi there," she smiled, gently teasing him. "I hear you're quite the hero."

His stern face immediately changed at the sight of her, and he sent her a wry smile. "Mike threatened to rat me out to you."

She put her things down, kicked her shoes off, and crawled into bed to be close to him. He scooted over to make more room for her beside him.

"I talked to him briefly. We passed each other in the lobby as he was leaving the hospital."

Andrew used his stronger arm to hug her close to him, before he deliberately changed the subject. "Did Haley get off all right?"

"Uh huh." Vanessa snuggled her head on his shoulder.

"I've missed you." Andrew moved the hair out of her eyes, gently placing a kiss on the top of her head.

"I've missed you too. When can you go home?" His body felt warm and suddenly she relaxed in his arms, her eyes drifting closed.

"Tomorrow. I'll call you in the morning to let you know what time." Andrew hugged her gently with his good arm, enjoying the feel of her close to him, slowly running his warm hand up and down the cool skin of her arm.

"I don't think I'm going to make it home tonight..." Vanessa almost purred, feeling so content. "Do you mind if I stay here with you?" she asked, gazing dreamily up at him. He kissed her with intensity, responding with such pent up passion, that she felt her toes curl.

"Nothing would make me happier," he said, his husky, low voice filled with arousal.

Feeling greedy, Andrew wanted every minute of Vanessa's time, while he could still get it. Come Monday morning, she'd return to her job. *Gemma* represented her entire life's endeavors. He was well aware that her decision could assure that all of their leisurely time spent together would come to a screeching halt. Tonight, he would love and cherish her. He'd persuade her that he was her first priority, miles ahead of *Gemma*.

Neglecting her usual bedtime rituals, Vanessa nuzzled into Andrew's arms, where nothing else in the world seemed to matter. The last couple of weeks had been like an emotional roller coaster for her. Now, with just the two of them alone at last, everything seemed picture-perfect. Vanessa's world felt blissfully sunny whenever Andrew held her in his embrace. She'd always operated from a position of cynicism, but when she was with him, she felt optimistic and uncharacteristically hopeful about her future. She'd behaved her absolute worst around him. He'd even witnessed one of her usually private tantrums, confessed her most humiliating experiences, and not only had Andrew not flinched, he'd come back for more. Physically and emotionally exhausted, Vanessa remained free from obsessing over the random thoughts that percolated through her mind, and drifted off to sleep. But, before she slipped into a deep sleep, she wondered in her dreamy state of mind: *Could it be? Would the powers-that-be finally allow me to find my happy ending?*

Andrew however, lay awake, remaining perfectly still. He could tell by her soft, steady breathing that Vanessa had fallen asleep. Pulling the blanket tenderly over her, he made sure she wasn't too close to the edge of the bed. Smiling down appreciatively at the beautiful woman asleep beside him, he thought, *I've competed with cancer and lost, but I refuse to lose Vanessa to a magazine.*

He stared blankly at the TV, while he silently plotted a variety of strategies to get Vanessa to give up her job with *Gemma*. He knew that if she took the position of editor-in-chief, he'd ultimately lose her into the big, dark, corporate void. He needed to make sure Vanessa's desire was to spend her remaining years with him, instead of dedicating them to *Gemma* Magazine. He had to find a way to tantalize her with his irresistible dreams for their future. Dreams they could happily share for the rest of their lives.

Andrew's heavy lids closed, while his mind continued to actively create images of their spectacular future together. But his daydreams were rudely interrupted when a soft-spoken, middle-aged, attractive nurse appeared at his bedside with his medications. She noticed the woman sleeping soundly against him, and whispered softly to him, not wishing to disturb Vanessa.

"Thank you, Mary," he whispered back. "Would you mind turning off the TV and pulling the bed rail up behind Vanessa? I don't want her to fall out. I'd do it myself, only my good arm is preoccupied," he said, motioning with his head to the arm wrapped securely around Vanessa.

"Goodnight, Andrew," Mary smiled, quietly accomplishing what he'd requested without waking Vanessa. "Call me if you need anything, otherwise I'll check on you again in a couple of hours." Andrew sent her a charming smile, nodding appreciatively to her. *Why are all the good guys taken?* Mary thought as she left the room, softly closing his door behind her.

Andrew fell asleep thinking how wonderful it was to have Vanessa in his bed. If he had his way, she'd be in his bed *every* night.

Hours later, Vanessa awoke when she heard the beep of the machine checking Andrew's blood pressure. Now fully awake, she slowly looked around, orienting herself to her surroundings. Glancing up she saw a young girl beside Andrew's bed, taking his temperature. She also discovered a very contented-looking Andrew smiling down at her. *He seems fully awake*, she thought grumpily. Rubbing the sleep out of her eyes, she wanted to get up, but the bar at her back blocked her escape.

"What time is it?" Her parched throat made her voice sound raspy. The young girl responded in a chipper voice. "It's three a.m."

"Sorry we woke you," Andrew said sympathetically. He could see that she'd had a rude awakening. "Amy was trying to be quiet."

"No problem," Vanessa grumbled, still sounding raspy.

She managed to climb out of bed with some degree of dignity, slip on her shoes, and stagger sleepily down the empty hallway to the ladies' room. She refused to look in the mirror as she walked by. Sitting on the toilet, she yawned and quickly calculated that she'd already slept a solid seven hours. Knowing that made three a.m. seem less inhumane. As she walked to the sink to wash her hands, she realized how stiff her body felt. Looking at herself in the mirror over the sink, she was surprised to see the wrinkles from Andrew's t-shirt etched into the right side of her face. Splashing her face with warm water, she attempted to repair the damage and straighten her disheveled clothes. She wished she'd brought some clean clothes, along with her makeup bag, and travel iron. With any luck, Andrew would be released first thing in the morning, before she had to face *too* many curious people.

Walking into Andrew's room, she found the lights on. He sat smiling at her as he cheerfully sipped juice from a straw. Andrew noticed Vanessa's severely wrinkled outfit. Knowing how she felt about her appearance, he imagined that it must have been driving her crazy. "You know, I have a clean pair of shorts and a t-shirt in the closet. If you want to, you can change, and maybe let your clothes hang out for awhile?"

Vanessa's hopelessly wrinkled, off-white cotton pants and blouse hung on her at strange angles. Both had been so nice and crisp when she'd worn them to the airport earlier.

"I might have to take you up on that offer," she said, quickly locating his clean clothes. Before moving toward the bathroom to change. Vanessa was at the door when she paused, a mischievous gleam flashed in her eyes, as a wicked idea crossed her mind. "Do you expect your nurse back anytime soon?"

"No...Why?" Andrew wasn't sure why she'd asked, but the look she sent made him curious. *What was she contemplating?*

She shut his door tightly. Slowly, she began removing her clothing, provocatively, one piece at a time, while a pleasantly surprised Andrew watched in pure fascination. Enthusiastically he observed her performance, feeling like a horny schoolboy, as she leisurely tossed each item of clothing across the room. Detaching her bra with deliberate flirtatiousness, she threw it directly toward his face. Once completely naked, she hid partway behind his bathroom door while she pulled on his t-shirt and shorts. Andrew, feeling more than entertained by her spontaneous striptease, wanted her to come back to bed to him immediately.

Laughing at her own brazenness, Vanessa shook her head coyly. Instead, she quickly picked up her crumpled clothes and carefully hung them up. He watched her bend over as she retrieved her clothes from the floor. Vanessa seemed completely unaware of how his form-fitting clothes appeared on her voluptuous body, leaving absolutely no room for the imagination.

When Vanessa finally snuggled back in bed with Andrew, she let her hand drift down below his muscular belly, instantly impressed by the physical effects of her impromptu, erotic teasing. She searched his eyes, and he saw her questioning look.

"Do you have any idea how sexy you are?" he asked, his voice dropping to a low growl.

"Too bad we're in a hospital. It looks like we could really use some privacy," Vanessa laughed, teasing him with her gentle, intimate touch, while affectionately nuzzling his neck.

"I won't tell, if you won't," he suggested, sending her his wolfish, predatory smile.

"I don't want to hurt you," Vanessa whispered sincerely, only partially appalled by his provocative suggestion.

"Trust me, that's not the part of me that's broken."

Andrew switched off the lights from his bed, while Vanessa shed the clothes she'd just put on. Slowly she removed his shorts, impressed by the hard, ready sign of his arousal as it escaped its confinement. She gently climbed on top of him, lowering herself slowly onto him. As she enveloped him within her body, their union instantly exploded for both of them. Physically intense and involuntary, they simultaneously released their pent up lust. But even though his exertion had been brief, it left Andrew panting, as if he'd run a marathon. Vanessa frowned and quickly climbed off of him. She scooped up her clothes, washed herself quickly, and dressed noiselessly in the confines of his small bathroom. When she returned, Andrew was still struggling to catch his breath. She washed and dressed him tenderly, frowning with concern, as he continued to gasp for breath. His slow recovery seemed concerning after such a short exertion.

"Are you all right?" Vanessa nestled next to him and frowned. "Why are you still breathing so hard? I'm sorry, we should have waited until you were stronger."

"I'm fine—it was just so intense. Give me a minute—believe me—there's really nothing to worry about."

Vanessa rested her hand over his racing heart. She remembered what the doctor had told her, that Andrew didn't even have a heartbeat when he'd first arrived in the emergency room.

"Should I call the nurse?" She felt her own heart rate speeding up as she began to panic. "Your heart is beating really fast, and you're not breathing normally."

Andrew forced himself to take slow, deep breaths. He could hear Vanessa's concern and he gave her a reassuring hug with his left arm. "Just give me another minute or so, I'll be fine."

Vanessa felt his heart begin to slow, as his breathing finally returned to its normal pace. She knew that Andrew's response had not been normal. They had both been breathless after strenuous lovemaking before, but nothing like this, and certainly not for this long.

"You need to tell your doctor about this. It could be serious. Next time, medical help might be a lot farther away."

"Okay, if it will make you feel better," Andrew said, attempting to make light of the situation. "I'll have a little man-to-man chat with the doctor this morning." He seemed completely recovered now, so she snuggled close again, and he pulled the blanket up over them.

"Thank you," Vanessa sighed in relief. "You have no idea how traumatic it would be for me if you were to die while we were making love."

"I'm sure it would, so I'll try my best not to die while we're doing it," Andrew chuckled. "But you have to know, I really can't think of a better way to go. When it's my time to go that is."

"And what would they say when you arrived at the pearly gates?" Vanessa inquired, sarcastically.

"I'm sure there'd be a lot of high fiving as I passed through them." Andrew laughed at the thought.

Vanessa laughed too; after being alone for so many years, she really loved having someone to banter back and forth with. One of the things she loved most about Andrew was his quick wit, and his almost uncanny ability to lighten even the most serious of situations. A day without Andrew would seem gloomy and boring. The mere thought of living without him caused her to squirm and feel uneasy. "Promise me you'll talk to the doctor first thing today. I'm not kidding! I'm worried about what might happen next time."

"I promise." He refused to admit it to her, but he was a little worried himself. "Now that we have that settled, should we sleep some more, or would you like to discuss something else with me?"

"I'm sorry." Vanessa feared her nagging had negatively affected his mood. She may have pushed him too far. "Is there anything you'd like to talk about?"

"Actually..." he kissed the top of her head as a peace offering. "I'd like to talk about a sailing trip. Is there anywhere special you'd like to go?"

Vanessa exhaled the tense breath she'd been holding, relieved that he'd returned to his normal, congenial self. Although she hadn't decided if they could sail together anytime soon, she wanted him to relax, so she made an effort to play along. "I'm wide open. I haven't traveled much except to see my mother in France, so any place you take me will be a brand-new experience. What do you recommend, sailor?"

Just as he'd assumed, she'd spent her life chained to her desk job, failing to take any time out for her own pleasure. "Now that you've asked, I'd like to take a nice long trip all the way down to the tip of South America. We can take our time; stop at some of the extraordinary ports along the way. I think you'll be amazed by the way all of your senses come alive in that part of the world. It's truly remarkable."

Vanessa instantly felt uncomfortable and dishonest. Andrew seemed to be talking about a long, long trip, not just a week or two. She knew she would have too many other obligations to leave on any long trips, at least for a while. "Don't you think we should begin with a few short sailing trips first, like we discussed before? Your arm needs time to heal."

Vanessa's obligations to *Gemma* appeared to be more on her mind than his arm. Realizing he'd jumped the gun with this conversation, Andrew decided to back off. At least she'd have something to consider, and hopefully dream about. "You're probably right. We can plan more extensively, once my arm is back in commission. In the meantime, would you consider letting me 'teach you the ropes,' so to speak? Take a few day trips, just until I get my strength back?"

He heard Vanessa sigh wistfully, as she relaxed against his shoulder. "Sure, that sounds like fun."

A pause of quiet consideration followed, each lost in contemplation. Neither of them had been fooled by their veiled conversation. They both knew full well that each of them had a not-so-secret agenda regarding their future life together. Closing their eyes, they tried to rest, but it seemed only short time later that the nurse came in to check on Andrew.

"The doctor's making rounds on his patients, and he'll be in to see you shortly. I'm pretty sure you're going to be discharged today. Are you ready to leave?" She included Vanessa in her statement.

"Please, don't be offended, you've all been wonderful," Andrew smiled apologetically at her. "But I'd really like to sleep in my own bed tonight."

The nurse returned his smile. "Andrew, you've been an absolute pleasure. I'd tell you to come back anytime, but instead I'll tell you to stay healthy. Can I bring you both some clean towels, so you can take a shower?"

I can take a hint, Vanessa thought. "That would be wonderful, thank you, Mary."

She climbed off Andrew's bed in anticipation of the doctor's arrival. Her clothes were still hopelessly wrinkled, so she took them with her into Andrew's bathroom. She hoped the steam from the shower would improve their sad, bedraggled appearance. Knowing the doctor would be in to see Andrew momentarily, she flipped on the shower and carefully hung her clothes close to the steam. When she looked in the mirror at her R-rated reflection wearing Andrew's tight t-shirt, her eyes stretched wide open in shock. Amused, she shook her head. No wonder Andrew had reacted so quickly to her teasing last night.

The shower helped Vanessa immensely with her stiff joints. *I'm overdue for a good massage,* she thought distractedly. In the process of dressing in her slightly less wrinkled clothes, she overheard Andrew talking to his doctor.

"Well Andrew, any questions or concerns about your recovery?"

"Actually I do, Doc." Andrew hesitated for just a second. "Vanessa spent the night with me last night."

"I know, the nurses told me," he said, nonjudgmentally. The doctor wasn't sure where he was going with the topic yet.

"I'm sure what they didn't tell you was that we made love." Andrew took a breath as he launched into his explanation. "I'm a little concerned because it made my heart race. Also, it took a lot longer than normal for me to catch my breath."

The doctor sat down in the chair next to Andrew. His voice took on a serious tone. "You know, you came very close to dying, Andrew. You'll need to take things slow and easy for the next few weeks. It's going to take a while for you to be able to do the things you did before you were shot. I'll order a cardiac stress test for you in a few weeks." The doctor jotted down a note on his chart and looked back at Andrew with a grave expression. "In the meantime, although I know Vanessa's a very attractive woman, you'll need to refrain from having a physical relationship. That is, at least until after the test results. Any questions?"

Although Vanessa was completely dressed, she overheard their conversation, and had no intention of leaving the bathroom until after Andrew's doctor had left. She silently scolded herself. She was too old to act like an embarrassed teenager. She listened to Andrew's response, smiling to herself.

"Understood, Doctor, I'll try to resist, but it won't be easy."

"You're a lucky man, Andrew." The doctor stood up as he added, "Try not to push your luck."

"I want to thank you officially for saving my life." Andrew reached out with his left hand to shake the doctor's hand. "I *am* a very lucky man. I know I have a lot to live for. I promise, I'll follow your advice and take it easy until you give me the all-clear. I owe you my life, and if you ever need anything, please let me know."

"Be careful," the doctor chuckled. He was well aware of Andrew's net worth. "I might just take you up on that."

"I mean it—anything—just ask," Andrew looked him square in the eyes, making his meaning clear.

The doctor left the room shaking his head and chuckling over Andrew's tempting offer.

Vanessa waited until the silence in the room convinced her that the doctor had left, and then emerged from the bathroom. Andrew smiled and thought she looked adorable. Her wet hair hung straight down to her chin, her clothes remained hopelessly wrinkled, and she wore no makeup on her freshly washed face. She looked irresistible. He opened his arm to reach for her and she walked eagerly into his tender embrace, bending down to kiss him softly on the lips.

"It seems our relationship will be a platonic one, at least for a few weeks."

"I heard," she smiled, gazing into his beautiful blue eyes. "But... just because we can't be physical, doesn't mean we're going to be totally platonic," she whispered, nibbling suggestively on his earlobe.

"Um, I like how you think, lady." He nuzzled her, softly kissing her on the crook of her neck with playful affection.

Chapter 31
Homecoming

*A*fter what seemed an eternity to Andrew, he found himself home again, lounging comfortably in his own bed. Pillows stacked behind his back, his right arm propped up on a soft, fluffy support; he sat like a king on his throne. The bedrooms' french doors stood wide open, allowing the warm afternoon breeze to gently circulate through the room while fanciful sunbeams danced across the floor. Utterly content, he listened to the familiar sounds of the ocean waves, rhythmically colliding onto the shoreline below, before swiftly washing back out to sea. Gratitude overwhelmed him. He was alive! Safe and sound, resting in his own bed as he listened to the ocean with the distant murmurs of the woman he loved downstairs. Sluggishly, he savored the euphoric feeling, slowly lapsing into a deep, soothing afternoon slumber.

Vanessa sat in the living room deep in conversation with Haley via video chat. Haley looked like a vulnerable, innocent child, sitting cross-legged in the midst of the powder-blue bedroom she now shared with her baby brother.

After discussing her flight home and the condition of her ankle, Vanessa cautiously asked, "So, how does it feel to be home again?"

"It's very strange." Haley lowered her voice, not risking her family overhearing her conversation. "My parents treat me like I never left. They seemed happy to see me when they picked me up at the airport, but on the ride home, they went over all the same house rules I had when I was fifteen. It's like stepping back in time."

Vanessa watched Haley's eyes tear up before she averted them. Haley had suffered unspeakable abuse and torment over the past few years. Vanessa knew this transition was going to be hard on all of them. Since it was only Haley's first day home, she tried not to interfere with the process. "How did that make you feel?" Vanessa asked.

"I'm not sure," Haley softly confided, chewing on her bottom lip. "Part of me felt loved, the other part of me felt insulted." Vanessa smiled, remembering what a sensitive soul Haley had.

"Maybe they're just trying to be clear about their expectations, in order to avoid any misunderstandings," Vanessa suggested, diplomatically.

"I guess so." Vanessa hid her smile as she watched Haley push out her bottom lip in a childlike pout.

"So, have you thought about returning to school yet?" Vanessa asked, tactfully changing the subject.

"I don't know what my parents are thinking, but I found an online GED program. I could have my high school diploma in as little as six months!" Haley smiled to herself, longing for her freedom again.

"That sounds good," Vanessa commented neutrally.

"The only problem is the cost." Haley's voice became flat, suddenly sounding discouraged. "I don't know if my parents will agree. It's kind of expensive. I could get a job to pay for it. I just don't know yet."

Vanessa would happily assist Haley with her education costs. But she struggled to control her impulse to help. She'd give Haley the opportunity to work it out with her parents first. "I'm sure if you decide that's the best program for you, a solution will come to you."

"Love has turned you into an optimist," Haley laughed, her mood instantly lightening.

"Speaking of Andrew, he's home."

"That's great, can I say hi to him?" Haley scooted closer to her computer excitedly.

"He's taking a nap right now..." Vanessa glanced up the staircase. "I'm sure you'll be able to talk to him when we chat next time."

"Saturday seems like forever," Haley moaned. "You're going back to work soon, aren't you? Did you find someone to watch out for Andrew while you're gone?"

"Actually, I haven't." Vanessa's forehead creased. "That reminds me, I need to call Diane to see if she'll do it this week."

"Can I video chat with Diane while she's there?" Haley perked up at the mention of Diane. "Then I could say hi to Andrew too."

"I don't see why not, you might even catch Father Patrick on one of his many visits." *Haley had developed so many lasting bonds*, Vanessa thought.

"I can hardly wait." Haley clapped her hands in excitement. "I miss everyone so much already."

"Haley, promise me you'll try hard to work things out with your family. You need to develop a close relationship with them, that way the next time you leave home, it will be with their blessing and support."

"I promise," Haley said, with a long sigh. "I'll do my best. I'm only here now because I know you want me to try. I would have run away from the hospital if it had been totally up to me. I owe you everything. I promise to behave myself and I'll become a part of my family again, for you."

"Honey, you don't owe me anything." Vanessa shook her head. "Please do this for you. You may not know this right now, but someday in the not too distant future you'll learn, family is everything. Take your time. Reestablish your rightful place with them. You'll be free to follow your dreams soon enough."

Haley acknowledged Vanessa with a nod of her head. The distant sound of her mom's voice calling her to dinner interrupted their brief conversation.

"Thanks for the chat, but I have to go now."

"Go have dinner." Vanessa wasn't ready to let Haley go so soon, although she knew she had no choice. "Maybe I'll check in with you tomorrow if Diane comes over."

"Thanks." Haley flashed her a broad smile. "That would be great, bye."

The screen went blank as Haley rushed off to have dinner with her family, sharing the first official meal with them in years.

Vanessa closed down her computer, sat back in the chair and allowed one tiny tear to run down her face. Quietly, she missed Haley and worried about her future. Jimmy had damaged Haley in ways that weren't apparent to most people. She'd worked hard to hide it. But Vanessa had seen through her protective façade the first time she'd fainted in her entryway.

The ringing of her phone rudely disturbed her pensive reflections. She glanced at it and smiled. It was Marie, just the person she needed to talk to. "I was just thinking about calling you."

"That's a relief, I think we need to talk," Marie said hesitantly, afraid she was disturbing Vanessa's homecoming with Andrew.

"I agree. Could you and Diane come over tomorrow afternoon?" Vanessa needed to see a friendly face. "I'd like to hire Diane to watch Andrew this week while we're at *Gemma*."

"I'm so relieved." Marie sighed, and the tension released from her tight shoulders. "I was afraid you weren't coming back to *Gemma* at all."

"You know me better than that," Vanessa chuckled. "I'll need you to bring the annual productivity reports for each of my junior executives. I've decided it's time to select my successor."

"Does that mean you're going to take the position of editor?" Marie's mouth fell open in shock.

"Let's not get ahead of ourselves." Vanessa glanced back up the stairs as she lowered her voice. "I haven't been offered it yet."

"You do know you have a meeting scheduled with Mr. Edwards, first thing Monday morning?"

"I guess I'll find out exactly what he's proposing then." Vanessa smiled thoughtfully to herself.

Vanessa had been so preoccupied with making arrangements with Marie that she failed to notice Andrew standing at the top of the stairs, or his hasty retreat back into his room. Up to use the bathroom, he'd overheard the tail end of Vanessa's conversation with Marie. His heart sank. Vanessa had clearly decided to become the editor-in-chief of *Gemma*!

Vanessa cocked her head, hearing the squeaking of the bed from upstairs. She had just begun to ascend the stairs to check on Andrew, when she heard a knock at the front door. Opening it, she found a smiling, very pleased Father Patrick.

"Vanessa, how lovely to see you."

"It's nice to see you too, Father," she smiled fondly, his cheerful mood contagious. "Come on in. Andrew will be glad to see you."

He stepped in and they both turned toward the stairway, witnessing Andrew's slow, painstaking descent. Father Patrick put his hands up.

"I would have come up to see you."

"Good to see you, Father." Andrew walked over to shake his hand with his strong one, his other hand resting limply in a sling. "I was just on my way to get some fresh air and sunshine; won't you join me by the pool?" Andrew seemed relaxed, more like his usual hospitable self. Vanessa smiled, relieved by his cheery mood.

"You two go ahead, I'll get you something to drink. Iced tea, Father?" Vanessa offered.

"Thank you, dear." Father Patrick patted Vanessa's arm. "I'll help Andrew. I'd like to have a few words with him." He winked and Vanessa got the message. He wanted to speak to Andrew in private.

Watching them through the kitchen window, Vanessa smiled as the elderly priest assisted Andrew into a chaise lounge, and then seated himself carefully in the chair beside him. Cradling his weak arm with his good arm, Andrew made himself comfortable. She watched Father Patrick lean in close to converse with him. Embarrassed to be caught spying, she turned away, busying herself with the task of making iced tea.

"So, how are you holding up?" Father Patrick inquired with a raised eyebrow.

"It's great to be home," Andrew sighed. "But—I'm worried about Vanessa. I just overheard her conversation with Marie. I think she's planning to assume the position of editor-in-chief at *Gemma* when she returns."

Father Patrick paused for a minute before responding. Considering he was a firm believer in never interfering with a couple's naturally forming relationship, he hesitated. But seeing the doubt in Andrew's eyes, he knew he was suffering and wanted to offer him some words of comfort.

"Do you trust Vanessa?"

Andrew nodded, returning his look of concern with complete sincerity. "With my life!"

"Well, isn't that what we're talking about here, your life?" Father Patrick soberly searched his face.

"I suppose," Andrew conceded. "I'm just afraid I can't compete. I'm afraid she'll be lured back to the glamor of her old life. After all, we've only been together for such a short time. I'm not sure I have enough left to offer her."

"I've spent some time with Vanessa..." Father Patrick responded carefully. "And my advice to you would be—trust her. She might think she wants a big prestigious job, but she's smart enough to know what she'd have to give up. She's experienced a lot of heartache and disappointment in her lifetime. I don't think she'll give up a chance of having a lasting, loving relationship with years of happiness, do you?"

Vanessa appeared in the doorway with a tray of cookies and iced tea. She paused on the threshold, unsure if she should interrupt. Father Patrick spotted her hesitation and sent her a broad, welcoming smile. "Oh my, you didn't need to go to so much bother."

"No trouble, Father." Vanessa approached with the tray. "I just found some cookies in the cupboard. I'm trying to get Andrew's strength up."

"This looks wonderful, please, come join us." He smiled, noting her attentiveness to Andrew.

"Yes please, Father Patrick was just trying to keep my spirits up," Andrew said, flashing her a weak smile.

"Alright." Vanessa sat down next to him.

Andrew quietly sipped his tea while munching on his favorite cookies. After a moment or two of silence, Father Patrick took up the conversation.

"I don't imagine Andrew will be able to attend church tomorrow, so

I'd like to come by, if that would be all right?"

"That would be perfect." Vanessa's voice perked up with genuine enthusiasm. "Marie and Diane will be visiting in the afternoon. I know Haley would like very much to video chat with both you and Diane."

"How wonderful." Father Patrick smiled broadly, genuinely pleased by the turn of events. "It will be delightful to see them, and to talk with Haley. Video chatting is such a wonderful invention. How is she getting on with her parents anyway?"

"It's an adjustment for her," Vanessa said. "But she's only just gotten home. I imagine it will take some time."

"She's a fortunate young woman to have such a fine family and caring friends." Father Patrick's smile included both Vanessa and Andrew. "What do you think, Andrew? How well do other children adjust after being abducted, or running away from their parents, when they've finally returned home?"

Andrew had not been following their conversation. He was lost in his own doubts about his continued relationship with Vanessa. But the question from Father Patrick was general enough; he was able to quickly respond in his usual thoughtful way. "No two cases are alike, Father. A lot depends on the age of the child, the circumstances of the estrangement, and the length of the separation. I believe Haley will adjust up to a point, but given her age and the length of time she was gone, I believe she'll leave home again fairly soon."

"I hope she stays long enough to reestablish her place in the family." Vanessa frowned at the idea of Haley running off again. "She needs to feel she's been forgiven, and reestablish her role as their firstborn child. It's important that the next time she leaves, it's with the support of her family. Don't you think so, Father?"

"Yes I do. So many of the troubled souls I counsel are carrying tremendous burdens of guilt. They often have strained or estranged relationships with their families."

"You're right," Andrew added, washing down his cookie with a gulp of tea. "These same individuals commit crimes. Many of them seem to suffer from feelings of worthlessness. They lack the security that comes from having family connections, even on murky terms."

"I hope Haley can release her sense of shame. She needs to feel like she's a valuable member of a family again." Vanessa bit at her lower lip.

The two men nodded in agreement. After a few moments, Father Patrick stood up, preparing to leave. "It's great to see you looking so well, but I must be off now. I have several other calls to make, so I'll simply bless you both and see you again tomorrow." Andrew reached up to shake hands with his good hand. Father Patrick placed his other hand over the top of the hand he continued to hold, gently reminding him, "Remember what we discussed today. Try to have faith."

"I will. Thank you for coming, Father. I look forward to your visit tomorrow."

"I'll walk you to the door." Vanessa stood, and once they were out of Andrew's earshot she cautiously remarked, "Thank you for coming, Father. Andrew is trying to fight it, but I know he's depressed about his condition. Your timely visit has cheered him up considerably."

"He's a good man, who's suffered a lot of sorrow in his life." He took both of Vanessa's hands in his, looking directly into her eyes. "His concerns are for more than just his own physical condition, you know."

She instantly knew to what he was referring, quickly realizing that Andrew must have discussed his fears regarding her return to work with the priest. "Perhaps I should have waited until I've made my final decision, before informing him. I know I'm being unfair, but I have so many factors to consider."

"This is your decision." Father Patrick remained solemn, bowing his head and tilting it to one side. "Just remember... whatever you decide, it will affect more than just your life. I will pray for you." With that being said, he gave her a fatherly kiss on her cheek and left.

Slowly closing the door, she leaned her back against it, and drew in a deep breath. Shoving her own guilty feelings aside, she returned to the only obstacle on her accelerated career path.

Stepping back outside into the blinding light, she found Andrew had reclined on his chaise lounge, and fallen fast asleep in the sunshine. He was still as weak as a kitten, she realized. His recovery would take a lot longer than he chose to admit.

Turning on her heel, she returned inside to locate a tablet of paper, planning to sit close to Andrew while she jotted down some notes about the individuals on her team, preparing for her meeting with Marie.

Vanessa mentally pictured several scenarios of how Monday might unfold. In one, she'd graciously accept the position of editor-in-chief, appoint her successor, and focus all her time and energy on her new position, restoring *Gemma* to its previous glory. In another, she'd agree to work with her successor for two weeks out of each month, while she vacationed with Andrew the other two weeks. Or her last choice, she'd quit all together, recommend her successor, and retire. She should never have trusted Max and Mindy to manage her accounts during her absence. Now returning to her previous position at *Gemma* was an option she would not willingly accept.

Quietly scribbling notes on a pad while Andrew slept, she methodically reviewed each of her team member's contributions and qualifications. She was determined to settle the question of who should succeed her as head of advertising, before she returned to *Gemma* Monday morning.

Jack had been with her the longest, she thought. Marie mentioned that he'd really stepped up to help during the recent crisis. He'd restored many of the accounts that had experienced cyber theft due to *Gemma's* computer breach. She placed his name at the top of her list of potential replacements. Maureen was too green. She still needed mentoring and support to manage her accounts. She might be a strong candidate in a few years, but not at this time. Odessa...she was smart, she'd also had several strong advertising experiences before joining *Gemma*. After nearly two years, she'd handled her own accounts without much coaching, and worked well with the rest of the team, definitely a contender. Matt had been with her for about eighteen months. He worked hard, but seemed stressed at times, and lacked confidence. She crossed him off the list of possible candidates. Alexis was also smart, quiet, and very efficient. She was the point person developing a market for *Gemma* in bilingual advertisements. Vanessa considered her a valuable member of her team, but not assertive enough to manage the other members. She crossed her off the list.

That narrowed her options down to Odessa and Jack. One of these two candidates would be her successor. Tomorrow she would review each of their productivity reports before making her final decision. Her first act as editor would be to promote one of them, and hire four new members to join the advertising team. Satisfied by her decisions, she set aside her notes.

The warm sunshine seeped into her weary body, while a gust of the cool ocean breeze blew her hair gently away from her face. Brow still furrowed, she noticed how beautiful the day was. Standing, she rolled her shoulders to relax away her lingering tensions, and she walked across the patio, where the peaceful, rolling ocean instantly mesmerized her. Stretching her arms over her head, she felt the exhilaration and sheer serenity of the tranquil scene before her. Vanessa became part of the soothing scene, unaware that Andrew's eyes had opened, or that his sad gaze guardedly followed her movements. He had peeked over at her several times while she'd sat concentrating on her notes. Her focus and intensity had deeply disturbed him. Watching the wheels turning in her brain as she plotted her strategies for Monday, he'd struggled to smother his feelings of resentment. Hurt, he hated that she'd excluded him from her plans.

Vanessa suddenly noticed him studying her, and the wary look in his eyes. He seemed moody again. "I didn't realize you were awake," she cheerfully responded to his probing look, still feeling relaxed and enjoying the magnificent day.

"Yeah, I just seem to nod off at a moment's notice these days." Andrew kept his tone neutral, struggling to shake off his feelings of dread.

"Everything takes time." Vanessa moved to sit beside him, reaching out for his good hand to give him a gentle, reassuring squeeze. "Please try to be patient. Trust me, everything will end up the way it's meant to be."

Andrew reached up, gently stroking his hand through the hair at the base of her neck, bent forward, placing a heart-wrenchingly tender kiss on her parted lips. "Forever and a day, you have my unending love and trust," he whispered.

Chapter 32
Complicated Sunday

*O*n a tiny island, off the coast of South America, Kate, the mastermind of the Bitton bank robbery and flamboyant nurse impersonator, smiled, enjoying the well-attended party. Standing out on the deck, away from the crowd inside, she gently swayed to the tympanic rhythm of the calypso band. The evening was warm, and the flaming torches scattered around the ground-level deck flickered seductively in the balmy ocean breezes, adding to the romantic ambiance of the night's social gathering.

Anna, Kate's realtor, had proven to be an invaluable resource for her ever since Kate's abrupt arrival onto the island two short weeks ago. As the only realtor on the island, Anna knew everything about everyone, and she loved to share. After listening endlessly to the woman's gossip, Kate had carefully protected her own shadowy story from the prying, chatty woman, sensibly shying away from Anna's persistent inquiries. The day Anna had sold Kate her fabulous beach house, she'd also graciously extended Kate a standing invitation to her weekly parties. Anna's lavish, intimate beach parties were legendary on the secluded island, and Kate loved being included in the festivities.

Standing away from the crowd, beside a tall, sandy-blond haired man, Kate remained transfixed; gazing adoringly into the softest, dreamy brown eyes she'd ever seen. She'd been instantly drawn to this handsome, athletic looking man, who called himself Brad. The thought 'love at first sight' drifted through her hazy, alcohol-soaked mind. Idly sipping her rum punch, she continued to ogle him, while Brad casually leaned in closer, steadily returning her warm gaze. An exquisitely suggestive smile slowly spread across his suntanned face. Bending nearer towards Kate's right ear, he whispered, "Let's get out of here."

Kate and Brad had met just a few hours before, during tonight's extravagant party. Anna had introduced them, explaining that Brad was her nephew, visiting indefinitely from California. No one on the island seemed the slightest bit suspicious about Brad's sudden appearance. Nor did anyone suspect that he was actually an undercover FBI agent, assigned to trail after Kate.

Brad and Kate said goodnight, graciously thanking Anna, before they leisurely walked hand in hand down the sandy shoreline in the direction of Kate's newly acquired beach house. She laughed at his jokes, and smiled *knowingly at his overt sexual innuendos. But, after the trying ordeal of having fled to this remote island for privacy, Kate planned to keep a low profile. No one, including Brad, could ever know that she was the only surviving member of the Bitton bank robbery, or of the piles of stolen bank bills neatly stashed inside her bedroom safe!*

Having spent a quiet evening together, Andrew and Vanessa had elected to retire early. They chatted pleasantly, snuggling intimately together in bed. Feeling talkative, Vanessa enjoyed sharing her opinions on a variety of subjects, thrilled that they both seemed to have so much in common. Andrew had patiently demonstrated his excellent listening skills, commenting only briefly when appropriate. They'd talked for hours like old friends, each carefully avoiding the sensitive topic of their impending future, or Vanessa's upcoming career choice.

Long after Vanessa had fallen asleep, Andrew lay awake. He stared blankly at the white ceiling, struggling to control his fears that Vanessa would choose her prominent career at *Gemma,* and she'd be lost to him forever. The suspense of waiting for her decision was killing him. He tenderly kissed the top of her sleeping head. *If only this useless arm was fully recovered*, he thought, *I could hold her, take her sailing, and I'd show her what she'd be missing*. He worked desperately to move the dormant muscles in his limp arm, but feeling defeated and betrayed by his body, his worries over their uncertain future persisted, until eventually exhaustion won out and he slept.

Just before dawn, Vanessa rolled to her side to watch Andrew sleep before she silently slipped out of his bed. Sitting peacefully out on the balcony, with Callie curled up on her lap, Vanessa wrestled with her options regarding her future at *Gemma.* Pale, calming morning light reflected softly over the ocean. The sun, still hidden from view, changed the feathery slow-moving white clouds into muted, watercolor pinks and lavenders. Then, as the sun first emerged from the mountaintops behind her, bright beams of sunlight streaked across the sky, causing the ocean to shimmer and sparkle as if a thousand tiny diamonds floated on its surface. Vanessa sat breathlessly. She would never tire of this morning spectacle, even if she watched it every day for the rest of her life. Turning around, she discovered Andrew standing quietly in the doorway, his gaze captured by the magnificent illustration created by the morning sun. Sharing this stunning moment with him made all previous thoughts of *Gemma* blur and fade away.

Reverently he watched the brilliantly illuminated sky, and whispered, "This is my favorite time of the day, with my favorite sunrise, and my favorite girl." Walking toward her, he bent down, giving her a gentle kiss, and then casually reached over to stroke Callie behind her ear. "Did you sleep all right?"

Vanessa smiled up at him. His sleep tussled hair fell perfectly into place as he flashed her a charming smile. *He always manages to look so handsome, any time of the day or night*, she thought. "I did. How about you? Did your arm hurt last night?"

"No, my arm feels surprisingly good today." Andrew stretched it tentatively. "I slept like a baby. It's so nice to be home again." He sent her a sly smile. "But I think I need a shower, and... I might need a little help."

Vanessa knew Andrew required her help. She also knew that he enjoyed the idea of playing the helpless patient in an attempt to lure her into the shower with him. Standing abruptly and dislodging her grumpy cat, she wrapped her arms around his waist. "I'd be more than happy to assist you, sir." In response he bent down to quickly kiss her upturned face.

"You know, I'm starting to think my arm might take a really long time to heal," he teased, and they headed for the bathroom while holding each other close.

Reaching over him carefully, she undressed Andrew for his shower. He enjoyed every minute of her touch; secretly knowing he wasn't entirely helpless. Once he'd stepped into the shower, she pulled off her sleep shirt and joined him. Showering together had always been a very sensuous endeavor, and this morning was no different. Unknowingly, she'd tormented Andrew as she slowly lathered his hair. Her breasts innocently brushing against his chest resulted in instantaneous evidence of his arousal, which she felt pressed firmly against her thigh.

"Do I have to douse you with cold water, mister?" she laughed, playfully.

"I'm sorry, I can't help the way my body reacts to yours," Andrew laughed. He pouted, pretending remorse.

"Maybe next time I'll have to wash your hair in the sink. I think you could probably manage to wash the rest," she said, abruptly turning to step out, but he grabbed her around her waist with his good arm, bending down to nuzzle the back of her neck.

"Ah, but this is so much fun," he murmured.

"Please, Andrew," Vanessa protested weakly, her breathy voice divulging her unspoken desire. "Remember what the doctor said."

"You're right, I'll behave." He reluctantly released her, seeing the split-second spark of alarm flash across her eyes. He knew she wanted him to continue, but she feared the unknown consequences.

Rinsing off, he stepped out of the shower and tried futilely to wrap the towel around his waist with one hand. Impatient and frustrated, he wished he could fast-forward his life to the point where he could be a whole man again.

Vanessa cursed herself for reminding him of his injury, as well as his other limitations. She wrapped a towel around herself sarong-style, and attempted to tease him back into his previously good mood. "Here, let me wrap up those family jewels." Bending down, she wrapped the towel around him, covering his now thoroughly deflated manhood, and then began drying him with another towel. As she bent down to dry his legs, her towel fell to the floor. Andrew's reaction was instantaneous, and poorly hidden beneath the loosely wrapped towel around his hips. He looked up to the ceiling, exhaling dramatically, "Maybe this wasn't such a good idea after all."

"Andrew, we're both adults." She wrapped herself up again, standing close in front of him. "I think we can restrain ourselves for a couple of weeks."

He pulled her close against his chest, where she rested her head against him. They stood silently for a few minutes while Andrew tried to regain his dignity. His efforts were clearly unsuccessful.

"Why don't you go sit out on the balcony while I get dressed," Vanessa suggested. "Then I'll go downstairs to make breakfast. Do you think you can dress yourself and join me?"

"Yes, I'm perfectly capable of dressing myself," he answered slowly, feeling embarrassed by his lack of control around her. "I'll go sit outside, since it seems I've turned into some kind of an uncontrollable sex maniac."

"Believe me, you've just paid me the highest compliment I've ever received," Vanessa grinned.

He returned her good-natured smile, bending forward to kiss her again, but she pushed back lightly against his chest, so that his intended kiss barely brushed across her face.

"All right Romeo, outside." She pointed to the door.

"I'm going." He tried to sound grumpy and rejected, but the grin on his face instantly gave him away.

Vanessa had finished putting the final touches on breakfast when Andrew appeared, as cheerful as always. He'd dressed casually and seemed in complete control of himself once again. He glanced appreciatively at the beautifully set table inside the dining room, tired of balancing food on his lap outside.

Since Andrew had consistently refused to take any pain pills, Vanessa made mimosas to have with the bacon, eggs and toast she served. Their morning breakfast discussion began on a relaxed and enjoyable note. However, the more they drank, the more animated and hilarious their conversation became. A sheepish look crossed Vanessa's face as she poured the last drop of a very large bottle of champagne into her glass. They'd been having such a good time that neither of them had noticed how much they'd imbibed. The laughter and alcohol seemed to have alleviated some of the unspoken tension between them, providing them with a much-needed release from their sexual constraints.

After breakfast, they unceremoniously dumped their dirty dishes into the sink. Since it was Sunday, and only moments before Father Patrick was expected to arrive, cleanup would have to wait.

The priest appeared on schedule and found them both in a surprisingly euphoric state. He struggled several times to gain their attention, but between their secretive glances and inane laughter, he found it difficult to capture their focus.

"Well, it seems you two are in fine spirits," he said, temporarily amused by their antics. But his good-natured smile quickly turned into a concerned frown when Vanessa and Andrew broke into hysterics over the word spirits. "Andrew, are you ready to receive communion?" Father Patrick asked, solemnly.

Andrew attempted to smother his uncontrollable laughter, responding with a simple nod. A knock at the front door distracted him before he could formulate a coherent verbal answer and an amused Vanessa quickly departed the awkward scene. Walking with exaggerated care, she stepped into the house, and Father Patrick turned to question Andrew. "What in heaven's name has gotten into you two?"

"I'm sorry, Father." Andrew struggled hopelessly to sound sober. "I'm afraid we had a few too many mimosas at breakfast this morning." Father Patrick hid his smile, slightly amused by Andrew's apologetic confession.

"I see… would you still like to receive communion this morning?"

"Yes, but go easy on the wine," Andrew smiled, guiltily.

"My dear boy," Father Patrick shook his head. "Your behavior never ceases to astound me."

Before he could begin the ritual, Vanessa returned, closely followed by Diane and Marie. Diane's eyes lit up with excitement when she spied Father Patrick. "Nice to see you again, Father."

"It seems like I just left you a few moments ago at church," he chuckled, standing to formally greet them. "It was an unexpected pleasure to see both of your smiling faces in church this morning."

Marie explained, for Vanessa and Andrew's benefit. "It made more sense, given our meeting here today."

"Diane will be looking after Andrew this week, and I needed to meet with Marie," Vanessa clarified briefly. "Why don't I show you his medications and exercises?" She addressed Diane. "Then you can video chat with Haley in her old room if you'd like." Vanessa motioned toward the house, assuming Andrew might want some privacy with Father Patrick.

"That would be great." Diane's eyes sparkled. "We've been texting every day since she left." Vanessa smiled and turned back to Father Patrick. "Haley would love to chat with you and Andrew as well, whenever you're finished of course."

"That would be grand," Father Patrick nodded, and Vanessa turned her attention to Marie.

"Now Marie…." A very loud hiccup escaped Vanessa's mouth before she could continue. *Darn*, Vanessa thought. Father Patrick tried unsuccessfully to hide his grin. Marie looked at each of them in confusion. They all obviously knew something she didn't.

"Please excuse me, we over-indulged on mimosas at breakfast this morning." Vanessa covered her mouth while endeavoring to sound proper and composed.

"I see." Marie smiled at her slightly inebriated boss.

"What I was about to suggest was, that you and I get settled in the living room to work. Did you bring the files I requested?"

"Of course, and I brought my work laptop in case you wanted to look up something else." Even intoxicated, Vanessa was sharper than most people were sober. Marie lifted the briefcase in her right hand.

"Wonderful." Vanessa waved her hand toward the house. "We'll see you gentleman later." With that, the women disappeared inside the house.

"How about we do this right out here, Father." Andrew motioned toward the patio with his good arm. Father Patrick smiled, gazing out at the shimmering ocean below.

"All right, it's certainly a glorious day for it."

While Father Patrick began the rite of Holy Communion, Andrew tried to confess, to follow the ritual, but his mind kept drifting back to thoughts of his unsettled future with Vanessa. Gazing covertly toward the house, his eyes narrowed as he visualized Vanessa sitting with her assistant, categorically destroying his hopes and future happiness.

Meanwhile, when Diane signed on to video chat with Haley from her old bedroom, she screamed with pleasure, immediately launching into an excited monologue. There were so many things Haley could talk to Diane about, things that no one else would understand. The adults at both homes were preoccupied, which gave them total privacy to talk. Haley took advantage of their confidential conversation and began openly discussing her thoughts of escaping from what she considered a smothering home life.

"Tell me, what are you planning to do, Haley?" Diane asked, quietly closing the bedroom door.

As they entered the living room, Marie asked, "Are you sure you're up for this today?"

"Of course, I am," Vanessa insisted. "Now, show me the productivity reports." It took Vanessa only a few minutes of looking over the reports to decide on Jack as the best candidate to assume her position. Marie agreed with her completely, which further confirmed her final decision. They spent the remainder of the time huddled over Marie's laptop, reviewing the demise of several of Vanessa's previously lucrative long-term accounts.

"After that sobering report, I think I need a stiff drink," Vanessa said, closing the laptop. She sat back, shutting her eyes briefly. Everything she'd reviewed with Marie appeared much bleaker than she'd anticipated.

"You may want to eat instead," Marie suggested.

"I think you may be right about that. Let's order some lunch," Vanessa said, closing her eyes and pinching her forefinger and thumb across her forehead. Standing up a little too fast, she swayed slightly. After silently watching her gain her bearings again, Marie pretended not to notice, knowing how much Vanessa valued her sense of dignity.

"Thank you for bringing me up to speed." Vanessa took a deep breath for strength. "I'm ready to face Mr. Edwards tomorrow morning. Now that I have the facts, and a much clearer picture of what's transpired in my absence, I believe I know exactly what needs to be done for *Gemma's* recovery," she said, as her mind silently calculated all of the tireless years of work that Max had originally put into growing *Gemma* from scratch.

Marie smiled. *Vanessa was definitely a force to be reckoned with, and Mr. Edwards doesn't know it yet, but he's met his match,* she thought. *Vanessa was the female version of him, only younger and smarter!*

Selecting a local restaurant, she knew would deliver, Vanessa carefully clung to the railing as she made her ascent up the stairs, leaving Marie with the task of collecting everyone's orders.

Marie intended to start with Diane's order, but she paused when she heard soft murmuring through the closed bedroom door. Diane was still video chatting with Haley and her tone of voice sounded preachy, as if she were trying to convince her of something important. Marie respected her daughter's privacy and decided to return later.

Stepping out into the sunshine, she waited for Andrew and Father Patrick to acknowledge her presence without interrupting their conversation. As a result, she overheard Andrew's last sentence.

"I know you think I should sit back and trust Vanessa, but it's driving me crazy."

Marie cleared her throat, and both men turned to face her. She was about to explain her presence, when Vanessa called down from the balcony, "Don't forget my salad."

"I'm taking lunch orders," Marie blushed, embarrassed by what she'd overheard Andrew say. "What can I get you?"

"None for me thank you." Father Patrick waved his hand. "I should get going. Mrs. Flanagan gets immense pleasure out of feeding me on Sundays." He patted his belly good-naturedly.

Toting her laptop, Diane joined them outside. "Don't leave yet, Father. Haley needs to talk to you."

"Ah, there you are, my dear," he chuckled, catching a glimpse of Haley's image on the screen, as Diane handed the laptop to him. "What a miracle it is to see you. How are you adjusting to being home again?"

"I don't know. I miss all of you so much." Haley's smile failed to match the sad look in her eyes.

"Haley, you know it's only been a couple of days." Father Patrick keenly observed her troubled expression, convincing him of her torment. "I know it's hard, but open your heart to your family. Give them a chance."

"I will," Haley sighed. "I promise, Father."

He talked briefly with her, trying to restore her faith. Before he ended the conversation, he made sure she knew how to contact him. Passing the computer off to Andrew, Father Patrick groaned as he rose to his feet and said his goodbyes.

Andrew also reassured Haley that her feelings were to be expected. She nodded solemnly, appearing to agree with him, but he wasn't buying it. Vanessa returned to add her own encouraging words, but Haley abruptly interrupted, "Oh my gosh, Vanessa, have you been drinking?" Her innocent outburst caught Vanessa completely off guard. She considered denying it, but her unfiltered brain responded, "I may have over-indulged a little on some champagne with breakfast this morning." Vanessa's dignified answer was instantly rewarded by the sound of Haley's genuine, spontaneous laughter. It grew to hysterics when Andrew piped in plaintively, "She got me drunk, too!"

Haley hedged when asked about her plans to reunite with her friends. Her gaze frequently fell to her lap whenever Vanessa probed her for information about school or her immediate future. Vanessa sensed Haley was hiding something from her. She felt she wasn't reaching Haley, and eventually signed off, promising to be sober for their next chat. Diane reached for the laptop, carrying it back inside the house to continue her previous conversation with Haley in private.

"I know I'm a little tipsy, but I'd swear that Haley's up to something," Vanessa reflected, as she sat down next to Andrew.

"I agree. Let's just hope it's not something dangerous," he nodded.

"You two need to hydrate. Lunch will be here shortly," Marie instructed, setting two large glasses of ice water beside them.

"Yes, Mom." They responded in unison, clinking their glasses together cheerfully, tipping them up to drink as they'd been told.

The three adults sat beside the shimmering pool surrounded by exotic tropical flowering plants, speculating on Haley and Diane's secretive behavior. Would Diane betray Haley? Would she let them know what schemes Haley had in mind, before she got into trouble? Their speculative conversation quickly hushed when Diane walked outside, accompanied by Officer Todd Kinsley, carrying their lunch.

"I answered the door and found Todd frisking the poor delivery boy, so I invited him to lunch," she gushed, smiling up at Todd affectionately.

"I hope it's all right if I join you, Detective Kelly. I'm on your detail again," Todd said, uncomfortable by the impromptu invitation.

It didn't take a detective to see the sparks flying between Officer Kinsley and Diane. Andrew felt protective of young Diane, and decided he'd need to monitor their interactions carefully. *Especially*, he thought, *since this young man will be on my surveillance detail while Diane stays here as my babysitter.* "Welcome, please sit down and have some lunch," he offered graciously. Andrew relaxed, but after a minute or so his investigative mind kicked into gear. "Todd...you're the officer I spoke to when Vanessa found the front door unlocked."

Todd had his mouth full, and quickly gulped down his food before he responded. "That's right, sir. Fortunately, the dog walker had simply left the door unlocked and ajar." Diane followed their exchange closely, her eyes darting inadvertently to each as they spoke.

"I don't know what we would have done if Todd hadn't been close by," Diane interjected, flashing him an appreciative smile.

"I wanted to thank you in person for sticking around that night and watching after the ladies. I hope you didn't have to stay past your shift," Andrew commented, informally.

"No, no, I'd just come on duty when the call came in." Todd squirmed under Andrew's close scrutiny.

Protective glances from both Vanessa and Diane warned Andrew to proceed lightly. *Obviously, now is not the right time or place for this line of questioning*, he decided. "I want to thank you for your continued protection, especially while I'm laid up." He smiled kindly at Todd, lifting his weak arm feebly to emphasize his point. The ladies exhaled and smiled in relief, while Todd visibly relaxed his shoulders. Before too long, Todd allowed his gaze to drift away from Andrew, and turned it slowly toward Diane.

The conversation from that point on remained lighthearted and informal. When the subject of Haley came up, Diane, who had been noticeably gazing at Todd, began concentrating on her food instead, silently allowing Vanessa to update Todd. Diane was unusually withdrawn during the entire conversation, failing to add any enlightenment into Haley's mindset or possible plans.

It wasn't long before Todd stood to leave. "I want to thank you all. This was much nicer than taking my break alone in the patrol car. Thank you again, for your hospitality."

"I found you, so I'll walk you out," Diane announced, standing immediately beside Todd. She casually reached for his hand, leading him possessively back through the house.

Marie set her lunch down abruptly. She'd been observing her daughter flirt outrageously with the awkwardly self-conscious man during the entire meal. The minute they left she scooted her chair closer toward Andrew's. "So, what can you tell me about that young man? And Vanessa, when exactly did Diane fall for this guy?"

"I really don't know much about him." Andrew's gaze followed the direction of their departure. "But I promise you, I intend to find out."

"All I can tell you is—I definitely felt the chemistry between those two the first moment they laid eyes on each other," Vanessa said, sending Marie a reassuring smile. "I don't believe they've seen each other again since that night, but I couldn't swear to it."

"Was he inappropriate with her at any time?" Andrew frowned.

"He was a perfect gentleman," Vanessa said primly, leaning over to pat his hand reassuringly. "I don't think they've even kissed."

Andrew fell silent, focusing out over the ocean, clearly brooding over the situation.

"I know my daughter," Marie said, assertively. "And I'm certain this is not the last time I'll be seeing Officer Todd Kinsley!"

Chapter 33
Moment of Truth

*A*ll the way home, Diane silently fumed and rolled her eyes at her mother, wondering how much longer she'd have to endure her mother's inquisition regarding her relationship with Todd. She attempted to tune out her mother's voice and focus outside the vehicle, watching the shadowy scenery as it passed her car window. But her mother's insistent tone kept interrupting her fanciful musings regarding the attractive, mysterious man in question.

"Mother please, I'm a grown woman. If I were away at school, you'd have no idea *who* I was dating. Besides, how much safer of a boyfriend would you want? He's a cop!"

Marie felt the blood rush to her head. "You're right. I wouldn't know. That doesn't mean I'll stand by and watch as you become involved with a man who is clearly inappropriate for you, or any young girl."

"Mom, he's only a few years older than I am. Dad's five years older than you!" Diane pointed out, feeling like a rebellious child.

Her emotional appeal was getting nowhere. *Time to try a rational approach,* Marie thought. "You'll be going back to school next week, and he'll be here working. You'll be living over two hundred miles apart. How do you see any kind of relationship working out?"

To be honest, Diane had to admit that although she found Todd intriguing, she expected nothing more to come of their brief meeting. Resentful of her mother's interference, Diane decided she'd toy with her a little. "I thought I could drop out of school. Then I could move in with Todd."

Marie's jaw fell open and the car swerved slightly on the freeway. "Please, tell me you're not serious?"

"No, I'm not serious," Diane laughed, and thought, *Got ya, Mom.* "Actually, I don't think I'll ever see Todd again." She abruptly ended the subject of Todd, and resumed peering idly out the passenger window.

Marie's death grip on the steering wheel slowly began to loosen. But then she remembered that Diane wouldn't begin her sophomore year at college until next Monday. She'd be looking after Andrew, with Todd conveniently posted directly outside his house. Marie stole a glance at her innocent child, the one who had just tried, and failed, to deceive her. She sighed. In order to prevent Diane's infatuation with Todd from going any further, she'd need to enlist Andrew's help. Andrew could keep Todd far away from her stubborn, starry-eyed daughter.

Once it was just the two of them again, Andrew heaved an exhausted sigh of relief, even though he'd enjoyed and welcomed the pleasant distraction. It was preferable to entertain visitors than to spend the whole day attempting to ignore the elephant in the room. Tomorrow Vanessa would return to *Gemma*! It would be the longest day of his life, while he sat at home, waiting to hear her decision. Andrew loved Vanessa with all of his heart, and no matter what choice she made regarding her career, he'd do his best to understand and support her.

Preparing for bed, Vanessa hummed absently while selecting one of the new outfits that René had talked her into buying. Preoccupied with locating all of her matching accessories, she failed to notice Andrew's frown as he lay watching her warily from the bed. He marveled at how much time and effort women put into appearing 'professional.' Occasionally, Vanessa would hold up an earring or a purse and ask him, "Which one do you think looks better? The blue or the black one?" Andrew, being color-blind, had no idea, so asking him was not the best idea. Vanessa would study them for a minute, and then make up her own mind without waiting for his reply.

As entertaining as it was to watch her get ready, he could barely keep his eyes open. Vanessa, preoccupied by putting together the perfect outfit, was unaware that Andrew had fallen asleep until she heard his slow, heavy breathing. Her final selections completed, she smiled down at Andrew, and thoughtfully switched off the lights.

Later, as she lay wide-awake beside him, she smiled Cheshire-like in quiet satisfaction. René had truly transformed her look. Her youthful appearance will shock her team in the morning when she arrives sporting her perky, new hairstyle, and recently updated wardrobe.

Too pumped up with anticipation to sleep, Vanessa decided to sit out on the balcony for a few minutes with a cup of warm chamomile tea to deliberate. Callie discovered her sitting there in the warm night air and agilely jumped onto her lap. The rhythmic sounds of the ocean surf and her purring kitty, combined with a warm cup of tea, went a long way to soothe her jumbled nerves. Eventually, she returned to bed feeling calmer, thinking, *No matter what Mr. Edwards proposes tomorrow, I can handle it!*

353

In the stillness of the eternal night, Vanessa cuddled closer to Andrew while Callie curled in a ball between the curve of her legs. She inhaled contentedly, realizing how much she valued Andrew's love and support. Finally, she'd found a place where she belonged. Feeling blessed, with a relaxed, contented smile across her face, a tranquil sigh softly escaping her lips, and she drifted into a peaceful slumber.

Vanessa woke with a sudden start, convinced that she'd overslept. Moonlight streamed into the room through the french doors. Rubbing her gritty eyes, she attempted to make sense of the darkness. A quick glance at her alarm clock confirmed it was five minutes until five a.m. She'd set it for five, so she reached over and turned it off. No need to disturb Andrew's much needed rest.

She'd given herself plenty of time to prepare for her big day. Vanessa paused, spending a few precious moments to watch Andrew as he slept peacefully beside her. Slipping quietly out of bed, using the moonlight to guide her, she tiptoed out the bedroom door. Closing the door softly, she flipped on the lights at the top of the stairs, making a beeline to the kitchen below.

A fortifying cup of coffee before her, Vanessa sat at the dining room table, carefully reviewing the handwritten notes she'd made over the weekend. She hoped Mr. Edwards would allow her to select her own replacement as head of advertising without interference. Leaning back in her chair, she mentally repeated, *I'm ready, I'm strong, and I will crush this*! She utilized the power of positive affirmations that she'd remembered from a confidence seminar she attended years ago in order to prepare for this morning's meeting with the formidable, Mr. Edwards.

Glancing at Andrew's driftwood wall clock, she gulped down her coffee. Tom should be dropping Diane off in about an hour. Even the mere thought of food made her stomach flip-flop, so with a fresh cup of coffee securely in hand, she ran back up the stairs to Andrew's bedroom.

An hour later she emerged from the bathroom showered, buffed, dressed, and ready to face the day. A fully awake Andrew sat propped up in bed. He looked her over, from the top of her fluffy short hair, to the tips of her sexy, periwinkle blue high heels, and a sensual smile of pure male appreciation materialized on his face.

"Very impressive, Ms. Golden," he growled. The timber of his voice made Vanessa want to crawl back into bed with him, curl up, and forget all about going to *Gemma*. But her dress might wrinkle, or the makeup that she'd just spent forever perfecting, might smear, so she simply smiled back at him and curtsied. "Thank you, kind sir."

Andrew climbed leisurely out of bed, intending to walk past her to the bathroom. Unable to resist the glowing blush on her face, he bent over to brush the softest whisper of a kiss across her ruby red lips. She remained transfixed, staring longingly at the bathroom door long after he'd gently closed it, feeling lonely the moment his masculine form disappeared from her sight. The tenderness of his kiss had left her trembling with desire, instantly erasing all thoughts of *Gemma* or Mr. Edwards.

A moment later, Vanessa shook her head to snap out of her trance. Andrew opened the door again to discover she hadn't moved from the spot where he'd left her. The frowning, bewildered look she sent him melted his heart.

"Come here." Andrew reached for her with his good arm, and Vanessa walked willingly into his comforting embrace. His slow, sensual massage of her upper back while holding her loosely against him, both comforted and confused her. He possessed the ability to magically infuse some of his own personal strength and power into her body, with only his mere touch. Although his wife had never worked, Andrew had learned how to hold a woman gingerly, especially after she'd painstakingly dressed for a charity ball or special event.

"Thank you." She pulled back, stepping reluctantly out of his tender embrace. "Thank you, for your constant support. I have friends, and I have my mother, but I'd never felt such unconditional love and support until I met you. I promise I won't let you down," she whispered.

"There's nothing you could say or do today that would ever change how I feel about you. This is your decision. I'll support anything you choose." Andrew tenderly brushed a strand of hair away from her face and bent to place another soft, painfully tender kiss on her parted lips. Then he continued in a hushed, sensual tone, "Don't worry about us. We'll make it work."

"I think—now's a good time for me to leave for the office," Vanessa whispered, feeling her heart race. "If I stay, I believe it wouldn't be too long before we'd both disregard your doctor's orders." She used humor to cover her arousal. Andrew chuckled, pleased by her intimate, uninhibited response.

"I know it's asking a lot, but please trust me." She reached up and caressed the side of his face with her hand. Andrew gently removed her hand from his face, lovingly placing a kiss in the center of her sensitive palm, before lifting his beautiful blue eyes to hers.

"With my life," he whispered, ardently. Shep's deep barking suddenly dissolved the romantic spell. "Oh no, that must be Diane," Vanessa whispered. "I've got to run."

Vanessa hurried down the stairs while Andrew followed at a slow, calm pace. Diane gazed at Vanessa's light blue dress with its matching bolero jacket, and gave her a wolf whistle as she descended the stairs. Vanessa smiled briefly in response to Diane's spontaneous appreciation of the meticulously professional look that she'd spent hours creating. Then in a whirlwind of activity, Vanessa frantically gathered her papers, shoving them hastily into her briefcase. Scurrying around the room, she gave rapid-fired instructions to Diane as she moved. Andrew stood at the base of the stairs, to receive his quick air kiss on the cheek before Vanessa breezed out the door, and off to *Gemma*.

Andrew and Diane stood quietly, momentarily stunned in the wake of Vanessa's flurry. Finally, after they heard the car pull away, Diane commented, "Wow, I've never seen Vanessa look so—incredible, and so official."

Andrew looked toward the door and smiled, knowing he'd given Vanessa something to ponder. "Have you eaten?" he asked. "Should we order something? Or, see what we can find in the kitchen?"

Willing her frazzled nerves to slowly settle, Vanessa eased back in the car. It would be a long ride to *Gemma*, and having nothing to work on to occupy her time, she leaned back against her seat and closed her eyes. Her mind tossed and tumbled as she imagined the consequences of each of the different decisions she'd been contemplating. But, even after a long, painfully quiet ride, when they pulled in front of *Gemma,* her final decision eluded her.

Getting off the elevator, she walked past the many small offices on the way to her spacious corner office, just as she had every day for years. Today however, she noticed the strained, serious faces of her coworkers as they squinted at their computer screens. She heard the constant noise of the many phones ringing, the din of the copiers, and felt the underlying sense of urgency and tension in the air. She used to thrive on all of this. Why did it feel so uncomfortably chaotic today?

"Good morning, Vanessa. Wow, you look incredible!" Marie said, sitting behind her desk. She stood to welcome her back with a cheerfully quick hug. "It's so nice to have you back. You have about twenty minutes before your meeting with Mr. Edwards."

"Thank you. Will you please buzz me five minutes before the meeting?" Vanessa said, forcing a smile as she halfheartedly took the stack of messages Marie handed her.

"Certainly," Marie responded, relieved to have Vanessa back in charge. After Vanessa closed her door, Marie frowned; she'd noticed that her boss seemed unusually hesitant and uncertain when she'd relayed the routine reminders to her. She seemed thoughtful and dazed, not her normal out-going, take-charge, confident self.

Setting her briefcase down on the corner of her desk, Vanessa regarded her office with new eyes. She'd taken all of her personal items home several weeks ago to make room for Mindy. It didn't feel much like *her* office anymore. This was the room where she'd spent most of her adult life! But it felt cold and impersonal, just a bunch of functional furniture set in an empty space. She slowly walked toward the window in detached wonder. She used to love her view, but now as she looked out over the city, all she saw was unimaginably cold concrete and glass buildings. Turning back from the window, she noted files stacked on the desk, and someone else's coffee mug sitting next to her computer. It was all so surreal. Vanessa felt disconnected, out of place.

The phone buzzed. "Five minutes until your meeting, Vanessa."

"Thanks," she said, automatically. After taking a long look around the room, she thought, *this office certainly doesn't feel like mine anymore; maybe I'll go try Max's office, see if I like that one better.*

"Do you know whose files and coffee cup are on my desk?" Vanessa asked, as she casually walked past Marie's desk.

"I'm sorry. I meant to check your office this morning." Marie stood up, starting toward the office. "Those are Jack's. He's been meeting with clients in your office. I hope you don't mind?"

"That's fine, I was just curious," Vanessa nodded. "It seems I made the right choice about my replacement after all. I certainly hope Mr. Edwards agrees."

Vanessa set off down the hall toward Max's extravagant office, the one displaying the most extraordinary view in the whole building. *That view,* she thought, *could end up being mine.* Her anxious, determined footsteps traveled rapidly down the plush, carpeted hallway, past photos decorating the walls with inspiring *Gemma* magazine covers.

She vaguely noticed the frantic level of hyper-activity around her, hearing for the first time the stressed-out voices within the crowded offices. The noise of the irritating phones and copiers became annoyingly loud, but they slowly began to fade away. Her mind muted the disharmonious sounds, as she began recalling the soothing sounds of the ocean waves crashing on the shore and the scolding cry of the occasional seagull in the distance. She paused, her footsteps faltering slightly. Shocked, she realized how emotionally detached she'd become from her beloved magazine in just two short weeks. Hesitantly, she continued, gradually approaching the far end of the hall, where she would seal her fate.

"We're all so glad you're here, Vanessa," Jane said, stepping out from behind her desk to greet her. "Mr. Edwards is waiting for you."

Vanessa suddenly realized that the rest of the magazine staff was counting on her to rescue their jobs. Father Patrick's words came back to her about how her decision would affect more than just her own life. She squared her shoulders, and thought carefully about the consequences of any decision she made, and who might be hurt by it. Sucking in a deep breath, she reached for the doorknob and prepared to face her destiny.

Sitting behind Max's desk in a wheelchair, a shriveled-up old Mr. Edwards peered at her over his spectacles. She wasn't fooled by his frail appearance. She knew from previous experience how extremely intelligent, shrewd, and incredibly powerful this man was.

"Well missy, what took you so long?" he demanded.

Vanessa had known the old man for years, and she knew she'd arrived on time for their meeting. She chose to ignore his comment. Instead of feeling pity for him or taking his bait, she got right to the point. "You wished to see me, Mr. Edwards?"

"You know full well why you're here," he blustered, shaking his finger at her. "Now tell me, I've waited all this time for you to come back to work, do you plan to except my offer?" he demanded, slapping his hands down on the desk before him.

"I'm sorry, Mr. Edwards, exactly what are you offering?" Vanessa feigned ignorance while maintaining direct eye contact, and although he hadn't, she seated herself opposite him.

His beady eyes looked at her over his glasses, staring directly into her eyes. His voice became strong, firm, and deadly serious. "Don't be coy with me, Vanessa. You know exactly why you're here. I want you to take over Max's position as editor-in-chief of this magazine."

There it was. Vanessa's heart pumped louder in her ears. She had just been offered her dream job! She couldn't speak; she simply sat there stunned. For a moment she was tempted to accept his offer. Then she gazed out of the window and Andrew's face reflected back at her from the glass. She thought of the ocean, the sailboat, the life filled with the kind of love she'd always dreamed of, and suddenly all of her long-time professional ambitions dissolved. Mr. Edwards cagily watched the expressions cross her face, and worried that he might have been wrong about her aspirations.

"Stop pussy-footing around, young lady. I've known you for years, and I know exactly how much you want to take it. If you do, I'll pour as much money as you need into *Gemma*, so you can bring her back to her former glory. If you reject my offer, you'll give me no choice but to close shop and go home. Which is it going to be?"

Instead of feeling threatened or pressured by his demanding tone, Vanessa suddenly felt calm, euphoric, and confident about her final decision. She smiled and leaned back, relaxing momentarily in her chair, feeling free. She'd made up her mind at last! Any desire she had to sit behind his desk and stress day and night over *Gemma,* was gone. Her only aspiration was to spend her life loving Andrew!

Now she had to finesse Mr. Edwards in order to make things right for those she cared about; the ones she'd be leaving behind. "Mr. Edwards, may I ask you a question?"

"What! I want an answer, not a question." He slammed his fist on the table, his eyes bulging with frustration.

"Please indulge me, then I'll answer your question." She smiled sweetly.

Hearing the firm tone of Vanessa's voice, he believed she'd be just stubborn enough to refuse to answer his question until he agreed to hear her out. Curiosity got the better of him and he leaned back in his chair and impatiently waved his bony hand at her. "Very well, shoot."

"I'm not a parent, but you are," she began respectfully. "If your child falls off a horse, what do you do?"

"What on earth are you talking about, woman?" he blustered, impatiently.

"Please humor me. Answer my questions and then I'll answer yours."

"You get him right back on the horse, so he's not afraid." Mr. Edwards eyed her suspiciously. Vanessa smiled, and despite his attempt to intimidate her she continued.

"And...if your child makes a mistake at school?"

"You make sure he has enough information to know the answer next time," he exhaled in frustration.

"One more question. If a bully takes advantage of him?" she said, knowing she was pushing her luck.

"You teach him how to stand up to bullies," he said, emphatically. "Now, what exactly are we talking about, Vanessa?" His face became beet red, and Vanessa feared she might have gone too far. Since she had nothing to lose, and everything to gain, she pushed on.

"Where is your son, Max, Mr. Edwards?" Vanessa asked. "I was taught that if you make a mess, you clean it up. I believe that Max..." she paused briefly, taking a deep breath while she considered how to approach the subject diplomatically. "Max is the only one who knows how to fix this mess." She held her breath and waited anxiously for his blistering response.

But Mr. Edwards surprised her. He looked down at his desk and began shuffling papers, avoiding eye contact with her. "He's in the Bahamas with his wife, trying to repair his disastrous marriage," he said, justifying Max's untimely absence.

Vanessa already knew the answer, but hoped Mr. Edwards would realize how shortsighted he'd been. She pushed him even farther, confident with her solution. "I said I would answer your question, now here's what I propose. Get Max back here. Give him the same support that you've just offered me. It's been pointed out to me that I have about a year's worth of vacation saved up. I'm willing to work three days a week for the next three months, in order to train a replacement of my choice, and assist Max as he gets *Gemma* back on track. Then I plan to retire. I strongly suggest that you let Max come back, and repair his mistakes. Let him retire from a successful company, instead of pushing him out now, simply to punish him."

Vanessa exhaled and leaned back. She waited, fully expecting Mr. Edwards to rage in response to her outrageous suggestions. He tented his fingers in front of his face while he sat perfectly still, quietly pondering the dilemma he faced. He seemed to be seriously considering what she'd just proposed. She had banked on his vanity and his love for his son, as well as his desire to secure *Gemma's* success. His legacy.

Finally, he answered softly, "What if I reject your proposal?" He looked over his tented fingers and glared at her.

Vanessa smiled sweetly, she refused to be bullied or intimidated by him. "Then I will return to my office and have Marie type up my letter of resignation."

"You've got gumption! I've always liked that about you, Vanessa," he suddenly laughed, throwing up his hands in surrender. "You win! We'll try it your way. I'll have Max back in this chair by tomorrow morning." He abruptly leaned forward and buzzed Jane. "Get me my car," he demanded. "I'm going home."

Vanessa stood, seeing that he was finished and anxious to leave. "Thank you, Mr. Edwards, for considering me for the position," she said, formally.

"Tell me..." he smiled up at her fondly. "Didn't you want to be the head of *Gemma* magazine?" he asked, curiously. The features of his face softened as he leaned wearily back in his wheelchair. Lifting his eyes inquisitively to hers, he searched for the true motive behind her unexpected rejection of his magnanimous offer.

"Another time—I might have." She held his gaze. "I've given *Gemma* all of my heart and soul for far too many years. It's time for me to give them to someone else." She walked around the desk, bent down and kissed Max's dad on the cheek. He blushed and smiled, but tried to sound gruff and annoyed. "Well, you picked a hell of a time to fall in love!" He realized that her priorities had definitely changed and that she no longer needed *Gemma*. He'd always thought of her as the daughter he'd never had. He'd miss her, but he wished her nothing but happiness. Secretly, he was very pleased that she'd found someone to love, even though she was too late to start a family.

"Give Max a chance." Vanessa patted the gruff old man on his arm. She had always been one of the few who had suspected that he kept a heart of gold hidden behind his bluster. "I know Max. He'll come through for you," she said emphatically, feeling more than confident that she'd made the right decision for her future, and the future of *Gemma*.

Blushing and grumbling something non-coherent, he waved her away.

Walking to the door, she smiled, calling over her shoulder, "Nice to see you again, Mr. Edwards."

Before closing the door behind her, she heard him bellow, "Jane, where's my damn car?"

Jane sent her a questioning look, which Vanessa returned silently, gesturing with a reassuring thumbs-up.

With a deep sense of relief, Vanessa smiled and greeted everyone she encountered in the hallway with unusual flamboyant enthusiasm. Walking away from the magnificent office and the position she'd always coveted, she felt surprisingly light-hearted and triumphant. Rounding the corner, she found Marie waiting for her, her eyes filled with questioning concern. "What happened? Jane called and said Mr. Edwards went home. He told her to take the rest of the day off!"

"One minute, and I'll explain." Vanessa held up her hand, needing a moment alone before she could discuss what had just transpired. Her voice remained calm and reassuring as she began directing her assistant. "First, call Jack. See if he can meet with me in about an hour. Then call my lawyer. Let him know that I'll need him to draw up a new contract for me. Call the car service. Inform them that I'll be leaving at four today. When you're done, come into my office. I'll tell you everything."

Vanessa's instructions rang out in a commanding tone, and Marie concentrated on keeping up. Vanessa seemed flushed and excited, more like her typical take-charge self. Marie smiled; this felt like the boss she'd known and loved all these years, and she felt sure that she'd just taken orders from the new editor-in-chief of *Gemma*.

Vanessa picked up the files and coffee cup that Marie had previously removed from her desk, and carried them purposefully back into the barren office that had once been hers. Seated in the leather chair, she swiveled toward the window. Gazing out at the familiar view, she frowned, experiencing a brief, bittersweet feeling of regret. Then she thought of Andrew, and her expression softened. *Changing of the guard*, she thought happily. She spun her chair around, and joyfully called Marie back into her office.

Chapter 34
Proposals

M ax loved his wife, but he'd had about all of their 'togetherness' he could stand. He wasn't used to spending every minute of every day with his beloved wife, Kitty. One more week of this farce, he thought, I can manage one more week.

Max's father had made two things quite clear; he had been permanently relieved from his position at Gemma, and he was expected to patch up his relationship with Kitty. If he elected to disobey his father, the consequences would prove to be enormously expensive. His father had coldly informed him that if he failed to repair his marriage, he would have his lawyers change his will, disinheriting Max, and leaving his entire estate to Kitty instead.

This two-week honeymoon in the Bahamas had been one of his father's dictates. Max counted his lucky stars that Kitty had gone along with his father's decree, and that she apparently had no idea of the financial power she held over his head.

So…relieved of his duties to Gemma, they'd flown off blissfully together to this exclusive, secluded Bahamian resort the following week. The private jet had landed just in time for them to share an elegant dinner on the terrace of their suite, compliments of his father. Since their arrival, Max had suffered through couple's massages, a dinner-dancing cruise, scuba diving, snorkeling, and a helicopter tour of the nearby islands. All of these activities had occurred during their first week at the resort. Kitty, the consummate tourist, had planned even more elaborate excursions, packing every activity she could find into next week's itinerary.

Today, Max trailed behind his wife, carting her purchases like a pack mule. He'd been pulled from store to store all morning. One helpful clerk gave his wife directions to an open-air market in a nearby plaza. So, he quietly followed his wife into a local, culturally colorful plaza. The magnificent fountain made of opaque blue dolphins rested in the center of the plaza. Scattered around the opulent fountain were a sizeable number of eclectic open-air stands, peddling everything imaginable.

His wife had immediately been attracted to a nearby vendor selling vibrant silk scarfs, and she rushed toward them eagerly, while Max slowly meandered behind her. Normally he hated shopping and would have preferred relaxing at the hotel instead, but he knew that accommodating all of Kitty's wants and desires was part of a necessary tactic to win back *her undying affection. He had a lot of neglect to make up for, and a whole lot to lose if he failed.*

As Max followed Kitty like a loyal puppy, he slowly gazed around the square as a distraction from his wife's enthusiastic shopping spree. The humidity felt uncomfortably high, with the temperature reaching a balmy one hundred degrees. Max smiled, watching as the local children amused themselves, laughing and splashing as they played in the spewing cool water of the fountain. Looking around the plaza, he calculated the number of vendors in the tiny square to be approximately fifty. Each booth was packed with diverse, brightly dressed tourists, along side of the locals. He wiped his brow with the back of his hand, feeling unpleasantly hot and sticky, sincerely hoping that Kitty would tire of shopping soon.

Max had momentarily lost sight of his wife and he paused, scanning the crowds for Kitty. Out of the corner of his eye he caught a mere glimpse of a familiar figure rushing away from him. He quickly located his wife, and then rushing to her side, he unceremoniously dropped the shopping bags down at her feet in a desperate attempt to follow the rapidly disappearing figure.

"I'll be right back," he said, anxiously. Kitty looked up briefly in confusion, but shifted her focus back to shopping, as a woman held up a beautifully handcrafted scarf.

Max dodged his way in and out of the crowded square. He'd know that body anywhere. It had to be Mindy! His heart beat faster, excitement surged through him and he felt more alive than he had all week. He searched the crowd frantically. Where had she gone? In desperation, he jumped up on the edge of the fountain amidst the playing children. From his viewpoint he could see the entire marketplace. He was determined to find Mindy. 'She didn't have to leave me holding the bag at Gemma,' he thought, 'I'd have gladly gone away with her.'

Kitty, who'd just bought what she thought was the perfect scarf, stood looking curiously across the plaza, wondering idly about Max's bizarre behavior. Spotting him in the middle of the plaza, she watched as a disappointed Max carefully stepped off the edge of the fountain and walked back toward her dragging his feet. It appeared he'd been searching for something or someone. His eyes continued to search the crowds as he approached her. Kitty shook her head, perplexed by his behavior. "Max? What on earth are you doing?"

Max bent down to begrudgingly retrieve her purchases, feeling extremely disappointed and frustrated. Before he could muster up a logical response to Kitty's question, his phone rang. They both knew by the obnoxious ring tone, that his father was calling. He hesitated, reluctant to answer; his father was the last person he wanted to talk to right now.

Kitty rolled her eyes and piped up sarcastically. "You'd better answer that, you wouldn't want to upset him." Kitty resented his father's interference in her life. She could care less about what his father had to say. Turning away, she wandered to another stand selling vibrantly garish, oversized catchall bags, leaving Max to deal with his father on his own.

Kitty had just put away her wallet, feeling pleased with the three bags she'd purchased, when Max returned to her side.

"Well, we have to go pack. It seems I'm being summoned back to the States. Our plane will be at the airport in approximately three hours."

Kitty, furious by his father's interference once again, became incensed. She'd been having the best time with Max, and she still had all kinds of plans for them. 'His father is always doing this,' she thought.

"Oooh Max, do we have to go now? I signed us up for a bike tour early tomorrow morning."

Max wanted to stay on the island to look for Mindy, but he was relieved to put an end to Kitty's constant tourist activities. Now that he finally had a solid lead on Mindy, he planned to send a private investigator back to find her. Satisfied by the turn of events, he returned his attention back to his sulking wife.

"I know. I'm sorry, but my dad wants me to return to Gemma first thing tomorrow. He's suddenly convinced that I'm the only one who can repair the damage to our reputation. He said he's expecting me to restore his precious magazine to its former glory. So, it seems my retirement was a bit premature; instead he's decided retirement will have to wait until I accomplish everything that he wants from me first."

Kitty scowled. She'd been waiting years to have her husband's undivided attention. She finally thought she had Max all to herself. 'Now he's going back to Gemma, it was so unfair!' "No!" she said, stomping her feet like a petulant child. "I can't take it anymore. I won't go back to a life where you're gone all the time. I refuse to sit home all alone waiting for you another minute."

Max panicked at her response. He had to appease her quickly, and so he said the first thing that popped into his head. He took her gently by the shoulders, kissing her seductively. He hadn't forgotten how to be charming when the need arose. He gazed sincerely into her eyes as he spoke. "I promise this time things will be different. I love you, Kitty, and I'll never risk losing you again."

Max could tell he had her by the love-struck look in his adoring wife's eyes. He grabbed her hand, pulling her forcefully through the crowd, calling to her over his shoulder, "Let's hurry, we have to pack, and I'm starving." Back in control, Max felt more like himself than he had in a long time.

Vanessa sat back in her seat. It was only four o'clock and she was on her way home to Andrew. A smiled slowly formed on her lips, as she thought, *I did it! I seized control!* She'd made her final decision at last. She had signed the draft of her new contract by noon, and Marie personally delivered it to HR minutes later. Taking a deep breath, she exhaled slowly as she reviewed the events of the day.

Jack had been thrilled to receive confirmation of his promotion. He knew he had been in line for it, but he hugged her ecstatically when Vanessa made it official. Jane, obviously relieved that old Mr. Edwards had departed for good, seemed unexpectedly happy to have Max returning. Marie remained distressed about Vanessa's impending retirement, but wished her the best. Marie appreciated that she'd be working with Jack, if she couldn't have Vanessa. He was respectful, kind, and easy to work with. Jack likewise recognized Marie as an asset, and begged her to stay on as his assistant. Vanessa had single-handedly saved everyone's positions at *Gemma*, including Max's. And, although Andrew was still in the dark about her ultimate decision, she had no doubt that he'd be happy too. Especially when she explained her new schedule, not to mention her upcoming retirement.

A huge sigh of relief slowly escaped her lips. *Father Patrick will be so proud of me.* She'd managed to give everyone what he or she wanted. Closing her eyes, Vanessa allowed herself a quiet moment of private remorse. She'd just willingly walked away from the one position she'd always dreamed of acquiring at *Gemma*.

As the car drew closer to Andrew's house, she became more and more convinced that she'd made the right decision. It was time to turn her devotions away from *Gemma*, and toward a happy, satisfying life with Andrew. *Gemma* represented her contented past, while Andrew represented her hopes for a joyful future. She'd always dreamed of a life with a man who'd constantly shower her with unconditional love. The prestige of heading *Gemma* couldn't compare to the full-hearted feeling of sharing her love with Andrew.

As the car pulled into the driveway, she could hardly wait to talk to him. Breezing into the house, she was surprised to find Diane soaking in the pool, and Todd sitting in a chair beside her. Todd leapt to his feet when he heard Vanessa approach.

"Relax Todd, it's good to see you're here entertaining Diane," Vanessa said kindly, before turning to address Diane. "The car is waiting for you outside. How did Andrew manage today?"

Diane hoisted herself out of the pool and began towel drying off, quickly throwing a sundress on over her revealing bathing suit. "Oh, I don't know, he spent most of the day upstairs talking on the phone. I feel kind of guilty. He didn't really need me to do much of anything for him today."

"That's fine," Vanessa replied offhandedly, smiling at her direct honesty. "I appreciate that you were here in case he needed some help."

Vanessa politely excused herself. Smiling, she lightly climbed the stairs to Andrew. *Apparently, he'd spent the entire day brooding in his room,* she mused, and toyed with the idea of torturing him a little longer. But she quickly changed her mind. Tonight, they would celebrate their love and commitment, and the beginning of their new life together!

Hearing Vanessa downstairs talking to Diane, Andrew slowly closed the lid on the box containing the diamond ring set he'd been contemplating for the past hour. The wedding rings had belonged to his favorite grandmother. When he'd married Grace, her father had insisted he buy her a particular wedding set from a famous jeweler in Paris. Andrew had felt resentful at the time, but now he was glad. Although he'd loved Grace, his grandmother's rings were special to him. They were meant for Vanessa! The love of his life! He returned the rings to his dresser drawer. *Now is not the right time to propose,* he decided. He'd be patient and wait until Vanessa gave him a sign that she'd be open to the idea, and ready to commit to a permanent relationship with him.

Vanessa knocked softly on the doorframe. Walking into the room, she found Andrew standing with his hand on the top dresser drawer. She was surprised by the somber look on his face, but his eyes immediately lit up at the sight of her, and a wide, genuine smile crossed his face. "You're home early. Is that a good sign?"

The hopeful sound of his voice tore at her heart. It had been unfair for her to keep him out of the loop, waiting at home in suspense. Stepping closer, she placed her arms around his neck, gazed deeply into his

367

beautiful blue eyes, and declared softly, "I did it!"

"Exactly what did you do?" Andrew frowned, holding her close with his good arm, suddenly fearing the worst-case scenario.

"I turned down the position of editor-in-chief, hired my replacement, and told them I plan to retire in three months," she said, beaming as brightly as the warm sunshine that filled the room.

Andrew wrapped his strong arm around her waist and swung Vanessa around in circles, laughing exuberantly. "I—love—you—so much!" He set her down, holding her close to him. Bending down, he slowly kissed her and then, reigning in his excitement, he pulled back. Reaching up, he tenderly caressed the side of her face. "Will you be all right? Is this what you truly want?"

Breathlessly leaning toward Andrew's body, Vanessa sensed the uncertainty in his questions. He needed to know the truth of why she'd decided to throw away her career at *Gemma,* choosing to be with him instead. Gazing up into his crystal blue eyes, she answered him sincerely. "I'll admit, I've always dreamed of running *Gemma. You* changed me. The thought of sitting day by day inside a stuffy office has lost its appeal. I'd rather be outside, sailing with you! When Mr. Edwards offered me the position, all I thought about was *you.* I don't need a job filled with stress and insurmountable obstacles to overcome. I only need *you,*" she whispered, wrapping her arms lovingly around him, nestling her head against his firm chest. Her eyes began spontaneously watering, filling with sentimentally inspired tears as she listened to the steady rhythm of his heartbeat. *Life is too short,* she thought silently, *and I don't want to miss one moment of sharing it with this man.*

Stunned, Andrew felt honored by Vanessa's confession. They remained motionless, standing within an all encompassing, quiet, whole-hearted embrace. The front of his shirt began warming with her wet, silent tears as he carefully gathered his thoughts enough to respond. Gently kissing the top of her head, he nuzzled at her ear. "I promise you, I'll do everything within my power to make sure you never regret your decision today."

She lifted her head and smiled, reassuring him, "You don't need to make promises to me. I never felt pressured by you. This is totally my choice, and whatever happens between us from now on, is on me."

Andrew didn't agree with her last statement, but no matter, she'd picked him and he was thrilled. He lifted the hem of his t-shirt and tenderly wiped her wet face. Then he kissed her passionately, physically marking the beginning of their new, exhilarating life.

That night, both feeling emotionally drained, they decided to relax and celebrate at an elegant, coastal seafood restaurant. Sitting alone at an intimate corner table by the window, Vanessa and Andrew enjoyed the quiet, relaxed atmosphere. They had a charming view of the old lighthouse, reflecting its light eerily out on the dark ocean, illuminating the mossy rocks far below. Andrew had called ahead to reserve all of the remaining tables, so they sat cozily in the room by themselves. Tonight, he wanted all of Vanessa's attention on him.

Watching her closely with quiet consideration, he smiled affectionately as she excitedly recounted her meeting with Mr. Edwards. He loved the way her eyes danced in the candlelight as she relayed the more amusing details of her conversation with the wily old man, expanding briefly on the remainder of her extraordinary day at *Gemma*. Mesmerized by her intelligence and business savvy, Andrew sat hypnotized by her sparkling eyes and quick smile. He briefly wondered how he'd succeeded in capturing such an incredibly beautiful woman to share his life. Vanessa noticed the adoring look on Andrew's face and wrapped up her story. Reaching for her hand, he looked into her eyes and they locked gazes as the cozy room filled with the soft sounds of a romantic violin concerto. When the champagne arrived, they sipped silently while they continued gazing lovingly into each other's eyes. The secretive smiles they shared, hinting at a playfully, loving future together.

After what seemed like an eternity, they broke eye contact and Vanessa slowly set down her glass, ready for a change of subject. Curious, she wondered whom Andrew had spent the day talking with on the phone. "So...Diane tells me you spent most of today on the phone. Anything important?"

"Actually, I talked to quite a few people today. Mike called first thing this morning. I'm to appear at a ceremony this Friday. Would you care to accompany me and be my date?" Andrew reached across the table to hold her hand and rub his thumb in circles over her wrist, waiting for her answer.

"I'm very proud of you, and I'd be honored to attend as your date."

"I also had an interesting call from Diane's mother today."

"Really, what did Marie want?"

"She asked me about Todd." He smiled and raised an eyebrow. "I told her that Todd checks out, he's a good guy." Andrew shrugged. "He's a little insecure because his father left the force under questionable circumstances, but no one seems to have a bad word to say about him."

Vanessa wondered if Marie had mentioned anything else to Andrew. "She didn't tell you about my meeting with Mr. Edwards this morning, did she?"

"I swear, she didn't tell me anything." Andrew laughed, and held his hand up to make the Boy Scout's sign with his fingers. "When we last talked, she'd been anxiously waiting for your return. Honestly, I spent the whole day in suspense."

Andrew paused as he began eating his salad that had just been served. "And...Haley's mother called this afternoon." He swallowed. "She's concerned that Haley's having trouble adjusting to the number of people in the house, the rules, her lack of privacy, and her isolation. She refuses to talk to any of her old friends. Instead she stays in her room all day, complaining about her siblings, and her parents' interference in her life."

Andrew could see the look of concern in Vanessa eyes. He inwardly cursed himself for interrupting their intimate, celebratory dinner with concerns about Haley.

"It's only been a few days; don't you think she'll adjust eventually?" Vanessa asked, calmly setting down her fork.

"Time will tell," he said dismissively, before changing the topic back to them. Vanessa simply nodded silently, wishing she could do something to help Haley.

"Let's put Haley on the back burner for now." Andrew suggested. "We're here to celebrate *our* future," he said, lifting his glass to salute her.

"All right." She lifted her own glass in response. Her eyes drifted out at the dark ocean below, before returning to gaze at Andrew's sincere expression. His eyes seemed to penetrate hers before he spoke reverently.

"I can't believe I found you again, after so many years apart. The wild attraction I'd felt for you so many years ago sprang to life again the minute I saw you standing in your doorway. You've haunted my dreams, and now, I can't imagine my life without you." He reached across to her, needing to touch her, to convince him that she wasn't merely a dream, but real, and actually here with him.

Vanessa smiled, tenderly cradling his searching hand intimately within her own. She knew she would never regret her decision to spend her life with him. She had high expectations for a lasting, loving relationship with this sexy man. He was the first man she'd trusted with her heart in many years, and she believed in him. Andrew could never betray her faith in him.

Being old-fashioned, Andrew wanted to ask her to marry him right then and there, but was afraid of scaring her away, so he settled for inviting her to live with him instead. "Vanessa Golden, I'd like to formally invite you to move in with me." His smooth, sensual tone spoke volumes regarding his intentions.

"Hum... I thought you already had?" she smiled, evasively.

"You originally moved in for my protection. Now, I asking you to live with me, permanently," he clarified, his voice low, soft, sexy, and suggestive. He turned her hand over in his as if he had just proposed to her.

The word *permanently* sent shivers of anticipation through Vanessa's body. *This is serious*, she thought. At least he wasn't proposing, she gently tugged her hand out of his and rested it primly in her lap. *It was much too soon for that!* She'd just assumed they'd live together, but now that he'd asked her in such a formal manner, she paused, wondering what he expected. She broke eye contact with him and glanced nervously around the room, chewing on her lower lip while she considered the meaning behind his words.

"You know...I promised to remain at *Gemma* for the next three months," she said, stalling for time. Searching his eyes, she leaned away from him, her hands safely in her lap.

"I'm well aware of the commitment you made earlier today. Believe me, it did not escape my attention. Will you move in with me? Even though *Gemma* will have your days for the time being, will you spend your nights sleeping beside me?" he leaned across the table, his sparkling blue eyes conveying his consuming need for her.

"I can think of nowhere else I'd rather be," she answered confidently, touched by his sincerity and realizing she needed him every bit as much as he needed her. Her misty eyes glistened in the candlelight as she professed, "I'll lay beside you each night and we can spend every weekend sailing until my time is up at *Gemma*. Then I'll be all yours." Having made her commitment to him, she exhaled a sigh of relief and reached over to caress his hand.

Exhaling the breath he'd been holding, he smiled, raised her hand to his lips and proceeded to kiss each of her fingertips. "Thank you," he whispered.

Her delightfully sentimental agreement meant the world to him. Feeling relieved and contented by Vanessa's answer, Andrew clarified another pressing issue. "Since you brought up sailing, I assume I now have every weekend to teach you to sail?"

"You know, I really love you, Andrew Kelly," she said, smiling. Her amused laughter bubbled joyously to the surface, breaking into the hushed, mellow atmosphere of the quiet restaurant. Maybe someday his love of sailing would capture her heart as well.

"I love you too, Vanessa Golden," Andrew said formally, before grinning humbly, and sharing her amusement and joy.

At that moment, delectable lobster and crab dinners arrived. Andrew couldn't remember when he'd felt so relaxed and enchanted by his dinner companion. He comfortably began regaling Vanessa with the beginnings of an enthusiastic crash course on sailing for the remainder of their meal. Just talking about the wind billowing in the sails, and the exhilaration of riding swiftly across the ocean with the thrill of untamed water surging beneath the hull, caused his eyes to dance with excitement.

While Andrew chatted merrily, passionately recounting the many techniques for sailing, try as she may, she couldn't concentrate. She smiled and nodded, but remained distractedly lost in her own contented thoughts. The man sitting across from her seemed too wonderful to be true. *My life is absolutely perfect now,* Vanessa thought. *I finally have everything I've ever dreamed of.* Sitting deep in contemplation, completely unaware of the slight crease in the middle of her forehead, Andrew immediately noticed her consternation. Covertly watching her ever-expressive eyes, he carefully read her unspoken thoughts. Although he rattled on, he observed Vanessa, as she unintentionally glanced down toward her left hand resting on the table, fixing her gaze on her naked ring finger. Andrew wondered if she'd been disappointed that he hadn't asked her to marry him, but Vanessa was simply thinking. *Maybe someday... I'll be brave enough to try marriage once again.*

Epilogue

M indy ducked out of sight from Max and hastily ran down the
*dock. She jumped into a small motorboat and sped across the
water to a luxurious white seventy-foot yacht. She kept frantically looking
behind her, as if she were being chased by demons. Tying off the small boat
to the back of the yacht, she scrambled up the ladder, struggling with the
large, cumbersome duffle bag slung across her back.*

*Walking into the opulent stateroom, she found Stephen, sitting in front
of his opened laptop, a silver beer stein in hand. Mindy dropped the duffle
bag at his feet and plopped down into the closest chair, struggling to catch
her breath.*

"You'll—never—guess—who I just saw," she panted.

*"I prefer not to guess, just tell me." Stephen peered over the top of his
computer screen, his spectacles pushed low across his pointed nose.*

*Winded, Mindy blurted out her shocking news. "Max, I just saw Max!"
Stephen set the computer next to him on the cherry wood table, and sipped
his beer thoughtfully.*

"Did he see you?" he asked, impatiently.

*"I don't think so." Mindy shook her head. "I ran as soon as I spotted him.
He's here with his wife, so I doubt they're looking for us."*

*"That's the beauty of staying on the yacht, we can simply leave. Did you
get all the money from the bank?" Stephen asked, peering inside the duffle.*

*"It's all in there," Mindy indicated with a wave of her hand. "I thought
there'd be more."*

*Stephen leaned back and sipped his beer again as he thought back over
the painful years he'd spent preparing for this day. A child computer whiz,
he'd spent his youth breaking through firewalls for fun. He'd barely
tolerated his simpering wife and whiny child; they were simply a means to
an end, helping to create his image. He'd developed the illusion of a "family
man," and had easily climbed the rungs of the corporate ladder, rapidly
reaching his goal of acquiring the highest level of Internet security access.
He frowned down into his beer. Now he was officially a criminal
mastermind, too clever and untraceable to ever get caught. He didn't need
them anymore; in fact he didn't need anyone!*

*"There will be a lot more cash when we get to the bank on the
Caymans," Stephen said, pacifying his temporary partner. "There'd been a
little less this time, because some of the companies discovered my spyware
and set up new firewalls. The next bank will have considerably more. It*

contains the money I siphoned the first few days, long before anyone knew what had happened." He set his beer aside and got to his feet. *"I'll move the boat to the next island, and we'll take off for the Caymans at first light tomorrow."*

Mindy watched Stephen leave the room. Then she dashed down the hall to her bedroom. She was grateful that Stephen had insisted they have separate sleeping quarters. She didn't like or trust Stephen. He'd made her take all the risks, while arrogantly believing he was the brains behind the operation.

They'd bought the yacht with cash in Florida. Stephen made Mindy sign all the paperwork, registering the boat under her own newly assumed deceased cousin's name. Stephen had always sent Mindy to retrieve the cash from the various banks. He claimed it made her a valuable partner. Once they'd withdrawn the last of the cash, Mindy knew he'd consider her a dispensable liability. She had no plans of conveniently becoming lost at sea, and had purchased a small handgun for protection. She'd been so preoccupied with concealing her new weapon that she'd nearly bumped right into Max, and his simpering wife!

* * * * *

Max frequently relived the day he'd caught a glimpse of Mindy in the midst of the busy open-air market in the Bahamas. It had been six months since that day and Max's detectives hadn't been able to locate any trace of Mindy in the Bahamas, or anywhere else. No sign of the cyber-criminals, Mindy and Stephen, had surfaced anywhere, and his detectives finally convinced him to give up his search. But although Max had put his heart and soul into reviving Gemma, he couldn't stop thinking about Mindy, or what could have been.

* * * * *

Meanwhile, on a tiny South America island, Kate rolled over in her crumpled sheets, a fan swooshing overhead. Brad still slept soundly on his belly, facing away from her, the sheet partially covering his muscular, beautifully naked body. Kate slipped out of the bed unnoticed, grabbing her short, silky robe off the floor, and making a beeline straight to her bathroom without looking back. Last night had been another one of many long, hot, sensually steamy nights with Brad. All Kate wanted now was a

374

strong cup of coffee and a few precious moments alone. Descending the cool marble stairs, she made her way into her impressively large kitchen. Within minutes she sat outside in a comfy wicker chair on her veranda with steam rising from a clear glass mug of black coffee. Kate watched in fascination as dense, dark clouds sped across the gloomy sky. She felt no sense of dread or apprehension, simply curiosity and wonder at the dark shapes forming above her.

Kate and Brad had been inseparable for the past six months, ever since the night they'd first met at his 'aunt's' party. They'd spent countless intimate hours getting to know each other and sharing their beloved childhood memories. But neither of them had been totally truthful. Especially not regarding the unusual events that had led each to their mysterious arrivals on the tiny, secluded island. Fortunately, Brad's 'aunt' had decided, just this once, that it might be in her best interest to be discreet. She was keeping both of their secrets safe, at least for the time being.

Brad knew Kate had been lying to him; he also knew why she had to lie. Following Kate had become far more of a pleasure than a job for Brad. But for the past few weeks, his superiors had begun pressuring him to produce some concrete evidence against Kate, or risk being replaced. He couldn't, wouldn't allow anyone else to take his place, not with his Kate.

Brad had actually been awake when Kate left the room. Watching her now from the upstairs window, he could tell she'd settled comfortably on the open veranda below. The darkening sky caught his attention, and he watched with growing alarm the threatening clouds, and stormy, high waters below. Brad had been given a rare opportunity that he couldn't pass up, but he only had a few minutes before he'd need to hustle the blissfully unaware Kate into a safe shelter, before the rapidly brewing storm hit the island.

Moving quickly, Brad carefully lifted the white framed, seascape painting that hung directly over Kate's massive bed. He cracked open the hidden safe behind the painting in a matter of seconds and peered inside. Shaking his head in incredulity, he couldn't believe how careless Kate had been. The bills sported their original wrappers labeled "Bitton Bank" still secured around each stack. Removing one of the incriminating wrappers, he replaced the loosened, unmarked bills under the bottom stack in the back of the safe. Carefully he closed the safe, returned the painting, and bent down to stuff the wrapper he'd removed into the pocket of his nearby cut-off shorts. Sliding his loose shorts over his naked body, not bothering *with much else, he headed downstairs. Hair bed-tousled, chest shirtless, and barefoot, he joined Kate outside on the veranda below.*

Standing silently in front of Kate, he looked down affectionately into her tranquil, unsuspecting eyes. Pleased to see him, she smiled up at him in greeting. Reaching down for her hand, Brad returned her smile. He could tell by the musty smell of the air that they were in for a wickedly fierce storm, very soon. "A storm's coming," he said. "Let's lock up and take shelter."

* * * * *

Haley opened the gate that led to the beach to happily romp along the seashore with Shep. She'd arrived several days ago to housesit, while Andrew and Vanessa sailed down the Mexican coast, toward the tip of South America.

The past six months had been a struggle for Haley. The first week she'd arrived home, her mother had lost her home clothing design business. Fortunately, she had also received another employment offer, one with higher pay and benefits. The difficulty arose when her new position required her mother to go into an office downtown daily, to work closely with a full team of designers. Although she thought she could handle the time away from home, her regular nanny got married unexpectedly, leaving for an extended honeymoon, and suddenly leaving her without childcare.

Unable to find a suitable replacement for her long-time nanny, her mother offered Haley the position. She reassured Haley that for most of the day her siblings would be in school, including her baby brother, who'd just started nursery school. In exchange for Haley's help, her mother agreed to pay for the online GED course that Haley had asked for. They moved Haley out of her baby brother's room and into her mother's now vacant office, and bought her a used car. The gift of the car had been contingent on Haley passing all of her courses, remaining dependable, and obtaining her driver's license.

Haley had easily met all of her obligations over the past six months. She'd completed her GED in record time, passed her driving test on the first attempt, and had been an excellent, reliable nanny.

She'd also worked hard to reconnect personally with each and every member of her large family, just as Vanessa had asked. But, after six months, although she loved them all dearly, she knew she couldn't continue to live with them. Haley admired her mother, but she had no desire to live her mother's life. Tired of being a nanny, she became impatient and anxious to find her own way in the world.

Informing her parents of her plans to leave had been difficult. She'd assured them that she'd remain in close contact, and once she'd heard about Andrew and Vanessa's plans for an extended sailing trip to South America, she immediately offered her services to housesit. As it happened, her mother's previous nanny had just returned to live close-by, the timing fit perfectly. The car her parents had bought for her could easily make the trip to California. Despite returning to the area where Jimmy had tortured her and held her captive, she felt confident, especially since he was no longer a threat, and she'd be perfectly safe with Vanessa, Andrew, Diane, and Father Patrick. With so much support, she believed it would be a good place to begin her new life on her own.

As Haley drove past the exit that led to the dilapidated apartment she'd shared with Jimmy, she held her breath and cringed. Arriving at Andrew's house felt safe, like coming home again. Vanessa welcomed Haley with open arms, moving her back into her old room downstairs and eagerly helping her to settle in. Haley's ankle had healed nicely, and she looked forward to swimming and running along the beach.

Vanessa, delighted by the way Haley had worked things out with her family, helped Haley register at the local community college for the fall, and Andrew gladly welcomed Haley to his home. He respected that she'd stuck it out with her family, and insisted on paying her generously for housesitting, claiming it was his way of "investing" in her educational pursuits.

Even though he'd retired, Andrew had kept track of Todd. One perk of being a retired detective was the continued patrol of his residence during his absence. He requested that Todd be a part of his surveillance detail during their trip. He knew if Todd were around, Diane would also be a regular visitor. Despite Marie's objections, Todd and Diane had developed close ties. Haley was overjoyed at the idea of spending time with Diane, even if it meant she had to share Diane's attention with Todd.

Father Patrick had checked in briefly before Andrew and Vanessa set sail, to wish them happy sailing, and say goodbye. He'd spent time with Haley, and had even video chatted with her parents, giving them proper assurances that he would watch over her. Haley had always appreciated the Father's uncanny ability to read her innermost thoughts and fears, magically appearing to provide her with comfort whenever she needed it most. She promised to faithfully attend his tiny church on the bluff during her stay at Andrew's.

Enjoying an absolutely perfect, sunny day at the beach, Haley inhaled deeply, filling her lungs with the moist, warm, sea air she'd been craving. Shep happily romped and played in the surf, while Callie trotted slowly behind, delicately picking her way through the dry sand with quiet dignity and disdain. Haley threw the ball for Shep, feeling pleased that she'd gone home and been able to spend time with her family for a while. She exhaled and laughed, ecstatic to be back, feeling free. Peacefully on her own at last!

* * * * *

Somewhere down the Mexican coastline, Vanessa sat in the stern of the gently rocking sailboat, relaxing on soft overstuffed cushions with her face tilted up to the warm sun. She leaned her head back, drinking in the radiant sunshine, inhaling the fresh, salty air.

The first couple of days on the boat had been exceedingly rough. To Vanessa's embarrassment, it had seemed an eternity before she acquired her sea legs, along with a strong sea-worthy stomach. Seasickness had caught her off guard. Their previous one-day sailing trips hadn't bothered her, not like this trip. Andrew had fussed over her and catered to her every desire. He'd even adjusted his meticulous timetable, allowing her to spend as much time on shore as she needed. But she'd finally acclimated, and declared herself a sturdy sailor, capable of fully enjoying her sailing adventure with Andrew. Tonight, she was determined to sleep onboard the rocking boat all night long. Not wimp out and beg for solid ground in a hotel on land, which she had done every night since they'd left home.

The past six months had turned out much different than Vanessa had originally pictured in her mind. First off, she'd had to convince Max that she had a limited timeline, and if he didn't sign her new contract, she'd simply quit. Max had tried countless strategies to convince Vanessa to stay on full time. He'd been counting heavily on Vanessa's help. But

Vanessa had stuck to her guns. Exasperated, Max had switched his strategy from coercing, to threatening Vanessa with breach of her previous contract. Finally, she'd heard enough out of him, and in utter frustration, she informed him coldly that he'd receive her letter of resignation that very day.

Max realized that he had lost the fight, and that part of Vanessa was better than none. Before Vanessa had reached her office, he'd sheepishly called Marie. He asked Marie to inform Vanessa that he'd send her the signed copy of her new contract immediately, and promptly booked a four-hour meeting with Vanessa for the following day.

After their initial blow up, Max and Vanessa had worked in perfect synchrony. They had a comprehensive plan to improve *Gemma's* sales within the first week, including its projected price tag.

Max had insisted that Vanessa come with him when he met with Mr. Edwards. His father seemed thrilled by the new plan, and immediately handed them a check to finance the full amount. The stunned look on Max's face as he shook hands with his challenging father made Vanessa smile. But she'd also noticed the obvious pride for Max glowing in Mr. Edward's eyes. Covertly, while Max had his back turned, Mr. Edwards smiled and winked at her. She smiled back and shrugged her shoulders, indicating to him that she'd known all along that Max could handle *Gemma's* resurrection, given the chance. On the way back to the office, Max kept repeating how easy things had gone with his father. She simply smiled; father and son had clearly reached a new level of understanding, and discovered a newfound respect for one another.

Her old advertising team had grown, and had been reshaped. They'd recovered old accounts, and brought in new ones. Their plans showed early indicators of success under Jack's superb leadership as the new advertising director. Vanessa left him alone to lead the new team, and spent most of her working hours supporting Max.

As the time drew near for Vanessa's retirement, Max began pitching new ideas to her. All of which had subtle undertones to keep Vanessa working, and readily accessible to him. Max counted on her, and he freely acknowledged how she'd helped him to develop *Gemma's* winning business strategy. Panicking as Vanessa's time grew shorter, Max worried that he'd be lost without her. Vanessa reluctantly agreed to stay attached to *Gemma*, but only for consultations, and only by phone. Her new contract had been specifically limited to three months and she'd deliberately made her fee exorbitantly high enough to discourage Max from calling her. Max had agreed, without the slightest reservations, and began by calling Vanessa at least twice weekly. Shortly, word of *Gemma's* resurgence as an advertising powerhouse, coupled with Vanessa and Max's arrangement leaked into the business community. Soon other companies began calling Vanessa as well. Although flattered, she was truly bewildered by the sudden consideration she received. Ultimately, Vanessa decided she deserved a break from the business world, and informed them all that although she *might* consider setting up a consulting firm, it wouldn't be in the foreseeable future.

While Vanessa had busily taken the business world by storm, Andrew had recovered from his injury. After suffering through countless hours of grueling, painful therapy, he'd regained full strength and use of his right arm. His hard work over the past six months had paid off. Now he could do everything he did before the shooting. He swam, jogged, worked out, and most importantly, he could sail again.

Andrew delighted in his new retired life with Vanessa. She'd moved in and he felt loved for the first time in years. They'd managed to talk about everything under the sun, and had developed an extraordinary level of respect and trust, one that many couples never achieve.

Proudly, Vanessa had stood by Andrew's side as he'd received his award from LAPD, even though he'd felt embarrassed by what he considered unfounded attention. At least he'd been able to ensure that Mike and his team both received recognition as well, along with a hefty fund to support their efforts to deal with the ongoing LA County drug trafficking crimes.

Andrew continued to keep close tabs on Kate through his FBI contacts, needing constant reassurance that Vanessa and Haley remained safe. And John, the security guard from the bank, moved in with his granddaughter after a brief stay in a rehabilitation facility. Andrew enjoyed spending afternoons with the resilient elderly man, and had met with him several times for coffee. John had a new girlfriend, and he was full of shrewd advice about how to develop and maintain a lasting, loving relationship.

But it was Vanessa who had been Andrew's rock. She'd kept him going when he became frustrated and discouraged by his slow, painful recovery. She'd helped him with his physical therapy, praising him for even the most miniscule improvement. He remembered their first long weekend together, when they'd gone sailing for a few hours. She'd had to use her own arm muscles to hoist the riggings, when Andrew's arm had failed him. She'd surprised him, demonstrating unusual strength for such a petite woman. Feigning insult at his comments about her sturdy arms, she laughed it off, explaining that years of swimming laps had paid off.

Now, finally completely free from any and all responsibilities to *Gemma*, Vanessa had left the company that had been her family and home for many years. She'd not only helped Max restore *Gemma*'s reputation, she'd made it superior to the one they'd previously enjoyed. The new advertising team had negotiated an unprecedented number of new contracts, and repaired relationships with old clients as well. Vanessa had walked out of *Gemma* for the last time feeling proud. She left *Gemma* without any qualms; Andrew had become her new life and family!

* * * * *

After dining on freshly caught fish, under a sky sparkling with stars, feeling better than she had since they'd begun sailing toward South America, the clinking of glasses in the galley caught Vanessa's attention. Andrew walked up the steps from the galley with two full champagne glasses. Impressed by the fact that he hadn't spilled a drop, but unsure how her seasick stomach would handle alcohol, Vanessa hesitated. "I'm not sure I can drink any alcohol just yet," she cautioned.

"It's ginger ale," he smiled, handing her a chilled glass. "I just need to ask you something, that I hope will require a celebratory toast." He felt the time was finally right, and he wasn't about to let anything postpone what he had to say.

Easing down beside her, he reached for her left hand, and began thoughtfully, "I've had the extreme privilege of sharing my life with two very beautiful, sensitive, accomplished women. The night Grace died, I felt as if my own life had ended as well. But when you first opened your door to me, I was stunned. The mysterious woman who had haunted my dreams for years stood right in front of me, materializing unexpectedly. Just the sight of you caused my heart to beat again. I felt it begin to thaw. My hidden passions sprung back to life. During the past months we've spent together, I've fallen deeper in love with you than I could have ever imagined. You are my heart and soul. My life would be meaningless without you beside me."

Vanessa held her breath in anticipation as Andrew set down his glass, got down on one knee, reached inside his pocket and slowly opened the jewelry box containing his grandmother's stunning diamond ring. His heart beat wildly within his chest, his palms moistened, and he had a worse case of nerves than he had when he'd asked his first wife. Grace had always wanted to be married and have a family. He feared Vanessa might prefer to keep their relationship looser, with no binding strings attached.

"Vanessa Golden, will you do me the honor of becoming my wife?" He held his breath, waiting for her answer.

Tears pooled in her eyes and her vision blurred as she set aside her glass. She placed both of her hands gently on the sides of his face, leaned forward in what seemed to Andrew as an eternity, before she kissed him tenderly on his lips. She had all but given up hope that he'd ask her. In her heart she had already decided, on the day that he'd tenderly held back her hair while she was seasick, that she was ready to marry him. She pulled back, gazing at him through teary eyes, and whispered, "I would be honored to be your wife, Andrew Kelly,"

Andrew reverently slid his grandmother's ring on Vanessa's left ring finger, and as he'd expected, it fit her perfectly.

They embraced, sharing a deep, passionate kiss before easing back to lie together on the deck cushions under a canopy of astonishingly brilliant stars. Sparks flew as they made love with an undying passion that sealed their commitment to one another, as husband and wife. They created shooting stars of their own, as their hearts, bodies and souls fused together. They had a loving relationship symbolized by their spiritual unity, and embodied in a world of limitless possibilities yet to come. They'd established a bond with each other, unlike any either had experienced before. Exploding together in their intimate embrace, their emotional release left them both pleasurably drained. Soon they drifted off, sleeping serenely as they floated on the gently rocking bed, their bodies intertwined, one merely an extension of the other.

Vanessa woke up alone and stretched contentedly across the soft captain's bed. The exhilarating feeling of the boat surging through the water meant that Andrew must be at the helm, steering them out to sea. Her seasickness had improved, but the feel of the pitching boat caused her stomach to flutter. Vanessa made her way cautiously to the galley. While fresh coffee dripped into her cup, she smiled as she inspected the beautiful, antique diamond ring resting securely on her finger. Fiercely independent and ambitious, she never thought she'd marry again. But Andrew was so different from any other man she'd met before. He was kind, considerate, charming, loving, sexy, and best of all, wild about her.

Glowing and pleased by the events of the previous night, Vanessa carried two steaming cups of coffee up the stairs, out onto the windy deck. Andrew stood at the helm wearing his captain's hat, looking wild and virile, the wind gusting in his face. Clear sailing and blue skies overhead, he steered the speeding boat bare-chested through the choppy waters, sails billowing, stretched taught in the wind. Vanessa, wearing nothing but his large white shirt and a diamond ring, appeared at his side, placing the coffee in the holders beside him. Squeezing in between Andrew and the large wooden ship's wheel, she wound her arms around his neck, and nuzzled his chest. "We're traveling mighty fast, sailor," she yelled over the wind.

Andrew smiled down at her, raising his eyebrow at her scant attire. The exhilaration of their speed, coupled with the feeling of Vanessa in his arms, intoxicated him. He'd never felt this happy before in his life! He bent close, his low tone reverberating seductively in Vanessa's ear. "See how the sails are tight and full of air, that means we're sailing at maximum speed. You know, full sail ahead."

Vanessa purred back at Andrew, playfully tipping his hat back on his head. "Okay sailor, I guess that makes us full-sailed lovers. I surrender to you, my captain." Vanessa's teasing eyes sparkled and the wind blew her hair across her face, giving her a look of wild, sensual abandonment.

Wordlessly, Andrew bent down to kiss her, slowly deepening his kiss, teasing her mercilessly with his tongue until their passion pushed them beyond the boiling point of uncontrollable desire. Vanessa's ardent response was his undoing. Andrew stepped back away from the helm and quickly dropped the sails. His low throaty laughter filled the ocean air as he boldly carried her below deck like a wayward pirate.

Andrew intended to show Vanessa exactly what her full-sailed surrender really meant, today and forever!

FOLLOW VANESSA AND ANDREW ON THEIR SAILING ADVENTURE IN THE SEQUEL COMING SOON.

Made in the USA
San Bernardino, CA
06 June 2019